PURE Robert Frost

佛羅斯特永恆詩選

佛羅斯特　著

曹明倫　譯

Contents 目錄

波士頓以北 NORTH OF BOSTON

跨越時空的心靈之友

　　2003年我一個人在北京清華大學擔任特聘教授，也開始嘗試翻譯英文詩歌，常常在冬天的寒夜中緊裹著外套，踽踽獨行穿越清華大學黑暗的校園，邊走邊念著佛羅斯特〈暗夜的故友〉中的句子：

I have stood still and stopped the sound of feet

When far away an interrupted cry

Came over houses from another street,

But not to call me back or say good-by;

也曾停下腳步屏息傾聽

遠方傳出斷續的呼叫聲

越過屋宇　來自另一個街頭

不是召喚　不在道別

　　詩人在這首詩中想要傳達的哲理是什麼呢？每一個人儘可以有不同的領悟和解釋，但也會不約而同地產生一份相似的感覺——孤獨。這份孤獨，也許像寒風中瑟縮的遊子，緊裹著外套，踽踽地獨行在異鄉，失落了什麼？懷念著什麼……，這就是我當時的心情了。

　　我很喜歡佛羅斯特的詩，是因為他能用淺顯易懂的語言，創造出意象鮮明的詩句，唸起來節奏順暢，而且深寓哲理，充滿了感情和人文關懷。以其另一首〈雪夜在林邊停留〉為例，不但文字樸實，韻律工整（每行八個母音；每段第三行之偏韻即為下一段之主韻），還充滿了視覺（幽林、冰湖、暗夜、積雪）和音覺（輕風聲、馬鈴聲、飄雪聲）的想像，以及生命的關懷（人、馬、大自然）。詩人用馬兒的鈴聲和風雪的旋律交融，象徵旅人對於回歸自然以解脫勞累的嚮往，用幽暗的樹林象徵死亡和歇息的誘惑，營造出一幅飄逸蒼涼的意境。然而詩人終究想到 "But I have promises to keep," 決定「再疲倦也得走下去」。最後以重覆兩次 "And miles to go before I sleep." 「前路迢迢我還不能入睡」收尾，真是動人心弦，餘韻無窮。

在一個初秋的早晨，風意微寒，太陽尚未昇起；一個孤獨的旅人走到了黃樹林邊，眼前有兩條路；一條看起來像是岔路，但是旅人沒有把握，該走哪一條呢？結果旅人選擇了那一條他以往不會走的岔路。那是一段更美的旅程嗎？旅人會後悔嗎？誰知道呢？多年以後旅人也許會突然想起這個早晨，然後深深地嘆息。因為這個早晨的一念之間，改變了他後來的一生。

I shall be telling this with a sigh

Somewhere ages and ages hence:

Two roads diverged in a wood, and I——

I took the one less traveled by,

And that has made all the difference.

多年後的某時某地

我回憶此刻將輕聲嘆息：

樹林裏岔開兩條路 而我——

我走了人跡較少的那一條

因此有了完全不同的人生

　　這是佛羅斯特最有名的一首〈末走之路〉，表面上描述旅人在樹林裡遇到岔路而躊躇不決的心情，實際上卻是在告訴大家：我們的人生道路是靠自己決定的，有得必有失，能捨才能得。這首詩最打動我心弦的一個字是 "Both that morning equally lay" 中的equally這個字，它代表一個選擇、一種平等，和一份自由。無分賢愚貴賤，每個人的人生當中都有過一些這樣的選擇機會。人生之無奈，固由於選擇之無可回頭；人生之美，豈不也來自對自己選擇的無怨無悔？

　　每一個人的人生都是一首自己的詩，這是我從佛羅斯特的詩中得到的最大的體會──詩人是我跨越時空的心靈之友。

尤克強

在平凡中見大智慧

如果說20世紀的美國有一位民族詩人，那他毫無疑問就是佛羅斯特；如果說在傳統詩歌和現代詩歌的交替時期有一位「交替性的詩人」，那他毫無疑問就是佛羅斯特；如果說有一位既是非凡的創造者又是普普通通的人的詩人，那他就是佛羅斯特；如果說有一位懂得如何用最少的語言表達最多的思想和感情的詩人，那他就是佛羅斯特。

佛羅斯特（Robert Lee Frost, 1874～1963）是20世紀美國最有影響的一位詩人，也是美國有史以來最具民族性的詩人。他的詩在美國可謂家喻戶曉，就像中國學童能隨口背誦「床前明月光」一樣，美國學生也能張口就背「金色的樹林中有兩條岔路」。佛羅斯特的詩歌承襲了傳統詩歌的形式，但不像浪漫派詩歌和唯美派詩歌那樣矯揉造作。他詩歌的內容往往是新英格蘭的自然景物和風土人情，但其中融入了他對宇宙人生的思考。佛羅斯特一生經歷了整個現代主義時期，然而，我們雖然沒有理由說他不是個現代詩人，但由於下文陳述的原因，我們以往關注現代詩歌時卻對他關注不夠。佛羅斯特的語言樸實無華，言近旨遠，讀來既是一種享受，又會受到一種啟迪。

一、少年的心願

羅伯特・李・佛羅斯特於1874年3月26日生於加利福尼亞州的舊金山。他父親是北方人（新英格蘭人），但在南北戰爭期間卻不滿北方當局而參加了南部同盟由李將軍指揮的北弗吉尼亞軍團，他於1873年結婚後遷居加州，從事新聞事業（佛羅斯特的教名和中間名「羅伯特・李」便是為了紀念南軍總司令羅伯特・李將軍）。佛羅斯特的母親是蘇格蘭人，她曾自己寫詩，還創作出版過童話故事《水晶國》。佛羅斯特從小就喜歡聽母親講聖女貞德以及《聖經》、神話和童話中人物的故事，喜歡聽她朗讀莎士比亞、華茲華斯、丁尼生、司各特、彭斯、愛倫坡、愛默生和朗費羅等人的詩篇。他是從母親那裏接受的文學啟蒙和宗教啟蒙。1885年，佛羅斯特的父親因病去世，他母親攜全家回到祖籍新英格蘭。

幼年的佛羅斯特獨處時常聽見有說話聲。他母親說這是得自於她的遺傳，天生就具有「超凡的聽覺」和「預見力」。他14歲迷戀上詩歌，在麻薩諸塞州勞倫斯中學上學時，他曾在放學回家的路上一邊走一邊寫詩，結果沒趕上祖母家的晚飯。他15歲時在的《勞倫斯中學校刊》上發表第一首詩〈傷心之夜〉，19歲在勞倫斯市的《獨立》周刊上正式發表詩作《我的蝴蝶：一曲哀歌》並收到第一筆稿費。他母親為此而感到自豪，但家中其他人卻深感不安。他祖父對他說，「誰也不能靠寫詩養家糊口，但我還是給你一年時間。如果你一年內寫不出名堂。那就別再寫詩了。你看怎麼樣？」

「給我20年吧──20年！」19歲的佛羅斯特向祖父討價還價。

　　不知是命運有意捉弄，還是他自己本身就是一個天才的預言家，此後他果真度過了艱苦、憂慮、甚至差點使他絕望的20年。幾乎是在20年後的同一個月，他才實現了少年時的心願，在異國出版了自己的第一部詩集。

二、成功的道路

　　在那漫長的20年中，佛羅斯特當過記者、農夫和教師。他妻子埃莉諾‧懷特是他中學的同學。他倆於1892年中學畢業，1895年結婚。此後，佛羅斯特在哈佛大學就學兩年，攻讀英語、希臘語、拉丁語和哲學。1899年，佛羅斯特離開哈佛，來到了他祖父為他在新罕布夏州買下的一座農場。他與妻子及四個孩子在那裡一住便是13個年頭。那些日子對佛羅斯特來說是灰暗的、憂慮的，他甚至想到過自殺。但正是在那些日子裡，佛羅斯特開始同鄉村景色和自然風光親近起來。他重新提筆寫詩。尤其是在1906至1907年期間，他寫出了後來收在《波士頓以北》（North of Boston, 1914）和《山間低地》〈Mountain Interval, 1916〉裡的一些重要詩篇。1912年，佛羅斯特決定全身心投入創作，他賣掉了經營多年的農場，辭掉了在州立師範學校的教職，攜妻帶子遠渡重洋，移居到了英國。

　　1913年，佛羅斯特在倫敦出版了他的第一部詩集《少年的心願》（A Boy's Will）。他簡潔樸實的詩行和詩中寓意深刻的哲理立刻贏得了詩人和評論家的好評，葉慈讀過《少年的心願》後對龐德說：「這是很久以來在美國寫出的最好的詩。」但如果說《孩子的心願》激起了評論家們的熱情，那緊接著出版的

《波士頓以北》可以說是讓評論家和讀者都入癡入迷。在20世紀各種流派競相標新立異、駁雜紛陳的歐美詩壇上，佛羅斯特的詩可以說是清風甘露，令人耳目一新，耐人細細玩味。評論家們從各個角度讚譽他的詩篇。

　　1915年，在英國僑居了三年之久的佛羅斯特，這位離開美國時一文不名的人，載譽歸國，成為了「美國詩歌新潮流」的領袖。美國開始印行並出版他的詩。他開始穩步地成為享有世界聲譽並深受讀者歡迎的美國第一流詩人。他1923年出版的《新罕布夏》（New Hampshire）、1928年出版的《小河西流》（West-Running Brook）、1936年出版的《山外有山》（A Further Range）和1942年出版的《見證樹》（A Witness Tree）分別獲得1924年、1931年、1937年和1943年的普利茲詩歌獎。

　　在返回美國後的40年間，他長期不懈的努力形成了自己獨特的詩歌藝術風格，贏得了大西洋兩岸成千上萬讀者的心。他一生中獲得了各種各樣的榮譽，其中包括牛津、劍橋和哈佛在內的40餘所大學授予的榮譽學位，而他所獲得的最高榮譽則是1961年應甘乃迪總統的邀請在其總統就職典禮上朗頌他創作的詩篇。佛羅斯特為此專門準備了一首題為〈為甘乃迪總統的就職典禮而作〉的詩。但寒冷的疾風和刺眼的陽光使他未能讀成那首詩，結果他即席背誦了他早年的愛國詩篇《徹底奉獻》。就職慶典之後他派人送去了那首未讀成的詩稿。他在那首詩中預言道，美國的未來將展現「下一個奧古斯都時期的榮耀」，將迎來「一個詩和力量的黃金時代」。

三、詩歌特色

佛羅斯特詩作的一個重要特點是口語的運用和具有地方色彩。他的第一部詩集剛一出版，吉卜林就指出對英國這個「舊世界」的讀者來說，佛羅斯特由於他的「異鄉方言」而顯得陌生。然而，佛羅斯特堅持道，語言習慣的差異可以使一種文化的不同分支接受另一種別有風味的方言，並從中品出「陌生人的新鮮味」。他還強調說，這種由民族或地區的語言特色所產生的陌生感或「疏隔感」，基本上與由不同意象或其他手段所產生的陌生感，同於因比喻而轉換字詞所產生的新奇感，而正是這些陌生感或新奇感賦予詩歌以特性。他直言不諱地宣稱「所有民間語言本身就富有音樂感」，民間語言之源泉可以通過發展「意義聲調」（sound of sense）而轉換成詩的語言。

佛羅斯特堅持口語入詩是和他詩歌內容的地方色彩分不開的。在去英國之前，他在祖父為他買的那座農場上居住了13年；重返美國之後，他又先後在新罕布夏州和佛蒙特州買下農場定居。雖然他經常外出演講並擔任過數所大學的「駐校詩人」和「文學顧問」，但他更多的時候是居住在固定的鄉村環境。他熱愛鄉村的生活，熱愛身邊那些勤勞而平凡的人。他的詩著意描寫日常生活，描寫日常生活中的人和物，抒發對人和大自然的熱愛。因此，他的詩讀起來總給人一種清新流暢、樸素自然的感覺。難怪大多數評論家對他的「異鄉方言」備加讚賞，極力推崇。評論家吉布森（Wilfrid Wilson Gibson）寫道：「佛羅斯特先生已把普通男女的日常語言變成了詩。」而另一位評論家則說：「佛羅斯特先生懂得如何用最少的語言表達最多的思想和感情。」的確，佛羅斯特詩歌的口語化和地方色彩使他的詩具有一種清新、美妙、使人產生聯想的魅力，無論是新英格蘭人還是其他地方的美國人都能感受到這種魅力。他詩歌的地方色彩不但為他的詩構成了一種文學上或描述上的技巧，還構成了比喻上的技巧。

我們說佛羅斯特的詩給人一種清新流暢、樸素自然的感覺，並不是說他的詩都明白易懂。其實，佛羅斯特許多詩篇所表現的情緒是難以把握的。佛羅斯特追求一種「詩始於歡欣，終於智慧」的詩學理念。他說：「世間有兩種現實主義者，一種拿出的土豆總是沾滿了泥，以表明他們的土豆是真的；可另一種則要把土豆弄乾淨才感到滿意。我傾向於第二種現實主義者。在我看來，藝術要為生活做的就是淨化生活，去蕪存真。」他始終堅持這些原則，善於從看起來平淡無奇的日常生活中發掘出詩的情趣和哲理，使人窺見智慧的光芒。當然，只有「追求他這位追求者的人」（見〈逃避現實者──絕不是〉一詩）才能窺見這種光芒。基於他的詩學理念，他的詩便成了一種象徵或比喻：〈補牆〉中那堵總要倒塌的牆表現了詩人欲消除人與人之間隔閡的願望，〈未走之路〉道出了詩人對人生道路選擇的態度，〈白樺樹〉暗示了人總想逃避現實但終究要回到現實的矛盾，〈小樹林中〉的枯葉新芽展示了人類社會新陳代謝的規律，〈摘蘋果之後〉中的「睡眠」和〈雪夜在林邊停留〉中的「安歇」則成了「死亡」的象徵。佛羅斯特把這種象徵稱為「隱喻」即一種「指東說西，以此述彼」的暗示。而正是這種暗示使讀者自然而然地去探索他詩中所描述的難以言狀的微妙關係，去尋找人與大自然或上帝之間的關聯，去評估一位摘蘋果的人彌留之際的道德價值，去思索一片樹葉、一株小草、一顆星星、一點流螢所包含的人生意義。

　　然而，佛羅斯特詩中的暗示並不都是容易被人領悟的。如果說一向酷愛大自然的佛羅斯特在〈意志〉、〈曾臨太平洋〉等詩中把大自然變成了黑暗、暴力和邪惡的化身使人感到詫異的話，那他在〈望不遠也看不深〉這首詩中所表現的情緒則可以說是叫人難以捉摸。乍一看，這首詩所表現的是人們對未知世界的嚮往，但這種理解恰好是片面的。從這首詩生動的比喻、強烈的節奏以及象徵性的畫面來看，這是一首抒情詩；但據其直截了當的陳述風格和散文化的遣詞造句，這首詩又具有反傳統詩的特點。這種形式上的矛盾正好與內容情緒上的矛盾相符。對那些專心致志但又徒勞無益地眺望大海的人，詩人是藐視還是讚賞？看來是二者皆有。一方面，那些被佛羅斯特稱為「人們」的人全然忽視他們固有的領域——陸地。他們看見的極少，他們所見的船，船體大部分都在水平線之下；他們所見的海鷗，不過是映在水汪汪的沙灘上的影子。如此直率的筆觸，其本身就暗示出眺望者缺乏想像力。但從另一方面來看，這首詩又使人聯想到大海本身及其神秘性那永恆的魅力，暗示出大海也是「真實」的領域。這樣，眺望者們對大海「終日眺望」也就無可非議了。

　　佛羅斯特某些詩中所表現出來的情緒上的不一致，或多或少源自於他生活中的矛盾。他家祖祖輩輩從1632年起就定居在新英格蘭，可他偏偏出生在加利福尼亞；他是20世紀最偉大的美國詩人，卻偏偏在英國最初被人賞識；他的詩在形式上是最傳統的，卻偏偏被奉為「美國詩歌新潮流」的領袖；他從不相信也從不參加任何競爭和比賽，但卻偏偏四次獲得普利茲詩歌獎；他的「獨白詩」和「對話詩」被認為是用「方言俚語」寫成的，可他的抒情詩則被認為具有無比優雅的音樂美；他本人及其詩歌都表現出十足的地方色彩，但同時又具有最普遍的意義。佛羅斯特用一行詩解釋了他詩中情緒的矛盾。他在〈今天這一課〉最末一行寫道：「我與這世界有過一場情人間的爭吵」。過去、現在和將來都不會再有一位評論家能對詩人的精神做出如此精闢的總結。是的，詩人的心靈是一個沈思的世界。他直率地質問，直率地批評，但對他所質問和批評的世界卻總是懷著一種寬容的理解，懷著一種最誠摯的愛。

四、藝術追求

佛羅斯特的詩歌一般都遵從了傳統詩歌的韻律和形式 —— 押韻的雙行詩、四行詩、素體詩和十四行詩。他始終堅持「英語詩中實際上只有兩種格律，即嚴謹的抑揚格和稍加變化的抑揚格。」他雖然偶爾也寫出一兩首自由詩，但他並不贊成這種詩體。他認為「如果沒有多年的格律詩功夫，自由詩會自由得一無是處」。他多次宣稱「寧願打沒有球網的網球，也不願寫自由詩」。

佛羅斯特雖然遵從傳統但卻不抱殘守闕。他注意到了20世紀的詩人都在走創新的道路，但他不贊成有些人寫詩不用標點符號，不用大寫字母，不用可調節音韻節奏的格律，尤其不贊成有些人只用視覺意象而不用聽覺意象，因為他發現聽覺意象是構成詩歌的更重要的元素。他20歲之前就注意到了這樣一個事實：有時候人們在閒聊中會實實在在地觸及到那種只有在最好的文學作品中才能觸及的東西。接著他意識到，要衝破書面語言陳詞濫調的禁錮，就必須到日常生活中去搜尋尚未被寫進文學作品的聲調，而這種聲調並非某些詩人（如斯溫伯恩和丁尼生）所追求的母音和輔音的和諧，而是佛羅斯特自己發現的、總是自由地隨著意義的變化而變化的「意義聲調」。這種聲調是詩中最富於變化的部分，同時也是最重要的部分。沒有這種聲調語言就會失去活力，詩也會失去生命。他在1915年致朋友的一封信中說：「大約10年前的某一天，我開始懷疑我喜歡聽鄰居閒聊僅僅是為了閒聊本身……我喜歡閒聊的實在，喜歡閒聊的親昵，從這種實在和親昵中獲取的東西就是一個藝術家能達到的最高目的。」

佛羅斯特不僅從日常生活中發現了「意義聲調」，還發現了把這些聲調串起來的「句子聲調」（sentence sound）。儘管佛羅斯特認為「詩是日常語言的聲調的複製品」（All Poetry is a reproduction of the tones of actual speech.），但日常語言之聲調畢竟是還沾著泥的土豆，而佛羅斯特的「聲調」則是已經洗乾淨的土豆。所以他的「意義聲調」和「句子聲調」實際上是經他提煉過的聲調，提煉的目的是為了將它們鑲入傳統的格律。於是佛羅斯特在藝術上走了一條他所說的「創新的老路」，讓人們通過傳統的詩行聽到了新英格蘭普通男女日常聊天的聲調，感受到了他們的真實感情。人們讀他的詩，尤其是讀他的「獨白詩」和「對話詩」，有時會覺得恍若置身于英格蘭鄉間，在聽一位睿智的新英格蘭農夫聊天。所以有人把佛羅斯特稱為「新英格蘭的農民詩人」。然而正如艾略特1957年在倫敦為佛羅斯特祝酒時所說：「我認為詩中有兩種鄉土感情，一種鄉土感情使其詩只能被有相同背景的人接受，而另一種鄉土感情則可以被全世界的人接受，那就是但丁對佛羅倫斯的感情、莎士比亞對沃里克郡的感情，歌德對萊茵蘭的感情、佛羅斯特對新英格蘭的感情。」

的確，正是懷著對祖先故土的深厚感情，佛羅斯特才把方言的措辭節奏用得那麼嫻熟巧妙，把姿態與景物的畫面表現得那麼令人信服，把新英格蘭鄉村的日常生活和自然風光創造的那麼真實，把現實與理想的題材與傳統形式結合的那麼完美，以致他的詩比同樣親近大自然的華茲華斯和愛默生等人的詩都更加接近現實生活，更具有普遍性。評論家們認為佛羅斯特是處在傳統詩歌和現代派詩歌交替時期的「交替性詩人」，認為他與艾略特同為美國新詩的兩大中心。

曹明倫

少年的心願
A BOY'S WILL

進入自我

我的心願之一是那黑沉沉的樹林，
那古樸蒼勁、柔風難吹進的樹林，
並不僅僅是看上去的幽暗的偽裝，
而應伸展延續，直至地老天荒。

我不該被抑制了，而在某一天
我該悄悄溜走，溜進那茫茫林間，
任何時候都不怕看見空地廣袤，
或是緩緩車輪灑下沙粒的大道。

我看不出有何理由要回頭返程，
也不知那些此刻還惦念我的友人，
那些想知我是否記得他們的朋友，
爲何不沿我足跡動身，把我趕上。

他們將發現我沒變，我還是自己——
只是更堅信我思索的一切是眞理。

Into My Own

One of my wishes is that those dark trees,

So old and firm they scarcely show the breeze,

Were not, as 'twere, the merest mask of gloom,

But stretched away unto the edge of doom.

I should not be withheld but that some day

Into their vastness I should steal away,

Fearless of ever finding open land,

Or highway where the slow wheel pours the sand.

I do not see why I should e'er turn back,

Or those should not set forth upon my track

To overtake me, who should miss me here

And long to know if still I held them dear.

They would not find me changed from him they knew —

Only more sure of all I thought was true.

荒屋

我居住在一座荒僻的小屋裡，
我知道小屋多年前曾經消失，
　那時只剩下地窖的斷壁殘牆，
　破敗的地窖白天能透進陽光，
還生長著野生的紫梗覆盆子。

越過葡萄藤遮掩的圍欄殘木，
樹林又在昔日的草場上復甦；
　果樹椿已長成一片萌生新林，
　新果林中有啄木鳥啄木聲聲；
通往水井的小道也已經修復。

　　　　心兒懷著一種奇異的疼痛，
　　　　我住在那座曾經消失的屋中，
　　　　　小屋遠離被人遺忘的大路，
　　　　　大路不再爲蟾蜍揚起塵土。
　　　　夜晚降臨，黑蝙蝠紛紛竄騰；

　　　　那三聲夜鷹就要開始叫喊，
　　　　牠會忽靜忽鳴，並振翅盤旋；
　　　　　大老遠我就聽牠敞開嗓門，
　　　　　一遍又一遍地叫個不停，
　　　　直到牠終於暢所欲言。

Ghost House

I dwell in a lonely house I know
That vanished many a summer ago,
And left no trace but the cellar walls,
And a cellar in which the daylight falls
And the purple-stemmed wild raspberries grow.

O'er ruined fences the grapevines shield
The woods come back to the mowing field;
The orchard tree has grown one copse
Of new wood and old where the woodpecker chops;
The footpath down to the well is healed.

I dwell with a strangely aching heart
In that vanished abode there far apart
On that disused and forgotten road
That has no dust-bath now for the toad.
Night comes; the black bats tumble and dart;

The whippoorwill is coming to shout
And hush and cluck and flutter about:
I hear him begin far enough away
Full many a time to say his say
Before he arrives to say it out.

這是在一個夏夜，月光陰晦。
我不知這些沉默的鄰居是誰，
　雖他們與我同住這荒郊野地——
　但肯定有被苔蘚覆蓋的名字
刻在屋外矮樹叢下那些墓碑。

他們不會煩人，但令人傷感，
不過最近的兩位是少女少男——
　他倆沒什麼可以傳頌的故事，
　但考慮到這世上的諸多東西，
他們倒是一對最可愛的夥伴。

It is under the small, dim, summer star.

I know not who these mute folk are

Who share the unlit place with me —

Those stones out under the low-limbed tree

Doubtless bear names that the mosses mar.

They are tireless folk, but slow and sad —

Though two, close-keeping, are lass and lad —

With none among them that ever sings,

And yet, in view of how many things,

As sweet companions as might be had.

深秋來客

當我的憂愁來做客時，
　她覺得秋雨綿綿的陰天
比任何日子都更美麗；
她喜歡掉光葉片的枯枝，
　她愛走濕漉漉的牧場小路。

她的快活不容我抑制。
　她愛說話，我樂於傾聽：
她喜歡鳥兒都向南飛去，
她喜歡她樸實的灰色毛衣
　被拂不開的薄霧染成銀色。

她那麼真切地感覺到美，
　從地之褪色，從天之陰沉，
從樹之孤單，從林之荒廢。
她以為我看不見山秋的秀媚，
　並一再追問是什麼原因。

我並非昨天才學會領悟
　在冬天的雪花飄落之前
這蕭瑟秋景的可愛之處，
但告訴她這點也於事無補，
　她的讚美使秋景更好看。

My November Guest

My sorrow, when she's here with me,
Thinks these dark days of autumn rain
Are beautiful as days can be;
She loves the bare, the withered tree;
She walks the sodden pasture lane.

Her pleasure will not let me stay.
She talks and I am fain to list:
She's glad the birds are gone away,
She's glad her simple worsted gray
Is silver now with clinging mist.

The desolate, deserted trees,
The faded earth, the heavy sky,
The beauties she so truly sees,
She thinks I have no eye for these,
And vexes me for reason why.

Not yesterday I learned to know
The love of bare November days
Before the coming of the snow,
But it were vain to tell her so,
And they are better for her praise.

愛情和一道難題

黃昏時一名異鄉客來到門前，
　開口與屋裡的新郎寒暄。
他手裡拄著一根灰綠色枴杖，
　他心事重重，愁眉不展。
他用眼睛而不是用嘴唇
　請求讓他借宿一晚，
然後他轉頭遙望路的遠方，
　暮色中沒有燈火閃現。

新郎從屋裡走到門廊，
　說：「客人喲，讓我和你
先來看看今晚的天色，
　然後再商量過夜的事。」
紫藤的落葉已鋪滿庭院，
　藤上的莢果也都變紫，
秋風中已有冬天的滋味；
　「客人喲，但願我能確知。」

新娘正坐在昏暗的屋裡，
　獨自俯身在溫暖的火上，
她的臉被爐火映得通紅，
　使她臉紅的還有心之欲望。
新郎望著使人困乏的小路，
　看見的卻是屋裡的新娘，
他真想把她的心裝進金盒，
　再用一把銀鎖將它鎖上。

該不該施捨金錢和麵包，
　或虔誠地為窮人祈禱，
或是詛咒天下的富人，
　新郎認為都無關緊要；
而一個男人該不該允許
　其新婚之夜被人打擾，
讓新房裡有潛在的禍根，
　新郎真希望他能知道。

Love and A Qiestopm

A Stranger came to the door at eve,
And he spoke the bridegroom fair.
He bore a green-white stick in his hand,
And, for all burden, care.
He asked with the eyes more than the lips
For a shelter for the night,
And he turned and looked at the road afar.
Without a window light.

The bridegroom came forth into the porch
With, "Let us look at the sky,"
And question what of the night to be,
"Stranger, you and I."
The woodbine leaves littered the yard,
The woodbine berries were blue,
Autumn, yes, winter was in the wind;
"Stranger, I wish I knew."

Within, the bride in the dusk alone
Bent over the open fire,
Her face rose-red with the glowing coal
And the thought of the heart's desire.
The bridegroom looked at the weary road,
Yet saw but her within,
And wished her heart in a case of gold
And pinned with a silver pin.

The bridegroom thought it little to give
A dole of bread, a purse,
A heartfelt prayer for the poor of God,
Or for the rich a curse;
But whether or not a man was asked
To mar the love of two
By harboring woe in the bridal house,
The bridegroom wished he knew.

黃昏漫步

我漫步穿越收割後的草場，
　但見草茬生發的新草
像帶露的茅屋頂光滑平整，
　半掩著通往花園的小道。

當我漫步走進那座花園，
　忽聽一陣淒清的鳥鳴
從纏結的枯草叢中傳出，
　比任何聲音都哀婉動人。

一株光禿的老樹孤立牆邊，
　樹上只剩下一片枯葉，
孤葉準是被我的沉思驚擾，
　晃晃悠悠向下飄跌。

我沒走多遠便止住腳步，
　從正在凋謝的紫花翠菊
採下一朵藍色的小花，
　要再次把花奉獻給你。

A Late Walk

When I go up through the mowing field,
The headless aftermath,
Smooth-laid like thatch with the heavy dew,
Half closes the garden path.

And when I come to the garden ground,
The whir of sober birds
Up from the tangle of withered weeds
Is sadder than any words.

A tree beside the wall stands bare,
But a leaf that lingered brown,
Disturbed, I doubt not, by my thought,
Comes softly rattling down.

I end not far from my going forth,
By picking the faded blue
Of the last remaining aster flower
To carry again to you.

星星

不計其數，聚集在夜空，
　　在騷動的雪地之上，
在凜凜寒風呼嘯的時候，
　　雪流動，以樹的形狀——

彷彿關注著我們的命運，
　　擔心我們會偶然失足
於一片白色的安息之地，
　　天亮後難覺察之處——

然而既無愛心也無仇恨，
　　星星就像彌涅瓦雕像
那些雪白的大理石眼睛，
　　有眼無珠，張目亦盲。

Stars

How countlessly they congregate
O'er our tumultuous snow,
Which flows in shapes as tall as trees
When wintry winds do blow! —

As if with keenness for our fate,
Our faltering few steps on
To white rest, and a place of rest
Invisible at dawn —

And yet with neither love nor hate,
Those stars like some snow-white
Minerva's snow-white marble eyes
Without the gift of sight.

害怕風暴

當風暴在黑暗中與我們作對，
當這頭野獸挾著雪
不停地撞擊矮屋的東窗
並用一種壓低的聲音
吠叫：
「出來！出來！」——
這時要出去非得經過內心的掙扎，
啊，的確！

我計算我們的力量，
兩個成人和一個孩子，
不眠的我們正忍住不去注意
爐火熄滅後寒冷爬得多近——
外面的積雪堆得多高，
門前庭院和未鋪平的路，
甚至連給人安慰的穀倉都變得遙遠，
於是我心中生出一種疑惑：
是否我們有力量隨日出而起
並自己拯救自己。

Storm Fear

When the wind works against us in the dark,

And pelts with snow

The lower-chamber window on the east,

And whispers with a sort of stifled bark,

The beast,

"Come out! Come out!" —

It costs no inward struggle not to go,

Ah, no!

I count out strength,

Two and a child,

Those of us not asleep subdued to mark

How the cold creeps as the fire dies at length —

How drifts are piled,

Dooryard and road ungraded,

Till even the comforting barn grows far away,

And my heart owns a doubt

Whether 'tis in us to arise with day

And save ourselves unaided.

風與窗台上的花

戀人們，忘卻你的愛，
　　來聽聽這段相思幽情，
她是窗台上嬌花一朵，
　　他是冬日裡微風一陣。

當冰與霜凝成的窗紗
　　在中午時分冰消霜融，
關在鳥籠中的金翅雀
　　在她頭頂上囀鳴詠誦。

他透過玻璃注意看她，
　　身不由己，情不自禁，
中午才打她眼前飛過，
　　可天一黑又再次飛臨。

他是冬日裡一陣寒風，
　　關心的是白雪與堅冰，
關心的是枯草與孤鳥，
　　但卻幾乎不懂得愛情。

可他在那窗台上嘆息，
　　他輕輕地搖動那窗扉，
室內的她目睹了一切，
　　因為她徹夜未能入睡。

也許他差點兒就成功
　　說服她與他一道私奔，
從那溫煦的火爐旁邊，
　　從那火光映照的明鏡。

但那花兒只微微傾身，
　　想不出應該說的話語，
而當黎明來到的時候，
　　風早已吹出一百英里。

Wind and Window Flower

Lovers, forget your love,
And list to the love of these,
She a window flower,
And he a winter breeze.

When the frosty window veil
Was melted down at noon,
And the caged yellow bird
Hung over her in tune,

He marked her through the pane,
He could not help but mark,
And only passed her by
To come again at dark,

He was a winter wind,
Concerned with ice and snow,
Dead weeds and unmated birds,
And little of love could know.

But he sighed upon the sill,
He gave the sash a shake,
As witness all within
Who lay that night awake.

Perchance he half prevailed
To win her for the flight
From the firelit looking-glass
And warm stove-window light.

But the flower leaned aside
And thought of naught to say,
And morning found the breeze
A hundred miles away.

致春風

攜雨一道來吧，喧囂的西南風！
帶來唱歌的鳥，送來築巢的蜂，
爲枯死的花兒帶來春夢一場，
讓路邊凍硬的雪堆融化流淌，
從白雪下面找回褐色的土地；
但不管今夜你要做什麼事，
都得來吹我的窗戶，讓它流動，
讓它像冰解雪化一般地消融；
融化掉玻璃，只留下窗框，
使它像隱居教士的十字架一樣；
然後吹進我狹窄的房間，
讓牆頭的圖畫隨你旋轉；
吹開嘩嘩書頁，
讓詩篇散落在地板
再把這詩人趕到外面。

To The Thawing Wind

Come with rain, O loud Southwester!

Bring the singer, bring the nester;

Give the buried flower a dream;

Make the settled snowbank steam;

Find the brown beneath the white;

But whate'er you do tonight,

Bathe my window, make it flow,

Melt it as the ice will go;

Melt the glass and leave the sticks

Like a hermit's crucifix;

Burst into my narrow stall;

Swing the picture on the wall;

Run the rattling pages o'er;

Scatter poems on the floor;

Turn the poet out of door.

春日祈禱

啊，讓我們歡樂在今日的花間；
別讓我們的思緒飄得那麼遙遠，
別想未知的收穫；讓我們在此，
就在這一年中萬物生長的時日。

啊，讓我們歡樂在白色的果林，
讓白天無可比擬，夜晚像精靈；
讓我們快活在快活的蜜蜂群中，
蜂群正嗡嗡圍繞著美麗的樹叢。

啊，讓我們快活在疾飛的鳥群，
蜂群之上的鳥鳴聲忽然間可聞，
忽而用喙劃破空氣如流星墜下，
忽而靜靜地在半空如一樹繁花。

因為這是愛，是世間唯一的愛，
是注定要由上帝使之神聖的愛，
上帝聖化此愛是為了祂的宏願，
但此愛此願卻需要我們來實現。

A Prayer in Spring

Oh, give us pleasure in the flowers today;
And give us not to think so far away
As the uncertain harvest; keep us here
All simply in the springing of the year.

Oh, give us pleasure in the orchard white,
Like nothing else by day, like ghosts by night;
And make us happy in the happy bees,
The swarm dilating round the perfect trees.

And make us happy in the darting bird
That suddenly above the bees is heard,
The meteor that thrusts in with needle bill,
And off a blossom in mid-air stands still.

For this is love and nothing else is love,
The which it is reserved for God above
To sanctify to what far ends He will,
But which it only needs that we fulfill,

採花

與你別離在黎明，
在清晨的霞光之中
你曾走在我身邊，
使我感到離別的悲痛。
還認得我嗎？在這日暮黃昏，
蒼白憔悴，還有漫遊的風塵？
你是因不認得我而無言，
還是因認得我而噤聲？

隨我去想！就沒有半句話
問問這些凋謝的花，
它們竟使我離開你身邊，
去了這麼漫長的一天？
這些花是你的，請作為量尺，
量一量你珍藏它們的價值，
量一量那短短的一會兒，
我曾遠遠離去的一會兒。

Flower-Gathering

I left you in the morning,
And in the morning glow
You walked a way beside me
To make me sad to go.
Do you know me in the gloaming,
Gaunt and dusty gray with roaming?
Are you dumb because you know me not,
Or dumb because you know?

All for me? And not a question
For the faded flowers gay
That could take me from beside you
For the ages of a day?
They are yours, and be the measure
Of their worth for you to treasure,
The measure of the little while
That I've been long away.

紅朱蘭

一片浸透水的草地，
　小如寶石，形如太陽，
一片圓形的草地，
　不比周圍的樹林寬敞；
那兒吹不進一絲風，
　那兒的花芬芳馥郁，
那兒的空氣不流動──
　一座供奉熱的廟宇。

我們曾在炎熱中俯身，
　那是太陽應得的禮拜，
俯身採擷千朵朱蘭，
　誰也不會對它們不理睬；
因為那兒蘭草雖稀疏，
　但每一片梗葉的葉尖
似乎都長有紅色的翼瓣，
　把周圍染成通紅一片。

在離開那地方之前，
　我們作了個簡短的祈禱，
願每年割草的季節，
　那地方能被人忘掉；
若得不到長久的恩寵，
　也望博得一時的歡心，
當花與草分不清的時候，
　願人人都能刀下留情。

Rose Pogonias

A saturated meadow,
Sun-shaped and jewel-small,
A circle scarcely wider
Than the trees around were tall;
Where winds were quite excluded,
And the air was stifling sweet
With the breath of many flowers —
A temple of the heat.

There we bowed us in the burning,
As the sun's right worship is,
To pick where none could miss them
A thousand orchises;
For though the grass was scattered,
Yet every second spear
Seemed tipped with wings of color
That tinged the atmosphere.

We raised a simple prayer
Before we left the spot,
That in the general mowing
That place might be forgot;
Or if not all so favored,
Obtain such grace of hours
That none should mow the grass there
While so confused with flowers.

等待

有些什麼會入夢，當我像一個幽靈
飄過那些匆匆垛成的高高的草堆，
獨自闖進那片只剩草茬的土地，
那片割草人的聲音剛消失的土地，
在落日餘暉的殘霞之中，
在初升滿月的清輝之中，坐下
在灑滿月光的第一個乾草堆旁邊，
隱身在無數相同的草垛中間。

我會夢見在月亮占上風之前，
與月光對立的日光阻止陰暗；
我會夢見夜鷹充斥整個天空，
相互環繞盤旋，發出可怕的怪聲，
或尖叫著從高處向下俯衝；
我會夢見蝙蝠表演滑稽啞劇，
那蝙蝠似乎已發現我的藏身之處，
只有當牠旋轉時才失去目標，
然後又盲目而急速地不停尋找；

Waiting — Field at Dusk

What things for dream there are when specter-like,

Moving among tall haycocks lightly piled,

I enter alone upon the stubble field,

From which the laborers' voices late have died,

And in the antiphony of afterglow

And rising full moon, sit me down

Upon the full moon's side of the first haycock

And lose myself amid so many alike.

I dream upon the opposing lights of the hour,

Preventing shadow until the moon prevail;

I dream upon the nighthawks peopling heaven,

Each circling each with vague unearthly cry,

Or plunging headlong with fierce twang afar;

And on the bat's mute antics, who would seem

Dimly to have made out my secret place,

Only to lose it when he pirouettes,

And seek it endlessly with purblind haste;

我會夢見最後一隻燕子掠過；夢見
因我的到來而中斷，
我身後香氣深處唧唧喓喓的蟲鳴，
在一陣沉寂之後又重試嗓音，
一聲、兩聲、三聲，看我是否還在；
我會夢見那本用舊的《英詩金庫》，
我雖沒把它帶上，但它彷彿在手邊，
在充滿枯草香味的空氣中清晰可見；
但我最可能夢見一個不在場的人，
這些詩行就是為了要呈現在她眼前。

On the last swallow's sweep; and on the rasp

In the abyss of odor and rustle at my back,

That silenced by my advent, finds once more,

After an interval, his instrument,

And tries once — twice — and thrice if I be there;

And on the worn book of old-golden song

I brought not here to read, it seems, but hold

And freshen in this air of withering sweetness;

But on the memory of one absent, most,

For whom these lines when they shall greet her eye.

在一個山谷裡

我年輕時曾住在一個山谷裡，
　在多霧並徹夜有聲的沼澤旁，
所以我熟悉那些美麗的少女，
臉色蒼白的少女常拖著裙裾
　穿越過蘆葦叢走向一窗燈光。

沼澤地裡有各種各樣的野花，
　每一種都像一張少女的臉龐，
像一種常響在我屋裡的聲音，
從屋外黑暗越窗而入的聲音。
　每一位都單獨來自她的地方，

但她們每晚全都披薄霧而來；
　常常帶來許許多多的消息，
她們爭說知曉的重要事情，
一位孤獨者是那麼喜歡傾聽，
　往往聽到星星都快要隱去，

最後一名少女才會披露回還，
　披一身晨露返回她來的地方——
那兒百鳥正等待著振翮翩躚，
那兒百花正等待著昂首吐艷，
　那兒的鳥和花全都一模一樣。

正因為如此，我才這般知悉
　花為何有芳香，鳥為何啼鳴。
你只需問我，而我會告訴你。
是啊，我沒有白在那兒獨居，
　沒有白白在長夜裡用心傾聽。

In a Vale

When I was young, we dwelt in a vale
By a misty fen that rang all night,
And thus it was the maidens pale
I knew so well, whose garments trail
Across the reeds to a window light.

The fen had every kind of bloom,
And for every kind there was a face,
And a voice that has sounded in my room
Across the sill from the outer gloom.
Each came singly unto her place,

But all came every night with the mist;
And often they brought so much to say
Of things of moment to which, they wist,
One so lonely was fain to list,
That the stars were almost faded away

Before the last went, heavy with dew,
Back to the place from which she came —
Where the bird was before it flew,
Where the flower was before it grew,
Where bird and flower were one and the same.

And thus it is I know so well
Why the flower has odor, the bird has song.
You have only to ask me, and I can tell.
No, not vainly there did I dwell,
Nor vainly listen all the night long.

夢中的痛苦

我早已躲進森林，而我的歌
也總讓被風吹走的樹葉吞沒；
有一天你來到那森林的邊緣
（這是夢）並久久地張望思索，
你很想進入森林，但沒進來，
你憂慮地搖頭，似乎是想說：
「我不敢──他的足跡太偏──
他若迷途知返，定會來找我。」

並不遠，我就站在矮樹後面，
把林外一切都看得清清楚楚；
不能告訴你我所見依然存在，
這使我感到一陣劇烈的痛苦。
但我這樣離群索居並非真實，
因森林會醒來，你就在這裡。

A Dream Pang

I had withdrawn in forest, and my song

Was swallowed up in leaves that blew alway;

And to the forest edge you came one day

(This was my dream) and looked and pondered long,

But did not enter, though the wish was strong:

You shook your pensive head as who should say,

"I dare not — too far in his footsteps stray —

He must seek me would he undo the wrong."

                  Not far, but near, I stood and saw it all,

                  Behind low boughs the trees let down outside;

                  And the sweet pang it cost me not to call

                  And tell you that I saw does still abide.

                  But 'tis not true that thus I dwelt aloof,

                  For the wood wakes, and you are here for proof.

被人忽視

他們把我倆丟在我們選的路上，
　作為兩個已證明被他們誤解的人，
我倆有時候愛坐在路邊張望，
用淘氣、無邪、游移的目光，
　看我們能不能覺得沒被人拋棄。

In Neglect

They leave us so to the way we took,

As two in whom they were proved mistaken,

That we sit sometimes in the wayside nook,

With mischievous, vagrant, seraphic look,

And try if we cannot feel forsaken.

地利

要是厭了樹，我又會去找人，
　我知道去哪兒──在拂曉之時
　去一片有牛群守護青草的坡地。
斜躺在枝椏低垂的杜松樹林，
別人看不見我，而我可以遙看
　遠離人家的地方，看更遠之處，
　看對面山上白界內的座座墳墓，
生者和死者對此都不會有意見。

如果中午時我已把這些看夠，
　那我只需換只胳臂倚傍，你瞧，
　太陽烤熱的山坡使我的臉發燒，
我的呼吸像微風使野花搖頭，
　我可以聞聞泥土和草木的氣息，
　可以從蟻穴洞口看裡面的螞蟻。

The Vantage Point

If tired of trees I seek again mankind,

Well I know where to hie me — in the dawn,

To a slope where the cattle keep lawn.

There amid lolling juniper reclined,

Myself unseen, I see in white defined

Far off the homes of men, and farther still,

The graves of men on an opposing hill,

Living or dead, whichever are to mind.

And if by noon I have too much of these,

I have but to turn on my arm, and lo,

The sunburned hillside sets my face aglow,

My breathing shakes the bluet like a breeze,

I smell the earth, I smell the bruised plant,

I look into the crater of the ant.

割草

靜悄悄的樹林邊只有一種聲音，
那是我的長柄鐮在對大地低吟。
它在說些什麼？我也不甚知曉；
也許在訴說烈日當空酷熱難耐，
也許在訴說這周圍過於安靜──
這也是它低聲悄語說話的原因。
它不夢想得到不勞而獲的禮物，
也不希罕仙女精靈施捨的黃金；

因凡事超過真實便顯得不正常，
就連割倒壘壘乾草的誠摯的愛
也並非沒有割掉些嬌嫩的花穗，
並非沒有驚動一條綠瑩瑩的蛇。
真實乃勞動所知曉的最甜蜜的夢。
我的鐮刀低吟，留下成堆的乾草。

Mowing

There was never a sound beside the wood but one,

And that was my long scythe whispering to the ground.

What was it it whispered? I knew not well myself;

Perhaps it was something about the heat of the sun,

Something, perhaps, about the lack of sound —

And that was why it whispered and did not speak.

It was no dream of the gift of idle hours,

Or easy gold at the hand of fay or elf:

Anything more than the truth would have seemed too weak

To the earnest love that laid the swale in rows,

Not without feeble-pointed spikes of flowers

(Pale orchises), and seared a bright green snake.

The fact is the sweetest dream that labor knows.

My long scythe whispered and left the hay to make.

取水

門邊的那口井已乾枯，
　於是我們帶上水罐水桶
穿過屋後的那片田野
　去看小河是否還在流動；

眞高興有藉口去河邊，
　因爲秋夜雖涼卻迷人，
因爲那片田野是我們的，
　因爲河邊有我們的樹林。

我們疾走，像是去迎月亮，
　月亮正在樹後慢慢上升，
枯枝上沒有一片樹葉，
　沒有鳥兒，也沒有微風。

但一進樹林我倆便停住，
　像躲開月亮藏匿的地神，
只等著當她把我們發現，
　再笑著找新的地方藏身。

我倆互相用手止住對方，
　在敢張望之前先仔細傾聽，
在我倆共創的寂靜之中
　我們知道自己聽見了水聲。

像從一個地方傳來的音樂，
　一道叮咚作響的細細水簾
飄掛在河灣的深潭之上，
　時而像珍珠，時而像銀劍。

Going for Water

The well was dry beside the door,
And so we went with pail and can
Across the fields behind the house
To seek the brook if still it ran;

Not loth to have excuse to go,
Because the autumn eve was fair
(Though chill), because the fields were ours,
And by the brook our woods were there.

We ran as if to meet the moon
That slowly dawned behind the trees,
The barren boughs without the leaves,
Without the birds, without the breeze.

But once within the wood, we paused
Like gnomes that hid us from the moon,
Ready to run to hiding new
With laughter when she found us soon.

Each laid on other a staying hand
To listen ere we dared to look,
And in the hush we joined to make
We heard, we knew we heard the brook.

A note as from a single place,
A slender tinkling fall that made
Now drops that floated on the pool
Like pearls, and now a silver blade.

啟示

在揶揄嘲弄的話語後面，
　我們總愛留點言外之意，
可在別人真正領悟之前，
　我們總會感到心中焦慮。

若情況要求（讓我們假設）
　為了讓朋友一聽就了然，
我們最終只能直話直說，
　這又會使人感到遺憾。

但都一樣，從遙遠的上帝
　到愛玩捉迷藏的孩子，
要是他們藏匿得過於隱蔽，
　就只能自己說自己藏在哪裡。

Revelation

We make ourselves a place apart

Behind light words that tease and flout,

But oh, the agitated heart

Till someone really find us out.

' Tis pity if the case require

(Or so we say) that in the end

We speak the literal to inspire

The understanding of a friend.

But so with all, from babes that play

At hide-and-seek to God afar,

So all who bid too well away

Must speak and tell us where they are.

生存考驗

就連死於疆場的最勇敢的人
　　也不會掩飾他們心中的詫異
當他們醒來發現在天國仙境
　　也像在人世一樣由勇氣統治；
他們赤手空拳地在天國尋找
　　那片常春花永遠開放的平原，
結果發現對勇敢的最高獎賞
　　居然還是什麼都不怕的勇敢。

普照天國的光是完整的白光，
　　從不分解成紅橙黃綠青藍紫，
天國之光永遠是黎明的曙光；
　　山坡都像牧場一般青翠碧綠；
一群群活潑的天使來來往往，
　　嬉笑著把可勇敢面對的尋找——
寂靜的冰雪便是所有的阻擋，
　　擋住了遠方洶湧澎湃的波濤。

從懸崖頂上傳來一聲召喚，
　　宣布靈魂集合，準備再生，
這種再生被叫做生存考驗，
　　人世間最令人費解的事情。
歪歪倒倒成群而過的靈魂，
　　來來往往川流不息的靈魂，
只能側耳傾聽其悅耳之聲，
　　想聽出它暗示些什麼夢境！

The Trial by Existence

Even the bravest that are slain
Shall not dissemble their surprise
On waking to find valor reign,
Even as on earth, in paradise;
And where they sought without the sword
Wide fields of asphodel fore'er,
To find that the utmost reward
Of daring should be still to dare.

The light of heaven falls whole and white
And is not shattered into dyes,
The light forever is morning light;
The hills are verdured pasturewise;
The angel hosts with freshness go,
And seek with laughter what to brave —
And binding all is the hushed snow
Of the far-distant breaking wave.

And from a cliff top is proclaimed
The gathering of the souls for birth,
The trial by existence named,
The obscuration upon earth.
And the slant spirits trooping by
In streams and cross-and counter-streams
Can but give ear to that sweet cry
For its suggestion of what dreams!

更多的遊魂會被轉過來，

　　又一次看那些靈魂作犧牲，

它們爲了某種已知的福分，

　　將心甘情願地放棄這天國。

一群發出白色微光的靈魂

　　像潮水般湧向上帝的寶座，

要親眼目睹上帝最寵愛的

　　那些虔誠的靈魂交上好運。

被選中的只有自願的靈魂，

　　當那些靈魂第一次聽見宣布

人世間交織著禍與福的生存，

　　心中不會有一絲一毫的疑問；

上帝把人世生存的短暫的夢，

　　描繪得非常完美，充滿溫情，

但沒有什麼可減弱或沖淡

　　天國樂園至高無上的特徵。

靈魂群中也不缺乏勇敢者，

　　有個靈魂愚蠢地挺身而出，

面對塵世間最遙遠的地方

　　赤裸裸地顯示出英雄氣概。

太陽下那些極不體面的事

　　在那兒聽來比世間更高貴；

於是頭腦發昏，心裡歡喜，

　　眾靈魂齊聲爲那勇敢者喝采。

And the more loitering are turned
To view once more the sacrifice
Of those who for some good discerned
Will gladly give up paradise.
And a white shimmering concourse rolls
Toward the throne to witness there
The speeding of devoted souls
Which God makes His especial care.

And none are taken but who will,
Having first heard the life read out
That opens earthward, gook and ill,
Beyond the shadow of a doubt;
And very beautifully God limns,
And tenderly, life's little dream,
But naught extenuates or dims,
Setting the thing that is supreme.

Nor is there wanting in the press
Some spirit to stand simply forth,
Heroic in its nakedness.
Against the uttermost of earth.
The tale of earth's unhonored things
Sounds nobler there than? neath the sun;
And the mind whirls and the heart sings,
And a shout greets the daring one.

但最後通常是由上帝說話：

　「這位勇者也許有一種記憶，
由於想到衝突紛爭的痛苦，

　他曾爲朋友而選擇生存方式；
但你們將接受的純粹命運

　不允許有任何選擇的記憶，
不然苦難就不是人世的苦難，

　不是你們都齊聲同意的苦難。」

於是選擇必須被重新作出，

　但最後的選擇仍與先前一樣；
這時候敬畏超過了驚嘆，

　喝采聲也變成了一片寂靜。
而上帝已經採下一朵金花，

　將其打碎，用花中的魔環
把靈魂縛牢，並使其具有

　幻覺意識，直到死亡來臨。

這就是人世間生存的本質，

　雖然我們都非常認眞地選擇，
但仍缺乏清晰而持久的記憶，

　記不得我們受苦受難的生活
不過是我們莫名其妙的選擇；

　於是我們被完全剝奪了自尊，
在只有一種結局的痛苦之中

　我們任生活被搗碎並變成迷惑。

But always God speaks at the end:
"One thought in agony of strife
The bravest would have by for friend,
The memory that he chose the life;
But the pure fate to which you go
Admits no memory of choice,
Or the woe were not earthly woe
To which you give the assenting voice."

And so the choice must be again,
But the last choice is still the same;
And the awe passes wonder then,
And a hush falls for all acclaim.
And God has taken a flower of gold
And broken it, and used therefrom
The mystic link to bind and hold
Spirit to matter till death come.

'Tis of the essence of life here,
Though we choose greatly, still to lack
The lasting memory at all clear,
That life has for us on the wrack
Nothing but what we somehow chose;
Thus are we wholly stripped of pride
In the pain that has but one close,
Bearing it crushed and mystified.

花叢

有一次我去翻曬已被割下的牧草，
有人早在清晨的露水中將其割倒。

在我看見那塊平坦坦的草場之前，
磨礪他那柄鐮刀的露水已經消散。

我曾繞到一片小樹林後把他找尋，
也期待過微風吹來他磨刀的聲音。

但他早已離開草場，因草已割完，
而我只能像他剛才一樣孤孤單單，

我心中暗想：正如人都注定孤單，
不管他們是一起幹活兒還是單幹。

我正這樣思忖，一隻迷惘的蝴蝶
舞著翅膀從我身邊迅疾地飛越，

懷著因隔夜而已變得模糊的牽掛，
牠在找一朵昨天使牠快活的野花。

起初我看見牠老在一處飛舞盤旋，
因爲那兒有朵枯萎的花躺在草間。

The Tuft of Flowers

I went to turn the grass once after one
Who mowed it in the dew before the sun.

The dew was gone that made his blade so keen
Before I came to view the leveled scene.

I looked for him behind an isle of trees;
I listened for his whetstone on the breeze.

But he had gone his way, the grass all mown,
And I must be, as he had been — alone,

"As all must be," I said within my heart,
"Whether they work together or apart."

But as I said it, swift there passed me by
On noiseless wing a bewildered butterfly,

Seeking with memories grown dim o'er night
Some resting flower of yesterday's delight.

And once I marked his flight go round and round,
As where some flower lay withering on the ground.

接著牠又飛向我目力所及的遠方，
然後又抖動著翅膀飛回到我身旁。

我在把一些沒有答案的問題思考，
而且正打算轉身翻曬地上的牧草；

可蝴蝶先飛回來，並把我的目光
引到小河岸邊一叢高高的野花上，

蘆葦叢生的河邊被割得寸草不留，
但那柄鐮刀偏對一叢花高抬貴手。

晨露中那位割草人如此喜愛它們，
留它們昂首怒放，但不是爲我們，

也不是爲了引起我們對他的注意，
而是因爲清晨河邊那純粹的歡愉。

但儘管如此，那隻蝴蝶和我自己
仍然從那個清晨得到了一種啓示，

那啓示使我聽見周圍有晨鳥啼鳴，
聽見他的鐮刀對大地低語的聲音，

And then he flew as far as eye could see,

And then on tremulous wing came back to me.

I thought of questions that have no reply,

And would have turned to toss the grass to dry;

But he turned first, and led my eye to look

At a tall tuft of flowers beside a brook,

A leaping tongue of bloom the scythe had spared

Beside a reedy brook the scythe had bared.

   The mower in the dew had loved them thus,

   By leaving them to flourish, not for us,

   Nor yet to draw one thought of ours to him,

   But from sheer morning gladness at the brim.

   The butterfly and I had lit upon,

   Nevertheless, a message form the dawn,

   That made me hear the wakening birds around,

   And hear his long scythe whispering to the ground,

感覺到一種與我同宗同源的精神，
於是我今後幹活不再是孑然一身；

而彷彿是與他一道，有他當幫手，
中午困乏時則共尋樹蔭同享午休；

睡夢中二人交談，好像親如弟兄，
而我原來並沒有指望能與他溝通。

「人類一起工作，」我由衷地對他說，
「不管他們是獨自還是在一起幹活。」

And feel a spirit kindred to my own;

So that henceforth I worked no more alone;

But glad with him, I worked as with his aid,

And weary, sought at noon with him the shade;

And dreaming, as it were, held brotherly speech

With one whose thought I had not hoped to reach.

"Men work together," I told him from the heart,

"Whether they work together or apart."

潘與我們在一起

有一天潘從森林裡出來——
他的皮膚、毛髮和眼睛都是灰色，
是牆頭上苔蘚的那種灰色——
　　他站在陽光下盡情觀看
　　樹木繁茂的幽谷和山巒。

他迎著微風，手持蘆笛，
在光禿禿牧場的高處站立；
在他統轄的所有土地之內
　　他不見人家，也不見煙火。
　　這真好！他用力把蹄一踩。

他熟悉安靜，因為沒人來
這貧瘠的牧場，除了一年一度
有人來為野放的牛群餵鹽，
　　或有提著木桶的鄉下孩子，
　　他們孤陋寡聞，講不出故事。

他揚起蘆管，新世界的歌
實在難教，他力所不能及，
林中的鳥叫、天邊的鷹鳴
　　已足以成為森林的象徵，
　　對於他已是夠美的音樂。

事過境遷，今非昔比，
這種蘆管已不具魔力，
還比不上毫無目的的柔風，
　　吹不動杜松掛果的樹枝，
　　吹不動一簇簇嬌弱的野菊。

它們是多神教徒尋歡的樂器，
而這個世界已找到新的價值。
他在太陽烤熱的土地上躺下，
　　揉碎一朵花，然後極目遠望——
　　吹奏？吹奏？他該吹奏什麼？

Pan With Us

Pan came out of the woods one day —
His skin and his hair and his eyes were gray,
The gray of the moss of walls were they —
And stood in the sun and looked his fill
At wooded valley and wooded hill.

He stood in the zephyr, pipes in hand,
On a height of naked pasture land;
In all the country he did command
He saw no smoke and he saw no roof.
That was well! and he stamped a hoof.

His heart knew peace, for none came here
To this lean feeding, save once a year
Someone to salt the half-wild steer,
Or homespun children with clicking pails
Who see so little they tell no tales.

He tossed his pipes, too hard to teach
A new-world song, far out of reach,
For a sylvan sign that the blue jay's screech
And the whimper of hawks beside the sun
Were music enough for him, for one.

Times were changed from what they were:
Such pipes kept less of power to stir
The fruited bough of the juniper
And the fragile bluets clustered there
Than the merest aimless breath of air.

They were pipes of pagan mirth,
And the world had found new terms of worth.
He laid him down on the sunburned earth
And raveled a flower and looked away.
Play? Play? — What should he play

造物主的笑聲

那是在遠方那座無變化的森林，
　我高興地發現了造物主的蹤跡，
不過我知道我追尋的不是真神。
　就在日光開始漸漸暗下來之際
我忽然聽見了我須聽見的一切；
那聲音已伴我度過了許多歲月。

當時聲音在我身後，而非在前，
　是種懶洋洋但半嘲半諷的聲音，
好像發聲者對什麼都不會在乎。
　那半神從泥沼出現，發出笑聲，
一邊走一邊擦去他眼上的污泥；
而我完全領會了他笑聲的含意。

我忘不了他的笑聲是怎樣發出。
　被他撞見使我覺得自己像白痴，
於是我突然止步，並裝模作樣，
　假裝是在找落葉間的什麼東西
（但不知他當時是否把我理睬）。
然後我就靠著一棵樹坐了下來。

The Demiurge's Laugh

It was far in the sameness of the wood;
I was running with joy on the Demon's trail,
Though I knew what I hunted was no true god.
It was just as the light was begirning to fail
That I suddenly heard — all I needed to hear:
It has lasted me many and many a year.

The sound was behind me instead of before,
A sleepy sound, but mocking half,
As of one who utterly couldn't care.
The Demon arose from his wallow to laugh,
Brushing the dirt from his eye as he went;
And well I knew what the Demon meant.

I shall not forget how his laugh rang out.
I felt as a fool to have been so caught,
And checked my steps to make pretense
It was something among the leaves I sought
(Though doubtful whether he stayed to see).
Thereafter I sat me against a tree.

現在請關上窗戶吧

現在請關上窗戶吧,讓原野沉寂;
　　如果樹要搖曳,讓它們搖也無聲;
眼下不會再有鳥鳴,萬一還有,
　　就把它算作我的損失。

要很久以後沼澤地才會復甦,
　　要很久以後最早的鳥才會飛回;
現在請關上窗戶吧,別聽風聲,
　　只消看萬物在風中搖動。

Now Close the Windows

Now close the windows and hush all the fields:

If the trees must, let them silently toss;

No bird is singing now, and if there is,

Be it my loss.

It will be long ere the marshes resume,

It will be long ere the earliest bird:

So close the windows and not hear the wind,

But see all wind-stirred.

在闊葉林中

片片相同的枯葉一層復一層！
它們向下飄落從頭頂的濃蔭，
爲大地披上一件褪色的金衣，
就像皮革剪裁那樣完全合身。

在新葉又攀上那些枝椏之前，
在綠葉又遮蔽那些樹幹之前，
枯葉得飄落，飄過土中籽實，
枯葉得飄落，落進腐朽黑暗。

腐葉定將被花籽的萌芽頂穿，
腐葉定將被埋在花的根下面。
雖然這事發生在另一個世界，
但我知人類世界也如此這般。

In Hardwood Groves

The same leaves over and over again!

They fall from giving shade above,

To make one texture of faded brown

And fit the earth like a leather glove.

Before the leaves can mount again

To fill the tress with another shade,

They must go down past things coming up.

They must go down into the dark decayed.

They must be pierced by flowers and put

Beneath the feet of dancing flowers.

However it is in some other world

I know that this is the way in ours.

風暴之歌

挾著風暴的破碎的烏雲在飛馳。
　　大路上終日冷冷清清，
路面上數不清的白石塊隆起，
　　蹄痕足跡都蕩然無存。
路邊野花太潮濕，蜜蜂也不採，
　　枉然度過艷麗的青春。
走過小山來吧，隨我去遠方，
　　到風雨中來做我的愛人。

在森林世界被撕碎的絕望之中
　　鳥兒幾乎都停息了歌聲，
此刻喧囂的是那些千年的精靈，
　　雖然鳥兒仍在林中棲身；
森林的歌聲全都被撕碎，就像
　　易遭摧殘的野玫瑰凋零。
到這潮濕的林中來吧，做我的愛人，
　　這兒枝葉滴雨，當風暴來臨。

強勁的疾風在我們身後驅策，
　　疾風會傳播我們的歌聲，
一汪汪淺水被厲風吹起漣漪，
　　快撩起你那墜地的長裙。
我們逕自去向西方又有何妨，
　　即便讓鞋襪沾上水痕？
因為滴雨的金菊──野生的胸針
　　會弄濕你美麗的胸襟。

摧枯拉朽的東風從未這般強勁，
　　可這似乎像是海歸的時辰，
大海復歸古老的陸地，在遠古
　　海在這兒留下貝殼粼粼。
這似乎也像是愛情復歸的時刻，
　　疑惑之後，我們的愛甦醒。
哦，來吧，走進這風暴與騷動，
　　到風雨中來做我的愛人。

A Line-Storm Song

The line-storm clouds fly tattered and swift.
The road is forlorn all day,
Where a myriad snowy quartz-stones lift,
And the hoofprints vanish away.
The roadside flowers, too wet for the bee,
Expend their bloom in vain.
Come over the hills and far with me,
And be my love in the rain.

The birds have less to say for themselves
In the wood-world's torn despair
Than now these numberless years the elves,
Although they are no less there:
All song of the woods is crushed like some
Wild, easily shattered rose.
Come, be my love in the wet woods, come,
Where the boughs rain when it blows.

There is the gale to urge behind
And bruit out singing down,
And the shallow waters aflutter with wind
From which to gather your gown.
What matter if we go clear to the west,
And come not through dry-shod?
For wilding brooch, shall wet your breast
The rain-fresh goldenrod.

Oh, never this whelming east wind swells
But it seems like the sea's return
To the ancient lands where it left the shells
Before the age of the fern;
And it seems like the time when, after doubt,
Our love came back amain.
Oh, come forth into the storm and rout
And be my love in the rain.

十月

哦，靜寂而柔和的十月之晨，
你的樹葉已熟成這金秋；
明天的風若是恣意放盪，
會把樹葉兒全都颳離枝頭。
烏鴉在森林上空成群啼叫，
也許明天就要結伴飛走。
哦，靜寂而柔和的十月之晨，
開始今天要用緩慢的節奏。
使我們覺得一天不那麼短暫，
讓我們並不討厭你的欺瞞，
用你所知的方法把我們騙誘。

拂曉時讓一片樹葉凋落，
中午時再讓另一片飄遊；
一片零落在我們眼前，
一片飄墜在天的盡頭；
用淡雲薄霧纏住疾行的太陽，
用紫霞碧靄迷住平原山丘。
緩緩，悠悠！
為了那些葡萄，即使只為葡萄，
它們的蔓葉已被嚴霜燒透，
為了那些攀緣在牆頭的葡萄，
不然它們的果實定難存留。

October

O hushed October morning mild,

Thy leaves have ripened to the fall;

Tomorrow's wind, if it be wild,

Should waste them all.

The crows above the forest call;

Tomorrow they may form and go.

O hushed October morning mild,

Begin the hours of this day slow.

Make the day seem to us less brief.

Hearts not averse to being beguiled,

Beguile us in the way you know.

Release one leaf at break of day;

At noon release another leaf;

One from our trees, one far away.

Retard the sun with gentle mist;

Enchant the land with amethyst.

Slow, slow!

For the grapes' sake if they were all,

Whose leaves already are burnt with frost,

Whose clustered fruit must else be lost ―

For the grapes' sake along the wall.

我的蝴蝶

你狂戀過的花兒如今也都凋謝，
那經常恐嚇你的襲擊太陽的瘋子
如今也逃走，或者死去；
除我之外
（如今這對你也不是悲哀！）
除我之外
原野上沒人留下來把你哀悼。

灰色的草上才剛剛灑落有雪花，
兩岸還沒有堵住河水流淌，
但那是很久以前──
彷彿已過了很久──
自從我第一次看見你掠過，
和你那些色彩艷麗的夥伴，
輕盈地飛舞嬉戲，
輕率地相親相戀，
追逐，盤旋，上下翻飛，
像仙女舞中一個軟軟的玫瑰花環。

那時候我惆悵的薄霧
還沒有籠罩這整片原野，
我知道我為你高興，
也為我自己高興。

My Butterfly

Thine emulous fond flowers are dead, too,

And the daft sun-assaulter, he

That frighted thee so oft, is fled or dead:

Save only me

(nor is it sad to thee!) —

Save only me

There is none left to mourn thee in the fields.

The gray grass is scarce dappled with the snow;

Its two banks have not shut upon the river;

But it is long ago —

It seems forever —

Since first I saw thee glance,

With all thy dazzling other ones,

In airy dalliance,

Precipitate in love,

Towed, tangled, whirled and whirled above,

Like a limp rose-wreath in a fairy dance.

When that was, the soft mist

Of my regret hung not on all the land,

And I was glad for thee,

And glad for me, I wist.

當時高高翻飛的你並不知道
命運創造你是爲了取悅於風，
用你無憂無慮的寬大翅膀，
而且我那時候也不知道。

還有一些別的情況：
似乎上帝曾讓你飛離祂輕握的手，
接著又擔心你飛得太遠，
飛到祂伸手不及的地方，
所以又過於熱切地一把將你抓走。

啊！我記得
與我作對的陰謀
曾如何充滿我的生活——
生活的柔情，夢一般的柔情；
波動的芳草攪亂我的思緒，
微風吹來三種香氣，
一朵寶石花在嫩枝上搖曳！

後來當我心煩意亂時，
當我不能説話時，
鹵莽的西風從側面吹來，
把什麼東西猛然拋在我臉上——
那竟然是你沾滿塵土的翅膀！

今天我發現那翅膀已破碎！
因爲你已死去，我説，
不相識的鳥也這麼説。
我發現破碎的翅膀和枯葉一道
散落在屋檐下面。

Thou didst not know, who tottered wondering on high,

That fate had made thee for the pleasure of the wind,

With those great careless wings,

Nor yet did I.

And there were other things:

It seemed God let thee flutter from His gentle clasp,

Then fearful he had let thee win

Too far beyond Him to be gathered in,

Snatched thee, o'ereager, with ungentle grasp.

Ah! I remember me

How once conspiracy was rife

Against my life —

The languor of it and the dreaming fond;

Surging, the grasses dizzied me of thought,

The breeze three odors brought,

And a gem-flower waved in a wand!

Then when I was distraught

And could not speak,

Sidelong, full on my cheek,

What should that reckless zephyr fling

But the wild touch of thy dye-dusty wing!

I found that wing broken today!

for thou art dead, I said,

And the strange birds say.

I found it with the withered leaves

Under the eaves.

不情願

我已穿過原野和樹林，
　　我已越過那些石牆，
我已登過視野開闊的高地，
　　看過這世界又步下山崗，
我已沿著大路回到家裡，
　　瞧！凡事都有個收場。

大地上的樹葉都已凋零，
　　只有一些橡葉還殘留樹枝，
等著被一片一片地吹落，
　　窸窸窣窣飄墜落地，
慢慢擦過凍硬的積雪，
　　當其他枯葉正在安息。

枯葉無聲地擠做一團，
　　再也不會被風四處吹散；
最後一朵寂寞的翠菊已枯萎；
　　金縷梅的花兒也都凋殘；
心兒依然在苦苦尋求，
　　但腳步卻問：「該去哪邊？」

唉，識時知趣地順水行舟，
　　體體面面地服從理智，
不管是愛情或季節到頭，
　　都聽從天命，接受現實，
不知這樣做在世人心中
　　何時才不被看成一種叛逆？

Reluctance

Out through the fields and the woods
And over the walls I have wended;
I have climbed the hills of view
And looked at the world, and descended;
I have come by the highway home,
And lo, it is ended.

The leaves are all dead on the ground,
Save those that the oak is keeping
To ravel them one by one
And let them go scraping and creeping
Out over the crusted snow,
When others are sleeping.

And the dead leaves lie huddled and still,
No longer blown hither and thither;
The last lone aster is gone;
The flowers of the witch hazel wither;
The heart is still aching to seek,
But the feet question "Whither?"

Ah, when to the heart of man
Was it ever less than a treason
To go with the drift of things,
To yield with a grace to reason,
And bow and accept the end
Of a love or a season?

波士頓以北

NORTH OF BOSTON

補牆

有一種不喜歡牆的東西，
它總讓牆腳的泥土凍得膨脹，
它在光天化日之下掀掉牆頭的礫石，
它撕開的豁口兩人能並肩來往。
獵人們毀牆則用另一種方式，
我常跟在他們身後壘石補牆，
他們總不把掰開的牆石壘回原處，
卻常常把野兔趕出藏身的石縫，
讓狂吠的獵犬歡暢。我是說
沒人見過石牆裂塌或聽見裂塌的聲響，
可一到春天那些牆總是百孔千瘡。

我與山那邊的鄰居相約，
同一天雙雙來到那殘垣斷牆。
我們又讓那道牆隔在我倆之間。
我們一邊走一邊把豁口補上。
各自拾起掉在自家牆腳的石塊。
石塊有的像麵包，有的呈球狀，
要放穩它們，我倆不得不唸句咒語：
「好好呆著吧，直到我們轉過身去！」
搬壘石塊磨粗了我們的手掌。
唉，這真像另一種室外遊戲，
一人在一邊，這只算是一種遊戲，
因為壘牆的地方我們並不需要牆；

Mending Wall

Something there is that doesn't love a wall,

That sends the frozen-ground-swell under it

And spills the upper boulders in the sun,

And makes gaps even two can pass abreast.

The work of hunters is another thing:

I have come after them and made repair

Where they have left not one stone on a stone,

But they would have the rabbit out of hiding,

To please the yelping dogs. The gaps I mean,

No one has seen them made or heard them made,

But at spring mending-time we find them there.

        I let my neighbor know beyond the hill;

        And on a day we meet to walk the line

        And set the wall between us once again.

        We keep the wall between us as we go.

        To each the boulders that have fallen to each.

        And some are loaves and some so nearly balls

        We have to use a spell to make them balance:

        "Stay where you are until our backs are turned!"

        We wear our fingers rough with handling them.

        Oh, just another kind of outdoor game,

        One on a side. It comes to little more:

        There where it is we do not need the wall:

他那邊種的松樹，我這邊栽的蘋果，
我的蘋果樹絕不會越過邊界
去偷吃他樹下的松果，我對他講。
可他只說：「籬笆牢實鄰居情久長。」
春天對我真是一場災害，我納悶
是否我能讓他有這樣一種思想：
「籬笆為什麼能使鄰居和睦？難道它
不是該豎在有牛的地方？但這兒沒牛。
我在壘牆之前就應該問清楚
我會圍進什麼，又把什麼圍在牆外，
我有可能把誰的感情挫傷。
世上有一種不喜歡牆的東西，

它希望牆都倒塌。」我可以對他說
那是「精靈」，可又不盡然，我寧願
他自己能說出那是什麼。我見他
一隻手抓緊一塊石頭，就像
舊石器時代的野蠻人手持武器一樣。
我覺得他彷彿進了一片黑暗，
那黑暗不僅僅因樹陰遮蔽了日光。
他不願去推敲父輩的那句格言，
倒喜歡把那句老話常記心上，
他還會說：「籬笆牢固鄰居情久長。」

He is all pine and I am apple orchard,

My apple trees will never get across

And eat the cones under his pines, I tell him.

He only says, "Good fences make good neighbors."

Spring is the mischief in me, and I wonder

If I could put a notion in his head:

"Why do they make good neighbors? Isn't it

Where there are cows? But here there are no cows.

Before I built a wall I'd ask to know

What I was walling in or walling out,

And to whom I was like to give offense.

Something there is that doesn't love a wall,

That wants it down." I could say "Elves" to him,

But it's not elves exactly, and I'd rather

He said it for himself. I see him there,

Bringing a stone grasped firmly by the top

In each hand, like an old-stone savage armed.

He moves in darkness as it seems to me,

Not of woods only and the shade of trees

He will not go behind his father's saying,

And he likes having thought of it so well

He says again, "Good fences make good neighbors."

雇工之死

瑪麗若有所思地盯著桌上的油燈，
等沃倫回家。一聽見他的腳步聲
她就踮起腳尖跑過黑漆漆的走廊
去門口迎接他，告訴他一個消息，
好讓他有所預防。「賽拉斯回來了，」
她一邊說一邊推著他一起到門外，
並關上身後的房門，「請對他好點。」
她接過沃倫從市場上買回的東西，
將它們放在門廊上，然後拉著他
並肩在門廊前的木製台階上坐下。

「我究竟在什麼時候對他不好過？
但我不會讓這傢伙回來。」他說。
「夏天割草時我難道沒告訴過他？
我說他那時要走就永遠別再回來。
他有什麼本事？別人誰會雇他？
年紀一大把，能幹的活兒已不多。
即使他還能幹活兒也完全靠不住。
他總是在我最需要他時離我而去。
他老覺得我應該付他一份工資，
至少應該夠他買點菸草，
這樣他就不會因討煙而欠下人情。

The Death of The Hired Man

Mary sat musing on the lamp-flame at the table,

Waiting for Warren. When she heard his step,

She ran on tiptoe down the darkened passage

To meet him in the doorway with the news

And put him on his guard. "Silas is back."

She pushed him outward with her through the door

And shut it after her. "Be kind," she said.

She took the market things from Warren's arms

And set them on the porch, then drew him down

To sit beside her on the wooden steps.

"When was I ever anything but kind to him?

But I'll not have the fellow back," he said.

"I told him so last haying, didn't I?"

If he left then, I said, that ended it.

What good is he? Who else will harbor him

At his age for the little he can do?

What help he is there's no depending on.

Off he goes always when I need him most.

He thinks he ought to earn a little pay,

Enough at least to buy tobacco with,

So he won't have to beg and be beholden.

『好哇，』我說，『我希望我能付，
但我付不起任何固定工資。』
『有人付得起。』『那有人將不得不付。』
如果他那樣說僅僅是爲了抬高自己，
我本不該介意。但你可以相信
他開始那樣說時，他背後總會有人
在設法用一點零花錢哄他過去——
在割草曬草難找幫工的時候。
到冬天他又回來。但我的活已幹完。」
「噓！小聲點！他會聽見的，」瑪麗說。
「我就想讓他聽見，他遲早都會聽見。」

「他累壞了。他正在火爐邊睡覺。
我從羅家回來時發現他在這兒，
在牲口棚門外縮成一團睡得正香，
那模樣眞可憐，也眞可怕——
你可別笑——當時我沒認出他來——
我沒想到會看見他——他完全變了。
待會兒你自己看吧。」

　　　　　　「他說他前陣子在哪兒？」

'All right,' I say, 'I can't afford to pay
Any fixed wages, though I wish I could.'
'Someone else can.' 'Then someone else will have to.'
I shouldn't mind his bettering himself
If that was what it was. You can be certain,
When he begins like that, there's someone at him
Trying to coax him off with pocket money —
In haying time, when any help is scarce.
In winter he comes back to us. I'm done."
"Sh! not so loud: he'll hear you," Mary said.
"I want him to: he'll have to soon or late."

                              "He's worn out. He's asleep beside the stove.
                              When I came up from Rowe's I found him here,
                              Huddled against the barn door fast asleep,
                              A miserable sight, and frightening, too —
                              You needn't smile — I didn't recognize him —
                              I wasn't looking for him — and he's changed.
                              Wait till you see."
                                        "Where did you say he'd been?"

「他沒講。我把他拉進了屋子，
讓他喝茶，還想讓他抽煙。
我也試過讓他談談自己的經歷。
但什麼都沒成。他只是不停打瞌睡。」
「他說過什麼？他說過任何話嗎？」
「沒說什麼。」

　　　「沒說什麼？瑪麗，老實講
他說他想來爲我的草場挖溝排水。」

　　「沃倫！」

　　「他說了嗎？我只是想知道。」
「他當然說了。你想要他說什麼呢？
你肯定不會不讓那可憐的老人
用某種卑微的方式保全他的自尊。

他還說，如果你眞想知道，
他還打算清理高處的那片牧場。
這聽起來和你以前聽到過的一樣？
沃倫，你要是也能聽他說就好了，
他當時東拉西扯，有好幾次
我都停下來看——我覺得他很古怪——
看他是不是在睡夢中胡言亂語。
他老是說起威爾遜——你記得——
四年前你雇來割草的那個小伙子。
他已念完了書，現在學校當老師。
賽拉斯斷言你將不得不弄他回來。
他說他倆將成爲一對幹活兒的搭檔，
他們會把這牧場收拾得平整漂亮！

"He didn't say. I dragged him to the house,

And gave him tea and tried to make him smoke.

I tried to make him talk about his travels.

Nothing would do: he just kept nodding off."

"What did he say? Did he say anything?"

"But little."

    "Anything? Mary, confess

He said he'd come to ditch the meadow for me."

"Warren!"

    "But did he? I just want to know."

"Of course he did. What would you have him say?

Surely you wouldn't grudge the poor old man

Some humble way to save his self-respect.

        He added, if you really care to know,

        He meant to clear the upper pasture, too.

        That sounds like something you have heard before?

        Warren, I wish you could have heard the way

        He jumbled everything. I stopped to look

        Two or three times — he made me feel so queer —

        To see if he was talking in his sleep.

        He ran on Harold Wilson — you remember —

        The boy you had in haying four years since.

        He's finished school, and teaching in his college.

        Silas declares you'll have to get him back.

        He says they two will make a team for work:

        Between them they will lay this farm as smooth!

他認爲威爾遜是個有出息的小伙子，
只是傻乎乎地要念書——你知道
那年七月他們在日頭下如何鬥嘴，
當時賽拉斯在馬車上裝草，
威爾遜則在下面把草叉上馬車。」
「是的，我當時儘量避開他們的吵聲。」
「唉，那些日子像折磨賽拉斯的夢。
你想不到會這樣。有些事忘不掉！
威爾遜那種大學生的自信惹他生氣。
都過了這麼多年，他卻還在搜尋
他覺得他當時本可以用上的巧辯。

　　　　　　　　　　我體諒他。我知道那是種什麼感覺，
　　　　　　　　　　當你想到該說的話卻爲時太晚。
　　　　　　　　　　他老把威爾遜和拉丁語連在一起。
　　　　　　　　　　威爾遜曾說他學拉丁語就像學提琴，
　　　　　　　　　　他問我認爲威爾遜這話是什麼意思。
　　　　　　　　　　因爲他喜歡學唄——那是個理由！
　　　　　　　　　　他說他沒法讓那個小伙子相信
　　　　　　　　　　他可以用一柄榛木草杈找到泉水——」

The way he mixed that in with other things.

He thinks young Wilson a likely lad, though daft

On education — you know how they fought

All through July under the blazing sun.

Silas up on the cart to build the load.

Harold along beside to pitch it on."

"Yes, I took care to keep well out of earshot."

"Well, those days trouble Silas like a dream.

You wouldn't think they would. How some things linger!

Harold's young college-boy's assurance piqued him.

After so many years he still keeps finding

Good arguments he sees he might have used.

I sympathize. I know just how it feels

To think of the right thing to say too late.

Harold's associated in his mind with Latin.

He asked me what I thought of Harold's saying

He studied Latin, like the violin,

Because he liked it — that an argument!

He said he couldn't make the boy believe

He could find water with a hazel prong —

Which showed how much good school had ever done him.

He wanted to go over that. But most of all

He thinks if he could have another chance

To teach him how to build a load of hay —"

「我知道，那是賽拉斯的拿手絕活。
他把每一杈乾草都堆在該堆的地方，
就像替草捆貼了標籤，加了編號，
這樣卸車時他就能依序找到它們。
賽拉斯幹這活兒真是無可挑剔。
他卸草捆就像是在摘一個個鳥巢。
你絕不會看見他站在他堆的草上，
他總能盡力使自己的手抬得夠高。」
「他認爲如果他能教會威爾遜堆草，
他也許就對這世上的某人有過用處。
他不願看到一個只會念書的傻小子。
可憐的賽拉斯，他那麼關心別人，
但自己的過去卻沒有什麼值得自豪，
自己的將來也看不到任何希望，
所以他永遠都不會有任何變化。」

半個月亮正在西天慢慢墜落，
正拽著整個天空一道墜下山坡。
柔和的月光灑在她懷中。她看見了它
並向它揮了揮圍裙。她把手
伸在被露水繃緊的牽牛花藤之間，
從花台爬向屋檐的花藤像豎琴琴弦，
彷彿她奏出了一支無聲的曲調，
一支對身邊的他有影響的曲調。
「沃倫，」她說，「他是回家來死，
這次你不用擔心他會離你而去。」

"I know, that's Silas' one accomplishment.

He bundles every forkful in its place,

And tags and numbers it for future reference,

So he can find and easily dislodge it

In the unloading. Silas does that well.

He takes it out in bunches like big birds' nests.

You never see him standing on the hay

He's trying to lift, straining to lift himself."

"He thinks if he could teach him that, he'd be

Some good perhaps to someone in the world.

He hates to see a boy the fool of books.

Poor Silas, so concerned for other folk,

And nothing to look backward to with pride,

And nothing to look forward to with hope,

So now and never any different."

Part of a moon was falling down the west,

Dragging the whole sky with it to the hills.

Its light poured softly in her lap. She saw it

And spread her apron to it. She put out her hand

Among the harplike morning-glory strings,

Taut with the dew from garden bed to eaves,

As if she played unheard some tenderness

That wrought on him beside her in the night.

"Warren," she said, "he has come home to die:

You needn't be afraid he'll leave you this time."

「家！」沃倫譏諷道。

　　　　　　「對，不是家是什麼？
這完全取決於你心中對家的定義。
當然，他與我們毫無關係，就像
那條從森林中來過我家的陌生獵犬，
牠當時因追獵物而累得精疲力盡。」
「家就是在你不得不進去的時候，
他們不得不讓你進去的地方。」

　　　　　　「我倒想把家叫做
某種不一定非要值得才享有的東西。」
沃倫俯身向前走了一兩步，
拾起一根枯枝，又走回台階，
然後將枯枝折斷並扔在一旁。

「你認為賽拉斯更有理由投靠我們
而不是找他兄弟？只有十三英里遠，
路上的風吹也能把他吹到那裡。
賽拉斯今天肯定也走了那麼多路。
他幹嘛不去那兒？他兄弟有錢，
是個人物——在銀行裡當經理。」
「他沒跟我們說起過。」

　　　　　　「可我們知道這事。」
「我當然認為他兄弟該幫他一把。
有必要我會去過問這事。他按理
該把他接去，而且說不定他願意——
他也許比他看上去更慷慨仁慈。

"Home," he mocked gently.

   "Yes, what else but home?

It all depends on what you mean by home.

Of course he's nothing to us, any more

Than was the hound that came a stranger to us

Out of the woods, worn out upon the trail."

"Home is the place where, when you have to go there,

they have to take you in."

   "I should have called it

Something you somehow haven't to deserve."

Warren leaned out and took a step or two,

Picked up a little stick, and brought it back

And broke it in his hand and tossed it by.

     "Silas has better claim on us you think

     Than on his brother? Thirteen little miles

     As the road winds would bring him to his door.

     Silas has walked that far no doubt today.

     Why doesn't he go there? His brother's rich,

     A somebody — director in the bank."

     "He never told us that."

        "We know it, though."

     "I think his brother ought to help, of course.

     I'll see to that if there is need. He ought of right

     To take him in, and might be willing to —

     He may be better than appearances.

但替賽拉斯想想。難道你認為
如果他對聲稱有兄弟感到自豪；
如果他指望從他兄弟得到任何東西，
這些年來他還會對他隻字不提？」
「真不知他倆之間是怎麼回事。」
　　　　　　　　「我可以告訴你。
賽拉斯就是這樣，我們不常在意他，
但他正是親戚們難容忍的那種人。
他從沒幹過一件真正的壞事。
他不明白為什麼他不能和別人
一樣好。雖說他一文不名，
他卻不屑蒙羞含恥去討好他兄弟。」

　　　　　　　　　　　　「我倒真想不出他傷害過什麼。」
　　　　　　　　　　　　「是呀，可他今天卻使我傷心，
　　　　　　　　　　　　那樣躺著，頭在硬椅背上轉動。
　　　　　　　　　　　　他無論如何也不讓我扶他到床上。
　　　　　　　　　　　　你必須進去看看，看你能做什麼。
　　　　　　　　　　　　我已為他鋪好床讓他過夜。
　　　　　　　　　　　　你看見他定會吃驚──他完全垮了。
　　　　　　　　　　　　他再也不能幹活──這點我敢肯定。」
　　　　　　　　　　　　「我倒不想急著下結論。」
　　　　　　　　　　　　「我也不想。去吧，自己去看看。
　　　　　　　　　　　　可是，沃倫，記住是怎麼回事，
　　　　　　　　　　　　他來是想要幫你為荒地挖溝排水。

But have some pity on Silas. Do you think

If he had any pride in claiming kin

Or anything he looked for from his brother,

He'd keep so still about him all this time?"

"I wonder what's between them."

                        "I can tell you.

Silas is what he is — we wouldn't mind him —

But just the kind that kinsfolk cant abide.

He never did a thing so very bad.

He don't know why he isn't quite as good

As anybody. Worthless though he is,

He won't be made ashamed to please his brother."

                "I can't think Si ever hurt anyone."

                "No, but he hurt my heart the way he lay

                and rolled his old head on that sharp-edged chair-back.

                He wouldn't let me put him on the lounge.

                You must go in and see what you can do.

                I made the bed up for him there tonight.

                You'll be surprised at him — how much he's broken.

                His working days are done; I'm sure of it."

                "I'd not be in a hurry to say that."

                "I haven't been. Go, look, see for yourself.

                But, Warren, please remember how it is:

                He's come to help you ditch the meadow.

他有一套想法。你千萬別笑話他。

他也許不會提這事；也許會提。

我就坐在這兒，看那片小小的浮雲

是撞上還是錯過月亮。」

　　　　　　浮雲撞上了月亮。

於是三者在朦朧的夜色中排成一行——

半輪月亮，銀色的小小浮雲和她。

沃倫回來——她覺得回來得太快——

悄悄坐到她身邊，握住她的手等待。

「沃倫？」她問。

　　　　「死了。」便是他的全部回答。

He has a plan. You mustn't laugh at him.

He may not speak of it, and then he may.

I'll sit and see if that small sailing cloud

Will hit or miss the moon."

It hit the moon.

Then there were three there, making a dim row,

The moon, the little silver cloud, and she.

Warren returned — too soon, it seemed to her —

Slipped to her side, caught up her hand and waited.

"Warren?" she questioned.

        "Dead," was all he answered.

山

大山把小城罩在一片陰影之中。
有次我羈留小城，臨睡前看山，
發現我看不見西天的星星，
那黑沉沉的山擋住了西方天際。
山顯得很近，我覺得它像一堵牆，
一堵使我免遭風吹的高牆。
但當我清晨出去觀光的時候，
我發現在小城與大山之間
有田野，有條河，河那邊還有田野。
那條河當時正值枯水季節，
河水漫過大卵石嘩嘩流過，
但仍能看到它春天泛濫過的痕跡：

被沖出溝壑的草原，草叢間的
沙埂，還有被剝了皮的漂流木。
我過了那條河，轉身朝向大山
迎面看見一人趕著一輛裝滿的牛車，
頭上有白斑的騾牛走得慢慢騰騰，
看來讓趕車人把車停下也無妨。
「這是哪個城鎮？」我問。

　　　　「這嘛？盧嫩堡。」
如此說來我錯了，我所羈留的
橋那邊的小城不屬這座山的城鎮，
只是在夜裡會感到山影的存在。

The Mountain

The mountain held the town as in a shadow.

I saw so much before I slept there once:

I noticed that I missed stars in the west,

Where its black body cut into the sky.

Near me it seemed: I felt it like a wall

Behind which I was sheltered from a wind.

And yet between the town and it I found,

When I walked forth at dawn to see new things,

Were fields, a river, and beyond, more fields.

The river at the time was fallen away,

And made a widespread brawl on cobblestones;

But the signs showed what it had done in spring:

Good grassland gullied out, and in the grass

Ridges of sand, and driftwood stripped of bark.

I crossed the river and swung round the mountain.

And there I met a man who moved so slow

With white-faced oxen, in a heavy cart,

It seemed no harm to stop him altogether.

"what town is this?" I asked.

"This? Lunenburg."

Then I was wrong: the town of my sojourn,

Beyond the bridge, was not that of the mountain,

But only felt at night its shadowy presence.

「你們的市鎮在哪兒？離這兒遠嗎？」
「這兒沒市鎮，只有零散的農場。
上次選舉我們鎮上有六十人投票。
實際上我們這兒不可能人丁興旺，
因為那傢伙太占地方！」他一邊說
一邊揮動趕牛棒指了指那座大山。
山腳下的牧場往上延伸了一小截，
然後就是一排可見樹幹的大樹，
大樹後面只見層層疊翠的樹梢，
蔥籠林海中有懸崖峭壁時隱時現。
一條乾涸的河溝從山腳樹林
伸進牧場。
　　　　「那兒看上去像條路。
那就是從這兒通往山頂的路嗎？──
我今天不上山，但下次會上的；
這會兒我必須趕回去吃早飯。」

「我不贊成你從這邊上山。
這邊沒有正經的路，但據我所知
那些上過山的人都從拉德客店出發。
往回走五英里，你能找到那地方，
就在山坡上，他們去年冬天才開店。
我想把你帶去，可惜不順路。」
「你沒爬上過山頂？」
　　　　「我爬上過山腰，
去獵鹿釣魚。那兒有條小河

"Where is your village? Very far from here?"

"There is no village — only scattered farms.

We were but sixty voters last election.

We can't in nature grow to many more:

That thing takes all the room!" He moved his goad.

The mountain stood there to be pointed at.

Pasture ran up the side a little way,

And then there was a wall of trees with trunks;

After that only tops of trees, and cliffs

Imperfectly concealed among the leaves.

A dry ravine emerged from under boughs

Into the pasture.

        "That looks like a path.

Is that the way to reach the top from here? —

Not for this morning, but some other time:

I must be getting back to breakfast now."

           "I don't advise your trying from this side.

There is no proper path, but those that have

Been up, I understand, have climbed from Ladd's.

That's five miles back. You can't mistake the place:

They logged it there last winter some way up.

I'd take you, but I'm bound the other way."

           "You've never climbed it?"

                "I've been on the sides,

Deer-hunting and trout-fishing. There's a brook

就從山間流出──我聽人家說
那源頭正好在山頂上──真是怪事。
但讓你覺得更怪的是那條河的水,
它永遠是夏天清涼,冬天暖和。
而它最值得讓人親眼見識的奇觀
是它冬天會像牛噴氣一樣冒蒸氣,
蒸氣會使小河兩岸低矮的灌木
都裹上一英寸長的針狀的凝霜──
你知道那種霜。然後讓陽光照在上面!」
「要不是森林一直覆蓋到山頂,
這樣一座山倒應該是天下一景。」
透過深林茂葉的屏障,我看見了
光影交錯之中的花崗岩階地,
突出的岩石可借人攀登時踏腳──
何懼身後就是百呎懸崖深淵。
攀登者也可轉身坐下極目眺望,
手肘挨著從岩縫間長出的羊齒蕨。

「天下一景我不敢說。但在峰頂
聽說有一股泉水,有點像噴泉。
值得一看。」

　　　　　「要是真有那泉水的話,
你從沒親眼見過?」

　　　　　「我猜山上一定
有那股泉水,但我從沒親眼見過。
它也許並不是恰好在山頂,
因為從山間流出來的流水,

That starts up on it somewhere — I've heard say

Right on the top, tip-top — a curious thing.

But what would interest you about the brook,

It's always cold in summer, warm in winter.

One of the great sights going is to see

It steam in winter like an ox's breath,

Until the bushes all along its banks

Are inch-deep with the frosty spines and bristles —

You know the kind. Then let the sun shine on it!"

"There ought to be a view around the world

From such a mountain — if it isn't wooded

Clear to the top." I saw through leafy screens

Great granite terraces in sun and shadow,

Shelves one could rest a knee on getting up —

With depths behind him sheer a hundred feet —

Or turn and sit on and look out and down,

With little ferns in crevices at his elbow.

          "As to that I can't say. But there's the spring,

          Right on the summit, almost like a fountain.

          That ought to be worth seeing."

                   "If it's there.

          You never saw it?"

                   "I guess there's no doubt

          About its being there. I never saw it.

          It may not be right on the very top:

          It wouldn't have to be a long way down

並不一定非從老高的山頂冒出，
而那些爬了很長一段路的登山人
很可能沒注意到遠處的山頂。
有一次我請一位來爬山的遊客
到頂上看看並告訴我那股泉如何。」
「他說什麼？」

　　　　　「他說在愛爾蘭什麼地方
有一個湖就正好在山頂。」
「湖是另一回事，那股泉水呢？」
「他爬得不夠高，沒看見泉水。
這也是我不主張你從這邊爬的原因。
他就是從這邊上山的。我一直都
想上去親眼看看，不過這是不可能的：
一輩子都圍著山腳打轉，
真要去爬它反而覺得沒意思。

我上山去幹嘛？要我穿著工作服，
拿著趕牛棒去趕到擠奶時間
還沒從山坡上回牲口棚的乳牛？
還是要我拿著獵槍去找迷路的黑熊？
只為爬山而爬山好像挺不實惠。」
「要是我不想爬山我也不會去爬──
不會為爬山而爬山。這山叫什麼名字？」
「我們管它叫霍爾山，但不知對不對。」
「可以繞山而行嗎？繞一圈遠嗎？」

To have some head of water from above,

And a good distance down might not be noticed

By anyone who'd come a long way up.

One time I asked a fellow climbing it

To look and tell me later how it was."

"What did he say?"

                "He said there was a lake

Somewhere in Ireland on a mountain top."

"But a lake's different. What about the spring?"

"He never got up high enough to see.

That's why I don't advise your trying this side.

He tried this side. I've always meant to go

And look myself, but you know how it is:

It doesn't seem so much to climb a mountain

You've worked around the foot of all you life.

                What would I do? Go in my overalls,

                With a big stick, the same as when the cows

                Haven't come down to the bars at milking time?

                Or with a shotgun for a stray black bear?

                "Twouldn't seem real to climb for climbing it."

                "I shouldn't climb it if I didn't want to —

                Not for the sake of climbing. What's its name?"

                "We call it Hor: I don't know if that's right."

                "Can one walk around it? Would it be too far?"

「你可以駕車繞一圈而不出盧嫩堡，
不過你能做到的也就是這些，
因爲盧嫩堡鎮界就貼著山腳環繞。
霍爾山就是城鎮，城鎮就是霍爾山——
有些零星的房舍散佈在山腳四周，
就像從懸崖上崩裂的岩石
沿著山坡朝前多滾了一截。」
「你剛才說，那河水冬暖夏涼？」
「其實我並不認爲水溫有什麼變化。
你我都非常清楚，說它暖
是和冷相比，說它冷是和熱比。
有趣的是，看你怎麼解釋吧。」

「你一輩子都住在山下？」
　　　　　　　「自從霍爾山
還不如……」不如什麼，我沒聽見。
他揮棒碰了碰牛的鼻子和肋腹，
拽了拽韁繩，吆喝了兩聲，
然後趕著那輛牛車慢悠悠地遠去。

"You can drive round and keep in Lunenburg,

But it's as much as ever you can do,

The boundary lines keep in so close to it.

Hor is the township, and the township's Hor —

And a few houses sprinkled round the foot,

Like boulders broken off the upper cliff,

Rolled out a little farther than the rest."

"Warm in December, cold in June, you say?"

"I don't suppose the water's changed at all.

You and I know enough to know it's warm

Compared with cold, and cold compared with warm.

But all the fun's in how you say a thing."

        "You've lived here all you life?"

            "Ever since Hor

Was no bigger than a —" What, I did not hear.

He drew the oxen toward him with light touches

Of his slim goad on nose and offside flank,

Gave them their marching orders and was moving.

一百條襯衫領

蘭開斯特生了他——那樣一座小鎮，
這樣一個大人物。但最近些年小鎮
不常見他，他保留著原有家宅
並讓妻子兒女去那兒過夏天，
過無拘無束、稍有點放縱的夏天。
有時候他也會去陪家人住一兩天，
並看看他不知何故有些距離的老朋友。
朋友們喜歡晚飯後在雜貨店與他相會，
滿腦子都想著難以對付的郵件，
他說話時他們也在偷偷看信。
他們顯得有顧慮。他本不想這樣，
因為他雖是大學者，但有民主精神，
若非發自內心，至少也出於原則。

最近在北上去蘭開斯特的途中，
他的火車誤點，誤了換乘的列車，
深夜已過十一點的時候，
他得在伍茲維爾站等四個小時。
他太累，不想在候車室裡受折磨，
於是他轉身去旅店想睡上一覺。
「沒房間，」夜班櫃台說，「除非——」
伍茲維爾充滿了喧囂、遊動的燈光
和轟隆隆的車輛，但只有一家旅店。
「你說『除非』。」

A Hundred Collars

Lancaster bore him — such a little town,

Such a great man. It doesn't see him often

Of late years, though he keeps the old homestead

And sends the children down there with their mother

To run wild in the summer — a little wild.

Sometimes he joins them for a day or two

And sees old friends he somehow can't get near.

They meet him in the general store at night,

Preoccupied with formidable mail,

Rifling a printed letter as he talks.

They seem afraid. He wouldn't have it so:

Though a great scholar, he's a democrat.

If not at heart, at least on principle.

Lately when coming up to Lancaster.

His train being late, he missed another train

And had four hours to wait at Woodsville Junction

After eleven o'clock at night. Too tired

To think of sitting such an ordeal out,

He turned to the hotel to find a bed.

"No room," the night clerk said. "Unless — "

Woodsville's a place of shrieks and wandering lamps

And cars that shock and rattle — and one hotel.

"You say 'unless.' "

　　　　「除非你不介意與
另一個人共住一個房間。」
　　　　　　　「什麼人？」
「男人。」
　　　「我想也是。什麼樣的男人？」
「我認識他，人不錯。男人就是男人。
當然是各睡各的床，這你明白。」
接待員挑戰似地朝他眨眼睛。
「睡在接待室椅子上的男人是誰？
難道他拒絕我現在這個機會？」
「他害怕被人搶竊，或被謀殺。
你怕嗎？」
　　　　「我得上床睡覺。」

櫃台領他上了三階樓梯，
然後穿過一條有許多門的走廊。
他敲了敲盡頭一扇房門，進了房間。
「萊夫，有個人想與你分租這間房。」
「帶他進來吧。我可不怕他。
我還沒醉到不能照顧自己的地步。」
櫃台拍了拍臥床的床架，
「你睡這張床。晚安。」說完離去。
「我想萊夫是姓？」
　　　　　　　「對，萊夫耶特。
你聽過就會記得。你姓什麼？」

"Unless you wouldn't mind

Sharing a room with someone else."

"Who is it?"

"A man."

"So I should hope. What kind of man?"

"I know him: he's all right. A man's a man.

Separate beds, of course, you understand."

The night clerk blinked his eyes and dared him on.

"Who's that man sleeping in the office chair?

Has he had the refusal of my chance?"

"He was afraid of being robbed or murdered.

What do you say?"

"I'll have to have a bed."

The night clerk led him up three flights of stairs

And down a narrow passage full of doors,

At the last one of which he knocked and entered.

"Lafe, here's a fellow wants to share your room."

"Show him this way. I'm not afraid of him.

I'm not so drunk I can't take care of myself."

The night clerk clapped a bedstead on the foot.

"This will be yours. Good-night," he said, and went.

"Lafe was the name, I think?"

"Yes, Layfayette.

You got it the first time. And yours?"

「馬貢。

馬貢博士。」

「博士？」

「也是個教授。」

「絞盡腦汁異想天開的教授？

等等，我腦子裡好像有件事，

一直想問問我碰巧結識的第一人，

不過我現在一下子想不起來。

待會兒再問你──請別讓我忘了。」

博士打量了萊夫後移開目光。

男人？粗人？上身一絲不掛，

醉醺醺地坐在燈光下，格外刺眼，

他正笨手笨腳地打開一件襯衫的鈕扣。

「我正想換一件大一點的襯衫。

我近來覺得不舒服，但不知為什麼，

今晚才發現毛病出在哪裡。

我就像苗圃裡的一棵樣本樹，

樹幹長粗了但名牌箍卻沒換大。

我以前只怪我們這兒天氣太熱，

原來只是我這該死的背

不肯坦白地承認我已經長胖了。

這是十八號襯衫。你穿多大尺寸？」

博士突然嗓子發硬，結結巴巴地說：

「哦──呀──十四號──十四號。」

        "Magoon.

Doctor Magoon."

        "A Doctor?"

        "Well, a teacher."

"Professor Square-the-circle-till-you're-tired?

Hold on, there's something I don't think of now

That I had on my mind to ask the first

Man that knew anything I happened in with.

I'll ask you later — don't let me forget it."

The Doctor looked at Lafe and looked away.

A man? A brute. Naked above the waist,

He sat there creased and shining in the light,

Fumbling the buttons in a well-starched shirt.

        "I'm moving into a size-larger shirt.

        I've felt mean lately; mean's no name for it.

        I just found what the matter was tonight:

        I've been a-choking like a nursery tree

        When it outgrows the wire band of its name tag.

        I blamed it on the hot spell we've been having.

        'T was nothing but my foolish hanging back,

        Not liking to own up I'd grown a size.

        Number eighteen this is. What size do you wear?"

        The Doctor caught his throat convulsively.

        "Oh — ah — fourteen — fourteen."

「你說十四號！

我還記得我穿十四號的時候。

細想起來，我家裡肯定還有

一百多條襯衫領，十四號的。

浪費了真可惜。你收下它們吧。

它們是你的了，請允許我寄給你。——

你幹嘛那樣站在那裡？

凱克離去後你就沒挪動過一步。

你那模樣好像是不想進這房間。

坐下或躺下吧，朋友；你讓我緊張。」

博士順從地快步衝到床前，

像走投無路似地靠上枕頭。

「你不能把鞋放在凱克的白床單上。

你不能穿著鞋睡，讓我幫你脫掉。」

「別碰我——我說請別碰我。

我不會讓你侍候我上床，老兄。」

「隨你便吧。你想怎麼睡都行。

你叫我『老兄』？你說話像個教授。

不過說到咱倆究竟誰怕誰，

我想如果碰巧出點什麼差錯，

我會比你遭受更大的損失。

誰想砍斷你穿十四號領的脖子呢？

讓我們都露個底，作為互相信任

的證明。這兒是九十美元，

過來看看，如果你不害怕。」

"Fourteen! You say so!

I can remember when I wore fourteen.

And come to think I must have back at home

More than a hundred collars, size fourteen.

Too bad to waste them all. You ought to have them.

They're yours and welcome; let me send them to you. —

What makes you stand there on one leg like that?

You're not much furtherer than where Kike left you.

You act as if you wished you hadn't come.

Sit down or lie down, friend; you make me nervous."

The Doctor made a subdued dash for it,

And propped himself at bay against a pillow.

"Not that way, with your shoes on Kike's white bed.

You can't rest that way. Let me pull your shoes off."

"Don't touch me, please — I say, don't touch me, please.

I'll not be put to bed by you, my man."

"Just as you say. Have it your own way, then.

'My man' is it? You talk like a professor.

Speaking of who's afraid of who, however,

I'm thinking I have more to lose than you

If anything should happen to be wrong.

Who wants to cut your number fourteen throat!

Let's have a showdown as an evidence

Of good faith. There is ninety dollars.

Come, if you're not afraid."

像我通常那樣把錢壓在身下睡覺，
夜裡有生人睡在一旁我總不放心。」
「要是我就把錢放在這床單上，
你能信任我嗎？——我就信任你。」
「你可以這麼說，老兄。我是收款員，
這九十美元不是我的，你可能想不到，
我東奔西走爲《新聞週報》
一個美元一個美元地收款，
那報在鮑鎮出版。你知道那報嗎？」

「我從年輕時就讀它了。」
　　　　　　「這下你就明白了。
現在咱們正聚在一起——一起交談。
我爲《新聞週報》當先鋒，
我的差事就是要了解讀者的想法，
他們花錢訂報，所以應該有想法。
費爾班克對我說——他是編輯——
『摸清公眾的感情』——他總是這麼說。
說眞的，我的待遇還算不錯。
唯一的麻煩是我和他政見不同，
我是佛蒙特州的民主黨人——

"I'm not afraid.

There's five: that's all I carry."

"I can search you?

Where are you moving over to? Stay still.

You'd better tuck your money under you

And sleep on it, the way I always do

When I'm with people I don't trust at night."

"Will you believe me if I put it there

Right on the counterpane — that I do trust you?"

"You'd say so, Mister Man. — I'm a collector.

My ninety isn't mine — you won't think that.

I pick it up a dollar at a time

All round the country for the Weekly News,

Published in Bow. You know the Weekly News?"

"Known it since I was young."

"Then you know me.

Now we are getting on together — talking.

I'm sort of Something for it at the front.

My business is to find what people want:

They pay for it, and so they ought to have it.

Fairbanks, he says to me — he's editor —

'Feel out the public sentiment' — he says.

A good deal comes on me when all is said.

The only trouble is we disagree

In politics: I'm Vermont Democrat —

而《新聞週報》則持共和黨觀點。
可知這意味著什麼？
費爾班克對我說：『今年幫幫我們，』
意思是要我們的選票。『不，』我說，
『我不能也不會！你們上台已夠久，
現在該轉過來支持我們。
如果你想要我選比爾‧塔夫脫，
你付我的周薪就必須多過十美元。
何況能否那樣做我還拿不準呢。』」
「你似乎可以左右那份報的方針。」

「你會看出我與誰都相處得很好。
我幾乎和他們一樣熟悉他們的農場。」
「你走南闖北？一定非常有趣。」
「都是出公差，但我不能說它沒趣。
我喜歡農場的位置各不相同，
有時鑽出樹林會突然看見一座；
有時翻過一座山或轉過彎道就會看到。
我喜歡看見人們春天時走出屋子，
用耙清掃庭院，在房前屋後幹活。
接著他們便到遠離房屋的田裡。
有時除了牲口棚所有的門都關著，
一家人都在某處偏遠的草地。
時辰一到，會有一車車乾草運回。
之後他們全都被冬天趕回屋裡；

You know what that is, sort of double-dyed:

The News has always been Republican.

Fairbanks, he says to me, 'Help us this year.'

Meaning by us their ticket. 'No,' I says,

'I can't and won't. You've been in long enough:

It's time you turned around and boosted us.

You'll have to pay me more than ten a week

If I'm expected to elect Bill Taft.

I doubt if I could do it anyway.' "

"You seem to shape the paper's policy."

"You see I'm in with everybody, know 'em all.

I almost know their farms as well as they do."

"You drive around? It must be pleasant work."

"It's business, but I can't say it's not fun.

What I like best's the lay of different farms,

Coming out on them from a stretch of woods,

Or over a hill or round a sudden corner.

I like to find folks getting out in spring,

Raking the dooryard, working near the house.

Later they get out further in the fields.

Everything's shut sometimes except the barn;

The family's all away in some back meadow.

There's a hay load a-coming — when it comes.

And later still they all get driven in:

那時牧場被割成了草坪，小塊菜園
變得光禿禿的，楓樹也只剩下
樹幹和樹枝。四處看不見人影，
只有屋頂的煙囪冒著輕煙。
我愛懶洋洋地讓馬遊走。只有
當迎面有人走來；或我那匹母馬
想停步時才收韁——我告訴牠何時該走。
杰邁瑪已經被我慣壞，
牠習慣一見到房舍就轉彎，
彷彿牠有某種毛病，
也不管我去那些房舍是否合宜。

牠以為我好交際。我也許是那樣，
不過除了吃飯我很少下馬。
人們通常在廚房門口款待我，
往往是全家人出來，小孩也在內。」
「一般人會認為他們並不像你
喜歡見到他們那樣，喜歡見到你。」
　　　　　　　　「噢，
因為我要他們的錢？我並不想要
他們拿不出的東西。我從不催債。
我來了，他們想付就順便付給我。
我上哪兒都不為收款，只是路過。
可惜這兒沒杯子，不能讓你喝一杯。
我愛就著瓶口喝——不是你的風格。
你也來一口？」

The fields are stripped to lawn, the garden patches

Stripped to bare ground, the maple trees

To whips and poles. There's nobody about.

The chimney, though, keeps up a good brisk smoking.

And I lie back and ride. I take the reins

Only when someone's coming, and the mare

Stops when she likes: I tell her when to go.

I've spoiled Jemima in more ways than one.

She's got so she turns in at every house

As if she had some sort of curvature,

No matter if I have no errand there.

She thinks I'm sociable. I maybe am.

It's seldom I get down except for meals, though.

Folks entertain me from the kitchen doorstep,

All in a family row down to the youngest."

"One would suppose they might not be as glad

To see you as you are to see them."

"Oh,

Because I want their dollar? I don't want

Anything they've not got. I never dun.

I'm there, and they can pay me if they like.

I go nowhere on purpose: I happen by. —

Sorry there is no cup to give you a drink.

I drink out of the bottle — not your style.

Mayn't I offer you — ?"

「不，不，不，謝謝。」
「悉聽尊便。那就祝你健康。──
現在我必須離開你一會兒。
也許我不在時你會睡得更安穩──
別起來──輕鬆點──睡個好覺。
但讓我想想──我想問你什麼來著？
哦，那些領子，要是我回來時你沒醒，
我該把它們寄到什麼地方？」
「朋友，我不要──你也許還用得著。」
「除非我變瘦，那時它們早過時了。」
「說實在的，我有不少襯衫領。」

「我真不知有誰願意要它們，
它們只會在那兒慢慢地發黃。
但還是一句老話，要不要由你決定。
我這就熄燈，你不要等我回來，
我的夜晚才開始。你睡一會兒吧。
我回來時會這樣嘟嘟敲兩聲，
你就知道是誰在敲門。
我最怕的就是被嚇破膽的人。
我可不想讓你一槍打掉我的腦袋。
我這是幹嘛，拎著酒瓶往外走？
好啦，你睡一會兒吧。」
　　　　　　　　他關上了房門。
博士稍稍放平了枕頭。

"No, no, no, thank you."

"Just as you say. Here's looking at you, then. —

And now I'm leaving you a little while.

You'll rest easier when I'm gone, perhaps —

Lie down — let yourself go and get some sleep.

But first — let's see — what was I going to ask you?

Those collars — who shall I address them to,

Suppose you aren't awake when I come back?"

"Really, friend, I can't let you. You — may need them."

"Not till I shrink, when they'll be out of style."

"But really I — I have so many collars."

"I don't know who I rather would have have them.

They're only turning yellow where they are.

But you're the doctor, as the saying is.170

I'll put the light out. Don't you wait for me:

I've just begun the night. You get some sleep.

I'll knock so-fashion and peep round the door

When I come back, so you'll know who it is.

There's nothing I'm afraid of like scared people.

I don't want you should shoot me in the head. —

What am I doing carrying off this bottle? —

There now, you get some sleep."

    He shut the door.

The Doctor slid a little down the pillow.

家庭墓地

他從樓梯下面看見了她，在她
看見他之前。她當時正要下樓，
可又回過頭去看什麼可怕的東西。
她遲疑地走了一步，接著又退回，
然後又踮起腳張望。他一邊上樓
一邊問她：「你總是站在樓上看，
究竟在看什麼——我倒想知曉。」
她轉過身來，隨即坐在裙子上，
臉上的神情從駭然變成了木然。
「你在看什麼？」他輕聲地問，
爬上樓讓她蜷縮在他跟前。
「這次我要弄清楚——
你得告訴我，親愛的。」

她坐在地板上，拒絕了他的攙扶，
倔強地轉過頭去，一聲不吭。
她任他張望，心想他肯定看不見，
這個睜眼瞎果然好一陣啥也沒看見。
但最後他終於輕輕地「哦」了兩聲。
「你看到什麼啦——什麼？」她問。
　　　　　　「看到我正看到的。」
「你沒有，」她懷疑地問，「告訴我是什麼。」
「奇怪的是我沒能一眼就看出來。
以前我從這兒經過時從沒注意，
——我想一定是看太多反而沒注意，

Home Burial

He saw her from the bottom of the stairs

Before she saw him. She was starting down,

Looking back over her shoulder at some fear.

She took a doubtful step and then undid it

To raise herself and look again. He spoke

Advancing toward her: "What is it you see

From up there always? — for I want to know."

She turned and sank upon her skirts at that,

And her face changed from terrified to dull.

He said to gain time: "What is it you see?"

Mounting until she cowered under him.

"I will find out now — you must tell me, dear."

She, in her place, refused him any help,

With the least stiffening of her neck and silence.

She let him look, sure that he wouldn't see,

Blind creature; and awhile he didn't see.

But at last he murmured, "Oh," and again, "Oh."

"What is it — what?" she said.

"Just that I see."

"You don't." she challenged. "Tell me what it is."

"The wonder is I didn't see at once.

I never noticed it from here before.

I must be wonted to it — that's the reason.

那塊埋著我親人的小小的墓地！
小得窗戶可以把它整個框在裡面。
比臥室大不了多少，你說是不是？
那兒有三塊灰石和一塊大理石墓碑，
就在那兒，在陽光照耀的山坡上，
寬寬的小石碑，我們一直忽視了它們。
但我明白，你不是看那些舊碑，
而是在看孩子的新墳──」
　　　「別，別，別說了，」她嚷道。
她縮起身子，從他扶著
樓梯欄杆的手臂下離開，
悄悄下了樓梯，
並用一種恐嚇的目光回頭看他，
他在回過神來之前已說了兩遍：
「難道男人就不能提他夭折的孩子？」

「你不能！哦，我的帽子在哪裡？
唉，我用不著它！我得出去透透空氣。
我真不知道男人能不能提這種事。」
「艾米！這時候別上鄰居家去。
你聽我說。我不會下這樓梯。」
他坐了下來，用雙掌托住下巴。
「親愛的，有件事我想問你。」
「你不會問事情。」
　　　　　　　「那就教教我吧。」
她的回答就是伸手去抽門閂。

The little graveyard where my people are!

So small the window frames the whole of it.

Not so much larger than a bedroom, is it?

There are three stones of slate and one of marble,

Broad-shouldered little slabs there in the sunlight

On the sidehill. We haven't to mind those.

But I understand: it is not the stones,

But the child's mound — ''

        ''Don't, don't, don't, don't,'' she

  cried.

She withdrew, shrinking from beneath his arm

That rested on the banister, and slid downstairs;

And turned on him with such a daunting look,

He said twice over before he knew himself:

''Can't a man speak of his own child he's lost?''

          ''Not you! — Oh, where's my hat? Oh, I don't need it!

          I must get out of here. I must get air. —

          I don't know rightly whether any man can.''

          ''Amy! Don't go to someone else this time.

          Listen to me. I won't come down the stairs.''

          He sat and fixed his chin between his fists.

          ''There's something I should like to ask you, dear.''

          ''You don't know how to ask it.''

              ''Help me, then.''

          Her fingers moved the latch for all reply.

「我幾乎一開口就惹你生氣，
我真不知如何說話，才能讓你高興。
但我認為我或許能夠學習，
只是不知怎樣才能學會。
與女人一起生活，男人就得讓步。
我們可以商量商量，
這樣我就能夠管住自己的嘴巴，
不提任何你特別介意提到的事情，
不過我並不喜歡相愛的人來這一套。
不相愛的夫妻不來這套會沒法生活；
但相愛的人來這一套真沒法過日子。」
她稍稍抽動門閂。「別──別走，
這個時候別把心事帶到鄰居家。
跟我說說吧，只要那是能說的事。

讓我分擔你的憂傷，我和別人
並沒有什麼不同，不像你
想像的那樣。給我個機會吧。
不過我真認為你稍稍有點兒過火。
你作為母親失去了第一個孩子，
固然難過但愛情還在，
那到底為什麼
使你這般傷心想不開？
你總認為應該老想著他才對──」
「你這是在取笑我！」

　　　　　　　「沒有，我沒有！
你真叫我生氣。我下樓來跟你談。
天哪，這種女人！事情竟會是這樣，
一個男人竟不能說起他夭折的孩子。」

"My words are nearly always an offense.

I don't know how to speak of anything

So as to please you. But I might be taught,

I should suppose. I can't say I see how.

A man must partly give up being a man

With womenfolk. We could have some arrangement

By which I'd bind myself to keep hands off

Anything special you're a-mind to name.

Though I don't like such things 'twixt those that love.

Two that don't love can't live together without them.

But two that do can't live together with them."

She moved the latch a little. "Don't — don't go.

Don't carry it to someone else this time.

Tell me about it if it's something human.

        Let me into your grief. I'm not so much

        Unlike other folks as your standing there

        Apart would make me out. Give me my chance.

        I do think, though, you overdo it a little.

        What was it brought you up to think it the thing

        To take your mother-loss of a first child

        So inconsolably — in the face of love.

        You'd think his memory might be satisfied —"

        "There you go sneering now!"

                "I'm not, I'm not!

You make me angry. I'll come down to you.

God, what a woman! And it's come to this,

A man can't speak of his own child that's dead."

「你不能，因為你不懂該怎樣說。
你要是有點感情該多好！你怎麼能
親手為他挖掘那個小小的墳墓？
我都看見了，就從樓上那個窗口，
你讓沙土飛揚在空中，就那樣
飛呀，揚呀，然後輕輕地落下，
落回墓坑旁邊那個小小的土堆。
我心想那個男人是誰？我不認識你。
當時我下了樓梯又爬上樓梯
再看一眼，你的鐵鏟仍然在揮舞。」

然後你進屋了。我聽見你粗聲大氣
在廚房裡說話，我不知為什麼，
但我來到了廚房邊要親眼看看。
你的鞋底還沾著你孩子墳頭上
的新土，但你居然能坐在那兒
大談你那些雞毛蒜皮的事情。
你早把鐵鏟豎著靠在牆上，
就在外面牆邊，我都看見了。」
「天哪，你真讓我笑掉大牙。
我要不信我倒霉，那我真是倒霉透了。」
「我可以重複你當時說的每一個字。
『三個有霧的早晨再加上一個雨天
就能讓編得最好的白樺籬笆爛掉。』
想想吧，在那個時候說那種事情！

"You can't because you don't know how to speak.

If you had any feelings, you that dug

With your own hand — how could you? — his little grave;

I saw you from that very window there,

Making the gravel leap and leap in air,

Leap up, like that, like that, and land so lightly

And roll back down the mound beside the hole.

I thought, Who is that man? I didn't know you.

And I crept down the stairs and up the stairs

To look again, and still your spade kept lifting.

Then you came in. I heard your rumbling voice

Out in the kitchen, and I don't know why,

But I went near to see with my own eyes,

You could sit there with the stains on your shoes

Of the fresh earth from your own baby's grave

And talk about your everyday concerns.

You had stood the spade up against the wall

Outside there in the entry, for I saw it."

"I shall laugh the worst laugh I ever laughed.

I'm cursed. God, if I don't believe I'm cursed."

"I can repeat the very words you were saying:

'Three foggy mornings and one rainy day

Will rot the best birch fence a man can build.'

Think of it, talk like that at such a time!

白樺樹條要多久才會爛掉，
跟家裡辦喪事有什麼關係呢？
你可以不在乎！但親朋好友本該
生死相隨，那麼叫人失望，
他們倒不如壓根兒就沒去墓地。
是呀，一個人一旦病入膏肓，
他就孤獨了，而且死了更孤獨。
親友們裝模作樣地去一趟墓地，
但人沒入土，他們的心早飛了，
一個個巴不得儘快回到活人堆中，
去做他們認為理所當然的事情。
世道就這麼壞。要是我能改變它
我就不這麼傷心了。哦，我就不會！」

　　　　　　　　　　　　「好啦，說出來就好受些了。
　　　　　　　　　　　　現在別走，你在哭。把門關上，
　　　　　　　　　　　　心事已經說出，幹嘛還想它呢？
　　　　　　　　　　　　艾米！有人沿著大路來了！」
　　　　　　　　　　　　「你──你以為說說就完了。我得走──
　　　　　　　　　　　　離開這棟屋子。我怎麼能讓你──」
　　　　　　　　　　　　「要是──你──走！」她把門推得更開。
　　　　　　　　　　　　「你要去哪兒？先告訴我個地方。
　　　　　　　　　　　　我要跟去把你拉回來。我會的！──」

What had how long it takes a birch to rot

To do with what was in the darkened parlor?

You couldn't care! The nearest friends can go

With anyone to death, comes so far short

They might as well not try to go at all.

No, from the time when one is sick to death,

One is alone, and he dies more alone.

Friends make pretense of following to the grave,

But before one is in it, their minds are turned

And making the best of their way back to life

And living people, and things they understand.

But the world's evil. I won't have grief so

If I can change it. Oh, I won't, I won't!"

"There, you have said it all and you feel better.

You won't go now. You're crying. Close the door.

The heart's gone out of it: why keep it up?

Amy! There's someone coming down the road!"

"You — oh, you think the talk is all. I must go —

Somewhere out of this house. How can I make you —"

"If — you — do!" She was opening the door wider.

"Where do you mean to go? First tell me that.

I'll follow and bring you back by force. I will! — "

黑色小屋

那天下午我們路過那兒的時候，
偶然發現它像在一幅別致的畫裡，
掩映在塗有瀝青的櫻桃樹林間，
坐落在遠離大道的荒草叢中，
當時我們正在談論的那幢小屋，
那幢正面只有一門二窗的小屋
剛被陣雨沖過，黑漆光潔柔和。
我們——牧師和我——停下來看。
牧師逕自上前，彷彿要去摸摸它；
或是要去拂開那些遮住它的枝葉。
「真美，」他說，「來吧，沒人會在意。」

通往屋子的小路幾乎隱沒在草中，
我倆循路來到遭風雨侵蝕的窗前。
我們把臉貼近窗口。「你看，」他說，
「一切都和她生前一樣原封未動。
她的兒子們不願賣掉這房子或家具，
他們說想回這曾經度過童年的地方
過夏天。他們今年還沒回來。
他們住得很遠——有一個在西部——
所以要他們履行諾言其實也很難。
但至少他們不會讓這地方被攪亂。」
一張馬尾襯躺椅伸著雕花扶手，
躺椅上方的牆頭有一幅炭筆肖像，
肖像是依據一幀銀板法老照片繪成。

The Black Cottage

We chanced in passing by that afternoon
To catch it in a sort of special picture
Among tar-banded ancient cherry trees,
Set well back from the road in rank lodged grass,
The little cottage we were speaking of,
A front with just a door between two windows,
Fresh painted by the shower a velvet black.
We paused, the minister and I, to look.
He made as if to hold it at arm's length
Or put the leaves aside that framed it in.
"Pretty," he said. "Come in. No one will care."

            The path was a vague parting in the grass
            That led us to a weathered windowsill.
            We pressed our faces to the pane. "You see," he said,
            "Everything's as she left it when she died.
            Her sons won't sell the house or the things in it.
            They say they mean to come and summer here
            Where they were boys. They haven't come this year.
            They live so far away — one is out West —
            It will be hard for them to keep their word.
            Anyway they won't have the place disturbed."
            A buttoned haircloth lounge spread scrolling arms
            Under a crayon portrait on the wall,
            Done sadly from an old daguerreotype.

「畫上就是父親出征前的模樣。
每當她談起那場遲早都要爆發的
戰爭，她總會在肖像前半跪下，
靠著那張有鈕扣裝飾的馬尾襯躺椅，
我不知道，在這麼多年之後，
那並不逼真的肖像是否還有力量
在她的心靈深處激起什麼感情？
他死在葛底斯堡或弗雷德里克斯堡，
我猜——當然兩個戰爭不一樣，
弗雷德里克斯堡不是葛底斯堡。
但現在我要說的是這樣一幢小屋
怎麼會一直都顯得早已被人遺棄；
因為她已離去，可在那之前——

我並不是說它被那些離開它的
人遺棄（先是父親，
然後是兩個兒子，直到她獨守空屋。
她無論如何也不肯跟著兒子離去；
儘管這棟小屋並不顯眼，而且她
尊重兒子們對它的忽視。）
我的意思是說它經常被路過的世人——
譬如今天下午我們就差點把它遺漏。
它在我看來永遠都是一個標幟，
可以量出五十年把我們帶了多遠。
幹嘛不坐下來，如果你不忙的話？
這些門階已很少有客人光顧。
要是沒人來踩踏，使它們維持功能，
這些變形的木板會使釘子自行脫落。
她凡事都有主見，我是說那老太太。

"That was the father as he went to war.

She always, when she talked about the war,

Sooner or later came and leaned, half knelt,

Against the lounge beside it, though I doubt

If such unlifelike lines kept power to stir

Anything in her after all the years.

He fell at Gettysburg or Fredericksburg,

I ought to know — it makes a difference which:

Fredericksburg wasn't Gettysburg, of course.

But what I'm getting to is how forsaken

A little cottage this has always seemed;

Since she went, more than ever, but before —

 I don't mean altogether by the lives

 That had gone out of it, the father first,

 Then the two sons, till she was left alone.

 (Nothing could draw her after those two sons.

 She valued the considerate neglect

 She had at some cost taught them after years.)

 I mean by the world's having passed it by —

 As we almost got by this afternoon.

 It always seems to me a sort of mark

 To measure how far fifty years have brought us.

 Why not sit down if you are in no haste?

 These doorsteps seldom have a visitor.

 The warping boards pull out their own old nails

 With none to tread and put them in their place.

 She had her own idea of things, the old lady.

而且她喜歡聊天，她見過加里森
和惠蒂埃，而且對他們自有說法。
人們要不了多久就可以了解
她認為那場內戰還有別的什麼目的，
戰爭不僅僅是為了保持國家統一
或解放奴隸，儘管這兩者都實現了。
她從不相信那兩個目的就足以
使她完全獻出她已經奉獻的一切。
她的奉獻多少觸及了那個基本信念；
所有的人都生而自由及平等。
你聽聽她那些奇談怪論──那些
與今人對那些事的看法相左的言論。
這就是傑弗遜那句話的費解之處。

他想說什麼呢？最簡單的理解
當然就是認定那壓根兒不是真話。
可能我說對了，我聽人這麼說過。
但不用擔心，那威爾斯人播下的
信念將會使我們煩惱一千年，
每一代人都得把它重新審視一番。
你沒法告訴她西部人在說些什麼；
或南方人對她的看法持什麼觀點。
她有某種聽話的訣竅，但從來
不聽這個世界最新的觀點意見。
白種人是她熟悉的唯一人種，
她很少見到黑人，黃種人則從沒見過。
同一雙手用同一種材料，
怎麼可能把人造得這麼不一樣？

And she liked talk. She had seed Garrison
And Whittier, and had her story of them.
One wasn't long in learning that she thought,
Whatever else the Civil War was for,
It wasn't just to keep the States together,
Nor just to free the slaves, thought it did both.
She wouldn't have believed those ends enough
To have given outright for them all she gave.
Her giving somehow touched the principle
That all men are created free and equal.
And to hear her quaint phrases — so removed
From the world's view today of all those things.
That's a hard mystery of Jefferson's.

          What did he mean? Of course the easy way
          Is to decode it simply isn't true.
          It may not be. I heard a fellow say so.
          But never mind, the Welshman got it planted
          Where it will trouble us a thousand years.
          Each age will have to reconsider it.
          You couldn't tell her what the West was saying,
          And what the South, to her serene belief.
          She had some art of hearing and yet not
          Hearing the latter wisdom of the world.
          White was the only race she ever knew.
          Black she had scarcely seen, and yellow never.
          But how could they be made so very unlike
          By the same hand working in the same stuff?

她一直認爲是戰爭決定了這些。
你對這種人的想法有什麼辦法？
奇怪的是這種無知如今卻大行其道。
如果有朝一日這世界上由武力
占上風，我也不會爲此感到驚奇。
你知道嗎，要不是因爲她的緣故，
我有段時間會稍稍改動教條措詞
去迎合教堂裡那些年輕的信徒，
更準確地說，去迎合我們今天都
不得不想到的教堂裡的非教徒？
這並不是因爲她曾要求我不改，
事情還沒到那地步；但只要想到
教堂會眾中她那頂抖動的舊帽子
和她那半睡的模樣，我就沒法改了。

唉，我可能會把她驚醒，嚇她一跳，
因爲要改的那句話是『降入冥府』，
而這對我們自由的青年顯得太異端。
你知道這句話曾受到普遍的攻擊。
可要是這句話不眞實，爲什麼老是
說它像異教信仰？我們可以刪掉它。
只是——教堂會眾中有那頂女帽。
這樣一個措詞也許對她意義不大。
不過假如她沒聽到聖經中這句話，
會像孩子沒聽到大人說晚安那樣
傷心地入睡——我會作何感想呢？

She had supposed the war decided that.

What are you going to do with such a person?

Strange how such innocence gets its own way.

I shouldn't be surprised if in this world

It were the force that would at last prevail.

Do you know but for her there was a time

When, to please younger members of the church,

Or rather say non-members in the church,

Whom we all have to think of nowadays,

I would have changed the Creed a very little?

Not that she ever had to ask me not to;

It never got so far as that; but she bare thought

Of her old tremulous bonnet in the pew,

And of her half asleep, was too much for me.

Why, I might wake her up and startle her.

It was the words ' descended into Hades '

That seemed too pagan to our liberal youth.

You know they suffered from a general onslaught.

And well, if they weren't true why keep right on

Saying them like the heathen? We could drop them.

Only — there was the bonnet in the pew.

Such a phrase couldn't have meant much to her.

But suppose she had missed it from the Creed,

As a child misses the unsaid Good-night .

And falls asleep with heartache — how should I feel?

我現在真高興她使我沒作改動，
因為，啊，為什麼要拋棄一個信仰，
僅僅因為它不再顯得真實？
只要持久地堅信，毫不懷疑，
它又會變真實，因為事情就是這樣。
我們以為親眼目睹的生活中的變化，
大多因為世人對真理時信時疑。
當我坐在這兒的時候，我常希望
我能成為一片荒涼土地的主宰，
我能將那片土地永遠奉獻給
那些我們可以不斷回歸的真理。

那土地必須荒涼貧瘠，必須
被夏天峰頂也有雪的山脈圍繞，
這樣就沒人覬覦，或認為它值得
花力氣去征服並迫使它改變。
那兒應有零星的供人住的綠洲，
但大部分是檉柳輕輕摟住的沙丘，
在安閒中一再忘卻自己的沙丘。
在初降的露水中，沙粒應使
誕生於荒漠的嬰兒可愛；沙暴
應把我畏縮的旅行隊阻在半路──
「這牆裡有蜂。」他敲了敲護牆板，
好鬥的蜂探頭探腦，轉動小小身軀。
我倆起身離去。晚霞在窗上燃燒。

I'm just as glad she made me keep hands off,

For, dear me, why abandon a belief

Merely because it ceases to be true.

Cling to it long enough, and not a doubt

It will turn true again, for so it goes.

Most of the change we think we see in life

Is due to truths being in and out of favor.

As I sit here, and oftentimes, I wish

I could be monarch of a desert land

I could devote and dedicate forever

To the truths we keep coming back and back to.

So desert it would have to be, so walled

By mountain ranges half in summer snow,

No one would covet it or think it worth

The pains of conquering to force change on.

Scattered oases where men dwelt, but mostly

Sand dunes held loosely in tamarisk120

Blown over and over themselves in idleness.

Sand grains should sugar in the natal dew

The babe born to the desert, the sandstorm

Retard mid-waste my cowering caravans —

"There are bees in this wall." He struck the clapboards,

Fierce heads looked out; small bodies pivoted.

We rose to go. Sunset blazed on the windows.

藍漿果

「你早該見過我今天在路上看見的，
就在穿過帕特森牧場去村裡的路上；
一粒粒藍漿果有你的拇指頭那麼大，
真正的天藍，沉甸甸的，就好像
隨時準備掉進第一個採果人的桶中！
所有的果子都熟透了，不是一些青、
而另一些熟透！這你早該見過了！」
「我不知道你在說牧場的什麼地方。」
「你知道他們砍掉樹林的那個地方──
讓我想想──那是不是兩年前的事──
不可能超過兩年──接下來的秋天
除了那道牆，一切都被大火燒得精光。」
「嗨，這麼短時間灌木叢還長不起來。
不過那種藍漿果倒總是見風就長；
凡是在有松樹投下陰影的地方，
你也許連它們的影子也見不到一個，
但要是沒有松樹，你就算放把火
燒掉整個牧場，直到蕨草連
一片葉子也不留──更不用說樹枝，
可眨眼工夫，它們又長得密密茂茂，
就像魔術師變法戲叫人難以猜透。」
「它們結果時肯定吸收了木炭的養料。
我有時嚐出它們帶有一股炭煙的味道。
另外它們的表面實際上是烏黑色，
藍色不過是風吹上去的一層薄霧，

Blueberries

"You ought to have seen what I saw on my way
To the village, through Patterson's pasture today:
Blueberries as big as the end of your thumb,
Real sky-blue, and heave, and ready to drum
In the cavernous pain of the first one to come!
And all ripe together, not some of them green
And some of them ripe! You ought to have seen!"
"I don't know what part of the pasture you mean."
"You know where they cut off the woods — let me see —
It was two years ago — or no! — can it be
No longer than that? — and the following fall
The fire ran and burned it all up but the wall."

"Why, there hasn't been time for the bushes to grow.
That's always the way with the blueberries, though:
There may not have been the ghost of a sign
Of them anywhere under the shade of the pine,
But get the pine out of the way, you may burn
The pasture all over until not a fern
Or grass-blade is left, not to mention a stick,
And presto, they're up all around you as thick
And hard to explain as a conjuror's trick."
"It must be on charcoal they fatten their fruit.
I taste in them sometimes the flavor of soot.
And after all, really they're ebony skinned:

你只要伸手一碰藍光就無影無蹤，
還不如摘果人曬紅的臉可保持幾天。」
「你認爲帕特森知道他地裡有漿果嗎？」
「也許吧，但他不在，就讓野鳥
幫他採摘——你了解帕特森的爲人，
他不會因爲自己擁有那片牧場，
就把我們這些外人趕走。」
「我真驚訝你沒看見洛倫在附近。」
「不，我還真看見了。好笑吧？
當時我正穿過牧場藏不住的漿果叢，
然後翻過那道石牆，走上大道；
這時他正好趕著馬車從那兒經過，
車上是他家那群嘰嘰喳喳的孩子，
至於做父親的洛倫是走著路趕車的。」

「那麼他看見你了？他都做了什麼？
他皺眉了嗎？」
「他只是不停地向我點頭哈腰，
你知道他碰上熟人時有多麼客氣。
但他想到了一件大事——我能看出——
實際上他的眼神暴露了他的心思：
『我想我真該責備自己把這些漿果
留在這兒太久，怕都熟過頭了。』」
「他比我認識的好多人都更節儉。」
「他當然要節儉，難道沒必要？
他有那麼多張小洛倫的嘴巴要餵！
別人說那群孩子是他用漿果餵大的，
就像餵鳥。他家總會儲存許多漿果，

The blue's but a mist from the breath of the wind,

A tarnish that goes at a touch of the hand,

And less than the tan with which pickers are tanned."

"Does Patterson know what he has, do you think?"

"He may and not care, and so leave the chewink

To gather them for him — you know what he is.

He won't make the fact that they're rightfully his

An excuse for keeping us other folk out."

"I wonder you didn't see Loren about."

"The best of it was that I did. Do you know,

I was just getting through what the field had to show

And over the wall and into the road,

When who should come by, with a democrat-load

Of all the young chattering Lorens alive,

But Loren, the fatherly, out for a drive."

"He saw you, then? What did he do? Did he frown?"

"He just kept nodding his head up and down.

You know how politely he always goes by.

But he thought a big thought — I could tell by his eye —

Which being expressed, might be this in effect:

' I have left those there berries, I shrewdly suspect,

To ripen too long. I am greatly to blame.' "

"He's a thriftier person than some I could name."

"He seems to be thrifty; and hasn't he need,

With the mouths of all those young Lorens to feed?

He has brought them all up on wild berries, they say,

Like birds. They store a great many away.

一年到頭都吃那玩意兒，吃不完的
他們就拿到商店賣錢好買鞋穿。」
「別在乎別人說什麼，那是種生活方式，
只索取大自然願意給予的東西，
不用犁杖釘耙去強迫大自然給予。」
「我真希望你也能看見他不停的哈腰
和那些孩子的表情！誰也沒回頭，
全都顯得那麼著急又那麼一本正經。」
「我要懂得他們懂得的一半就好了，
他們知道野漿果長在什麼地方，
比如蔓越橘生在沼澤，蔗莓則長在
有卵石的山頂，而且知道何時去採。

有一天我遇見他們，每人把一朵花
插在各自提的新鮮漿果中；
他們說那種奇怪的漿果還沒有名字。」
「我告訴過你我們剛搬來的時候，
我曾差點讓可憐的洛倫樂不可支，
當時我跑到他家門前，
問他知不知道有什麼野果子可摘。
那個騙子，他說要是他知道的話
會樂意告訴我，但那年年景不好，
原本有些漿果樹──全都死了。
他不說那些漿果原本長在哪兒。
『我肯定──我肯定──』他客氣極了，
對門裡的妻子說，『讓我想想，
媽媽，哪裡可以採果子？』
他當時能做到的就是沒有露出笑臉。」

They eat them the year round, and those they don't eat

They sell in the store and buy shoes for their feet."

"Who cares what they say? It's a nice way to live,

Just taking what Nature is willing to give,

Not forcing her hand with harrow and plow."

"I wish you had seen his perpetual bow —

And the air of the youngsters! Not one of them turned,

And they looked so solemn-absurdly concerned."

"I wish I know half what the flock of them know

Of where all the berries and other things grow,

Cranberries in bogs and raspberries on top

Of the boulder-strewn mountain, and when they will crop.

I met them one day and each had a flower

Stuck into his berries as fresh as a shower

Some strange kind — they told me it hadn't a name."

"I've told you how once, not long after we came,

I almost provoked poor Loren to mirth

By going to him of all people on earth

To ask if he knew any fruit to be had

For the picking. The rascal, he said he'd be glad

To tell if he knew. But the year had been bad.

There had been some berries — but those were all gone.

He didn't say where they had been. He went on:

'I'm sure — I'm sure' — as polite as could be.

He spoke to his wife in the door, 'Let me see,

Mame, we don't know any good berrying place?'

It was all he could do to keep a straight face."

「要是他以爲野果子都是爲他長的，
那他將發現自己想錯了。聽我説，
咱們今年就去摘帕特森牧場的漿果。
我們一大早就去，如果天氣晴朗，
出太陽的話，不然衣服會被弄濕。
好久沒去採漿果，我幾乎都忘了
過去咱倆常幹這事；我們總是先
四下張望，然後像精靈一般消失，
誰也看不見誰，也聽不到聲音，
除非當你説我正使得一隻小鳥
不敢回巢，而我説那應該怪你。
『好吧，反正是我倆中的一個。』小鳥
圍著我打轉抱怨。然後一時間
我們埋頭摘果，直到我擔心你走散，
我以爲把你弄丟了，於是扯開嗓門
大喊，想讓遠處的你聽見，可結果
你就站在我身邊，因爲你回答時
聲音低得像是在閒聊。還記得嗎？」
「我們可能享受不到那種樂趣——
不大可能，如果洛倫家孩子在那裡。
他們明天會去那兒，甚至今晚就去。
他們會很禮貌——但不會很友好——
因爲他們認爲在他們採果子的地方
別人就沒有權力去採。沒什麼，
你早該看見它們在雨中的模樣，
層層綠葉間果子和水珠交相輝映，
小偷若看花眼會以爲是兩種寶石。」

"If he thinks all the fruit that grows wild is for him,

He'll find he's mistaken. See here, for a whim,

We'll pick in the Pattersons' pasture this year.

We'll go in the morning, that is, if it's clear,

And the sun shines out warm: the vines must be wet.

It's so long since I picked I almost forget

How we used to pick berries: we took one look round,

Then sank out of sight like trolls underground,

And saw nothing more of each other, or heard,

Unless when you said I was keeping a bird

Away from its nest, and I said it was you.

'Well, one of us is.' For complaining it flew

Around and around us. And then for a while

We picked, till I feared you had wandered a mile,

       And I thought I had lost you. I lifted a shout

       Too loud for the distance you were, it turned out,

       For when you made answer, your voice was as low

       As talking — you stood up beside me, you know."

       "We shan't have the place to ourselves to enjoy —

       Not likely, when all the young Lorens deploy.

       They'll be there tomorrow, or even tonight.

       They won't be too friendly — they may be polite —

       To people they look on as having no right

       To pick where they're picking. But we won't complain.

       You ought to have seen how it looked in the rain,

       The fruit mixed with water in layers of leaves,

       Like two kinds of jewels, a vision for thieves."

僕人們的僕人

我先前沒讓你知道我有多高興，
真高興你能來我們農場上小住。
我曾指望有一天去你們南方，
看你們怎麼過日子，但現在難說！
有一屋子餓著肚子的人要餵，
我想你會發現……我似乎
我不太會表露自己的感情，就像
我不能提高嗓門或不想抬手一樣
（哦，我不得不抬手時也能抬起）
你有過這種感覺嗎？但願你沒有。
有時候我甚至沒法清楚地知道
我是高興還是難過，或別的感受。

心裡只剩下一種像聲音的東西，
它似乎是要告訴我該怎樣去感覺，
而要是我不完全犯病也會感覺。
就說這個湖吧，我朝它看呀看呀，
我看得出它是一片明淨可愛的水。
我可以站起來大聲說出
它所有的優點，那麼長那麼窄，
就像一條流淌的大河被砍去
了一頭一尾。它足足有五英里長，
從我洗碗的那個水槽前的窗口
一直向前伸進那座大山的峽谷，
這兒的風都從湖面撲向這棟房子，
風會把緩緩的波浪吹得越來越白。

A Servant to Servants

I didn't make you know how glad I was
To have you come and camp here on our land.
I promised myself to get down some day
And see the way you lived, but I don't know!
With a houseful of hungry men to feed
I guess you'd find .... It seems to me
I can't express my feelings, any more
Than I can raise my voice or want to lift
My hand (oh, I can lift it when I have to).
Did ever you feel so? I hope you never.
It's got so I don't even know for sure
Whether I am glad, sorry, or anything.

There's nothing but a voice-like left inside
That seems to tell me how I ought to feel,
And would feel if I wasn't all gone wrong.
You take the lake. I look and look at it.
I see it's a fair, pretty sheet of water.
I stand and make myself repeat out loud
The advantages it has, so long and narrow,
Like a deep piece of some old running river
Cut short off at both ends. It lies five miles
Straightaway through the mountain notch
From the sink window where I wash the plates,
And all our storms come up toward the house,
Drawing the slow waves whiter and whiter and whiter.

它曾讓我忘掉甜甜圈和蘇打餅，
在一個陽光明媚的早晨走到屋外
去抓耀眼的水，或當一場風暴
氣勢洶洶地從龍穴那邊逼過來，
一陣寒氣掠過湖面，我會去抓
繞在我身邊並鑽過我衣服的風。
我看出它是一片明淨可愛的水，
我們的威洛比！你是怎麼知道的？
不過我猜想人人都會知道它。
從一本寫蕨的書？它沒寫錯！
你多像候鳥有規律地去去來來，
來這兒小住。你喜歡這個湖嗎？
我看得出你喜歡。但我就不一定！

要是有更多的人來情況就不同了，
因為那樣這兒就會有更多的活兒。
萊恩照舊會建些小屋，我們有時出租，
有時則不。我們有個好湖灘，
它應該有點價值。
但我不像萊恩抱那麼大希望，
他凡事都只看到好的一面，
看我也是。他認為我吃點藥
就會好起來。但我需要的不是藥——
敢說這話的大夫只有洛厄——
我需要的是休息——你看我都說了——
我不想再為空腹的雇工們做飯，
不想再洗他們的盤子——不想再做
那些似乎永遠都做不完的雜事。

It took my mind off doughnuts and soda biscuit

To step outdoors and take the water dazzle

A sunny morning, or take the rising wind

About my face and body and through my wrapper,

When a storm threatened from the Dragon's Den,

And a cold chill shivered across the lake.

I see it's a fair, pretty sheet of water,

Our Willoughby! How did you hear of it?

I expect, though, everyone's heard of it.

In a book about ferns? Listen to that!

You let things more like feathers regulate

Your going and coming. And you like it here?

I can see how you might. But I don't know!

             It would be different if more people came,

             For then there would be business. As it is,

             The cottages Len built, sometimes we rent them,

             Sometimes we don't. We've a good piece of shore

             That ought to be worth something, and may yet.

             But I don't count on it as much as Len.

             He looks on the bright side of everything,

             Including me. He thinks I'll be all right

             With doctoring. But it's not medicine —

             Lowe is the only doctor's dared to say so —

             It's rest I want — there, I have said it out —

             From cooking meals for hungry hired men

             And washing dishes after them — from doing

             Things over and over that just won't stay done.

按理説，我不該有這麼多事
壓在肩上，但看來沒有別的辦法。
萊恩説要穩步發展就應該這麼做，
他説最好的出路都是走出來的。
我贊成他的説法，要不然我自己
就只能看到走路而看不到出路——
這至少是爲我——而且他們會相信。
萊恩也不是不想讓我過得好些。
這都是因爲他把家搬到湖邊的計劃，
從那天我指給你看過的那個地方，
那個去哪兒都得走上十英里的地方。
我們搬家並不是沒有付出些代價，

但萊恩立即著手要彌補損失。
他幹的當然是男人的活，趁黑起早，
他幹起活來和我一樣拼命——
雖説這種比較沒多少意義，
（但是男人女人仍然會進行比較。）
萊恩不只幹活兒，他太愛管事。
鎮上的事他樣樣都插手，今年
是修路，他爲太多的幫工
提供食宿，結果花費一堆。
他們不知羞恥地占他的便宜，
而且還因此暗中洋洋得意。
我們家住了四個，全都一無是處，
只知道攤手攤腿地在廚房裡閒聊，
等我替他們煎肉。他們啥也不在乎！

By good rights I ought not to have so much
Put on me, but there seems no other way.
Len says one steady pull more ought to do it.
He says the best way out is always through.
And I agree to that, or in so far
As that I can see no way out but through —
Leastways for me — and then they'll be convinced.
It's not that Len don't want the best for me.
It was his plan out moving over in
Beside the lake from where that day I showed you
We used to live — ten miles from anywhere.
We didn't change without some sacrifice,

But Len went at it to make up the loss.
His work's a man's, of course, from sun to sun,
But he works when he works as hard as I do —
Though there's small profit in comparisons.
(Women and men will make them all the same.)
But work ain't all. Len undertakes too much.
He's into everything in town. This year
It's highways, and he's got too many men
Around him to look after that make waste.
They take advantage of him shamefully,
And proud, too, of themselves for doing so.
We have four here to board, great good-for-nothings,
Sprawling about the kitchen with their talk
While I fry their bacon. Much they care!

即使我壓根兒就不在屋裡，
他們的言行也不能更令人難堪。
他們總是一波一波來來去去，
我不知他們姓什名誰，更不知
他們的品行，也不知讓他們住進
這四門不鎖的房子是否可靠。
不過我並不怕他們，只要他們
不怕我——有兩個人裝出不怕。
我愛胡思亂想，這是家族遺傳。
我父親的兄弟不對勁，他們把他
關了許多年，在原來那座農場上。

我離開過家——是的，離開過家，
去州立精神病院。我當時很反感，
我是不會把家裡人送到那種地方。
你知道那個老觀念——瘋人院
就是貧民院，那些家裡有錢的人
寧願把病人留在家裡也不肯往
那兒送；那顯得更有人情味。
但事實並非如此，那是精神病院，
那兒有各種適當的治療措施，
而且你不會攪亂家裡人的生活——
你犯病時對他們更糟，而他們
也沒法幫你；你不可能了解
在那種狀態時的意向和需要。
過去對付瘋子的事我聽得太多。

No more put out in what they do or say

Than if I wasn't in the room at all.

Coming and going all the time, they are:

I don't learn what their names are, let alone

Their characters, or whether they are safe

To have inside the house with doors unlocked.

I'm not afraid of them, though, if they're not

Afraid of me. There's two can play at that.

I have my fancies: it runs in the family.

My father's brother wasn't right. They kept him

Locked up for years back there at the old farm.

I've been away once — yes, I've been away.

The State Asylum. I was prejudiced;

I wouldn't have sent anyone of mine there;

You know the old idea — the only asylum

Was the poorhouse, and those who could afford,

Rather than send their folks to such a place,

Kept them at home; and it does seem more human.

But it's not so: the place is the asylum.

There they have every means proper to do with,

And you aren't darkening other people's lives —

Worse than no good to them, and they no good

To you in your condition; you can't know

Affection or the want of it in that state.

I've heard too much of the old-fashioned way.

我父親的兄弟很年輕時就瘋了。
有人認爲他曾經被一條狗咬過，
因爲他發瘋時就像一條狗，
會用嘴叼著他的枕頭跑來跑去；
但更有可能他發瘋是因爲失戀，
據説是這樣的，是爲某個姑娘。
總之他滿口説的都是愛情。
他們很快就看出若不嚴加管束，
他就可能對其他人造成傷害，
結果父親用桃木替他做了個籠子，
或者説在房間裡又建了個房間，
像牛棚的隔欄，從地板到屋頂——
四周只剩下一條窄窄的走道。

放進去的家具都被他砸成了碎片，
連給他睡覺的一張床也沒能倖免。
於是他們像鋪牲口棚一樣在那兒
鋪上乾草，以安慰他們的良心。
他們不得不允許他吃飯不用盤子。
他們設法讓他穿衣，但他把衣服
纏在胳膊上炫耀——所有的衣服。
聽起來眞慘。我想他們也盡了力。
而就在他瘋得最厲害的時候，
父親娶了母親，新娘子的母親來了，
幫著照料小叔子，
讓她年輕的生命適應他的——
那就是她嫁給父親的意義。

My father's brother, he went mad quite young.

Some thought he had been bitten by a dog,

Because his violence took on the form

Of carrying his pillow in his teeth;

But it's more likely he was crossed in love,

Or so the story goes. It was some girl.

Anyway all he talked about was love.

They soon saw he would do someone a mischief

If he wa'nt kept strict watch of, and it ended

In father's building him a sort of cage,

Or room within a room, of hickory poles,

Like stanchions in the barn, from floor to ceiling —

A narrow passage all the way around.

Anything they put in for furniture

He'd tear to pieces, even a bed to lie on.

So they made the place comfortable with straw,

Like a beast's stall, to ease their consciences.

Of course they had to feed him without dishes.

They tried to keep him clothed, but he paraded

With his clothes on his arm — all of his clothes.

Cruel — it sounds. I s'pose they did the best

They knew. And just when he was at the height,

Father and mother married, and mother came,

A bride, to help take care of such a creature,

And accommodate her young life to his.

That was what marrying father meant to her.

夜裡她不得不躺在床上聽他
用可怕的聲音大叫大嚷愛情。
他叫呀叫呀，用嚎叫來消耗精力，
直到他精疲力竭聲音才慢慢消失。
他常常像拉弓一樣拉籠子的木條，
直到它們像弓弦那樣繃一聲滑脫，
他的手把木條磨得像牛軛般光滑。
後來他愛學雞叫，彷彿他覺得
那種小孩玩的把戲是他唯一的樂趣。
不過我聽說他們設法止住了他的啼叫。
在我出世之前他死了，我沒見過他，
但那個木籠子仍放在那個地方，
仍然在廂房樓上那個房間裡，
像閣樓一樣堆滿了雜亂的東西。

我常常想到那些被磨光的桃木條，
我甚至曾常說──你知道這有點傻──
「該是輪到我進樓上牢籠的時候了」──
正如你所想，後來竟說成了習慣。
怪不得我很高興搬離那個地方。
不過我是等萊恩提出才搬的，
我不想事情萬一出錯怪到我頭上。
不過我們搬走時我高興得要死，
而且也顯得快活，如我所說，
我快活了一陣子──但現在難說了。
不知為什麼，變化像藥方一樣失效。

She had to lie and hear love things made dreadful

By his shouts in the night. He'd shout and shout

Until the strength was shouted out of him,

And his voice died down slowly from exhaustion.

He'd pull his bars apart like bow and bowstring,

And let them go and make them twang, until

His hands had worn them smooth as any oxbow.

And then he'd crow as if he thought that child's play —

The only fun he had. I've heard then say, though,

They found a way to put a stop to it.

He was before my time — I never saw him;

But the pen stayed exactly as it was,

There in the upper chamber in the ell,

A sort of catchall full of attic clutter.

        I often think of the smooth hickory bars.

        It got so I would say — you know, half fooling —

        "It's time I took my turn upstairs in jail" —

        Just as you will till it becomes a habit.

        No wonder I was glad to get away.

        Mind you, I waited till Len said the word.

        I didn't want the blame if things went wrong.

        I was glad though, no end, when we moved out,

        And I looked to be happy, and I was,

        As I said, for a while — but I don't know!

        Somehow the change wore out like a prescription.

我需要的不僅僅是窗前的風景
和住在湖邊。這已幫不了我的忙——
除非萊恩想到這點，但他想不到，
而我又不會求他——太沒把握了。
我想我不得不忍受現在這種生活，
別人都得忍受，幹嘛我不能忍呢？
我差點兒想我是否能像你一樣，
丟開一切到外面去住一陣子——
但天也許會黑，我不喜歡夜晚。
或下場大雨，我很快就會受不了，
就會高興頭頂上有個堅固的屋頂。

最近有幾夜我睡不著，老想到你，
我敢說比你想到自己的時候還多。
奇怪的是當你們睡在床上的時候，
你們頭頂上的帳篷竟沒被風颳走。
我從來都沒有勇氣去冒那種風險。
上帝保佑你，當然，你在耽誤我幹活，
但重要的是我需要有點兒耽誤。
要幹的活夠多了——永遠都幹不完；
耽擱就耽擱吧。你所能做的錯事
也就是讓我稍稍多耽擱一點兒。
反正我永遠也追不上。
我真不想讓你走，除非你非走不可。

And there's more to it than just window views
And living by a lake. I'm past such help —
Unless Len took the notion, which he won't,
And I won't ask him — it's not sure enough.
I s'pose I've got to go the road I'm going:
Other folks have to, and why shouldn't I?
I almost think if I could do like you,
Drop everything and live out on the ground —
But it might be, come night, I shouldn't like it.
Or a long rain. I should soon get enough,
And be glad of a good roof overhead.

I've lain awake thinking of you, I'll warrant,
More than you have yourself, some of these nights.
The wonder was the tents weren't snatched away
From over you as you lay in your beds.
I haven't courage for a risk like that.
Bless you, of course you're keeping me from work,
But the thing of it is, I need to be kept.
There' work enough to do — there's always that;
But behind's behind. The worst that you can do
Is set me back a little more behind.
I shan't catch up in this world, anyway.
I'd rather you'd not go unless you must.

摘蘋果之後

我用高高雙角梯穿過一棵樹
靜靜地伸向天空，
一只木桶沒裝滿，
放在梯子旁邊，或許有兩三個
沒摘到的蘋果還留在枝頭，
但我現在已經幹完了活兒。
冬日睡眠的氣氛瀰漫在夜空，
蘋果的氣味使我昏昏欲睡。
抹不去眼前那幅奇特的景象：
今晨我從水槽揭起一層薄冰
舉到眼前對著枯草的世界，
透過玻璃般的冰我見到奇特景象。
冰化了，我讓它墜地摔碎。

但在它墜地之前
我早已在睡眠之中，
而且我能說出
我就要進入什麼樣的夢境。
被放大了的蘋果忽現忽隱，
其柄端、萼端
赤褐色蘋果上的斑點。
我拱起的腳背不僅還在疼痛，
而且還在承受梯子橫檔的頂壓。
我會感到梯子隨壓彎的樹枝晃動。
我會繼續聽到從地窖傳來
一堆堆蘋果滾進去的
轟隆隆的聲音。

After Apple-Picking

My long two-pointed ladder's sticking through a tree

Toward heaven still,

And there's a barrel that I didn't fill

Beside it, and there may be two or three

Apples I didn't pick upon some bough.

But I am done with apple-picking now.

Essence of winter sleep is on the night,

The scent of apples: I am drowsing off.

I cannot rub the strangeness from my sight

I got from looking through a pane of glass

I skimmed this morning from the drinking trough

And held against the world of hoary grass.

It melted, and I let it fall and break.

But I was well

Upon my way to sleep before it fell,

And I could tell

What from my dreaming was about to take.

Magnified apples appear and disappear,

Stem end and blossom end,

And every fleck of russet showing clear.

My instep arch not only keeps the ache,

It keeps the pressure of a ladder-round.

I feel the ladder sway as the boughs bend.

And I keep hearing from the cellar bin

The rumbling sound

Of load on load of apples coming in.

因為我已經採摘了太多的
蘋果，我已非常厭倦
我曾期望的豐收。
成千上萬的蘋果需要伸手去摘，
需要輕輕拿，輕輕放，不能掉地。
因為所有
掉在地上的蘋果
即使沒碰壞，也未被殘茬戳傷，
都得送去榨果汁兒，
彷彿一文不值。
誰都能看出什麼會來打擾我睡覺，
不管這是什麼樣的睡覺。
要是土撥鼠還沒離去，
聽到我描述這睡覺的過程，
牠就能說出這到底是像牠的冬眠
還是只像某些人的睡眠。

For I have had too much

Of apple-picking: I am overtired

Of the great harvest I myself desired.

There were ten thousand thousand fruit to touch,

Cherish in hand, lift down, and not let fall.

For all

That struck the earth,

No matter if not bruised or spiked with stubble,

Went surely to the cider-apple heap

As of no worth.

One can see what will trouble

This sleep of mine, whatever sleep it is.

Were he not gone,

The woodchuck could say whether it's like his

Long sleep, as I describe its coming on,

Or just some human sleep.

規矩

三個人在小河邊的草原上做工，
把攤曬的乾草收攏，垛成草堆，
他們不時抬眼看看西邊的天色，
西方有一團鑲有金邊的不規則的
烏雲在移動，而在烏雲中央
始終橫著一柄閃亮的匕首。忽然
一名雇工把乾草杈往地上一扔，
轉身朝家裡走去，另一名則沒動，
那位城裡長大的牧場主人非常疑惑。
「出什麼事啦？」
　　　　　　「你剛才說的話。」
「我剛才說什麼來著？」
　　　　　　「說我們得快點堆草。」

　　　　　　「快點堆草──因為天快下雨？
　　　　　　我說這話至少是在半小時以前。
　　　　　　我那麼說也是在為我自己打打氣。」
　　　　　　「你不懂的，詹姆斯是個傻蛋，
　　　　　　他以為你在暗示說他幹活不賣力，
　　　　　　一般主人喊加油都有那種意思。
　　　　　　當然，詹姆斯得把話琢磨半天
　　　　　　才會作出反應；他是那麼認為的。」
　　　　　　「他要那樣想，那他真是個傻瓜。」

The Code

There were three in the meadow by the brook

Gathering up windrows, piling cocks of hay,

With an eye always lifted toward the west

Where an irregular sun-bordered cloud

Darkly advanced with a perpetual dagger

Flickering across its bosom. Suddenly

One helper, thrusting pitchfork in the ground,

Marched himself off the field and home. One stayed.

The town-bred farmer failed to understand.

"What is there wrong?"

        "Something you just now said."

"What did I say?"

        "About our taking pains."

        "To cock the hay? — because it's going to shower?

I said that more than half an hour ago.

I said it to myself as much as you."

"You didn't know. But James is one big fool.

He thought you meant to find fault with his work.

That's what the average farmer would have meant.

James would take time, of course, to chew it over

Before he acted: he's just got round to act."

"He is a fool if that's the way he takes me."

「別為這事煩心，你已學到點東西。
對於雇工有兩點千萬別說——
一是叫他幹得快點，二是叫他幹得好些。
我和其他熟手一樣難侍候，
但我對你盡心盡力，
因為我知道你並不懂我們的規矩。
你只是想到什麼就說什麼，甚至
說出我們想的，可你並沒有暗示。
我給你講一件曾經發生過的事情，
那時我就在這北邊的塞勒姆鎮
和四五個雇工一道替一戶叫桑德斯
的人家割草。誰也不喜歡那老板。
他長得活像是蜘蛛的某個變種，
四條手臂和腿又細又長又彎，
駝背的身體卻胖得像個烤圓餅。

但說到幹活，那傢伙可真拼命，
尤其是在他拼命也能讓雇工跟著
拼命的時候。我現在也不想否認
他對自己很嚴苛。我發現他自己
從來就沒有固定的作息時間，
太陽光和燈光對他都是一個樣，
我曾聽見他整夜都在穀倉裡幹活。
可他就是喜歡催他的雇工加把勁兒，
對那些帶不動的人他就緊逼緊催——
你知道在割草時可以來這一手——
鐮刀緊跟著他們的腳後跟，威脅
　　要把他們的雙腿割掉。

"Don't let it bother you. You've found out something.

The hand that knows his business won't be told

To do work better or faster — those two things.

I'm as particular as anyone:

Most likely I'd have served you just the same.

But I know you don't understand our ways.

You were just talking what was in your mind,

What was in all our minds, and you weren't hinting.

Tell you a story of what happened once:

I was up here in Salem at a man's

Named Sanders, with a gang of four or five

Doing the haying. No one liked the boss.

He was one of the kind sports call a spider,

All wiry arms and legs that spread out wavy

From a humped body nigh as big's a biscuit.

But work! that man could work, especially

If by so doing he could get more work

Out of his hired help. I'm not denying40

He was hard on himself. I couldn't find

That he kept any hours — not for himself.

Daylight and lantern-light were one to him:

I've heard him pounding in the barn all night.

But what he liked was someone to encourage.

Them that he couldn't lead he'd get behind

And drive, the way you can, you know, in mowing —

Keep at their heels and threaten to mow their legs off.

我一直很留神他那套擠壓把戲
（我們管那叫擠壓）並一直防著他。
所以有次割草時他要我做搭檔，
我就心想得留心別惹什麼麻煩。
我裝好一大車乾草並捆壓結實，
老桑德斯除去雜草，說了聲『好了！』
直到我們進入穀倉一切都很順利，
只等把乾草卸進堆草的隔倉。
你知道雖然堆草又慢又費力氣，
卸草卻是再輕鬆不過的事情，
卸草人只要站在車上往下扔，
一車草要不了多久就可以卸光。

你該不會認為幹這種輕鬆活兒
也需要大聲催促，對吧？
但是那個老傻瓜雙手緊握草杈，
從堆草坑裡抬起滿臉鬍鬚的臉，
像個軍官似地吼道：『讓他媽的來吧！』
我心想你真要他媽來？我沒聽錯吧？
於是我大聲問：『你剛才說什麼啊？
你說讓他媽來？』『對，讓他媽的來吧。』
他又說了一遍，但聲音溫和了些。
你就絕不會對雇工說這種髒話，
自重的人都不會說。老天作證，當時
我真恨不得把他和他的臭嘴一同除掉。

I'd seen about enough of his bulling tricks

(We call that bulling). I'd been watching him.

So when he paired off with me in the hayfield

To load the load, thinks I, Look out for trouble.

I built the load and topped it off; old Sanders

Combed it down with a rake and says, 'O.K.'

Everything went well till we reached the barn

With a big jag to empty in a bay.

You understand that meant the easy job

For the man up on top, of throwing down

The hay and rolling it off wholesale,

Where on a mow it would have been slow lifting.

You wouldn't think a fellow'd need much urging

Under those circumstances, would you now?

But the old fool seizes his fork in both hands,

And looking up bewhiskered out of the pit,

Shouts like an army captain, 'Let her come!'

Thinks I, D'ye mean it? 'What was that you said?'

I asked out loud, so's there'd be no mistake,

'Did you say, "Let her come"' 'Yes, let her come.'

He said it over, but he said it softer.

Never you say a thing like that to a man,

Not if he values what he is. God, I'd as soon

Murdered him as left out his middle name.

那車草是我裝的，我知道怎樣卸。
我先試著輕輕叉出兩三捆草，好像
在考慮從何下手，然後我一叉到底
把整車乾草朝他頭上傾卸下去。
透過騰起的灰塵我朝下瞥了一眼，
只見他像個溺水者仰著頭在掙扎，
像一隻被夾住的老鼠大聲尖叫。
『他媽的，』我說，『你這是活該！』
隨即他就沒了影子也沒了叫聲。
我弄乾淨草架便趕車出倉去消氣。
我坐下來一邊拭去脖子上的草籽
一邊等著有人來問我出了什麼事，
這時有人高聲問：『老傢伙在哪裡？』
『我把他埋在穀倉裡的乾草堆下。
你們要找他，可以去把他挖出來。』

見我擦拭脖子上的草籽，他們意識到
肯定發生了什麼不該發生的事情。
他們跑向穀倉，我則待在原地。
後來他們告訴我，他們把草坑裡
的乾草叉出來一大半。不見人影！
他們仔細傾聽，也未聞絲毫動靜。
我猜他們以為我剌穿了他的腦袋，
不然我不可能把他埋在乾草下面。
他們繼續挖掘。『別讓他妻子來穀倉。』
去攔他妻子的人朝一扇窗戶裡看，

I'd built the load and knew right where to find it.

Two or three forkfuls I picked lightly round for

Like meditating, and then I just dug in

And dumped the rackful on him in ten lots.

I looked over the side once in the dust

And caught sight of him treading-water-like,

Keeping his head above. 'Damn ye,' I says,

"That gets ye!' He squeaked like a squeezed rat.

That was the last I saw or heard of him.

I cleaned the rack and drove out to cool off.

As I sat mopping hayseed from my neck,

And sort of waiting to be asked about it,

One of the boys sings out, 'Where's the old man?'

'I left him in the barn under the hay.

If ye want him, ye can go and dig him out.'

They realized from the way I swabbed my neck

More than was needed, something must be up.

They headed for the barn; I stayed there I was.

They told me afterward. First the forked hay,

A lot of it, out into the barn floor.

Nothing! They listened for him. Not a rustle.

I guess they thought I'd spiked him in the temple

Before I buried him, or I couldn't have managed.

They excavated more. 'Go keep his wife

Out of the barn.' Someone looked in a window,

真他媽的，他居然已在廚房裡，
癱在一把椅子上，雙腳靠著火爐，
儘管那天是夏季最熱的一天。
從背後也能看得出他氣急敗壞，
所以沒人敢進去驚動他，甚至
不敢讓他察覺有人在背後看他。
顯而易見，我沒能把他埋掉
（我也許只把他撞倒了），但是
我想埋他的企圖傷了他的面子。
他逕自回到了屋裡，以免碰上我。
那天下午他一直遠遠躲著我們。
我們繼續為他割草。晚些時候

我們看見他到菜園裡去摘豌豆，
因為他老閒不住，總要找點事做。」
「發現他沒死你該鬆了口氣吧？」
「對！可也說不準——這很難說。
我當時的確是恨不得要他的命。」
「你對他下狠手，他開除了你嗎？」
「開除我？不！他知道我是按規矩做事。」

And curse me if he wasn't in the kitchen

Slumped way down in a chair, with both his feet

Against the stove, the hottest day that summer.

He looked so clean disgusted from behind

There was no one that dared to stir him up,

Or let him know that he was being looked at.

Apparently I hadn't buried him

(I may have knocked him down); but my just trying

To bury him had hurt his dignity.

He had gone to the house so's not to meet me.

He kept away from us all afternoon.

We tended to his hay. We saw him out

After a while picking peas in his garden:

He couldn't keep away from doing something."

"Weren't you relieved to find he wasn't dead?"

"No! and yet I don't know — it's hard to say.

I went about to kill him fair enough."

"You took an awkward way. Did he discharge you?"

"Discharge me? No! He knew I did just right."

世世代代

既然所有要來新罕布夏
尋祖尋宗的人有可能一起來，
所以這次宣布了一位新主管。
姓斯塔克的都聚集在鮑鎮──
一個農業已經衰退、遍布岩石的鄉鎮，
一片已被砍伐過、只剩新生樹苗的土地。
有人曾實實在在地住在這土中，
在小路旁的一個古老的地窖洞裡，
那兒就是斯塔克家族的發源地。
他們從那兒繁衍成許多分支，
以致於現在鎮上留下的所有房屋
怎麼安排也不夠讓他們避風躲雨，
只好在樹林和果園中搭起帳篷。

他們聚集在鮑鎮，但這還不夠，
他們還必須在規定的一天，聚集到
那個使他們來到世上的地窖邊緣，
努力去追根溯本，探究過去，
從中獲得某種不平凡的東西。
但雨毀了一切。那天一開始就不順，
烏雲低垂，不時有點濛濛細雨。
那些年輕人仍然抱有一點希望，
直到日近中午暴風驟起，吹得草
沙沙作響。「即使其他人在那兒又
有啥關係，」他們說，「反正不會下雨。」

The Generations of Men

A governor it was proclaimed this time,

When all who would come seeking in New Hampshire

Ancestral memories might come together.

And those of the name Stark gathered in Bow,

A rock-strewn town where farming has fallen off,

And sprout-lands flourish where the ax has gone.

Someone had literally run to earth

In an old cellar hole in a byroad

The origin of all the family there.

Thence they were sprung, so numerous a tribe

That now not all the houses left in town

Made shift to shelter them without the help

Of here and there a tent in grove and orchard.

They were at Bow, but that was not enough:

Nothing would do but they must fix a day

To sand together on the crater's verge

That turned them on the world, and try to fathom

The past and get some strangeness out of it.

But rain spooled all. The day began uncertain,

With clouds low-trailing and moments of rain that misted.

The young folk held some hope out to each other

Till well toward noon, when the storm settled down

With a swish in the grass. "What if the others

Are there," they said. "It isn't going to rain."

只有一個從附近農場來的青年
信步去那兒，但只是去閒逛，
他並沒指望會見到其他任何人。
一人，兩人，對，那兒有兩人，
沿著彎彎山路走來的第二位
是個姑娘。她在遠處停下腳步
觀察了一陣，然後拿定主意
至少該走過去看看那人是誰，
而且說不定還能聽他說說這天氣。
那人是某個她不認識的斯塔克。
「今天沒有聚會。」他點頭說。
　　　　　「看來是沒有。」
她抬頭看了天空一眼，忽然轉身。
「我只是來閒逛。」
　　　　　「我也是來閒逛。」

考慮到同一家族的成員互不相識，
有人早就為此做好了必要的準備，
某位熱心者精心設計了一份家譜——
一種像護照般的卡片，卡片上
詳細記載了持有人所屬的分支。
她伸手去摸她上衣的胸襟，
像要掏心似的。他倆同時笑了。
「斯塔克？」他問，「卡片不要緊。」
「對，斯塔克。你呢？」
　　　　　「我也姓斯塔克。」他掏出卡片。
「你知道我們或許不是或仍然是親戚；

Only one from a farm not far away

Strolled thither, not expecting he would find

Anyone else, but out of idleness.

One, and one other, yes, for there were two.

The second round the curving hillside road

Was a girl; and she halted some way off

To reconnoiter, and then made up her mind

At least to pass by and see who he was.

And perhaps hear some word about the weather.

This was some Stark she didn't know. He nodded.

"No fete today," he said.

     "It looks that way."

She swept the heavens, turning on her heel.

"I only idled down."

      "I idled down."

    Provision there had been for just such meeting

    Of stranger-cousins, in a family tree

    Drawn on a sort of passport with the branch

    Of the one bearing it done in detail —

    Some zealous one's laborious device.

    She made a sudden movement toward her bodice,

    As one who clasps her heart. They laughed together.

    "Stark?" he inquired. "No matter for the proof."

    "Yes, Stark. And you?"

        "I'm Stark." He drew his passport.

    "You know we might not be and still be cousins:

這鎮上有許多人姓蔡斯、洛厄和貝利，
全都聲稱具有斯塔克家族的血緣。
我母親家姓萊恩，但她可以
嫁給任何一個男人，而她的孩子
依然屬於斯塔克家族，今天無疑
也可以來到這裡。」
「你說起家世就像在打啞謎，
活像薇奧拉，叫人聽不明白。」
「我只是想說在幾代人之前，
我母親家也姓斯塔克，她嫁給父親
只是讓我們恢復了斯塔克這個姓。」
「你清楚的陳述家世，
真不該讓人覺得糊塗，
可我得承認你說的使我腦袋發昏。
這是我的卡片——看來你熟悉家譜——
看看你能否算出我倆的親緣關係。
咱們在這地窖牆頭坐上一會兒，
讓雙腳懸盪在山莓藤中間吧。」
「在家譜的庇護之下。」

「正是如此——那應是充分的保護。」
「可保不住不淋雨——我看就要下雨。」
「正在下雨。」
「不，正在起霧；請公正一些。
你覺得雨會使眼睛失去熱情嗎？」
那個地窖周圍的環境是這樣的：
小路彎彎曲曲通向半山腰，
然後在不遠處終止，消失。
沒人會從那條路回家。他倆
身後唯一的房舍是一片廢墟。

The town is full of Chases, Lowes, and Baileys,

All claiming some priority in Starkness.

My mother was a Lane, yet might have married

Anyone upon earth and still her children

Would have been Starks, and doubtless here today."

"You riddle with your genealogy,

Like a Viola. I don't follow you."

"I only mean my mother was a Stark

Several times over, and by marrying father

No more than brought us back into the name."

"One ought not to be thrown into confusion

By a plain statement of relationship,

But I own what you say makes my head spin.

You take my card — you seem so good at such things —

And see if you can reckon our cousinship.

Why not take seats here on the cellar wall

And dangle feet among the raspberry vines?"

"Under the shelter of the family tree."

"Just so — that ought to be enough protection."

"Not from the rain. I think it's going to rain."

"It's raining."

"No, it's misting; let's be fair.

Does the rain seem to you to cool the eyes?"

The situation was like this; the road

Bowed outward on the mountain halfway up,

And disappeared and ended not far off.

No one went home that way. The only house

Beyond where they were was a shattered seedpod.

廢墟下方有條樹叢遮掩的小河，
小河的流水聲對那地方是種寂靜。
他聆聽著水聲直到她開始推算。
「從父親那方來看，似乎我倆是──
　　　讓我想想──」
「別太拘泥字眼──你有三張卡片。」
「四張，你一張，我三張，每張都
記載了一個我屬於其中的家族分支。」
「你知道，如此攀附自己的家世，
你會被人認為是瘋子。」
　　　　「我也許是個瘋子。」

「你看上去也是，這樣坐在雨中
和你從未見過的我一起研究家譜。
具有祖先過人的驕傲，我們，
我們新英格蘭人會變成怎樣呢？
我想我們都瘋了。請你告訴我
我們為何被拉進這鎮上來到這洞邊，
就像暴風雨之前野鵝聚集在湖面？
我真想知道從這個洞裡會看見什麼。」
「印地安人有個芝加莫茨托神話，
芝加莫茨托意思是指人誕生的七個洞穴。
我們斯塔克人就是從這個洞出來的。」
「你真有學問。這是你從洞裡看見的？」

And below roared a brook hidden in trees

The sound of which was silence for the place.

This he sat listening to till she gave judgment.

"On father's side, it seems, we're — let me see —"

"Don't be too technical. — You have three cards."

"Four cards: one yours, three mine (one for each branch

Of the Stark family I'm a member of)."

"D' you know a person so related to herself

Is supposed to be mad."

           "I may be mad."

           "You look so, sitting out here in the rain

           Studying genealogy with me

           You never saw before. What will we come to

           With all this pride of ancestry, we Yankees?

           I think we're all mad. Tell me why we're here,

           Drawn into town about this cellar hole

           Like wild geese on a lake before a storm?

           What do we see in such a hole, I wonder."

           "The Indians had a myth of Chicamoztoc,

           Which means The-Seven-Caves-that-We-Came-Out-of.

           This is the pit from which we Starks were digged."

           "You must be learned. That's what you see in it?"

「那你會看見什麼呢？」

　　　　「是呀，我會看見什麼呢？
先讓我瞧瞧。我會看見山莓藤——」
「哦，要是你只想用眼睛看，那就
先聽聽我看見什麼。那是個小男孩，
朦朦朧朧就像是陽光下的火柴光；
他正摸索著在地窖裡找果醬，
他以為洞裡很黑，其實充滿了陽光。」
「那算什麼！聽我說，我能
清楚地看見老祖父斯塔克——
嘴裡叼著煙斗，還有他的水罐——
噢，哎呀，那不是老祖父，是老祖母，

但仍有煙斗、煙霧和那個水罐。
她在找蘋果汁，那個老太婆，她渴了；
但願她找到喝的並平平安安地出來。」
「跟我講講她，她長得像我嗎？」
「她應該像，不是嗎？你從那麼多
家族分支中繼承了她的血緣。我認為
她的確像你，請保持你的姿勢，
你們的鼻子簡直一模一樣，下巴也相同——
這是客觀的比較。」
「你可憐的親愛的曾曾曾曾祖母！」
「注意說對她的輩份。別讓她少了一輩。」

"And what do you see?"

"Yes, what do I see?

First let me look. I see raspberry vines — "

"Oh, if you're going to use your eyes, just hear

What I see. It's a little, little boy,

As pale and dim as a match flame in the sun;

He's groping in the cellar after jam —

He thinks it's dark, and it's flooded with daylight."

"He's nothing. Listen. When I lean like this

I can make out old Grandsir Stark distinctly —

With his pipe in his mouth and his brown jug —

Bless you, it isn't Grandsir Stark, it's Granny;

But the pipe's there and smoking, and the jug.

She's after cider, the old girl, she's thirsty;

Here's hoping she gets her drink and gets out safely."

"Tell me about her. Does she look like me?"

"She should, shouldn't she? — you're so many times

Over descended from her. I believe

She does look like you. Stay the way you are.

The nose is just the same, and so's the chin —

Making allowance, making due allowance."

"You poor, dear, great, great, great, great Granny!"

"See that you get her greatness right. Don't stint her."

「是呀，這很重要，但你並不這樣想。
我不是好欺負的，看我淋得多濕。」
「對，我們得走了，不能老待在這兒。
但等我幫你一個忙再走。
頭髮上掛點銀色的水珠
不會有損於你夏天的容貌。
我很想利用空谷間那條小河
嘩嘩的流水聲做一點實驗。
我們已見過幻象，現在來聽聽聲音。
我小時候乘坐火車時肯定得到過
某種啓示。過去我習慣利用轟鳴聲
使那些聲音清晰地說出啓示，
說出，唱出，或是用音樂奏出。
或許你也具有我有的這種本領。

但我從沒在河水的喧囂聲中傾聽過，
而這條小河又流得如此湍急。
它應該給出更明確的啓示。」
「這就像你把一個圖案映在紗窗上，
圖案的意思全憑你自己去想像；
那些聲音會給你你希望聽到的。」
「眞奇怪，它們想給你的是什麼東西？」
「這我就不知道了。那肯定夠奇怪。
我眞懷疑這是不是你的虛構，
你覺得你今天可能會聽見什麼呢？」

"Yes, it's important, though you think it isn't.

I won't be teased. But see how wet I am."

"Yes, you must go; we can't stay here forever.

But wait until I give you a hand up.

A bead of silver water more or less,

Strung on your hair, won't hurt your summer looks.

I wanted to try something with the noise

That the brook raises in the empty valley

We have seen visions — now consult the voices.

Something I must have learned riding in trains

When I was young. I used to use the roar

To set the voices speaking out of it,

Speaking or singing, and the band-music playing.

Perhaps you have the art of what I mean.

           I've never listened in among the sounds

           That a brook makes in such a wild descent.

           It ought to give a purer oracle."

           "It's as you throw a picture on a screen:

           The meaning of it all is out of you;

           The voices give you what you wish to hear."

           "Strangely, it's anything they wish to give."

           "Then I don't know. It must be strange enough.

           I wonder if it's not your make-believe.

           What do you think you're like to hear today?"

「根據我倆一直在一起的感覺——
何必說我可能會聽見什麼？
我可以告訴你那些聲音確實說了什麼。
你最好還是在原來的位置
再多坐一會兒。別催我，
不然我沒法用心去聽那些聲音。」
「你是要進入某種催眠狀態？」
「你得非常安靜，千萬別說話。」
「我會屏住呼吸。」
　　　　「那些聲音似乎說——」
「我在洗耳恭聽。」

　　　　　　　　「別說話！那些聲音似乎說：
管她叫璐西卡婭，那個敢於冒險、
不怕與生人結識的璐西卡婭。」
「我允許你這麼說吧——經過考慮。」
「我看不出你怎麼能不允許我說。
你想聽真話。我只是重複那些聲音，
你明白它們知道我不知你的名字，
不過在我倆之間名字有什麼關係——」
「我應該懷疑——」

　　　　　　　「請別做聲。那些聲音說：
管她叫璐西卡婭，並取一塊木頭，
你會發現它躺在燒焦的地窖裡
那些山莓叢間，然後將它劈成
在這古老的宅基上修建的新屋
的門檻，或劈成新屋的其他部分。

"From the sense of our having been together —
But why take time for what I'm like to hear?
I'll tell you what the voices really say.
You will do very well right where you are
A little longer. I mustn't feel too hurried,
Or I can't give myself to hear the voices."
"Is this some trance you are withdrawing into?"
"You must be very still; you mustn't talk."
"I'll hardly breathe."
            "The voices seem to say — "
"I'm waiting."

                        "Don't! The voices seem to say:
            Call her Nausica?, the unafraid
            Of an acquaintance made adventurously."
            "I let you say that — on consideration."
            "I don't see very well how you can help it.
            You want the truth. I speak but by the voices.
            You see they know I haven't had your name,
            Thought what a name should matter between us —"
            "I shall suspect —"
                        "Be good. The voices say:
            Call her Nausica?, and take a timber
            That you shall find lies in the cellar, charred
            Among the raspberries, and hew and shape it
            For a doorsill or other corner piece
            In a new cottage on the ancient spot.

生命還沒有從這古宅完全消失。
你可以把它當做你夏天的住屋，
可能她也會來，仍然無所畏懼，
會在敞開的門口坐在你面前，
懷裡捧著鮮花，直到花兒枯萎，
但她不會跨過那道神聖的門檻——」
「我真納悶你的神諭想說什麼。
你看得出這個神諭有點破綻，
或者說它應該講方言。它到底想
假冒誰的聲音？想必不是老祖父，
也不是老祖母。請想到他們吧。
在這兒最該聽到的是他們的聲音。」
「你好像特別偏愛我們的老祖母
（已過了九代。我說錯了請糾正）

她說的任何話都有可能被你
當做神諭。但讓我提醒你，
她那個時代的人聽到的都是大白話。
你認為此刻你應該叫她回來？」
「叫不叫她來取決於我們。」
「那好，這下是老祖母在說話：
『我說不好！也許我這麼說不對。
不過今天的族人與過去的不大相同，
他們絕不會按我的想法去想問題。
雖說老祖宗不該過分影響後代，
但今天貪圖舒適的人也太多了一點。
要是我能多見到些使他們的生活
有點艱辛的風險，我會感到輕鬆。

The lift is not yet all gone out of it.

And come and make your summer dwelling here,

And perhaps she will come, still unafraid,

And sit before you in the open door

With flowers in her lap until they fade,

But not come in across the sacred sill —"

"I wonder where your oracle is tending.

You can see that there's something wrong with it,

Or it would speak in dialect. Whose voice

Does it purport to speak in? Not old Grandsir's

Nor Granny's, surely. Call up one of them.

They have best right to be heard in this place."

"You seem so partial to our great-grandmother

(Nine times removed. Correct me if I err.)

You will be likely to regard as scared

Anything she may say. But let me warn you,

Folks in her day were given to plain speaking.

You think you'd best tempt her at such a time?"

"It rests with us always to cut her off."

"Well then, it's Granny speaking: ‘I dunnow!

Mebbe I'm wrong to take it as I do.

There ain't no names quite like the old ones, though,

Nor never will be to my way of thinking.

One mustn't bear too hard on the newcomers,

But there's a dite too many of them for comfort.

I should feel easier if I could see

More of the salt wherewith they're to be salted.

孩子，照我的話去做！取那塊木頭——
它和當初被砍倒時一樣結實——
重新開始——』好啦，她該在此打住。
不過你看得出是什麼使老祖母苦惱，
你難道不覺得我們有時過分看重
這古老的血緣？但重要的是他們的理想，
那些理想可以使一些人繼續努力。」
「我看得出我們就要成為好朋友。」
「我喜歡你說『就要』。你先前說過
天就要下雨。」

   「我知道，當時正在下雨。
我允許你這麼說。但我現在得走了。」

      「你允許我這麼說？經過考慮？
    在這種情況下我們怎麼可以說再見呢？」
「我們怎麼會？」
      「你願意把路留給我嗎？」
「不，我不相信你的眼睛。你已說夠了。
現在幫我那個忙吧——替我摘那朵花。」
「我們下次見面該在哪兒？」
       「在去別處相會之前，
我們得在這兒再見上一面。」
        「在雨中？」
「應該在雨中，雨中的某個時候。
在明天的雨中，好嗎？如果天下雨？
但非要再見面，陽光下也行。」她說著離去。

Son, you do as you're told! You take the timber —

It's as sound as the day when it was cut —

And begin over —' There, she'd better stop.

You can see what is troubling Granny, though.

But don't you think we sometimes make too much

Of the old stock? What counts is the ideals,

And those will bear some keeping still about."

"I can see we are going to be good friends."

"I like your ' going to be.' You said just now

It's going to rain."

"I know, and it was raining.

I let you say all that. But I must go now."

"You let me say it? on consideration?

How shall we say good-by in such a case?"

"How shall we?"

"Will you leave the way to me?"

"No, I don't trust your eyes. You've said enough.

Now give me your hand up. — Pick me that flower."

"Where shall we meet again?"

"Nowhere but here

Once more before we meet elsewhere."

"In rain?"

"It ought to be in rain. Sometime in rain.

In rain tomorrow, shall we, if it rains?

But if we must, in sunshine." So she went.

當家的

我不請自入地進入了那道廚房門。
「是你，」她說，「我起不來。原諒我
沒應你敲門。我再也不能請人進屋，
就像我再也不能不讓人進屋一樣。
我快老得不中用了，我告訴他們。
我現在還能活動的大概只有手指，
所以得找點樂趣。我能做針線活，
幫人家鑲這種珠邊湊合著還行。」
「你鑲邊的這雙軟底鞋可真漂亮。
它們是誰的？」

　　　「你是說——哦，某個小姐的。
我沒法子把別人家的女兒了解清楚。

啊，要是我能想像得出都是誰會穿著
我裝飾過的鞋去跳舞，那該有多好！」
　　　　　「約翰在哪兒？」
「你沒見到他？這真怪了，他上
你家去找你，你卻來他家找他。
按理你們不可能錯過。我知道了，
他肯定改變主意去了加蘭家。
他不會去得太久，你可以等等。
不過你或任何人還能有什麼用呢——
太晚了。你知道埃絲特爾已經走了。」
「我聽說了，怎麼回事？她什麼時候走的？」
「走了兩星期了。」

　　　　　「看來她真鐵了心。」

The Housekeeper

I let myself in at the kitchen door.

"It's you," she said. "I can't get up. Forgive me

Not answering your knock. I can no more

Let people in than I can keep them out.

I'm getting too old for my size, I tell them.

My fingers are about all I've the use of

So's to take any comfort. I can sew:

I help out with this beadwork what I can."

"That's a smart pair of pumps you're beading there.

Who are they for?"

       "You mean? — oh, for some miss.

I can't keep track of other people's daughters.

       Lord, if I were to dream of everyone

       Whose shoes I primped to dance in!"

               "And where's John?"

       "Haven't you seen him? Strange what set you off

       To come to his house when he's gone to yours.

       You can't have passed each other. I know what:

       He must have changed his mind and gone to Garland's.

       He won't be long in that case. You can wait.

       Though what good you can be, or anyone —

       It's gone so far. You've heard? Estelle's run off."

       "Yes, what's it all about? When did she go?"

       "Two weeks since."

               "She's in earnest, it appears."

「我肯定她不會回來，她藏在某個地方，

我不知道在哪兒，約翰以爲我知道。

他以爲我只要説句話她就會回來。

可是，哎喲，我雖然是她的母親——

卻沒法跟她説話，哦，但願我能！」

「約翰眞難受啊，他怎麼辦？

他不可能找到任何替代她的女人。」

「哦，如果你問我他怎麼辦，

他會只吃烘餅，而且三餐併一餐，

他會坐下來讓我告訴他每一件事：

需要什麼，要多少，問題所在。

但等我一走——我當然不能留在這兒，

埃絲特爾一安頓好就會來接我。

約翰和我只會是彼此的累贅。

不過我告訴他們不能趕我出門，

因爲我一直都是這個家的一部分。

我們在這兒已十五年了。」

　　　　　　　　　　「在一起

生活了這麼久，現在卻要拆散。

你看你們走了他怎樣過日子呢？

你們倆一走，就只剩一座空屋了。」

「我看他也過不了幾年日子，

這兒除了家具再沒別的東西。

我們走後我可不願再想起這個破地方，

不願想起從庭院旁邊流過的小溪，

不願想起只有幾隻雞的空空庭院。

"I'm sure she won't come back. She's hiding somewhere.

I don't know where myself. John thinks I do.

He thinks I only have to say the word,

And she'll come back. But, bless you, I'm her mother —

I can't talk to her, and, Lord, if I could!"

"It will go hard with John. What will he do?

He can't find anyone to take her place."

"Oh, if you ask me that, what will he do?

He gets some sort of bakeshop meals together,

With me to sit and tell him everything,

What's wanted and how much and where it is.

But when I'm gone — of course I can't stay here:

Estelle's to take me when she's settled down.

He and I only hinder one another.

I tell them they can't get me through the door, though:

I've been built in here like a big church organ.

We've been here fifteen years."

                              "That's a long time

To live together and then pull apart.

How do you see him living when you're gone?

Tow of you out will leave an empty house."

"I don't just see him living many years,

Left here with nothing, but the furniture.

I hate to think of the old place when we're gone,

With the brook going by below the yard,

And no one here but hens blowing about.

他要早賣了這地方該有多好，現在

　　他想賣也賣不掉，

因為沒有人願意在這兒過日子。

這兒破敗不堪，好像到了末日，

我想他要做的就是讓這一切完蛋。

他將靠咒罵度日。他是個笨蛋！

我從沒見過，一個男人讓家庭糾紛

如此影響他應該處理的事務。

他將一切都撒手不管，簡直像個孩子，

我看一切都怪他只由母親養大。

他已讓割下的乾草淋了三場雨。

昨天他為我鋤了一會兒地，

我想到菜園工作會對他有好處，

不知他有什麼不如意，竟把鋤頭

往空中一扔。我這會兒還能看見——

過來，我指給你看，在那蘋果樹上。

這可不是他那把年紀的人該做的事，

他都五十五了，還火氣這麼大。」

「你該不是怕他吧？那槍做什麼用？」

「哦，那是小雞出巢時用來嚇鷹的。

約翰會碰我！除非他不知誰好誰歹。

我該替他說句話，約翰從不耍威風，

不像有些男人。誰也不用怕他；

問題的關鍵是他早已拿定主意

不承擔他必須承擔的責任。」

If he could sell the place, but then, he can't:

No one will ever live on it again.

It's too run down. This is the last of it

What I think he will do, is let things smash.

He'll sort of swear the time away. He's awful!

I never saw a man let family troubles

Make so much difference in his man's affairs.

He's just dropped everything. He's like a child.

I blame his being brought up by his mother.

He's got hay down that's been rained on three times.

He hoed a little yesterday for me:

I thought the growing things would do him good.

Something went wrong. I saw him throw the hoe

Sky-high with both hands. I can see it now —

Come here — I'll show you — in that apple tree.

That's no way for a man to do at his age:

He's fifty-five, you know, if he's a day."

"Aren't you afraid of him? What's that gun for?"

"Oh, that's been there for hawks since chicken-time.

John Hall touch me! Not if he knows his friends.

I'll say that for him, John's no threatener

Like some menfolk. No one's afraid of him;

All is, he's made up his mind not to stand

What he has got to stand."

「埃絲特爾在哪兒？
沒人能跟她說上話嗎？她會說什麼？
你剛才說你不知道她在哪裡。」
　　　　　　「不想知道！
她認爲既然和他過日子沒面子，
當然就該離他而去。」
　　　　　　「她的想法是錯的！」
「嗯，可是他本來應該和她結婚。」
　　　　　　　　「這倒也是。」
「這些年來那種關係一直讓她夠受，
這事我無論如何也說不清楚。

有個男人是不同，至少約翰這種男人，
比一般男人更溫和。
『好得像結了婚比不結婚好，』
這就是他經常掛在嘴邊的話。
我知道他怎樣感覺——但一切照舊！」
「我眞不知道他爲什麼不和她結婚，
然後結束那種關係。」
　　　　　　「現在太遲了。她不會要他了。
他已經給了她時間去想別的事情。
這是他的錯。那寶貝知道我的心思
一直都是爲了阻止這個家被拆散。
這個家不錯，我不求更好的。
但每當我問『你們幹嘛不結婚呢？』
他都只是一句話，『幹嘛要結婚？』」

"Where is Estelle?

Couldn't one talk to her? What does she say?

You say you don't know where she is."

"Nor want to!

She thinks if it was bad to live with him,

It must be right to leave him."

"Which is wrong!"

"Yes, but he should have married her."

"I know."

"The strain's been too much for her all these years:

I can't explain it any other way.

It's different with a man, at least with John:

He knows he's kinder than the run of men.

Better than married ought to be as good

As married — that's what he has always said.

I know the way he's felt — but all the same!"

"I wonder why he doesn't marry her

And end it."

"Too late now: she wouldn't have him.

He's given her time to think of something else.

That's his mistake. The dear knows my interest

Has been to keep the thing from breaking up.

This is a good home: I don't ask for better.

But when I've said, Why shouldn't they be married?

He'd say, Why should they? — no more words than that."

「爲什麼非結婚不可呢？我認爲
約翰歷來都公道。他的就是她的。
他們從沒爲財產發生過爭執。」
「理由很簡單，他們壓根兒就沒財產。
這農場差不多歸一兩個朋友擁有，
就這個攤子，連抵押都沒人要。」
「我是說埃絲特爾一直管著錢袋。」
「這當中的實情就更難被人知曉，
我想是埃絲特爾和我裝滿那錢袋，
是我們使他有錢，不是他使我們。
約翰是個蹩腳農夫，我這不是怪他。
一年又一年，他總掙不了多少。

你知道我們來這兒只圖我有個家，
埃絲特爾做家務掙我倆的伙食。
但你看事情後來變成了這樣：
她不但包攬了家務，好像戶外活兒
也攬了一半，不過說到這點，
他總說她多幹活兒是因爲她喜歡。
你看我們值點錢的東西都在門外，
與像我們這樣兼點的人家相比，
我們養的雞牛豬都是最棒的，
四周比我們富一倍的人家也比不上。
他們的副業總沒法與農場並駕齊驅，
說到約翰有一點你不得不欣賞，
他喜歡好東西——有人會說太喜歡。

"And after all why should they? John's been fair

I take it. What was his was always hers.

There was no quarrel about property."

"Reason enough, there was no property.

A friend or two as good as own the farm,

Such as it is. It isn't worth the mortgage."

"I mean Estelle has always held the purse."

"The rights of that are harder to get at.

I guess Estelle and I have filled the purse.

'Twas we let him have money, not he us.

John's a bad farmer. I'm not blaming him.

Take it year in, year out, he doesn't make much.

> We came here for a home for me, you know,
>
> Estelle to do the housework for the board
>
> Of both of us. But look how it turns out:
>
> She seems to have the housework, and besides,
>
> Half of the outdoor work, though as for that,
>
> He'd say she does it more because she likes it.
>
> You see our pretty things are all outdoors.
>
> Our hens and cows and pigs are always better
>
> Than folks like us have any business with.
>
> Farmers around twice as well off as we
>
> Haven't as good. They don't go with the farm.
>
> One thing you can't help liking about John,
>
> He's fond of nice things — too fond, some would say.

但埃絲特爾不抱怨，這一點她像他，
她想把我們的雞養成這一帶最好的。
你絕不會看到在一次家禽展覽會前，
這屋裡會滿是半浸在水裡發抖的瘦雞，
一隻一個籠子，羽毛都經過修飾。
熱天裡濕羽毛的氣味可真難聞！
你剛才說和約翰住在一起不安全，
那你是不知道我們這家人有多溫和，
我們連雞都不會傷害！你應該看看
我們怎樣把雞從一處挪到另一處。
我們從不允許把雞倒提起來，
我們能做的只是抓住雞的雙腳。
一手抱一隻，一次挪動兩隻，
不管挪動的地方有多遠，也不管
我們得走多少趟。」

「你想說這是約翰的主意？」
「反正我們遵守規矩，要不然
我不知他會發什麼小孩子脾氣，
他總會設法支配他自己的農場，
他是當家的。但說到那些雞，
我們把花園雞舍都圍在籬笆裡。
什麼也不比它們值錢。我們說上算。
約翰喜歡提起別人向他開的價，
這隻公雞值二十元，那隻二十五。
但他從不出售。既然這些雞能賣
那麼多錢，養在家裡也能值那麼多。
但你知道這些都是花費。幫我個忙，
把櫥櫃架子上那個小盒子遞給我，

But Estelle don't complain: she's like him there.

She wants our hens to be the best there are.

You never saw this room before a show,

Full of lank, shivery, half-drowned birds

In separate coops, having their plumage done.

The smell of the wet feathers in the heat!

You spoke of John's not being safe to stay with.

You don't know what a gentle lot we are:

We wouldn't hurt a hen! You ought to see us

Moving a flock of hens from place to place.

We're not allowed to take them upside down,

All we can hold together by the legs.

Two at a time's the rule, one on each arm,

No matter how far and how many times

We have to go."

                                     "You mean that's John's idea."

                            "And we live up to it; or I don't know

                            What childishness he wouldn't give way to.

                            He manages to keep the upper hand

                            On his own farm. He's boss. But as to hens:

                            We fence our flowers in and the hens range.

                            Nothing's too good for them. We say it pays.

                            John likes to tell the offers he has had,

                            Twenty for this cock, twenty-five for that.

                            He never takes the money. If they're worth

                            That much to sell, they're worth as much to keep.

                            Bless you, it's all expense, though. Reach me down

                            The little tin box on the cupboard shelf —

上邊一排，鐵皮盒子，就是那個。
我讓你看看。在這兒。」
　　　　　　　「這是什麼？」
「花五十美元買隻狼山雞的收據。
那隻公雞現在就在院子裡。」
「不用玻璃籠子嗎？」
　　　　　　「牠需要個大的，
因為牠從地上啄食一頓能吃上一桶米。
正如你說，牠住過玻璃籠子——
倫敦的水晶宮。牠非常名貴，
約翰買回牠，用我們鑲珠的錢——
我們管那叫貝殼串珠。我們不抱怨。
但你看見了，不是嗎？我們得照料牠。」

「而且喜歡照料。這會使事情更糟。」
「好像是的。可這還不夠，我簡直
沒法給你說他那種一籌莫展的樣子。
有時他像著了魔似的——記賬，
想看這麼快錢都花在了什麼地方。
你知道男人會多麼荒唐可笑。
可他著魔時那副模樣真是滑稽——
你想他不修邊幅會是什麼樣子？」
「那會使事情更糟。你只能閉上眼睛。」
「那是埃絲特爾糟，你用不著對我說。」
「你我就不能來找找問題的根源？
癥結在哪兒？怎樣才會使她滿意？」

The upper shelf, the tin box. That's the one.
I'll show you. Here you are."
                    "What's this?"
"A bill —
For fifty dollars for one Langshang cock —
Receipted. And the cock is in the yard."
"Not in a glass case, then?"
                    "He'd need a tall one:
He can eat off a barrel from the ground.
He's been in a glass case, as you may say,
The Crystal Palace, London. He's imported.
John bought him, and we paid the bill with beads —
Wampum, I call it. Mind, we don't complain.
But you see, don't you, we take care of him."

                              "And like it, too. It makes it all the worse."
                              "It seems as if. And that's not all: he's helpless
                              In ways that I can hardly tell you of.
                              Sometimes he gets possessed to keep accounts
                              To see where all the money goes so fast.
                              You know how men will be ridiculous.
                              But it's just fun the way he gets bedeviled —
                              If he's untidy now, what will he be — ?"
                              "It makes it all the worse. You must be blind."
                              "Estelle's the one. You needn't talk to me."
                              "Can't you and I get to the root of it?
                              What's the real trouble? What will satisfy her?"

「我已說了，她甩了他，就這麼回事。」
「爲什麼呢，在她過好日子的時候？
是因爲沒鄰居，因爲沒朋友？」
            「我們有我們的朋友，
那不是原因，鄰居不怕與我們交往。」
「她爲這種關係發愁。你都不管她，
而你是她的母親。」
            「但我並非一直這樣。
一開始我也不喜歡這種關係。
但後來就習慣了。再說——
約翰說我太老，不該抱孫子。
但事到如今說這些還有什麼用呢？
她不會回來，更糟的是她不能回來。」

                        「你幹嘛這麼說話？你知道什麼？
                        你在說什麼？——她把自己弄傷了？」
                        「我是說她結婚了——和另一個男人。」
                        「喔唷！」
                                    「你不相信我？」
                                    「不，我相信，
                        太妙了。我就知道一定有什麼原因！
                        原來原因在這兒。她是個壞女人！」
                        「碰上結婚的機會結婚，算是壞女人？」
                        「荒唐！瞧她做了什麼！那人是誰？」
                        「誰會來這個爛雞窩把她娶走呢？
                        直話直說吧——是她的母親也無妨。

"It's as I say: she's turned from him, that's all."

"But why, when she's well off? If it the neighbors,

Being cut off from friends?"

            "We have our friends.

That isn't it. Folks aren't afraid of us."

"She's let it worry her. You stood the strain,

And you're her mother."

            "But I didn't always.

I didn't relish it along at first.

But I got wonted to it. And besides —

John said I was too old to have grandchildren.

But what's the use of talking when it's done?

She won't come back — it's worse than that — she can't."

                "Why do you speak like that? What do you know?

                What do you mean? — she's done harm to herself?"

"I mean she's married — married someone else."

"Oho, oho!"

                "You don't believe me."

                "Yes, I do,

Only too well. I knew there must be something!

So that was what was back. She's bad, that's all!"

"Bad to get married when she had the chance?"

"Nonsense! See what she's done! But who, but who — ?"

"Who'd marry her straight out of such a mess?

Say it right out — no matter for her mother.

那人是她自己找的，我最好不說出名字，
約翰也想像不出那人是誰。」
「那這事就完了。我想我該走了，
我可憐的埃絲特爾，
而且我也認爲她有一點值得同情。
這下你應該獨占這間廚房，
告訴他，他會得到這個工作。」
「你不必急著走。
約翰就快回來了，我看見有人
下了萊恩山，我想那人就是他。
正是他！這個盒子！快把它放好。
還有這收據。」
　　　　　　「慌什麼？他還要卸套呢。」

「不，他不會。他只會把韁繩一扔，
讓多爾連車帶套自己去草原。
牠走不遠，車輪就會被什麼東西擋住——
不會出事的。你瞧，他過來了！
天哪，看上去他肯定已聽說了！」
約翰推開了房門，但他沒有進屋。
「你好哇，老鄰居，我正想找你哩。
這難道不是地獄，我真想知道。
到這兒來吧，要是你想聽我說話。
老太婆，我待會兒再跟你說。
我聽到一個也許不算新聞的新聞，
這兩個女人，她們想對我幹嘛呢？」
「快跟他去吧，快止住他嚷嚷。」
她隨後衝進關上的房門大聲吼道：
「誰希罕聽你的新聞，你這討厭的白痴？」

The man was found. I'd better name no names.

John himself won't imagine who he is."

"Then it's all up. I think I'll get away.

You'll be expecting John. I pity Estelle;

I suppose she deserves some pity, too.

You ought to have the kitchen to yourself

To break it to him. You may have the job."

"You needn't think you're going to get away.

John's almost here. I've had my eye on someone

Coming down Ryan's Hill. I thought 'twas him.

Here he is now. This box! Put it away.

And this bill."

                                        "What's the hurry? He'll unhitch."

                             "No, he won't, either. He'll just drop the reins

And turn Doll out to pasture, rig and all.

She won't get far before the wheels hang up

On something — there's no harm. See, there he is!

My, but he looks as if he must have heard!"

John threw the door wide but he didn't enter.

"How are you, neighbor? Just the man I'm after.

Isn't it Hell?"   he said.   "I want to know.

Come out here if you want to hear me talk. —

I'll talk to you, old woman, afterward. —

I've got some news that maybe isn't news.

What are they trying to do to me, these two?"

"Do go along with him and stop his shouting."

She raised her voice against the closing door:

"Who wants to hear your news, you — dreadful fool?"

恐懼

提燈的燈光從牲口棚的深處
照射到大門邊一男一女的身上，
把他們的身影投向旁邊的一座房子，
那座房子的窗戶全都黑漆漆的。
一隻馬蹄叩了叩發出空響的地板，
他倆身邊那輛輕便馬車的車尾
動了一動。男的一把抓住車輪，
女的厲聲喝道：「吁，別動！
我剛才看見它清楚得像個白盤子。」
她說：「就在擋泥板的反光晃過路邊
灌木叢的時候——一張男人的臉。
你一定也看見了。」

　　　　　　　　　　「我沒看見。
你看清楚了？」

　　　　　　　　「對，看清楚了！」

　　　　　　　　「一張臉？」
「喬爾，我得去看看。我不能進屋，
我要搞清楚，門鎖著窗簾拉著，
我不知發生了什麼事。
每次夜裡回家，走近這幢空了
大半天的黑屋，我都感到不安，
而鑰匙在鎖孔裡格格嗒嗒的響聲
就好像是在警告什麼人趕快溜走，
趁我們進門時從後門溜走。
要是我的感覺是對的，有人一直——
別拉我的手！」

The Fear

A lantern-light from deeper in the barn
Shone on a man and woman in the door
And threw their lurching shadows on a house
Nearby, all dark in every glossy window.
A horse's hoof pawed once the hollow floor,
And the back of the gig they stood beside
Moved in a little. The man grasped a wheel.
The woman spoke out sharply, "Whoa, stand still! —
I saw it just as plain as a white plate,"
She said, "as the light on the dashboard ran
Along the bushes at the roadside — a man's face.
You must have seen it too."

                                        "I didn't see it.

             Are you sure —   "

                                        "Yes, I'm sure!"

                                        " — it was a face?"

"Joel, I'll have to look. I can't go in,
I can't, and leave a thing like that unsettled.
Doors locked and curtains drawn will make no difference.
I always have felt strange when we came home
To the dark house after so long an absence,
And the key rattled loudly into place
Seemed to warn someone to be getting out
At one door as we entered at another.
What if I'm right, and someone all the time —
Don't hold my arm!"

　　　　　「我說那是有人路過。」
「依你的說法，這好像是條道路囉。
你忘了我們是在哪兒？而且，
誰會在三更半夜這樣的時候，
在這兒走來走去？
他既是過路，爲什麼站在灌木叢中不動？」
「天不算太晚──只是有點黑。
其實事情也許並不像你想的。
他是不是長得像──？」
　　　　　　　　「他像任何人。
我要不弄清楚今晚就絕不睡覺。
把提燈遞給我。」
　　　　　　「你用不著燈。」
她推開他，自己把燈取在手上。

「你不用來，」她說。「這事算我的。
如果是解決它的時候，就讓我來
解決它。叫他永遠也不敢──
聽！他踢響了一塊石子。聽啊，聽！
他正朝我們走來。喬爾，你進屋去。
聽！我聽不見他了。但你進去吧。」
「首先你沒法叫我相信那是──」
「那──或許是他派來偵察的人。
現在該是跟他攤牌的時候了，
只要我們準確地弄清楚他在哪裡。
這次讓他溜掉，那他將在我們周圍
的任何地方從樹叢中朝我們窺望，
直到我夜裡再也不敢跨出房門。

"I say it's someone passing."

"You speak as if this were a traveled road.

You forget where we are. What is beyond

That he'd be going to or coming from

At such an hour of night, and on foot too?

What was he standing still for in the bushes?"

"It's not so very late — it's only dark.

There's more in it than you're inclined to say.

Did he look like — ?"

"He looked like anyone

I'll never rest tonight unless I know.

Give me the lantern."

"You don't want the lantern."

She pushed past him and got it for herself.

"You're not to come," she said. "This is my business.

If the time's come to face it, I'm the one

To put it the right way. He'd never dare —

Listen! He kicked a stone. Hear that, hear that!

He's coming towards us. Joel, go in — please.

Hark! — I don't hear him now. But please go in."

"In the first place you can't make me believe it's — "

"It is — or someone else he's sent to watch.

And now's the time to have it out with him

While we know definitely where he is.

Let him get off and he'll be everywhere

Around us, looking out of trees and bushes

Till I shan't dare to set a foot outdoors.

我受不了。喬爾，你讓我去吧！」
「真荒唐，他幹嘛要在意你？」
「你是說你不能理解他的在意？
哦，我想他還沒有在意夠呢——
喬爾，我不是那意思，我向你保證。
我們都別說氣話。你也不能說。」
「如果真要去看看，也該是我去！
你提著這燈，會讓他占了優勢。
我們站在明處，他有什麼不能做呢？
不過要是他想做的就只是看看，
那他早已看到了一切，然後走了。」
他似乎忘記了他的主力位置，
而是緊跟在她身後穿過草叢。

「你想幹什麼？」她對著黑夜高喊。
她昂然舉手，忘了手中的提燈，
灼熱的燈罩靠著她的裙子。
「這兒沒人，看來是你弄錯了，」他說。
　　　　　　　　　　　　「有人——
你想幹什麼？」她高聲問，接著
她被一聲真正的回答嚇了一跳。
「不幹什麼。」聲音沿著馬路傳來。
她伸手抓住喬爾，以便站穩身子，
因為烤焦的毛線味令她頭昏。
「你深更半夜在這房子周圍幹什麼？」
「不幹什麼。」然後好像沒再回話。

And I can't stand it. Joel, let me go!"

"But it's nonsense to think he'd care enough."

"You mean you couldn't understand his caring.

Oh, but you see he hadn't had enough —

Joel, I won't — I won't — I promise you.

We mustn't say hard things. You mustn't either."

"I'll be the one, if anybody goes!

But you give him the advantage with this light.

What couldn't he do to us standing here!

And if to see was what he wanted, why,

He has seen all there was to see and gone."

He appeared to forget to keep his hold,

But advanced with her as she crossed the grass.

"What do you want?" she cried to all the dark.

She stretched up tall to overlook the light

That hung in both hands, hot against her skirt.

"There's no one; so you're wrong," he said.

"There is. —

What do you want?" she cried, and then herself

Was startled when an answer really came.

"Nothing." It came from well along the road.

She reached a hand to Joel for support:

The smell of scorching woolen made her faint.

"What are you doing round this house at night?"

"Nothing." A pause: there seemed no more to say.

接著那聲音又說：「你們好像被嚇著了。
我現在就走到你們的燈光處來，
讓你們看見。」
「好，過來吧──喬爾，你到後邊去！」
她迎著逼近的腳步聲堅持著沒動，
但她的身體有點微微發抖。
「你看見啦？」那聲音問。

⠀⠀⠀⠀⠀「噢。」她使勁兒張望。
「你沒看見──我牽著一個孩子，
強盜不會帶著家人出來打劫。」
「深更半夜你帶孩子出來幹什麼？」

⠀⠀⠀⠀⠀⠀⠀⠀⠀「出來散步。每個孩子至少都應該
⠀⠀⠀⠀⠀⠀⠀⠀⠀有一次深夜散步的記憶。
⠀⠀⠀⠀⠀⠀⠀⠀⠀對不對，孩子？」
⠀⠀⠀⠀⠀⠀⠀⠀⠀「我認爲你應該設法找個
⠀⠀⠀⠀⠀⠀⠀⠀⠀散步的地方──」

⠀⠀⠀⠀⠀⠀⠀⠀⠀⠀⠀「碰巧我們走上這馬路──
⠀⠀⠀⠀⠀⠀⠀⠀⠀我們在迪恩家做客，要住兩星期。」
⠀⠀⠀⠀⠀⠀⠀⠀⠀「原來是這樣──喬爾──你明白──
⠀⠀⠀⠀⠀⠀⠀⠀⠀你不該胡思亂想。你能原諒嗎？
⠀⠀⠀⠀⠀⠀⠀⠀⠀你知道我們不得不小心謹慎。
⠀⠀⠀⠀⠀⠀⠀⠀⠀這是一個非常，非常荒僻的地方。
⠀⠀⠀⠀⠀⠀⠀⠀⠀喬爾！」她說話時好像不能回頭似的。
⠀⠀⠀⠀⠀⠀⠀⠀⠀搖搖晃晃的提燈墜到了地上，
⠀⠀⠀⠀⠀⠀⠀⠀⠀磕磕撞撞，叮叮噹噹，然後熄滅。

And then the voice again: "You seem afraid.

I saw by the way you whipped up the horse.

I'll just come forward in the lantern-light

And let you see."

"Yes, do. — Joel, go back!"

She stood her ground against the noisy steps

That came on, but her body rocked a little.

"You see," the voice said.

        "Oh." She looked and looked.

"You don't see — I've a child here by the hand.

A robber wouldn't have his family with him."

"What's a child doing at this time of night — ?"

        "Out walking. Every child should have the memory

        Of at least one long-after-bedtime walk.

        What, son?"

        "Then I should think you'd try to find

        Somewhere to walk —"

            "The highway, as it happens —

        We're stopping for the fortnight down at Dean's."

        "But if that's all — Joel — you realize —

        You won't think anything. You understand?

        You understand that we have to be careful.

        This is a very, very lonely place. —

        Joel!" She spoke as if she couldn't turn.

        The swinging lantern lengthened to the ground,

        It touched, it struck, it clattered and went out.

謀求私利的人

「威利斯，今天我本不想見到你，
因爲公司的那位律師今天要來。
我要出賣我的靈魂，準確地說是賣腳。
你知道，這雙腳值五百美元。」
「對你來說這雙腳幾乎就是靈魂，
如果你打算把它們賣給那個魔鬼，
我倒想親眼看見。他什麼時候來？」
「我差點兒還以爲你知道哩，以爲
你來是要幫我做一筆更好的買賣。」
「喔，就算這樣吧！你的腳可不一樣。
那律師並不知道他要買的是什麼：
你沒法再走那些你也許曾經走過的路。
你還沒找到你要找的四十種蘭花。
他懂什麼呢？——這雙聖足怎樣？

醫生肯定你今後還能夠走路嗎？」
「他認爲會有點跛，腿腳都不方便。」
「它們一定很可怕——我是說看上去。」
「我一直不敢看它們解開繃帶的樣子。
透過床上的毯子我會聯想到
一隻攤開身體滿背尖刺的海星。」
「沒傷著你的腦袋，可眞是個奇蹟。」
「很難告訴你我當時是怎樣躲過的。
當我發現輪軸纏住了我的外套，
我沒有死抱著用力掙脫的念頭，

The Self-Seeker

"Willis, I didn't want you here today:
The lawyer's coming for the company.
I'm going to sell my soul, or rather, feet.
Five hundred dollars for the pair, you know."
"With you the feet have nearly been the soul;
And if you're going to sell them to the devil,
I want to see you do it. When's he coming?"
"I half suspect you knew and came on purpose
To try to help me drive a better bargain."
"Well, if it's true! Yours are no common feet.
The lawyer don't know what it is he's buying:
So many miles you might have walked you won't walk.
You haven't run your forty orchids down.

What does he think? — How are the bless?d feet?
The doctor's sure you're going to walk again?"
"He thinks I'll hobble. It's both legs and feet."
"They must be terrible — I mean, to look at."
"I haven't dared to look at them uncovered.
Through the bed blankets I remind myself
Of a starfish laid out with rigid points."
"The wonder is it hadn't been your head."
"It's hard to tell you how I managed it.
When I saw the shaft had me by the coat,
I didn't try too long to pull away,

也沒想去摸出小刀把外套割掉，
我只是緊抱著輪軸和它一起旋轉——
直到韋斯切斷了輪槽的水源。
我想正是這樣我才保住了腦袋，
但我的雙腿卻被天花板撞傷。」
「見鬼？他們幹嘛不扔掉那根皮帶，
而讓它完全滑進了那個輪槽？」
「他們說那根皮帶已有些日子了。
那根條紋舊皮帶不怎麼喜歡我，
因為我讓它在我的連軸上爆出火花，
就像富蘭克林當年玩風箏線那樣。
一定是皮帶，它不正常已有些日子。
那天有個女工就拿它沒辦法，
當時它轉動時帶頭老是壓帶尾，
通過那銀色皮帶輪時總左偏右滑。

假如我沒出事，一切仍如以往。
你仍能聽見小鋸低聲唱歌，大鋸則
向村子周圍的山嶺發出呼喊，
當它們鋸木的時候。那是我們的音樂。
你應該像個好村民那樣喜歡它。
它無疑具有一種興旺繁榮的聲音，
而且它是我們的生機。」
「是呀，如果它不是我們的死亡。」
「聽你說來它好像並非總是生機。
須知我們賴以生者即賴以死者。
我的律師在哪兒？他的火車已到了。
我想早點了事。我覺得又熱又累。」

Or fumble for my knife to cut away,

I just embraced the shaft and rode it out —

Till Weiss shut off the water in the wheel pit.

That's how I think I didn't lose my head.

But my legs got their knocks against the ceiling."

"Awful. Why didn't they throw off the belt

Instead of going clear down in the wheel pit?"

"They say some time was wasted on the belt —

Old streak of leather — doesn't love me much

Because I make him spit fire at my knuckles,

The way Ben Franklin used to make the kite string.

That must be it. Some days he won't stay on.

That day a woman couldn't coax him off.

He's on his rounds now with his tail in his mouth,

Snatched right and left across the silver pulleys.

                    Everything goes the same without me there.

                    You can hear the small buzz saws whine, the big saw

                    Caterwaul to the hills around the village

                    As they both bite the wood. It's all our music.

                    One ought as a good villager to like it.

                    No doubt is has a sort of prosperous sound,

                    And it's our life."

                    "Yes, when it's not our death."

                    "You make that sound as if it wasn't so

                    With everything. What we live by we die by. —

                    I wonder where my lawyer is. His train's in.

                    I want this over with; I'm hot and tired."

「你是在準備去做一件蠢事。」
「去看看他好嗎？威爾？領他進來。
我倒寧願科爾賓太太不知道這事，
我寄宿她家太久，她把我當家裡人。
沒有她，你就夠難應付的了。」
「我打算變得更難應付，
你得告訴我這事已進行到什麼地步，
你答應過任何代價嗎？」
　　　　　　　　　「五百美元。

五百——五——五！一二三四五。
你用不著盯住我看。」
　　　　　　「我不相信你。」

「威利斯，你一進來我就告訴過你。
別對我太苛刻。我不得不接受
我能得到的。你看他們都有腳，
這使他們在那個行當占有優勢。
我無論如何也不會有雙好腳了。」
「可你的花，朋友，你是把花給賣了。」
「是呀，也可以這麼說——所有的花，
這個地區每個地方的每一種花，
為今後的四十年——就說四十年吧。
但我不會賣它們，我會獻出它們，
它們絕不會為我賺回一分錢，
因為若失去了它們金錢也沒法彌補。
不，那五百美元是他們說的數，
用來支付醫療費並幫我渡難關。

"You're getting ready to do something foolish."

"Watch for him, will you, Will? You let him in.

I'd rather Mrs. Corbin didn't know;

I've boarded here so long, she thinks she owns me.

You're bad enough to manage, without her."

"I'm going to be worse instead of better.

You're got to tell me how far this is gone:

Have you agreed to any price?"

   "Five hundred.

Five hundred — five — five! One, two, three, four, five.

You needn't look at me."

   "I don't believe you."

       "I told you, Willis, when you first came in.

       Don't you be hard on me. I have to take

       What I can get. You see they have the feet,

       Which gives them the advantage in the trade.

       I can't get back the feet in any case."

       "But your flowers, man, you're selling out your flowers."

       "Yes, that's one way to put it — all the flowers

       Of every kind everywhere in this region

       For the next forty summers — call it forty.

       But I'm not selling those, I'm giving them;

       They never earned me so much as one cent:

       Money can't pay me for the loss of them.

       No, the five hundred was the sum they named

       To pay the doctor's bill and tide me over.

不然就打官司，而我不想打官司——
我只想安安穩穩地過我的日子，
就像將要過的日子，嚐嚐它的艱辛，
或者甜蜜——那也許不會太糟。
公司還答應給我我想釘的套板。」
「你那個關於山谷的花卉譜呢？」
「你問倒我了。但是你——你不會
認為它對我也值錢吧？我得承認，
要是不完成它，我就無法用它去
結交朋友。那可不大好。
順便告訴你，我收到伯勒斯的來信，
關於我的女王蘭；
他說在這麼靠北的地區還沒有記載。

聽！門鈴響了。是他。你下去
接他上來，但別讓科爾賓太太——
哦，我們將很快了結這事。我累了。」
威利斯帶上來那位波士頓律師，
還帶上來一位赤腳的小姑娘，
木板房裡響起一陣沉重的腳步聲
和那位律師傲氣十足的男中音，
小姑娘一時未被注意，她背著雙手
羞澀地站在一旁。

　　「啊，怎麼樣，這位先生——」
律師已經打開了他的皮包，
好像要找出文件，看看上面
他沒記住的那個名字。「你得原諒我，
我順便去工廠耽擱了一會兒。」

It's that or fight, and I don't want to fight —

I just want to get settled in my life,

Such as it's going to be, and know the worst,

Or best — it may not be so bad. The firm

Promise me all the shooks I want to nail."

"But what about your flora of the valley?"

"You have me there. But that — you didn't think

That was worth money to me? Still I own

It goes against me not to finish it

For the friends it might bring me. By the way,

I had a letter from Burroughs — did I tell you? —

About my Cypripedium regin?;

He say it's not reported so far north. —

                There! there's the bell. He's rung. But you go down

                And bring him up, and don't let Mrs. Corbin. —

                Oh, well, we'll soon be through with it. I'm tired."

                Willis brought up besides the Boston lawyer

                A little barefoot girl, who in the noise

                Of heavy footsteps in the old frame house,

                And baritone importance of the lawyer,

                Stood for a while unnoticed, with her hands

                Shyly behind her.

                                "Well, and how is Mister . . . ?"

                The lawyer was already in his satchel

                As if for papers that might bear the name

                He hadn't at command. "You must excuse me,

「我想是去到處看看。」威利斯說。

　　　　　「是呀，

　　　　　　喔，是的。」

「打聽到什麼可能有用的情況嗎？」

那受傷者看見了小姑娘，「嗨，安妮。

你要什麼，親愛的？過來，到床邊來。

告訴我那是什麼？」安妮只是用背著

的雙手晃了晃裙子。「猜猜。」她說。

「哦，猜哪隻手？哎喲！從前

我知道個訣竅，只消朝耳朵裡

一看就能猜中，但我現在忘了。

嗯，讓我想想。我想該猜右手，

就猜右手吧，哪怕是猜錯。

　　　　　　　　　　拿出來呀！別換手──一株羊角蘭！

　　　　　　　　　　羊角蘭！我真想知道，要是我猜

　　　　　　　　　　左手會得到什麼。伸出左手來呀。

　　　　　　　　　　又一株羊角蘭！你在哪兒找到的？

　　　　　　　　　　在哪棵山毛櫸下？在哪個水獺窩上？」

　　　　　　　　　　安妮瞥了一眼身旁的大個子律師，

　　　　　　　　　　覺得她不應該冒險回答這問題。

　　　　　　　　　　「那邊就這兩株？」

　　　　　　　　　　　　　　　　　　「那邊有四五株。

　　　　　　　　　　我知道你不會讓我把它們都採來。」

　　　　　　　　　　「我不會──不會。你真是個好姑娘！

　　　　　　　　　　你們看安妮已記住了她學的課程。」

I dropped in at the mill and was detained."

"Looking round, I suppose," said Willis.

"Yes,

Well, yes."

"Hear anything that might prove useful?"

The Broken One saw Anne. "Why, here is Anne.

What do you want, dear? Come, stand by the bed;

Tell me what is it?"

Anne just wagged her dress,

With both hands held behind her. "Guess," she said.

"Oh, guess which hand? My, my! Once on a time

I knew a lovely way to tell for certain

By looking in the ears. But I forget it.

Er, let me see. I think I'll take the right.

That's sure to be right, even if it's wrong.

Come, hold it out. Don't change. — A Ram's Horn orchid!

A Ram's Horn! What would I have got, I wonder,

If I had chosen left. Hold out the left.

Another Ram's Horn! Where did you find those,

Under what beech tree, on what woodchuck's knoll?"

Anne looked at the large lawyer at her side,

And thought she wouldn't venture on so much.

"Were there no others?"

"There were four or five.

I knew you wouldn't let me pick them all."

"I wouldn't — so I wouldn't. You're the girl!

You see Anne has her lesson learned by heart."

「我希望明年那邊還會有羊角蘭。」
「你當然希望。你留下了其餘的種籽，
也爲水獺留下了籽殼。眞是好姑娘！
水獺特別喜歡羊角蘭籽的莢殼，
對一隻胃口挑剔的水獺來説，
那可比農場上的豆莢還好吃。
不過羊角蘭很少被大量發現——
所以你花錢也難買到。可是，安妮，
我感到不安；你對我説出了一切嗎？
你還有所隱瞞，那可和撒謊一樣。
不信你問這位律師先生，當著
律師的面發現你説謊不太好。
對我，你應該毫不隱瞞，安妮。
你該不是要告訴我在你發現羊角蘭
的地方，竟然沒發現一株黃杓蘭？

我是怎麼教你的？我該替你臉紅。
你不想解釋？如果那兒有黃杓蘭，
現在它在什麼地方？」
「這個——黃杓蘭太普通了。」
「普通？那麼紫杓蘭更普通囉？」
「我沒給你帶紫杓蘭來。我想——
對你來説——它們都沒什麼了不起。」
律師一邊翻文件一邊笑出聲，
彷彿是因爲安妮話中的責備意味。
「我已經使安妮改掉了採花束的習慣，
這對孩子不公平，但也沒有辦法，

"I wanted there should be some there next year."

"Of course you did. You left the rest for seed,

And for the backwoods woodchuck. You're the girl!

A Ram's Horn orchid seedpod for a woodchuck

Sounds something like. Better than farmer's beans

To a discriminating appetite,

Though the Ram's Horn is seldom to be had

In bushel lots — doesn't come on the market.

But, Anne, I'm troubled; have you told me all?

You're hiding something. That's as bad as lying.

You ask this lawyer man. And it's not safe

With a lawyer at hand to find you out.

Nothing is hidden from some people, Anne.

You don't tell me that where you found a Ram's Horn

You didn't find a Yellow Lady's Slipper.

What did I tell you? What? I'd blush, I would.

Don't you defend yourself. If it was there,

Where is it now, the Yellow Lady's Slipper?"

"Well, wait — it's common — it's too common."

"Common?

The Purple Lady's Slipper's commoner."

"I didn't bring a Purple Lady's Slipper.

To you — to you I mean — they're both too common."

The lawyer gave a laugh among his papers

As if with some idea that she had scored.

"I've broken Anne of gathering bouquets.

It's not fair to the child. It can't be helped, though:

因爲幹一行就得有幹一行的樣子。
我會設法補償她的——她會看到。
她將替我到野外去搜尋蘭花，
在一道道石牆和一根根木頭上；
她將替我去河邊找水生花卉，
有種漂心蓮，小葉片就像一顆心，
而且在水面下的彎節處有隻拳頭，
四根指頭握緊，一根指頭翹起
並伸出水面在陽光下開出小花，
彷彿在說：『你喲！你是心之欲望。』
安妮善於弄花，以此來彌補
她所失去的：她愛一條腿跪下，
用雙手輕輕把花湊到她面前，
呼喚它們的名字，然後留它們在原處。」

那位律師有一只奇特的懷錶，
錶殼設計精妙，他只要把錶殼一關，
錶殼發出一種類似槍響的聲音。
此刻他就把錶一關。
「好啦，安妮，去吧，我們等會兒再聊。
這位律師先生在擔心他的火車。
他走之前想給我很多很多的錢，
因爲我把自己給弄傷了。
我不知道這事會用他多少時間。
你先把花放在水裡。威爾，幫幫她；
那水罐太滿。這兒沒有杯子嗎？
就把它們放在水罐裡吧。
現在開始——請拿出你的文件！
你看我不得不堅持自己的喜愛，

Pressed into service means pressed out of shape.

Somehow I'll make it right with her — she'll see.

She's going to do my scouting in the field,

Over stone walls and all along a wood

And by a river bank for water flowers,

The floating Heart, with small leaf like a heart,

And at the sinus under water a fist

Of little fingers all kept down but one,

And that thrust up to blossom in the sun

As if to say, 'You! You're the Heart's desire.'

Anne has a way with flowers to take the place

Of what she's lost: she goes down on one knee

And lifts their faces by the chin to hers

And says their names, and leaves them where they are."

      The lawyer wore a watch the case of which

      Was cunningly devised to make a noise

      Like a small pistol when he snapped it shut

      At such a time as this. He snapped it now.

      "Well, Anne, go, dearie. Our affair will wait.

      The lawyer man is thinking of his train.

      He wants to give me lots and lots of money

      Before he goes, because I hurt myself,

      And it may take him I don't know how long.

      But put our flowers in water first. — Will, help her:

      The pitcher's too full for her. — There's no cup?

      Just hook them on the inside of the pitcher.

      Now run. — Get out your documents! You see

      I have to keep on the good side of Anne.

我是個會考慮自身利益的大孩子。
而就我的處境，你不能責備我。
除了我自己，誰還會關心
我的需要呢？」
　　　　　　　「一段美妙的插曲，」
律師説，「眞對不起，我的火車——
有幸的是條款内容大家都同意。
你只要簽上大名。這裡——這裡。」
「你，威爾，別扮鬼臉。到這邊来，
在這兒你就不能再扮鬼臉。
你要麼規矩點，要麼就出去陪安妮。」
「你沒打算不讀一下文件就簽字吧？」
「那你就別發呆，唸給我聽聽。
難道這不是我以前看過的東西？」

「你會發現是的，讓你朋友看看吧。」
「嗯，那太費時間，而我和你
一樣也巴不得這事早點辦完。
但讀吧，讀吧。不錯，到此爲止，
因爲我幾乎不知是什麼在使我不安。
你想説什麼，威爾？別幹蠢事，
你，把人家的法律文件揉成了一團。
你眞有什麼異議，不妨直説。」
「五百美元！」
　　　　　　　「那你説該是多少？」
「一千美元也不嫌多；
你清楚這點，律師先生。在他
確知自己還能不能再走路之前，

I'm a great boy to think of number one.

And you can't blame me in the place I'm in.

Who will take care of my necessities

Unless I do?"

                     "A pretty interlude,"

The lawyer said. "I'm sorry, but my train —

Luckily terms are all agreed upon.

You only have to sign your name. Right — there."

"You, Will, stop making faces. Come round here

Where you can't make them. What is it you want?

I'll put you out with Anne. Be good or go."

"You don't mean you will sign that thing unread?"

"Make yourself useful, then, and read it for me. —

Isn't it something I have seen before?"

                     "You'll find it is. Let your friend look at it."

                     "Yes, but all that takes time, and I'm as much

                     In haste to get it over with as you. —

                     But read it, read it. — That's right, draw the curtain:

                     Half the time I don't know what's troubling me. —

                     What do you say, Will? Don't you be a fool,

                     You, crumpling folks's legal documents.

                     Out with it if you've any real objection."

"Five hundred dollars!"

                         "What would you think right?"

"A thousand wouldn't be a cent too much;

You know it, Mr. Lawyer. The sin is

Accepting anything before he knows

要他接受任何協議都是罪過。
我覺得這是一種不光彩的欺詐。」
「我認爲——我認爲——據我今天
親自所見所聞——他歷來都不謹愼。」
「你聽到什麼,舉個例吧?」威利斯說。
「喏,事故發生的現場——」
那受傷者在床上扭了扭身體。
「這看來好像是你們之間的事,
我倒想知道我究竟算什麼角色?
你們面面相對就像一對公雞,
要鬥到外邊去鬥,別碰著我。
等你們鬥完回來我會簽好字。

鉛筆行嗎?請把你的鋼筆給我。
請你們中的一位把我的頭扶起來。」
威利斯從床邊走開。「我不鬥了——
我不是對手——也不想假裝是——」
律師莊重地擰緊鋼筆筆帽。
「你這是明智之舉,你不會後悔的。
我們都替你難過。」

　　　　　　威利斯譏諷道:
「我們是誰——波士頓那群股東?
見鬼!我得出去,再也不進來了。」
「威利斯,進來時把安妮帶回來。
哦,多謝關照。別介意威爾的粗魯。
他認爲你還應該賠償我那些花。
你弄不懂我說那些花是什麼意思。
但別停下來弄懂。你會耽誤火車的。
再見。」他說著揮了揮雙臂。

Whether he's ever going to walk again.

It smells to me like a dishonest trick."

"I think — I think — from what I heard today —

And saw myself — he would be ill-advised —"

"What did you hear, for instance?" Willis said.

"Now, the place where the accident occurred — "

The Broken One was twisted in his bed.

"This is between you two apparently.

Where I come in is what I want to know.

You stand up to it like a pair of cocks.

Go outdoors if you want to fight. Spare me.

When you come back, I'll have the papers signed.

Will pencil do? Then, please, your fountain pen.

One of you hold my head up from the pillow."

Willis flung off the bed. "I wash my hands —

I'm no match — no, and don't pretend to be —"

The lawyer gravely capped his fountain pen.

"You're doing the wise thing: you won't regret it.

We're very sorry for you."

Willis sneered:

"Who's we? — some stockholders in Boston?

I'll go outdoors, by gad, and won't come back."

"Willis, bring Anne back with you when you come.

Yes. Thanks for caring. — Don't mind Will: he's savage.

He thinks you ought to pay me for my flowers.

You don't know what I mean about the flowers.

Don't stop to try to now. You'll miss your train.

Good-by." He flung his arms around his face.

一堆木柴

一個陰天，我在冰凍的沼澤地散步，
我停下腳步說：「我將從這兒折返。
不，我還在往前走——咱們得看看。」
除了在有人不時走過的地方，凍雪
使我行走困難。身前身後能見到的
都是一排排整齊的又細又高的樹，
景色都那麼相似，以致我認不出
也叫不出地名，沒法據此斷定
我在此處或彼處，我只知離家已遠。
一隻小鳥在我前面飛過。當牠停下時，
小心地讓一棵樹隔在我倆之間，

並且一聲不響，不告訴我牠是誰，
而我卻傻乎乎地去想牠在想什麼。
牠以為我在追牠，為了一片羽毛——
牠尾巴上白色的那片；就像一個
會把每一片羽毛都據為己有的人。
其實牠只要飛出來就會明白真相。
接著出現了一堆木柴，我因此而
忘記了那隻小鳥，讓牠那點恐懼
把牠帶離了我本可以再走的路，
甚至沒想到要給牠說一聲晚安。
牠飛到柴堆後面，最後一次停下。

The Wood-Pile

Out walking in the frozen swamp one gray day,
I paused and said, "I will turn back from here.
No, I will go on farther — and we shall see."
The hard snow held me, save where now and then
One foot went through. The view was all in lines
Straight up and down of tall slim trees
Too much alike to mark or name a place by
So as to say for certain I was here
Or somewhere else: I was just far from home.
A small bird flew before me. He was careful
To put a tree between us when he lighted,

And say no word to tell me who he was
Who was so foolish as to think what he thought.
He thought that I was after him for a feather —
The white one in his tail; like one who takes
Everything said as personal to himself.
One flight out sideways would have undeceived him.
And then there was a pile of wood for which
I forgot him and let his little fear
Carry him off the way I might have gone,
Without so much as wishing him good-night.
He went behind it to make his last stand.

那是一考得槭木，砍好，劈好，
並堆好──標準的四乘四乘八。
我不可能見到另一個這樣的柴堆。
柴堆周圍的雪地上沒有任何足跡。
它肯定不是今年才砍劈的木柴，
甚至不是去年砍劈或前年砍劈的。
木色已經發灰，樹皮已開始剝落，
整個柴堆也有點下陷。克萊曼蒂斯
曾用細繩把它捆得像一個包裹。

柴堆一端的支撐是一棵還在生長
的樹，另一端是由斜樁撐著的豎樁，
這兩根木樁已快被壓倒。我心想
只有那種老愛轉去做新鮮事的人
才會忘記他自己的工作成果，忘記
他曾為之消耗過的斧頭、勞力和自身，
才會把柴堆留在遠離火爐的地方，
任其用緩慢的無煙燃燒──
在冰冷的沼澤腐朽。

It was a cord of maple, cut and split

And piled — and measured, four by four by eight.

And not another like it could I see.

No runner tracks in this year's snow looped near it.

And it was older sure than this year's cutting,

Or even last year's or the year's before.

The wood was gray and the bark warping off it

And the pile somewhat sunken. Clematis

Had wound strings round and round it like a bundle.

What held it, though, on one side was a tree

Still growing, and on one a stake and prop,

These latter about to fall. I thought that only

Someone who lived in turning to fresh tasks

Could so forget his handiwork on which

He spent himself, the labor of his ax,

And leave it there far from a useful fireplace

To warm the frozen swamp as best it could

With the slow smokeless burning of decay.

美好時光

我獨自漫步在冬日黃昏──
身邊沒有作伴交談的友人，
但我有那排小小的木屋
和它們在雪地裡閃亮的窗戶。

我想我擁有小屋中的鄰居；
我聽見小提琴的琴聲響起；
我透過窗簾的花邊看見
年輕的身影和年輕的容顏。

我有關係如此親密的朋友，
直到不見村舍我還在漫遊。
我轉身並後悔，但往回走時，
我看見所有窗戶都黑漆漆的。

我在雪地上嘎嚓作響的腳步
驚擾了已入睡的鄉村馬路，
請你們原諒我褻瀆安寧，
在一個冬夜，在十點時分。

Good Hours

I had for my winter evening walk —
No one at all with whom to talk,
But I had the cottages in a row
Up to their shining eyes in show.

And I thought I had the folk within:
I had the sound of a violin;
I had a glimpse through curtain laces
Of youthful forms and youthful faces.

I had such company outward bound.
I went till there were no cottages found.
I turned and repented, but coming back
I saw no window but that was black.

Over the snow my creaking feet
Disturbed the slumbering village street
Like profanation, by your leave,
At ten o'clock of a winter eve.

山間低地

MOUNTAIN INTERVAL

未走之路

金色的樹林中有兩條岔路
可惜我不能沿著兩條路行走；
我久久地站在那分岔的地方，
極目眺望其中一條路的盡頭，
直到它轉彎，消失在樹林深處。

然後我毅然踏上了另一條路，
這條路也許更值得我嚮往，
因為它荒草叢生，人跡罕至；
不過說到其冷清與荒涼，
兩條路幾乎是一模一樣。

那天早晨兩條路都鋪滿落葉，
落葉上都沒有被踩踏的痕跡。
唉，我把第一條路留給未來！
但我知道人世間阡陌縱橫，
我不知未來能否再回到那裡。

我將會一邊嘆息一邊敘說，
在某個地方，在很久很久以後：
曾有兩條小路在樹林中分手，
我選了一條人跡稀少的行走，
結果後來的一切都截然不同。

The Road Not Taken

Two roads diverged in a yellow wood,
And sorry I could not travel both
And be one traveler, long I stood
And looked down one as far as I could
To where it bent in the undergrowth;

Then took the other, as just as fair,
And having perhaps the better claim,
Because it was grassy and wanted wear;
Though as for that, the passing there
Had worn them really about the same,

And both that morning equally lay
In leaves no step had trodden black.
Oh, I kept the first for another day!
Yet knowing how way leads on to way,
I doubted if I should ever come back.

I shall be telling this with a sigh
Somewhere ages and ages hence:
Two roads diverged in a wood, and I —
I took the one less traveled by,
And that has made all the difference.

聖誕樹
——一封寄給親友的聖誕賀函

城裡人都已經回城裡去了，
終於把鄉村留給了鄉下人；
當飛舞的雪花還沒堆積的時候，
當紛紛落葉還沒被覆蓋的時候，
一個陌生人驅車來到我家庭院，
他像是城裡人，但懂鄉下規矩，
他坐在車裡等，直到引我們出去
一邊扣外套鈕扣一邊問他是誰。
他果然是城裡人，現在回來
尋找一種城裡人留在鄉下的東西，
一種過聖誕節非用不可的東西。
他問我願不願賣些聖誕樹給他，

因為我的樹林，那些小小的冷杉
活像一座座聳著尖塔的教堂。
我還從沒想過它們就是聖誕樹。
我說不清當時是否受到過誘惑，
是否想把小樹賣掉，裝上汽車，
而讓屋後留下一片光禿禿的坡地，
此時那兒的陽光和月光一樣清冷。
我若動過此念也不願讓它們知道。
但除非和別人一樣留著樹不賣，
我更不願老留著我那些冷杉
直到過了有利可圖的銷售時間——
因任何東西都得經過市場的檢驗。

Christmas Trees

A Christmas Circular Letter

The city had withdrawn into itself

And left at last the country to the country;

When between whirls of snow not come to lie

And whirls of foliage not yet laid, there drove

A stranger to our yard, who looked the city,

Yet did in country fashion in that there

He sat and waited till he drew us out,

A-buttoning coats, to ask him who he was.

He proved to be the city come again

To look for something it had left behind

And could not do without and keep its Christmas.

He asked if I would sell my Christmas trees;

My woods — the young fir balsams like a place

Where houses all are churches and have spires.

I hadn't thought of them as Christmas trees.

I doubt if I was tempted for a moment

To sell them off their feet to go in cars

And leave the slope behind the house all bare,

Where the sun shines now no warmer than the moon.

I'd hate to have them know it if I was.

Yet more I'd hate to hold my trees, except

As others hold theirs or refuse for them,

Beyond the time of profitable growth —

The trial by market everything must come to.

我輕率地想著出售這個念頭，
然後不知是出於不合時宜的禮貌
還是擔心顯得笨口拙舌，或是
因為希望自己的東西被人誇獎，
我說：「它們不夠多，不值得費事。」
「我很快就能說出可以砍多少，
你領我去看看吧。」

　　　　　　　「你可以看看，
但別指望我會把它們賣給你。」
小樹長在牧場內，有些長得太密，
以致它們互相修剪了對方的樹枝，
但長得稀疏、樹葉勻稱的也不少。

　　　　　　　　　　他對長得勻稱的樹點頭稱道，
　　　　　　　　　　或是停在某棵更可愛的樹下
　　　　　　　　　　用買主節制的口吻說：「這還可以。」
　　　　　　　　　　我想也可以，但不想當著他的面說。
　　　　　　　　　　我們爬上南坡的牧場，橫穿而過，
　　　　　　　　　　然後下到北坡的牧場。

　　　　　　　　　　　　　　「一千棵，」他說。
　　　　　　　　　　「一千棵聖誕樹！——每棵多少？」
　　　　　　　　　　他覺得有必要對我公道一點：
　　　　　　　　　　「一千棵樹可以給你三十美元。」
　　　　　　　　　　於是我確信我絕沒有過要把樹
　　　　　　　　　　賣給他的意思。千萬別顯詫異！
　　　　　　　　　　但與我要砍光的一大片牧場相比，

I dallied so much with the thought of selling.

Then whether from mistaken courtesy

And fear of seeming short of speech, or whether

From hope of hearing good of what was mine,

I said, "There aren't enough to be worth while."

"I could soon tell how many they would cut,

You let me look them over."

    "You could look.

But don't expect I'm going to let you have them."

Pasture they spring in some in, clumps too close

That lop each other of boughs, but not a few

Quite solitary and having equal boughs

      All round and round. The latter he nodded "Yes" to,

      Or paused to say beneath some lovelier one,

      With a buyer's moderation, "That would do."

      I thought so too, but wasn't there to say so.

      We climbed the pasture on the south, crossed over,

      And came down on the north.

          He said, "A thousand."

      "A thousand Christmas trees! — at what apiece?"

      He felt some need of softening that to me:

      "A thousand trees would come to thirty dollars."

      Then I was certain I had never meant

      To let him have them. Never show surprise!

      But thirty dollars seemed so small beside

三十美元顯得太微不足道；三美分
（因爲算下來每棵樹只值三美分）
與城裡朋友要掏的錢相比太不起眼，
因爲我馬上就要寫信去的那些朋友
買這麼好一棵聖誕樹得花好多錢，
這種樹可以擺在主日學校的教室裡，
足以掛夠供孩子們摘取的禮物。
我以前並不知道我有一千棵聖誕樹！
正如稍稍一算便可明白的那樣，
賣三美分一棵還不如留下送人。
只可惜我不能把聖誕樹裝進信封。
我眞希望我能給你們寄來一棵，
同此信一道祝你們聖誕快樂。

The extent of pasture I should strip, three cents

(For that was all they figured out apiece) —

Three cents so small beside the dollar friends

I should be writing to within the hour

Would pay in cities for good trees like those,

Regular vestry-trees whole Sunday Schools

Could hang enough on to pick off enough.

A thousand Christmas trees I didn't know I had!

Worth three cents more to give away than sell,

As may be shown by a simple calculation.

Too bad I couldn't lay one in a letter.

I can't help wishing I could send you one

In wishing you herewith a Merry Christmas.

一個老人的冬夜

透過凝在空屋窗格上的薄霜，
透過一片片幾乎呈星形的凝霜，
屋外的一切都陰險地朝他窺視。
阻止他的目光朝外看的
是他手中那盞朝眼睛傾斜的燈。
他記不得是什麼把他引進那個空房，
而阻止他記憶的是他的年齡。
他站在一些木桶間——茫然困惑。

他的腳步聲剛驚嚇過腳下的地窖，
當他咯蹬咯蹬出來時又把它嚇了
一跳——而且還驚嚇了屋外的夜，
夜有它的聲音，很熟悉，很平常，
像林濤呼嘯樹枝斷裂的聲音，
但最像是猛敲一個木箱的聲音。
他是盞只能照亮他自己的燈，那個
此時已坐下、與他所知有關的自己，
一盞靜靜的燈，然後連燈也不是。

An Old Man's Winter Night

All out-of-doors looked darkly in at him

Through the thin frost, almost in separate stars,

That gathers on the pane in empty rooms.

What kept his eyes from giving back the gaze

Was the lamp tilted near them in his hand.

What kept him from remembering what it was

That brought him to that creaking room was age.

He stood with barrels round him — at a loss.

And having scared the cellar under him

In clomping here, he scared it once again

In clomping off — and scared the outer night,

Which has its sounds, familiar, like the roar

Of trees and crack of branches, common things,

But nothing so like beating on a box.

A light he was to no one but himself

Where now he sat, concerned with he knew what,

A quiet light, and then not even that.

他把屋頂的積雪和牆頭的冰柱
託付給月亮保管,雖然那是一輪
升起得太晚而且殘缺不全的月亮,
但說到保管積雪和冰柱,它
無論如何也比太陽更能勝任。
然後他睡了。火爐裡的木柴挪動
一下位置,驚得他也動了一動,
緩和了他沉重的呼吸,但他仍沉睡。
一個年邁的男人不能照料一棟房子、
一座農場、一片鄉村,即使他能,
也不過像他在一個冬夜裡所做的那樣。

He consigned to the moon — such as she was,

So late-arising — to the broken moon,

As better than the sun in any case

For such a charge, his snow upon the roof,

His icicles along the wall to keep;

And slept. The log that shifted with a jolt

Once in the stove, disturbed him and he shifted,

And eased his heavy breathing, but still slept.

One aged man — one man — can't keep a house,

A farm, a countryside, or if he can,

It's thus he does it of a winter night.

暴露的鳥窩

過去你總是能發現新的遊戲。
所以那次我看見你趴在地上
在新割下的牧草堆裡忙著時，
我還以為你是要把草重新豎起，
於是我過去，若你真想那樣做，
我會教你怎樣讓草迎風豎立；
要是你求我，我甚至會幫你
假裝讓草重新生根重新生長。
可那天你並非在玩什麼遊戲，
你真正關心的也不是那些草，
儘管我發現你手裡盡是乾枯的
蕨草、六月禾和變黑的紅花苜蓿。

地上是一個擠滿小鳥的鳥窩，
割草機剛剛從那裡咀嚼而過
（它沒嚐嚐肉味真是個奇蹟）
把無助的小鳥留給了灼熱和陽光。
你想使牠們馬上恢復正常，想把
什麼東西隔在牠們的視線和
這個世界之間——辦法總會有的。
我們每次移動那窩小鳥，牠們
都站起身來彷彿把我們當做媽媽，
當做那個遲遲不回家的媽媽。
我不禁想，那鳥媽媽會回來嗎？

The Exposed Nest

You were forever finding some new play.

So when I saw you down on hands and knees

In the meadow, busy with the new-cut hay,

Trying, I thought, to set it up on end.

I went to show you how to make it stay,

If that was your idea, against the breeze,

And, if you asked me, even help pretend

To make it root again and grow afresh.

But 'twas no make-believe with you today,

Nor was the grass itself your real concern,

Though I found your hand full of wilted fern,

Steel-bright June-grass, and blackening heads of clover.

'Twas a nest full of young birds on the ground

The cutter bar had just gone champing over

(Miraculously without tasting flesh)

And left defenseless to the heat and light.

You wanted to restore them to their right

Of something interposed between their sight

And too much world at once — could means be found.

The way the nest-full every time we stirred

Stood up to us as to a mother-bird

Whose coming home has been too long deferred,

Made me ask would the mother-bird return

遭此變故之後牠還會關心牠們嗎？
我們管閒事會不會使牠更害怕？
不過，我們無法等到答案。
我們看到了行善要擔的風險，
但儘管做這件善事也許會有害，
我們卻不敢不盡力去做；於是
建起了屏障，還給了小鳥陰涼。
我們想知道結果。那為何後來
不再提起？是因為我們忙其他事情。
我記不得——你記得嗎？——
我們在任何時候回去過那地方，
看小鳥是否活過了那天晚上，
看牠們是否學會了用翅膀。

And care for them in such a change of scene,

And might our meddling make her more afraid.

That was a thing we could not wait to learn.

We saw the risk we took in doing good,

But dared not spare to do the best we could

Though harm should come of it: so built the screen

You had begun, and gave them back their shade,

All this to prove we cared. Why is there then

No more to tell? We turned to other things.

I haven't any memory — have you? —

Of ever coming to the place again

To see if the birds lived the first night through,

And so at last to learn to use their wings.

一堆殘雪

一個角落裡有一堆殘雪，
　我居然一直猜想
那是被風刮走的一張報紙
　被雨沖在那兒休息。

雪堆上有點點污跡，像是
　報上小小的鉛字，
像我已忘記的某天的新聞——
　如果我讀過它的話。

A Patch of Old Snow

There's a patch of old snow in a corner,

That I should have guessed

Was a blow-away paper the rain

Had brought to rest.

It is speckled with grime as if

Small print overspread it,

The news of a day I've forgotten —

If I ever read it.

在最後階段

她站在廚房裡靠在水槽邊，透過
水槽上方一扇積滿灰塵的窗戶
看窗外因水槽的污水而長高的雜草。
她身上穿著披肩，手裡拿著帽子。
她身後那間廚房裡亂七八糟，
一些椅子被翻過來疊在別的椅子上，
就像是什麼人坐在那裡，
一些其他房間——客廳、飯廳、
臥室——的東西也被胡亂堆進廚房。
不時有一張被弄得烏鼻包眼的臉
從她身後的一道門探進來衝著她的
背影說話。她回應時總是頭也不回。

「這個桃木衣櫃該放哪兒，女主人？」
「放在哪裡還不都一樣，」
她笑著說，「哪裡能放下就放在
哪裡，然後走吧。天都快黑了，
你們要回城裡必須馬上動身。」
另一張灰頭土臉笑嘻嘻地探進來，
見她沒有回頭，便溫和地問道：
「你在看窗外什麼東西呀，女主人？」
「以前我從沒這樣被人叫做女主人。
我真想知道，被人這樣無數次的
稱做女主人，會不會使我成為
真正的女主人。」

In The Home Stretch

She stood against the kitchen sink, and looked

Over the sink out through a dusty window

At weeds the water from the sink made tall.

She wore her cape; her hat was in her hand.

Behind her was confusion in the room,

Of chairs turned upside down to sit like people

In other chairs, and something, come to look.

For every room a house has — parlor, bedroom,

And dining room — thrown pell-mell in the kitchen.

And now and then a smudged, infernal face

Looked in a door behind her and addressed

Her back. She always answered without turning.

"Where will I put this walnut bureau, lady?"

"Put it on top of something that's on top

Of something else," she laughed.   "Oh, put it where

You can tonight, and go. It's almost dark;

You must be getting started back to town."

Another blackened face thrust in and looked

And smiled, and when she did not turn, spoke gently,

"What are you seeing out the window, lady?"

"Never was I beladied so before.

Would evidence of having been called lady

More than so many times make me a lady

In common law, I wonder."

「我問的是：

你在看窗外什麼東西呀，女主人？」

「看我今後將常常看到的東西，

在今後的歲月，我會無數次地站在

這兒用毛巾洗擦一個又一個的盤子。」

「可那是什麼呢？你問東答西。」

「是荒草，喬，是比某些女人更喜歡

洗碗槽那樣喜歡洗碗水的荒草；

與你的牧場相連的一小塊荒草地，

不過望不了多遠視線就被樹林遮擋。

幾乎不足以被叫做風景。」

「你喜歡這個風景，親愛的？」

「這就是你急於想知道的！你希望

我喜歡。樓上有大家碰撞出的聲響，

對這樣一座木造結構的小房子，

那些大塊頭男人的每一步都使它

搖搖欲墜。等他們走後，親愛的，

你我上樓下樓穿堂過室都必須

放輕腳步；除非陣風使我們脫手，

誰也不許砰砰地使勁兒關門。」

「我認為你所看見的，比你喜歡

承認的那窗外的東西多得多。」

「不，除了我告訴你的那些東西，

我也看見歲月。它們來來去去，

隨著荒草、田野和樹林的變化。」

「什麼樣的歲月？」

"But I ask,

What are you seeing out the window, lady?"

"What I'll be seeing more of in the years

To come as here I stand and go the round

Of many plates with towels many times."

"And what is that? You only put me off."

"Rank weeds that love the water from the dishpan

More than some women like the dishpan, Joe;

A little stretch of mowing field for you;

Not much of that until I come to woods

That end all. And it's scarce enough to call

A view."

"And yet you think you like it, dear?"

"That's what you're so concerned to know! You hope

I like it. — Bang goes something big away

Off there upstairs. The very tread of men

As great as those is shattering to the frame

Of such a little house. Once left alone,

You and I, dear, will go with softer steps

Up and down stairs and through the rooms, and none

But sudden winds that snatch them from our hands

Will ever slam the doors."

"I think you see

More than you like to own to out that window."

"No; for besides the things I tell you of,

I only see the years. They come and go

In alternation with the weeds, the field,

The wood."

「以後的歲月呀——
不同於以前的歲月。」

　　　　「我也看見了。
你沒有清點過它們？」

　　　　「沒有，過去的歲月
已經攪成一團，所以我不想清點。
而且那些歲月絕不應該是我們想去
知道的數字，因爲我們已不再年輕。
那邊又有什麼砰砰的撞擊聲，
聽上去像是那些男人下樓來了。
彷彿每聲撞擊都意味著又有一個人
要回到我們熟悉、但爲鄉下的黑暗
而要放棄的燈火通明的城市街道。」

「來，離開那扇你已經看夠的窗戶，
到這邊來看看更能使人輕鬆的場景。
他們要走了。你看那個大塊頭
正翻過車輪坐上那個高聳的座位，
這會兒他在點煙斗，當他吸煙時，
他會瞇著眼睛，看他鼻尖下的火光。」
「你看煙斗映亮了他的鼻子，這
說明天已多黑。你能根據那火光
說出幾點了嗎？要麼就根據月亮！
那新月映出的是誰的肩頭？
新月像一截銀線，新得就像我們
對於這裡的一切。月光會很快隱去，

"What kind of years?"

        "Why, latter years —

Different from early years."

           "I see them, too.

You didn't count them?"

             "No, the further off

So ran together that I didn't try to.

It can scarce be that they would be in number

We'd care to know, for we are not young now. —

And bang goes something else away off there.

It sounds as if it were the men went down,

And every crash meant one less to return

To lighted city streets we, too, have known,

But now are giving up for country darkness."

                        "Come from that window where you see too much,

And take a livelier view of things from here.

They're going. Watch this husky swarming up

Over the wheel into the sky-high seat,

Lighting his pipe now, squinting down his nose

At the flame burning downward as he sucks it."

"See how it makes his nose-side bright, a proof

How dark it's getting. Can you tell what time

It is by that? Or by the moon?" The new moon!

What shoulder did I see her over? Neither.

A wire she is of silver, as new as we

To everything. Her light won't last us long.

不過要知道，在最初的兩個星期，
我們每天晚上都可以看見那月光，
而且它會一晚比一晚更亮。可是，
喬，爐子！快敲窗，叫他們等等！
請他們幫你把爐子立起來。快！
我們只顧遐想。快！快叫他們回來！」
「他們還沒走。」

　　　　　「不管我們缺什麼
也不能沒有爐子，還要一盞燈。
蠟燭在哪裡？萬一燈和油
混在雜物中找不出來？」

　　　　　　　　　　　　　　　　於是
屋子裡頓時又充滿了腳步聲，身影
朦朧的高大男人們衝進屋抬起爐子。
牆頭上有一個炮口般大小的洞，
他們憑目測將爐子對著洞裝好，
然後一齊動手舉起連接好的煙筒，
對他們的力氣來說煙筒實在太輕，
輕得幾乎就像充滿氣的氣球，
從他們笨拙的手中滑脫升上天花板。
「完全密合！」一個人拍著煙筒說，
「你們一搬進來裝爐子就這麼的運氣。
這可是好運的開始，不用擔心，
鄉下也不是那麼糟，安心過吧，
既然人人都在過日子。你們會喜歡的。」

It's something, though, to know we're going to have her

Night after night and stronger every night

To see us through our first two weeks. But, Joe,

The stove! Before they go! Knock on the window;

Ask them to help you get it on its feet.

We stand here dreaming. Hurry! Call them back!"

"They're not gone yet."

    "We've got to have the stove,

Whatever else we want for. And a light.

Have we a piece of candle if the lamp

And oil buried out of reach?"

        Again

    The house was full of tramping, and the dark,

    Door-filling men burst in and seized the stove.

    A cannon-mouth-like hole was in the wall,

    To which they set it true by eye; and then

    Came up the jointed stovepipe in their hands,

    So much too light and airy for their strength

    It almost seemed to come ballooning up,

    Slipping from clumsy clutches toward the ceiling.

    "A fit!" said one, and banged a stovepipe shoulder.

    "It's good luck when you move in to begin

    With good luck with your stovepipe. Never mind,

    It's not so bad in the country, settled down,

    When people're getting on in life. You'll like it."

喬説：「你們這些大小伙子也應該
找座農場當個好農夫，讓別的傢伙
去幹城裡的活兒。城裡的活兒不多，
不是人人都能找到活兒。」
「天哪！」一個人粗聲大氣地説，
「這話對傑米説吧。他需要一座農場。」
傑米扮了個鬼臉，裝出一副傻相，
骨碌碌轉動眼睛，彷彿是説他認爲
自己是農夫。接著一位法國小伙子
用一本正經的話把他們逗笑，
「我的朋友，你不知你在建議什麼。」

他説著摘下帽子用雙手捧在胸前，
行了個不倫不類的鞠躬禮，「我們
願把我們在農場上的機會讓給你。」
然後他們轉身，腳步聲震耳欲聾，
互相推著碰著操著出了那幢房子。
「跟他們再見吧！我們使他們困惑了。
他們以爲──我不知他們會怎麼看
我們在這裡看到的：那片好像是
某座農場後坡的坡地農場，還有你
在水槽窗邊看見的朝北延伸的樹林
彷彿都在等著，一旦我們垂下目光
或做別的事，它們就會偷偷朝我們
走近一步，就像小孩在玩『木頭人』遊戲。」

Joe said: "You big boys ought to find a farm,
And make good farmers, and leave other fellows
The city work to do. There's not enough
For everybody as it is in there."
"God!" one said wildly, and, when no one spoke:
"Say that to Jimmy here. He needs a farm."
but Jimmy only made his jaw recede
Fool-like, and rolled his eyes as if to say
He saw himself a farmer. Then there was a French boy
Who said with seriousness that made them laugh.
"Ma friend, you ain't know what it is you're ask."

He doffed his cap and held it with both hands
Across his chest to make as ʽtwere a bow:
"We're giving you our chances on de farm."
And then they all turned to with deafening boots
And put each other bodily out of the house.
"Good-by to them! We puzzle them. They think —
I don't know what they think we see in what
They leave us to: that pasture slope that seems
The back some farm presents us; and your woods
To northward from your window at the sink,
Waiting to steal a step on us whenever
We drop our eyes or turn to other things,
As in the game ʽten-stepʼ the children play."

「他們看上去都是好小伙子，讓他們
去愛城市吧。當你建議他們來鄉下
做有用的農夫時，他們只會說『天哪！』」
「他們有沒有使你感到幾分孤單寂寞？
不過他們還不足以使你——使我們
厭倦我們的農場。他們留下了
我們，像留下一對不可理喻的白痴，
這差點兒使我動搖。」

　　　　　　「這一切正是
我們一直所希望的，但我承認
這個暫時看起來的糟糕，使得情況
好像更糟糕，結果使人心情抑鬱。
沒什麼，只是因為他們在夜裡離去。
人們離去時我心裡向來不好受。

搬家第一天晚上客人走後，房子
總顯得有幽靈出沒或無遮無掩。
我總會留心在睡覺前親自鎖好門窗，
不過這種陌生感很快就會消失。」
他從一道門後面取出一盞舊提燈。
「這兒有我們沒失去的！還有這些。」
他從口袋裡摸出幾根火柴，「至於食物，
我們已經吃進肚裡的誰也拿不走。
我希望這世上的每樣東西都像我們
已吃下肚的一樣穩當。至少我希望
我們尚未吃的一日三餐會是這樣。
你知道你能在哪兒找到什麼吃的嗎？」

"Good boys they seemed, and let them love the city.

All they could say was ' God! ' when you proposed

Their coming out and making useful farmers."

"Did they make something lonesome go through you?

It would take more than them to sicken you —

Us of our bargain. But they left us so

As to our fate, like fools past reasoning with.

They almost shook me."

    "It's all so much

What we have always wanted, I confess

Its seeming bad for a moment makes it seem

Even worse still, and so on down, down, down.

It's nothing; it's their leaving us at dusk.

I never bore it well when people went.

       The first night after guests have gone, the house

       Seems haunted or exposed. I always take

       A personal interest in the locking up

       At bedtime; but the strangeness soon wears off."

       He fetched a dingy lantern from behind

       A door. "There's that we didn't lose! And these!" —

       Some matches he unpocketed. "For food —

       The meals we've had no one can take from us.

       I wish that everything on earth were just

       As certain as the meals we've had. I wish

       The meals we haven't had were, anyway.

       What have you you know where to lay your hands on?"

「我們路過那家商店時買的麵包。
大概還能找出些奶油。」
　　　　　「讓我們吃麵包吧。
我這就生起爐火，讓它與你做伴，
你這段時間不會有其他的夥伴，
直到埃德星期天出城來
看我們，並開始給我們出主意：
什麼地方需要修整、翻蓋或拆除。
他總能一下就知道如果他是我們
他應該做什麼。他會為我們計劃，
並幫我們，但他會以此抵債。

　　　　　　　　好吧，你可以先把麵包擺上桌子。
　　　　　　　　讓我們看你找出麵包，我這就生火。
　　　　　　　　我希望這些疊在其他椅子上的椅子
　　　　　　　　不會給女主人——」
　　　　　　　　　　　　「你又來了，喬！
　　　　　　　　你累了。」
　　　　　　　　　　　　「我都累得糊塗了，
　　　　　　　　別介意我的話。這一天可真夠嗆，
　　　　　　　　把一幢房子裡的所有家具搬空，
　　　　　　　　再把十五英里外的另一幢房子填滿，
　　　　　　　　不過只是把它們傾倒在這屋裡。」
　　　　　　　　「我們被傾倒進了樂園，而且快活。」
　　　　　　　　「這正好是我一直希望的，
　　　　　　　　我簡直不敢相信你對此也嚮往。」

"The bread we bought in passing at the store.

There's butter somewhere, too."

                     "Let's rend the bread.

I'll light the fire for company for you;

You'll not have any other company

Till Ed begins to get out on a Sunday

To look us over and give us his idea

Of what wants pruning, shingling, breaking up.

He'll know what he would do if he were we,

And all at once. He'll plan for us and plan

To help us, but he'll take it out in planning.

                                Well, you can set the table with the loaf.

Let's see you find your loaf. I'll light the fire.

I like chairs occupying other chairs

Not offering a lady —"

                              "There again, Joe!

You're tired."

                              "I'm drunk-nonsensical tired out;

Don't mind a word I say. It's a day's work

To empty one house of all household goods

And fill another with 'em fifteen miles away,

Although you do no more than dump them down."

"Dumped down in paradise we are and happy."

"It's all so much what I have always wanted,

I can't believe it's what you wanted, too."

「難道你不想知道？」

　　　　　　　　「我想知道
這是不是你所希望的，還是你嚮往它
基本上是爲了我。」

　　　　　　「一顆不安的良心！
要是我不説出，你不會要我説吧？」
「我不想弄清不可能弄清的事。
但是誰最先説起要到這裡來呢？」

　　　　　　　　　「親愛的，
是最先想到這個念頭的人。喬，
你在尋求不存在的東西；我是説開始。
結束和開始──世上沒有這種東西。
只有中間的過程。」

　　　　　　　　　　　　「那這是什麼？」

　　　　　　　　　　　　　「這種生活？
我倆一起坐在這盞提燈的燈光下，
在原來那個家的這堆破爛中間？
你不能否認這盞燈並不是新的。
這爐子也不是，你對我也不是，
我對你也不是。」

　　　　　　　　「也許你從來就不是？」
「仔細説，在我們存在的地方一切都不
是新的，那我可能一輩子也説不完。
新只是城裡那些白痴們的一個字眼，
他們以爲新服裝新思想的更迭終將
達到什麼目的。我聽你也這麼説過。
不，這絕不是開始。」

"Shouldn't you like to know?"

   "I'd like to know

If it is what you wanted, then how much

You wanted it for me."

   "A troubled conscience!

You don't want me to tell if I don't know."

"I don't want to find out what can't be known.

But who first said the word to come?"

   "My dear,

It's who first thought the thought. You're searching, Joe,

For things that don't exist; I mean beginnings.

Ends and beginnings — there are no such things.

There are only middles."

     "What is this?"

     "This life?

Our sitting here by lantern-light together

Amid the wreckage of a former home?

You won't deny the lantern isn't new.

The stove is not, and you are not to me,

Nor I to you."

     "Perhaps you never were?"

"It would take me forever to recite

All that's not new in where we find ourselves.

New is a word for fools in towns who think

Style upon style in dress and thought at last

Must get somewhere. I've heard you say as much.

No, this is no beginning."

「那這是結束？」
「結束是一個憂傷的字眼。」
　　　　「現在會不會太晚，
如果我拉你出去看看土丘上
那些老桃樹，向它們道聲晚安，
借著星光在草叢中找最後一顆桃，
當這座房子沒人住時，鄰居們也許
沒把它給撿去？我一直在留神：
不知他們是否給我們留下許多葡萄。
明天上午在動手收拾這房子之前，
我們要做的第一件事就是出去看看，

看看我們的蘋果、櫻桃、桃樹、
松樹、楦樹、牧場、水井和小溪。
這些就是一座農場。」
　　　　「這我知道得很清楚。
我現在打算讓你上床睡覺，即使
我首先得讓你搭床。來吧，燈。」
當廚房裡不再有提燈的燈光時，
點點火光從爐子的縫隙中透出，
像一個個金色的小人在天花板上跳舞，
跳得那麼自在，彷彿那兒一直是家。

"Then an end?"

"End is a gloomy word."

"Is it too late

To drag you out for just a good-night call

On the old peach trees on the knoll, to grope

By starlight in the grass for a last peach

The neighbors may not have taken as their right

When the house wasn't lived in? I've been looking:

I doubt if they have left us many grapes.

Before we set ourselves to right the house,

The first thing in the morning out we go

To go the round of apple, cherry, peach,

Pine, alder, pasture, mowing well, and brook.

All of a farm it is."

"I know this much:

I'm going to put you in your bed, if first

I have to make you build it. Come, the light."

When there was no more lantern in the kitchen,

The fire got out through crannies in the stove

And danced in yellow wrigglers on the ceiling,

As much at home as if they'd always danced there.

電話

「今天，我在我從這兒剛好能
步行到的地方，
曾有過一小段
靜寂的時辰，
當時我正把頭湊向一朵花，
忽然聽見你在說話。
別說我沒聽見，因為我聽見了——
你的話是從窗台上那朵花傳來的——
你還記得你當時說了什麼嗎？」
「你先告訴我你認為你聽見了什麼。」

「發現了那朵花並趕走一隻蜜蜂之後，
我朝花低下頭，
托起那枝花梗，
我仔細聆聽，我想我聽清了那個詞——
那是什麼來著？你叫過我的名字嗎？
或是你說——
有人說『來吧』——我俯身時聽見的。」
「我也許那麼想過，但沒說出聲。」
「那麼，我就來啦。」

The Telephone

"When I was just as far as I could walk

From here today,

There was an hour

All still

When leaning with my head against a flower

I heard you talk.

Don't say I didn't, for I heard you say —

You spoke from that flower on the windowsill —

Do you remember what it was you said?"

"First tell me what it was you thought you heard."

"Having found the flower and driven a bee away,

I leaned my head,

And holding by the stalk,

I listened and I thought I caught the word —

What was it? Did you call me by my name?

Or did you say —

Someone said 'Come' — I heard it as I bowed."

"I may have thought as much, but not aloud."

"Well, so I came."

相逢又分離

在我沿著那道石牆下山的途中
有一道柵門，我曾倚門看風景，
剛要離開時我第一次看見了你。
當時你正走上山來，我倆相逢。
但那天我們只是在夏日塵埃中
結合了我們倆大小不同的足跡，
像把我們的存在描成了大於一
但小於二的數字。你的傘一插
就標出了那個深深的小數點。
我們交談時你似乎一直在偷瞧
塵土中的什麼東西並對它露出笑臉。
（哦，那對我並沒有什麼不好！）
後來我走過了你上山時走過的路，
而你也走過了我下山時走過的路。

Meeting and Passing

As I went down the hill along the wall
There was a gate I had leaned at for the view
And had just turned from when I first saw you
As you came up the hill. We met. But all
We did that day was mingle great and small
Footprints in summer dust as if we drew
The figure of our being less than two
But more than one as yet. Your parasol
Pointed the decimal off with one deep thrust.
And all the time we talked you seemed to see
Something down there to smile at in the dust.
(Oh, it was without prejudice to me!)
Afterward I went past what you had passed
Before we met, and you what I had passed.

雨蛙溪

到六月我們的小溪就不再奔騰喧嘩。
在那之後尋找溪流，你將會發現
它要不是潛在地面之下摸索向前，
（帶著小溪裡各種各樣的雨蛙，
那些雨蛙一個月前還曾在霧中鳴叫，
就像朦朧雪地裡隱約的雪橇鈴聲）——
要不是微微冒出來浸潤鳳仙花
和嬌弱的枝葉，枝葉迎風彎腰，
甚至反朝著河水源頭的方向彎腰。
小溪的河床如今像一頁褪色的紙——
由被熱黏在一起的枯葉拼成的紙。
只有牢記它的人才知它是條小溪。
這條小溪，正如可以看出的一樣，
遠遠比不上歌中唱的別處的小溪。
但我們愛所愛之事物是因其真相。

Hyla Brook

By June our brook's run out of song and speed.

Sought for much after that, it will be found

Either to have gone groping underground

(And taken with it all the Hyla breed

That shouted in the mist a month ago,

Like ghost of sleigh bells in a ghost of snow) —

Or flourished and come up in jewelweed,

Weak foliage that is blown upon and bent,

Even against the way its waters went.

Its bed is left a faded paper sheet

Of dead leaves stuck together by the heat —

A brook to none but who remember long.

This as it will be seen is other far

Than with brooks taken otherwhere in song.

We love the things we love for what they are.

灶頭鳥

有一位人人都聽過其歌聲的歌手，
牠愛在仲夏時的樹林中敞開歌喉，
讓高大結實的樹幹發出回聲。
牠說樹葉已蒼老，牠說對於花，
若春天開放十成花，仲夏只開一成。
牠說大晴天不時飄來一陣雨，
當梨花櫻桃花在陣陣雨中落下，
最初的花飄花落時節就已經過完；
然後被叫做飄落的另一個秋天將至。
牠說那時路上的塵土將遮天蔽日。
若非牠懂得不在百鳥啼鳴時歌唱，
牠也許早就噤聲，像其他鳥一樣。
牠那個並非用字眼提出的問題
便是該如何去利用事物的衰替。

The Oven Bird

There is a singer everyone has heard,

Loud, a mid-summer and a mid-wood bird,

Who makes the solid tree trunks sound again.

He says that leaves are old and that for flowers

Mid-summer is to spring as one to ten.

He says the early petal-fall is past,

When pear and cherry bloom went down in showers

On sunny days a moment overcast;

And comes that other fall we name the fall.

He says the highway dust is over all.

The bird would cease and be as other birds

But that he knows in singing not to sing.

The question that he frames in all but words

Is what to make of a diminished thing.

約束與自由

愛有她所依附的地方，
有擁抱的手臂和環繞的山崗——
能阻擋恐懼的牆中之牆。
但思想並不需要這些東西，
因為他有一雙無畏的翅翼。

在雪地，在沙灘，在草坪，
我看見愛留下一種痕跡，
因為被這世界擁抱得太緊。
愛就是這樣並因此而滿足，
但思想已經擺脫這種約束。

思想能穿過星際的黑暗，
整夜坐在天狼星的表面，
直到白晝來臨才迅速回返，
他經過太陽，回到塵世，
根根羽毛發出燒焦的氣息。

他在天空獲得的便是他的擁有。
然而有人說愛擁有美的一切，
就因為她被約束並真正持久，
而思想得遠行至另一個星座，
發現愛擁有的一切在那兒融合。

Bond and Free

Love has earth to which she clings
With hills and circling arms about —
Wall within wall to shut fear out.
But Thought has need of no such things,
For Thought has a pair of dauntless wings.

On snow and sand and turf, I see
Where Love has left a printed trace
With straining in the world's embrace.
And such is Love and glad to be.
But Thought has shaken his ankles free.

Thought cleaves the interstellar gloom
And sits in Sirius' disc all night,
Till day makes him retrace his flight,
With smell of burning on every plume,
Back past the sun to an earthly room.

His gains in heaven are what they are.
Yet some say Love by being thrall
And simply staying possesses all
In several beauty that Thought fares far
To find fused in another star.

白樺樹

每當我看見白樺樹或左或右地彎下
與一排排較直且較黑的樹木相交，
我都會想到有個男孩在搖盪它們。
但搖盪不會像冰暴那樣使白樺樹
久久彎曲。在晴朗的冬日早晨，
在一場雨後，你肯定看見過它們
被冰凌壓彎。當晨風開始吹拂時，
當風力使它們表面的琺琅裂開時，
它們會喀嚓作響並變得色澤斑駁。
太陽很快會使它們的水晶外套滑落，
掉在凍硬的雪地上摔得粉碎——

若要你清除這樣一堆堆的碎玻璃，
你會以為是天堂的內頂塌落人間。
重壓可使它們觸到枯萎的蕨叢，
它們看上去不會折斷，不過一旦被
長久壓彎，它們就再也不會伸直；
在以後的歲月裡，你會在樹林中
看見它們枝幹彎曲，樹葉垂地，
就像姑娘們手腳並用趴在地上
任洗過的頭髮散在頭上讓太陽曬乾。
但我要說的是，即使真相已大白，
白樺樹的彎曲是由於冰暴的緣故，

Birches

When I see birches bend to left and right

Across the lines of straighter darker trees,

I like to think some boy's been swinging them.

But swinging doesn't bend them down to stay

As ice storms do. Often you must have seen them

Loaded with ice a sunny winter morning

After a rain. They click upon themselves

As the breeze rises, and turn many-colored

As the stir cracks and crazes their enamel.

Soon the sun's warmth makes them shed crystal shells

Shattering and avalanching on the snow crust —

Such heaps of broken glass to sweep away

You'd think the inner dome of heaven had fallen.

They are dragged to the withered bracken by the load,

And they seem not to break; though once they are bowed

So low for long, they never right themselves:

You may see their trunks arching in the woods

Years afterwards, trailing their leaves on the ground

Like girls on hands and knees that throw their hair

Before them over their heads to dry in the sun.

But I was going to say when Truth broke in

With all her matter of fact about the ice storm,

我仍然更喜歡有個孩子弄彎它們，
在他走出農舍去林中牽牛的時候——
一個離城太遠沒法學棒球的孩子，
他唯一的遊戲就是他自己的發明，
夏天或冬日，他能獨自玩得開心。
他把他父親的白樺樹當做馬騎，
一遍又一遍地挨個兒制伏它們，
直到他除掉了那些白樺樹的硬性，
沒剩下一棵不能彎曲，沒留下一棵
不能征服。他學會了應該學會的
技藝：開始爬樹時不要太快，
這樣就不會使樹過於彎向地面。
他始終都能保持住身體的平衡，

平穩地爬向樹梢，爬得很小心，
就像你平時往酒杯裡倒啤酒，
想讓酒滿杯，甚至稍稍冒出一點。
然後他嗖地一下蹬腳向外跳出，
踢著雙腿從半空中落到地面。
我曾經就是這樣一個盪樹的孩子。
而且我做夢都盪回到少年時代。
那是在我厭倦了思考的時候，
這時生活太像一座沒有路的森林，
你的臉因撞上蜘蛛網而發癢發燒，
你的一隻眼睛在流淚，因為一根
小樹枝在它睜著時抽了它一下。

I should prefer to have some boy bend them

As he went out and in to fetch the cows —

Some boy too far from town to learn baseball,

Whose only play was what he found himself,

Summer or winter, and could play alone.

One by one he subdued his father's trees

By riding them down over and over again

Until he took the stiffness out of them,

And not one but hung limp, not one was left

For him to conquer. He learned all there was

To learn about not launching out too soon

And so not carrying the tree away

Clear to the ground. He always kept his poise

        To the top branches, climbing carefully

        With the same pains you use to fill a cup

        Up to the brim, and even above the brim.

        Then he flung outward, feet first, with a swish,

        Kicking his way down through the air to the ground.

        So was I once myself a swinger of birches.

        And so I dream of going back to be.

        It's when I'm weary of considerations,

        And life is too much like a pathless wood

        Where your face burns and tickles with the cobwebs

        Broken across it, and one eye is weeping

        From a twig's having lashed across it open.

我真想離開這人世一小段時間，
然後再回到這裡重新開始生活。
但願命運別存心誤解我的意思，
只成全我心願的一半，把我攫去
而不送回。人世是適合愛的地方，
因爲我不知還有什麼更好的去處。
我喜歡憑著爬一棵白樺樹離去，
攀著黑色樹枝沿雪白的樹幹上天，
直到那棵樹沒法再承受我的體重，
低下頭把我又重新送回地面。
那應該説是不錯的離去和歸來。
而人之所爲可以比盪白樺樹更有害。

I'd like to get away from earth awhile

And then come back to it and begin over.

May no fate willfully misunderstand me

And half grant what I wish and snatch me away

Not to return. Earth's the right place for love;

I don't know where it's likely to go better.

I'd like to go by climbing a birch tree,

And climb black branches up a snow-white trunk

Toward heaven, till the tree could bear no more,

But dipped its top and set me down again.

That would be good both going and coming back,

One could do worse than be a swinger of birches.

豆棚

星期天做完禮拜後我獨自溜躂
　去約翰剛剛砍過樹的那個地區，
親自去整理那些白樺樹枝椏，
　約翰說我可以用來搭豆棚圍欄。

在剛砍了樹的那片狹長的空地
　就五月一日來說陽光實在太熱，
樹樁還在流著生命的液汁，
　炎熱與樹汁的氣味混合。

無論在何處只要有潮濕的窪地
　就有青蛙發出成千上萬的尖鳴，
牠們聽到我的腳步便息聲屏氣，
　靜觀我到這兒來做什麼事情。

空地上到處都堆著白樺樹枝！
　剛被斧子砍下，新鮮而結實。
不時有人趕著雙駕馬車來到，
　把白樺樹枝從野花背上搬去。

樹枝對菜園裡的豌豆會有好處，
　它們會伸出一根小指盤繞其上，
（就像你玩翻花繩時把線勾住，）
　然後攀著樹條離地向上生長。

樹枝對野生花草沒什麼好處，
　它們會使得許多延齡草彎腰，
延齡草在堆樹枝前就已抽芽，
　既然已經抽芽就必須長高。

Pea Brush

I walked down alone Sunday after church
To the place where John has been cutting trees,
To see for myself about the birch
He said I could have to bush my peas.

The sun in the new-cut narrow gap
Was hot enough for the first of May,
And stifling hot with the odor of sap
From stumps still bleeding their life away.

The frogs that were peeping a thousand shrill
Wherever the ground was low and wet,
The minute they heard my step went still
To watch me and see what I came to get.

Birch boughs enough piled everywhere! —
All fresh and sound from the recent ax.
Time someone came with cart and pair
And got them off the wild flowers' backs.

They might be good for garden things
To curl a little finger round,
The same as you seize cat's-cradle strings,
And lift themselves up off the ground.

Small good to anything growing wild,
They were crooking many a trillium
That had budded before the boughs were piled
And since it was coming up had to come.

下種

今天晚上你來叫我停下活回去，
說晚餐已上桌，我們將看看
是否我能停止掩埋這些白色的
從蘋果樹上落下的嬌嫩的花瓣，
（嬌嫩的花瓣並非完全無用，
可與這些或光或皺的豆種做伴）
而跟你回家，或是否你已忘記
來地裡幹什麼，變得和我一般，
成為對土地懷一腔熱情的奴僕。
這腔熱情多熾烈，當你把豆種
埋入土中並等待它們破土而出，
那該是在土裡生出雜草的時候，
茁壯的籽苗將彎曲著身子抽芽，
頂開它的路，抖掉身上的泥渣。

Putting in The Seed

You come to fetch me from my work tonight

When supper's on the table, and we'll see

If I can leave off burying the white

Soft petals fallen from the apple tree

(Soft petals, yes, but not so barren quite,

Mingled with these, smooth bean and wrinkled pea),

And go along with you ere you lose sight

Of what you came for and become like me,

Slave to a springtime passion for the earth.

How Love burns through the Putting in the Seed

On through the watching for that early birth

When, just as the soil tarnishes with weed,

The sturdy seedling with arched body comes

Shouldering its way and shedding the earth crumbs.

一段聊天的時間

當一個朋友從路上叫我
並意味深長地放慢腳步，
我那片坡地還沒有鋤完，
所以我沒停下來張望，
而是原地大聲問：「什麼事？」
不，雖然沒有聊天的時間，
我還是把鋤頭插進沃土，
五英尺長的鋤頭鋤口朝上，
然後我慢慢走向那道石牆，
為了一次友好的聊天。

A Time to Talk

When a friend calls to me from the road
And slows his horse to a meaning walk,
I don't stand still and look around
On all the hills I haven't hoed,
And shout from where I am, "What is it?"
No, not as there is a time to talk.
I thrust my hoe in the mellow ground,
Blade-end up and five feet tall,
And plod: I go up to the stone wall
For a friendly visit.

蘋果收穫時節的母牛

近來有某種東西使那頭母牛
不利用大門就像不利用牆頭，
不考慮修牆人就像不考慮傻瓜。
她的臉上到處沾著蘋果渣，
嘴邊滴著蘋果汁。嚐到了鮮果，
她不屑再去牧草已枯萎的草原。
她從一棵樹到一棵樹，樹下
落有因蟲蛀留下疤痕的蘋果。
當她不得不逃走時，落果已被咬。
她愛在一個土丘上對著人吼叫。
她的乳汁已枯竭，乳房已縮小。

The Cow in Apple Time

Something inspires the only cow of late

To make no more of a wall than an open gate,

And think no more of wall-builders than fools.

Her face is flecked with pomace and she drools

A cider syrup. Having tasted fruit,

She scorns a pasture withering to the root.

She runs from tree to tree where lie and sweeten

The windfalls spiked with stubble and worm-eaten.

She leaves them bitten when she has to fly.

She bellows on a knoll against the sky.

Her udder shrivels and the milk goes dry.

邂逅

在一個孕育著暴風雨的晴天，
當酷熱慢慢凝固，當太陽
似乎要被它自己的力量毀滅，
我正艱難地半擠半爬穿過一片
長滿雪松的沼澤。松油和
樹皮的氣味令我窒息，又累
又熱，真後悔離開我熟悉的路，
我停下來坐上一根彎曲的樹幹，
鋪著外套樹幹坐起來挺舒服，
既然四周沒有什麼東西可看，
我仰起頭來，但見襯著藍天
眼前豎立著一棵死而復生的樹，
一棵早倒下又重新站起的樹──

一個沒有樹皮的幽靈。
他停下腳步，彷彿擔心
會踩到我。
我見他兩隻手的姿勢很奇怪──
彎在肩頭上拖著個黃色網兜，
兜裡裝了些男人們用的東西。
「你是誰？」我說。「你從哪兒來？
有什麼消息，要是你知道的話？
告訴我你要去哪兒──蒙特利爾？
我？我從沒打算要上哪兒去。
有時我愛到僻靜的地方閒逛，
順便尋找卡呂普索蘭花。」

An Encounter

Once on the kind of day called "weather breeder,"
When the heat slowly hazes and the sun
By its own power seems to be undone,
I was half boring through, half climbing through
A swamp of cedar. Choked with oil of cedar
And scurf of plants, and weary and overheated,
And sorry I ever left the road I knew,
I paused and rested on a sort of hook
That had me by the coat as good as seated,
And since there was no other way to look,
Looked up toward heaven, and there against the blue,
Stood over me a resurrected tree,
A tree that had been down and raised again —

A barkless specter. He had halted too,
As if for fear of treading upon me.
I saw the strange position of his hands —
Up at his shoulders, dragging yellow strands
Of wire with something in it from men to men.
"You here?" I said. "Where aren't you nowadays?
And what's the news you carry — if you know?
And tell me where you're off for — Montreal?
Me? I'm not off for anywhere at all.
Sometimes I wander out of beaten ways
Half looking for the orchid Calypso."

射程測定

在戰鬥弄污一個人的胸膛之前
它撕裂了一張亮晶晶的蜘蛛網，
並把地上鳥巢邊的一株花折斷。
被折斷的花彎下腰垂下腦袋。
鳥媽媽依然頻頻回到小鳥身邊，
花折時被暫時撢走的一隻蝴蝶
在空中飛舞尋找牠的棲息之地，
然後輕輕降回花上拍動著翅膀。
昨夜，在那片光禿的高地牧場，
在野毛蕊花和拉緊的電纜之間，
那張蜘蛛網被銀色的露珠濕潤。
一粒突然穿過的子彈把它抖乾，
網中央那隻蜘蛛衝出來迎接蒼蠅，
但什麼也沒發現，只好悻悻退回。

Range-Finding

The battle rent a cobweb diamond-strung

And cut a flower beside a groundbird's nest.

Before it stained a single human breast.

The stricken flower bent double and so hung.

And still the bird revisited her young.

A butterfly its fall had dispossessed,

A moment sought in air his flower of rest,

Then lightly stooped to it and fluttering clung.

On the bare upland pasture there had spread

O'ernight 'twixt mullein stalks a wheel of thread

And straining cables wet with silver dew.

A sudden passing bullet shook it dry.

The indwelling spider ran to greet the fly,

But finding nothing, sullenly withdrew.

山妻（組詩）

I 孤獨——她的話

一個人不該非要這般掛念
　　像你和我這般掛念
當那對鳥兒飛來繞屋盤旋
　　彷彿是要説聲再見；

或這般關心，當牠們回來
　　唱著我們不懂的歌；
實情是我們因為一件事情
　　總會感到過分快活

就像為另一件事情過分悲傷——
　　因為鳥兒心裡只想著
牠們彼此，只想著牠們自己，
　　只想著築巢或棄窩。

II 害怕空屋

我要告訴你他們學會了害怕——
每天晚上當他們從田裡回家，
從遠處回到那孤零零的房子，
此時燈尚未點亮而爐火早熄，
他們學會了弄響鑰匙和鎖孔，
提前警告任何偶然溜進屋中
的入侵者，使其能溜之大吉；
更喜歡戶外而非屋內的黑夜，
他們學會了進屋後敞開房門
直到他們點亮屋裡的那盞燈。

The Hill Wife

I LONELINESS-Her Word

One ought not to have to care

So much as you and I

Care when the birds come round the house

To seem to say good-by;

Or care so much when they come back

With whatever it is they sing;

The truth being we are as much

Too glad for the one thing

As we are too sad for the other here —

With birds that fill their breasts

But with each other and themselves

And their built or driven nests.

II HOUSE FEAR

Always — I tell you this they learned —

Always at night when they returned

To the lonely house from far away,

To lamps unlighted and fire gone gray,

They learned to rattle the lock and key

To give whatever might chance to be,

Warning and time to be off in flight:

And preferring the out- to the indoor night,

They learned to leave the house door wide

Until they had lit lamp inside.

III笑容——她的話

我不喜歡他離去時的那種神情。
那種笑容！那絕不是出自高興。
你看見了嗎？我敢說他是偷笑！
也許是因為我們只給了他麵包，
所以那流浪漢知道我們很窘迫。
也許是因為他使我們主動施捨，
免去了他也許本想進行的搶劫。
他也許是嘲笑我倆過早把婚結，
嘲笑我們太年輕（而且他樂於
想像看見我們日漸衰老並死去）。
我不知他已順這條路走了多遠。
說不定他正從樹林朝我們窺視。

IV一再重覆的夢

她找不出任何恰當的字眼
　　來形容窗外那棵黑松，
黑松永遠在試圖撥開窗閂，
　　他倆就睡在那間屋中。

那些永不疲倦但徒勞的手
　　用每一次無益的手勢
使那棵大樹彷彿是隻小鳥
　　隔著窗玻璃顯得神秘！

黑松從來沒進過那個房間，
　　而這兩人中只有一人
在一個一再重覆的惡夢中
　　害怕黑松會做的事情。

III THE SMILE–*Her Word*

I didn't like the way he went away.

That smile! It never came of being gay.

Still he smiled — did you see him? — I was sure!

Perhaps because we gave him only bread

And the wretch knew from that that we were poor.

Perhaps because he let us give instead

Of seizing from us as he might have seized.

Perhaps he mocked at us for being wed,

Or being very young (and he was pleased

To have a vision of us old and dead).

I wonder how far down the road he's got.

He's watching from the woods as like as not.

IV THE OFT-REPEATED DREAM

She had no saying dark enough

For the dark pine that kept

Forever trying the window latch

Of the room where they slept.

The tireless but ineffectual hands

That with every futile pass

Made the great tree seem as a little bird

Before the mystery of glass!

It never had been inside the room,

And only one of the two

Was afraid in an oft-repeated dream

Of what the tree might do.

V 衝動

那裡對她來說真太寂寞，
　　而且太荒僻，
因為那裡只有他們兩人，
　　他倆沒孩子，

那屋裡的家務活實在太少，
　　她毫無約束，
她常跟他到地頭看他犁地
　　或看他鋸樹。

她愛倚著一根原木拋灑
　　新鮮的木屑，
嘴裡輕輕哼著一支唱給
　　自己聽的歌。

有一次她想去折黑檀樹
　　的一根枝椏。
她走得太遠差點沒聽見
　　他大聲喊她──

她沒有回應──沒有吭聲──
　　沒往回移動。
她呆呆站著，然後跑開
　　藏進了蕨叢。

他沒找到她，儘管他找遍
　　了所有旮旯，
最後他去到她母親家詢問
　　她是否在娘家。

娘家人說話那麼突兀迅疾
　　又那麼隨便，
他終於知道了後來的一切，
　　在她的墓邊。

V THE IMPULSE

It was too lonely for her there,

And too wild,

And since there were but two of them,

And no child,

And work was little in the house,

She was free,

And followed where he furrowed field,

Or felled tree.

She rested on a log and tossed

The fresh chips,

With a song only to herself

On her lips.

And once she went to break bough

Of black alder.

She strayed so far she scarcely heard

When he called her —

And didn't answer — didn't speak —

Or return.

She stood, and then she ran and hid

In the fern.

He never found her, though he looked

Everywhere,

And he asked at her mother's house

Was she there.

Sudden and swift and light as that

The ties gave,

And he learned of finalities

Besides the grave.

火堆

「啊，讓我們上山去嚇唬嚇唬自己，
今晚就像他們最棒的那樣無所顧忌，
去點燃我們親手堆積的所有枯枝，
別等著哪天下雪，或哪天下雨。
哦，別為了什麼安全而等雨雪天。
那堆枯枝是我們的，是我們從
黑魆魆的松林一根一根拖出來的。
今晚我們犯不著在乎把它怎麼樣。
分成小堆？不！就讓它一起燃燒，
像我們堆它時那樣。讓人們去說吧，
一團火光將從某處映亮他們的壁紙，
將把他們通通都吸引到窗戶前面。

把他們都驚醒吧，任他們直率或
不那麼直率地說要怎麼處置我們，
為了那件他們最好等我們做完的事。
讓我們叫這座古老的火山重新噴發，
如果這座山過去真是一座火山的話——
嚇唬我們。讓野火蔓延，我們要……」

「那也會嚇住你嗎？」孩子們齊聲問。

「怎麼不會嚇住我呢？讓一場火
從燼煙火堆開始，而同時又知道
我可能還會記起，如果我後悔的話，

The Bonfire

"Oh, let's go up the hill and scare ourselves,
As reckless as the best of them tonight,
By setting fire to all the brush we piled
With pitchy hands to wait for rain or snow.
Oh, let's not wait for rain to make it safe.
The pile is ours: we dragged it bough on bough
Down dark converging paths between the pines.
Let's not care what we do with it tonight.
Divide it? No! But burn it as one pile
The way we piled it. And let's be the talk
Of people brought to windows by a light
Thrown from somewhere against their wallpaper.

Rouse them all, both the free and not so free
With saying what they'd like to do to us
For what they'd better wait till we have done.
Let's all but bring to life this old volcano,
If that is what the mountain ever was —
And scare ourselves. Let wild fire loose we will —"
"And scare you too?" the children said together.
"Why wouldn't it scare me to have a fire
Begin in smudge with ropy smoke, and know
That still, if I repent, I may recall it,

但不是在此刻：熊熊的火堆只要
有一點兒蔓延，那就只有火本身
才能滅火。而且我知道，火滅火
靠的是燒光一切，而在燒光之前
火將呼嘯躍騰，火星會碰到星星，
火焰會像一柄旋轉的火劍橫掃一切，
使樹林向四周後退讓出一個大圈——
因此我不知要是我能夠控制火，
那麼有什麼我想造成的毀壞它不能夠。
好啦，但願它今晚別從什麼地方
引來一陣強風，別像
有一年四月它給我惹禍那般。
當時刮了一冬的風已減弱，
弱得似乎令藍背鳥也感到失望，

怎麼老也飛不到要去的棲息之地；
而當我燒著我的火堆巡視時
它還像一根尖柱似的直衝雲天。
屋外總有風，你們知道這格言。
一陣風驟起。你們過去習慣以為
是樹搧動空氣而生風，因為你們
知道只要有風就會看見樹木搖動。
但那陣風是由某物或某人引起。
風使火舌傾斜向地面並用其舌尖
舔食地上剛過了冬天的枯草，
就像你們用舌頭舔手上的糖或鹽。

But in a moment not; a little spurt

Of burning fatness, and then nothing but

The fire itself can put it out, and that

By burning out, and before it burns out

It will have roared first and mixed sparks with stars,

And sweeping round it with a flaming sword,

Made the dim trees stand back in wider circle —

Done so much and I know not how much more

I mean it shall not do if I can bind it.

Well if it doesn't with its draft bring on

A wind to blow in earnest from some quarter,

As once it did with me upon an April.

The breezes were so spent with winter blowing

They seemed to fail the bluebirds under them

                Short of the perch their languid flight was toward;

                And my flame made a pinnacle to heaven

                As I walked once around it in possession.

                But the wind out-of-doors — you know the saying.

                There came a gust. (You used to think the trees

                Made wind by fanning, since you never knew

                It blow but that you saw the trees in motion.)

                Something or someone watching made that gust.

                It put the flame tip-down and dabbed the grass

                Of over-winter with the least tip-touch

                Your tongue gives salt or sugar in your hand.

火焰所到之處頓時就被燒黑。
在大白天看那兒幾乎是一片黑色，
與此相比濃煙不過是一縷青煙，
火焰則細得像是一根根獐耳草、
血根草，很快又像是朵朵紫羅蘭。
但那黑色就像黑死病一樣蔓延，
當時天空也是一片漆黑，
彷彿冬天和夜晚一起降臨。
當時要考慮的事真是太多太多，
我來不及細想就把那片土地朝北
伸延的方向和太陽落下的小溪
的方向留給了火去蔓延，還把

朝公路那個方向也留給了火焰，
儘管我擔心路邊枯萎的灌木叢、
深深的野草、已經變白的金穗花
以及被野葡萄藤纏糾的橙樹
會成為烈火衝過公路所需的燃料。
我選擇的滅火方向是朝鎮上這邊，
我跪下來動手滅火，並把臉避開。
滅這種火要靠輕捂而不能重拍。
最好是用寬木板，如果你有的話。
我是用外套。哦，我知道，我知道，
並大聲喊出，我受不了這麼近的
煙薰火烤；但一想到所有樹林
和整個城鎮將被我點燃，想到
全鎮人要找我算帳──我仍堅持。

The place it reached to blackened instantly.

The black was almost all there was by daylight,

That and the merest curl of cigarette smoke —

And a flame slender as the hepaticas,

Bloodroot, and violets so soon to be now.

But the black spread like black death on the ground,

And I think the sky darkened with a cloud

Like winter and evening coming on together.

There were enough things to be thought of then.

Where the field stretches toward the north

And setting sun to Hyla brook, I gave it

To flames without twice thinking, where it verges

> Upon the road, to flames too, though in fear
>
> They might find fuel there, in withered brake,
>
> Grass its full length, old silver goldenrod,
>
> And alder and grape vine entanglement,
>
> To leap the dusty deadline. For my own
>
> I took what front there was beside. I knelt
>
> And thrust hands in and held my face away.
>
> Fight such a fire by rubbing not by beating.
>
> A board is the best weapon if you have it.
>
> I had my coat. And oh, I knew, I knew,
>
> And said out loud, I couldn't bide the smother
>
> And heat so close in; but the thought of all
>
> The woods and town on fire by me, and all
>
> The town turned out to fight for me — that held me.

我相信小溪會擋住火，但卻擔心
公路會失敗；實際上在公路那邊
火滅前發出木頭辟啪的聲響──
燒著的不僅僅是易燃的雜草──
那使我站起身來去那邊滅火，
我仍然彎下身子，就像有韁繩
纏在我脖子上，而我在犁地。
我贏了！但我敢說，與我那天
弄黑的那一大片空間相比，
沒人能用另一種顏色塗十分之一。
從鎮上趕來的鄰居們簡直沒法
相信，怎麼他們剛剛才轉過身，
那兒就變成了一片黑土，因爲
當他們一小時前經過那兒彎到
另一條路時，他們並沒有看見黑色。

他們到處尋找那個闖此大禍的人，
但周圍不見人影。我正在某個地方
驚嘆我的疲勞到哪兒去，爲什麼
穿著笨重的鞋，我卻走得那麼輕鬆，
雖說我有種被烤焦的獨立日感情。
想起那事我怎麼會不感到害怕？」

「要是連你都怕火，我們怎麼辦？」

「害怕！但要是你們因害怕而退縮，
那麼戰爭降臨你們時怎麼辦？
而這正是我有理由想知道的──
你們是否能給我一個滿意的回答？」

I trusted the brook barrier, but feared

The road would fail; and on that side the fire

Died not without a noise of crackling wood —

Of something more than tinder-grass and weed —

That brought me to my feet to hold it back

By leaning back myself, as if the reins

Were round my neck and I was at the plow.

I won! But I'm sure no one ever spread

Another color over a tenth the space

That I spread coal-black over in the time

It took me. Neighbors coming home from town

Couldn't believe that so much black had come there

While they had backs turned, that it hadn't been there

When they had passed an hour or so before

Going the other way and they not seen it.

They looked about for someone to have done it.

But there was no one. I was somewhere wondering

Where all my weariness had gone and why

I walked so light on air in heavy shoes

In spite of a scorched Fourth-of-July feeling.

Why wouldn't I be scared remembering that?"

"If it scares you, what will it do to us?"

"Scare you. But if you shrink from being scared,

What would you say to war if it should come?

That's what for reasons I should like to know —

If you can comfort me by any answer."

「但戰爭與孩子無關，那是大人的事。」

「目前我們幾乎要自掏腰包給中國。
親愛的孩子們，你們想過的事──
我們都想過。所以你們的錯是我們的。
但你們難道沒聽說過被戰爭擊沉的
民船，沒聽說過那些被戰爭蹂躪的
城鎮，（戰爭在夜晚從雲端呼嘯而至，
而在那之前雲端只有天使和星星？）
你們沒聽說過船上和城鎮裡有孩子？
沒聽說過人類用生命換來的教訓？
這教訓並不新鮮，只是被我們忘了：
戰爭人人都有份，孩子也不例外。
我不打算也不可能給你們說清楚戰爭。
最好的辦法就是隨我一起上山，
去點燃火堆並歡笑，同時也害怕。」

"Oh, but war's not for children — it's for men."

"Now we are digging almost down to China.
My dears, my dears, you thought that — we all thought it.
So your mistake was ours. Haven't you heard, though,
About the ships where war has found them out
At sea, about the towns where war has come
Through opening clouds at night with droning speed
Further o'erhead than all but stars and angels —
And children in the ships and in the towns?
Haven't you heard what we have lived to learn?
Nothing so new — something we had forgotten:
War is for everyone, for children too.
I wasn't going to tell you and I mustn't.
The best way is to come uphill with me
And have our fire and laugh and be afraid."

一個姑娘的菜園

我們村裡有一位鄰居
　　愛講她做過的一樁傻事，
那是在某一年的春天，
　　當她還是個農家少女。

有一天她要求她父親
　　給她一小塊菜園
讓她自己耕種自己收穫，
　　父親說：「爲什麼不呢？」

在尋找耕地的時候，
　　他想起一塊有牆的空地，
空地上曾有過一家商店，
　　他說：「就是這裡。」

他說：「你可以在這裡
　　弄成你心目中的個人農場，
而且它會給你一個機會
　　鍛煉你瘦弱的臂膀。」

她父親還說那菜園太小，
　　不適宜使用耕畜，
所以她幹活兒只能用手，
　　但她現在並不在乎。

她沿著一條延伸的小路
　　用手推車去運肥料；
但她常常拋下運肥小車
　　一個人掉頭就跑，

A Girl's Garden

A neighbor of mine in the village

Likes to tell how one spring

When she was a girl on the farm, she did

A childlike thing.

One day she asked her father

To give her a garden plot

To plant and tend and reap herself,

And he said, "Why not?"

In casting about for a corner

He thought of an idle bit

Of walled-off ground where a shop had stood,

And he said, "Just it."

And he said, "That ought to make you

An ideal one-girl farm,

And give you a chance to put some strength

On your slim-jim arm."

It was not enough of a garden.

Her father said, to plow;

So she had to work it all by hand,

But she don't mind now.

She wheeled the dung in the wheelbarrow

Along a stretch of road;

But she always ran away and left

Her not-nice load,

為的是躲開來往的行人。
　　然後她要來了種子。
她說她打算除野草之外，
　　什麼作物都種種看。

於是一個坑只栽一種作物；
　　蘿蔔萵苣豌豆馬鈴薯
甜菜蠶豆南瓜玉米和番茄，
　　甚至還有各種果樹。

是的，長久以來她一直不相信
　　今天還長在那裡的
蘋果樹是她的，
　　或至少可能是她的。

在一切都說了並做了之後，
　　她的收穫真是五花八門，
每樣東西都有那麼一點點，
　　但沒有一樣夠斗量秤稱。

如今每當她在村裡看見
　　各種事務在進行，
每當事情顯得有點眉目時，
　　她總會說：「這我知道！」

「這就像我當年種地時一樣——」
　　但她絕非是有何高見！
而且她絕不會對同一個人
　　把這個故事講上兩遍。

And hid from anyone passing.

And then she begged the seed.

She says she thinks she planted one

Of all things but weed.

A hill each of potatoes,

Radishes, lettuce, peas,

Tomatoes, beets, beans, pumpkins, corn,

And even fruit trees.

And yes, she has long mistrusted

That a cider-apple tree

In bearing there today is hers,

Or at least may be.

Her crop was a miscellany

When all was said and done,

A little bit of everything,

A great deal of none.

Now when she sees in the village

How village things go,

Just when it seems to come in right,

She says, "I know!"

"It's as when I was a farmer..."

Oh, never by way of advice!

And she never sins by telling the tale

To the same person twice.

關在屋外——寫給一個孩子

當我們在晚上關門閉窗，
我們總會把花兒關在屋外，
使它們照不到窗內的燈光。
每次我幻想有人試圖開門，
袖口上的鈕扣擦著門框，
這時花兒就在小偷身旁。
但他們誰也沒去欺侮花朵！
我們曾發現一朵旱金蓮
折斷了花梗倒在腳印上。
我也許已因此責備過自己，
因為我常想，它說不定
就是我曾逗弄過的那朵花，
當我坐在暮色中看月亮落下。

Locked Out

As told to a child

When we locked up the house at night,

We always locked the flowers outside

And cut them off from window light.

The time I dreamed the door was tried

And brushed with buttons upon sleeves,

The flowers were out there with the thieves.

Yet nobody molested them!

We did find one nasturtium

Upon the steps with bitten stem.

I may have been to blame for that:

I always thought it must have been

Some flower I played with as I sat

At dusk to watch the moon down early.

藍背鳥的留言
—— 寫給一個孩子

我出門時遇見隻烏鴉
用一種低沉嗓音對我說話：
「嘿，我正在找你呢。
你好嗎？我來是為了
叫你去告訴萊絲利
（你會告訴她嗎？）
她那隻小小的藍背鳥
要我幫牠把口信捎，
說昨晚的那場北風
那場使星星明亮的北風，
那場使水槽結冰的北風
使得牠咳嗽，差點兒沒
咳掉牠尾巴上的羽毛。

所以牠只好飛走！
但牠跟她說再見，
並叫她多多保重，
叫她要戴好紅兜帽，
當她拿起一柄斧頭
在雪地裡找臭鼬的蹤跡——
牠還祝她事事順利！
也許等明年春暖花開
牠又會唱著歌回來。」

The Last Word of a Bluebird

As told to a child

As I went out a Crow

In a low voice said, "Oh,

I was looking for you.

How do you do?

I just came to tell you

To tell Lesley (will you?)

That her little Bluebird

Wanted me to bring word

That the north wind last night

That made the stars bright

And made ice on the trough

Almost made him cough

His tail feathers off.

He just had to fly!

But he sent her Good-by,

And said to be good,

And wear her red hood,

And look for skunk tracks

In the snow with an ax —

And do everything!

And perhaps in the spring

He would come back and sing."

「熄滅吧，熄滅──」

場院裡的電鋸時而咆哮時而低吟，
濺起鋸末並吐出適合爐膛的木條，
微風拂過時木條散發出陣陣清香。
人們從場院裡抬眼就可以看見
有五道平行的山脈一重疊一重
在夕陽下伸向遠方的佛蒙特州。
電鋸咆哮低吟，電鋸低吟咆哮，
當它或是空轉、或是負荷之時。
一切平平安安，一天活就要幹完。
他們要早點說一天活結束就好了，
給那孩子半小時空閒讓他高興。

那孩子會非常看重半小時空閒。
那孩子的姐姐繫著圍裙站在一旁
告訴他們晚餐好了。此時那電鋸
好像是要證明它懂得什麼是晚餐，
突然跳向孩子的手──似乎是跳向──
但想必是他伸出了手。可不管怎樣，
電鋸和手沒避免相遇。那隻手喲！
那男孩的第一聲慘叫是一聲慘笑，
他猛地轉身朝他們舉起那隻手，
像是在呼救，但又像是要阻止生命

"Out, Out —"

The buzz saw snarled and rattled in the yard

And made dust and dropped stove-length sticks of wood,

Sweet-scented stuff when the breeze drew across it.

And from there those that lifted eyes could count

Five mountain ranges one behind the other

Under the sunset far into Vermont.

And the saw snarled and rattled, snarled and rattled,

As it ran light, or had to bear a load.

And nothing happened: day was all but done.

Call it a day, I wish they might have said

To please the boy by giving him the half hour

That a boy counts so much when saved from work.

His sister stood beside them in her apron

To tell them "Supper." At the word, the saw,

As if to prove saws knew what supper meant,

Leaped out at the boy's hand, or seemed to leap —

He must have given the hand. However it was,

Neither refused the meeting. But the hand!

The boy's first outcry was a rueful laugh,

As he swung toward them holding up the hand,

Half in appeal, but half as if to keep

從那隻手溢出。這時他看清了——
因爲他已經是大孩子，已經懂事，
雖說有孩子的心，但幹的大人的活——
他看見血肉模糊。「別讓他砍我的手——
姐姐，醫生來了別讓他砍掉我的手！」
好吧，可那隻手已經與胳膊分離。
醫生來了，用麻醉藥使他入睡。
他躺在那兒鼓起雙唇拼命喘息。
後來——聽他脈膊的人猛然一驚。
誰都不相信。他們又聽他的心跳。
微弱，更弱，消失——到此爲止。
不再有指望了。於是他們都轉身
去忙各自的事，因爲他們不是死者。

The life from spilling. Then the boy saw all —

Since he was old enough to know, big boy

Doing a man's work, though a child at heart —

He saw all spoiled. "Don't let him cut my hand off —

The doctor, when he comes. Don't let him, sister!"

So. But the hand was gone already.

The doctor put him in the dark of ether.

He lay and puffed his lips out with his breath.

And then — the watcher at his pulse took fright.

No one believed. They listened at his heart.

Little — less — nothing! — and that ended it.

No more to build on there. And they, since they

Were not the one dead, turned to their affairs.

布朗下山

布朗的農場在高高的山上，
　冬日裡一過下午三點半時分，
只要他在幹農場上的雜活，
　人們老遠就能看見他的提燈。

想必許多人都看到有天夜裡
　他曾瘋狂地衝下那座高山，
越過耕地、石牆和一切，
　手中的提燈劃出道道光環。

當時他在農舍與穀倉間搬東西，
　忽然間有一陣狂風刮來
把他吹向了包裹著地面的冰殼，
　於是他就開始連滾帶摔！

石牆都被雪掩，樹木也稀少，
　他看出除非靴跟能鑿孔
不然他就沒法在冰面上停住。
　然而儘管他一直口腳並用

一邊跺腳一邊自語，但有時
　有些事似乎只能順其自然，
他跺腳沒能跺出立足之處，
　而是繼續旅程，滑行下山。

有時他的雙臂像翅膀張開，
　他瘦長的身子則像一根中軸，
他就像表演旋轉舞似的滑行，
　這種姿勢頗有尊嚴和風度。

Brown's Descent

Brown lived at such a lofty farm
That everyone for miles could see
His lantern when he did his chores
In winter after half-past three.
And many must have seen him make
His wild descent form there one night.
'Cross lots, 'cross walls, 'cross everything,
Describing rings of lantern-light.
Between the house and barn the gale
Got him by something he had on
And blew him out on the icy crust
That cased the world, and he was gone!

Walls were all buried, trees were few:
He saw no stay unless he stove
A hole in somewhere with his heel.
But though repeatedly he strove
And stamped and said things to himself,
And sometimes something seemed to yield,
He gained no foothold, but pursued
His journey down from field to field.
Sometimes he came with arms outspread
Like wings, revolving in the scene
Upon his longer axis, and
With no small dignity of mien.

或快或慢他自己沒法掌握，
　　或蹲或立卻由他自己決定，
這全看他敢不敢為保住衣服
　　而讓脖子或思想做出犧牲。

他始終沒讓那盞提燈脫手，
　　有人也聲稱曾遠遠地注意
布朗用燈光發出過信號，
　　「我不懂那信號是什麼意思，

在深更半夜那樣一個時辰！
　　他是在慶祝什麼特別的事。
我不知是他賣掉了他的農場
　　還是當上了格蘭其的分會主席。」

他磕磕跌跌撞撞一溜歪斜，
　　他滑倒時提燈碰得劈里啪啦，
（但他設法沒讓燈光熄滅。）
　　直滑到山腰他還想止住下滑，

他不相信自己會如此倒霉。
　　後來他終於變得隨遇而安，
徹底放棄了想停住的努力，
　　像個玩耍的孩子直滑下山。

「好吧，我──」他就說了這麼多，
　　當他躺直滑過冰凍的小河
他回頭沿著那道滑溜溜的山坡，
　　望了望（兩英里外）他的住所。

我作為一名汽車方面的權威，
　　有時候人們會要求我回答
是否我們的股票已徹底崩盤，
　　這就是我認真的回答：

Faster or slower as he chanced,

Sitting or standing as he chose,

According as he feared to risk

His neck, or thought to spare his clothes.

He never let the lantern drop.

And some exclaimed who saw afar

The figures he described with it,

"I wonder what those signals are

Brown makes at such an hour of night!

He's celebrating something strange.

I wonder if he's sold his farm,

Or been made Master of the Grange."

He reeled, he lurched, he bobbed, he checked;

He fell and made the lantern rattle

(But saved the light from going out).

So halfway down he fought the battle,

Incredulous of his own bad luck.

And then becoming reconciled

To everything, he gave it up

And came down like a coasting child.

"Well — I — be —" that was all he said,

As standing in the river road

He looked back up the slippery slope

(Two miles it was) to his abode.

Sometimes as an authority

On motorcars, I'm asked if I

Should say our stock was petered out,

And this is my sincere reply:

咱們北方佬仍和過去一樣。

　　別因爲布朗爬不上那光溜
的山坡，就以爲他會放棄
　　重新返回山頂家園的希望；

更不要以爲他會站在山腳下
　　等來一月的解凍季節
融化掉地殼那層光滑的表面。
　　他體面地順從了自然法則，

然後按股票攀升的方式，
　　憑他的雙腳一步步繞路上山；
千萬別替那些人過分擔心，
　　因爲在那樣一種特殊時間，

他們的感覺肯定非常良好。
　　即使腳下走的是羊腸小路，
他們也覺得彷彿是康莊大道——
　　我說別替他們過分擔心，

不然做不成一個男子漢——
　　一個有閒暇時間的政治家。
我一直讓布朗在山下挨凍，
　　雖然我找了理由替他說話；

但現在他朝山上看了兩三眼，
　　然後晃了晃他的提燈，說：
「上路吧！」然後他就上路，
　　上了那條有幾英里遠的盤山路。

Yankees are what they always were.

Don't think Brown ever gave up hope

Of getting home again because

He couldn't climb that slippery slope;

Or even thought of standing there

Until the January thaw

Should take the polish off the crust.

He bowed with grace to natural law,

And then went round it on his feet,

After the manner of our stock;

Not much concerned for those to whom,

At that particular time o'clock,

                  It must have looked as if the course

                  He steered was really straight away

                  From that which he was headed for —

                  Not much concerned for them, I say;

                  No more so than became a man —

                  And politician at odd seasons.

                  I've kept Brown standing in the cold

                  While I invested him with reasons;

                  But now he snapped his eyes three times;

                  Then shook his lantern, saying, "Ile's

                  'Bout out!" and took the long way home

                  By road, a matter of several miles.

採樹脂的人

一天清晨，在下山的路上，
有個人趕上來與我同行，
他拎著個空空的口袋，
口袋的上半截繞在他手上。
他讓我與他同行的五英里路
比讓我乘車騎馬都更舒暢。
山路沿著一條嘩嘩的小溪，
我倆説話都像在大聲嚷嚷。
我先告訴他我從哪兒來，
我住在山區的什麼地方，
此時我正沿著那條路回家，
然後他也講了些他的情況。

他來自很高很高的山坳
在那兒河川源頭沖刷著的
是從山體裂出的一塊塊岩石，
那看上去真足以令人絕望——
因岩石的風化層只夠生苔蘚，
永遠也形不成能長草的土壤。
他在樹林邊建了間小木屋。
那只能是間低矮的木屋，
因為對烈火與毀滅的恐懼
常常驚擾林區人的夢鄉：
夢中半個世界被燒得烏黑，
太陽在濃煙中蜷縮變黃。

The Gum-Gatherer

There overtook me and drew me in
To his downhill, early-morning stride,
And set me five miles on my road
Better than if he had had me ride,
A man with a swinging bag for load
And half the bag wound round his hand.
We talked like barking above the din
Of water we walked along beside.
And for my telling him where I'd been
And where I lived in mountain land
To be coming home the way I was,
He told me a little about himself.

He came from higher up in the pass
Where the grist of the new-beginning brooks
Is blocks split off the mountain mass —
And hopeless grist enough it looks
Ever to grind to soil for grass.
(The way it is will do for moss.)
There he had built his stolen shack.
It had to be a stolen shack
Because of the fears of fire and loss
That trouble the sleep of lumber folk:
Visions of half the world burned black
And the sun shrunken yellow in smoke.

我們熟悉帶山貨進城的山民，
他們馬車座下或有些漿果，
他們兩腳之間或有籃雞蛋；
這個人布袋裡裝的樹脂，
從山上的雲杉樹採的樹脂。
他讓我看那些芳香的樹脂塊，
它們像尚未雕琢的寶石。
它們的顏色在齒間呈粉紅，
但在上市之前卻成為金黃。

我告訴他那是一種愜意的生活：
終日在陰暗的林間樹下，
讓樹皮貼近你的胸膛，
伸出你手中的一柄小刀，
將樹脂撬鬆，然後採下，
高興時則帶著它們去市場。

We know who when they come to town

Bring berries under the wagon seat,

Or a basket of eggs between their feet;

What this man brought in a cotton sack

Was gum, the gum of the mountain spruce.

He showed me lumps of the scented stuff

Like uncut jewels, dull and rough.

It comes to market golden brown;

But turns to pink between the teeth.

I told him this is a pleasant life,

To set your breast to the bark of trees

That all your days are dim beneath,

And reaching up with a little knife,

To loose the resin and take it down

And bring it to market when you please.

架線工

他們像拓荒者一樣從這兒經過。
他們留下一個可爛不可砍的樹林。
他們為活人種下一棵棵死樹，
又用一根活線將死樹連成一串。
他們襯著藍天為一架樂器調琴弦，
往後不管是敲出還是說出的話語
經過琴弦時都會像思想一樣無聲，
但他們調弦時卻並不安靜，他們
向遠處吶喊：「嗨，把線拉緊囉！
千萬別鬆手，直到我們把它固定。
鬆手吧——完工了！」隨著笑聲，
隨著鎮民們藐視荒野的誓言聲，
他們為我們送來了電報和電話。

The Ling-Gang

Here come the line-gang pioneering by.

They throw a forest down less cut than broken.

They plant dead trees for living, and the dead

They string together with a living thread.

They string an instrument against the sky

Wherein words whether beaten out or spoken

Will run as hushed as when they were a thought.

But in no hush they string it: they go past

With shouts afar to pull the cable taut,

To hold it hard until they make it fast,

To ease away — they have it. With a laugh,

An oath of towns that set the wild at naught,

They bring the telephone and telegraph.

消失的紅色

據說約翰是阿克頓鎮的最後一個
紅種人。據說那磨坊主一直在笑——
如果你想把那種聲音叫做笑聲的話。
但他卻不給別人的笑聲發許可證，
因為他會突然扳起面孔，好像是說：
「這關誰的事——要是我把它攬下，
這關誰的事——可幹嘛眾人要議論？
既然這只是我贊成處置的一件事情。」

你沒法回到當時像他那樣目睹此事。
這話說來太長，現在已沒法說清。
除非你一直在那兒並經歷了一切。
然後你也許就不會只把它看成是
兩個種族間哪個先動手的問題。
當時那紅種人正在磨坊裡閒逛，
俯身於那個咯咯轉動的巨大磨盤，

The Vanishing Red

He is said to have been the last Red Man

In Acton. And the Miller is said to have laughed —

If you like to call such a sound a laugh.

But he gave no one else a laugher's license.

For he turned suddenly grave as if to say,

"Whose business — if I take it on myself,

Whose business — but why talk round the barn? —

When it's just that I hold with getting a thing done with."

You can't get back and see it as he saw it.

It's too long a story to go into now.

You'd have to have been there and lived it.

Then you wouldn't have looked on it as just a matter

Of who began it between the two races.

Some guttural exclamation of surprise

The Red Man gave in poking about the mill,

他粗聲大氣地發出驚訝的叫喊，
驚叫聲使磨坊主生理上產生反感，
因為聲音來自無權大聲呼叫的人。
「喂，約翰，」他說，「想看看輪槽嗎？」
他領他來到輪坑裡的一根橫樑下，
從地板上的檢修孔讓他看輪槽，
引木槽裡湍急的水像發瘋的魚，
像一尾尾甩動尾巴的鮭魚和鱘魚。
後來他關上了繫有鈴鐺的活板門，
鈴鐺的響聲甚至壓過了所有聲音，
然後他獨自上來──並開始那樣笑，
還對一個來磨麵的人說了些什麼，
但那個人沒能聽明白。──後來呢？
哦，對啦，他的確讓約翰見識了輪槽。

Over the great big thumping, shuffling millstone,

Disgusted the Miller physically as coming

From one who had no right to be heard from.

"Come, John," he said, "you want to see the wheel pit?"

He took him down below a cramping rafter,

And showed him, through a manhole in the floor,

The water in desperate straits like frantic fish,

Salmon and sturgeon, lashing with their tails.

The he shut down the trap door with a ring in it

That jangled even above the general noise,

And came upstairs alone?and gave that laugh,

And said something to a man with a meal-sack

That the man with the meal-sack didn't catch? then.

Oh, yes, he showed John the wheel-pit all right.

雪

三個人站著仔細聽狂風再次發威，
風剛才捲著大雪猛撞了一陣房子，
然後又無拘無束地呼嘯。科爾夫婦
本已上床，故衣服頭髮都顯凌亂，
梅澤夫身上的大皮衣使他更顯矮小。

梅澤夫先開口說話。他用手中的
煙斗從肩頭上向後指著外邊說：
「你簡直能看清那陣風掠過屋頂，
從屋頂朝天空展開一軸名冊長卷，
長得足以記下我們所有人的名字。——
我想我得給我妻子掛個電話，告訴
她我在這裡——待一會兒再上路。

我會只讓鈴響兩聲，要是她聰明
又已經入睡，她就不必醒來接電話。」
他只搖了三下手柄，然後拿起聽筒。
「嗨，萊特，還沒睡？我在科爾家。
是晚了點。我打電話是想在我回家
說早上好之前從這兒跟你說聲晚安——
我想我會——我知道——萊特，
我可以，但那有什麼意思？剩下的路
不會太糟——我一小時就能到——
喂，三小時到這兒！但那全是上坡；
剩下的是下坡路。哦，不，路不太糟。
馬都很鎮靜，走得不慌不忙，還覺得
好玩哩。牠們現在在牲口棚。

Snow

The three stood listening to a fresh access

Of wind that caught against the house a moment,

Gulped snow, and then blew free again — the Coles,

Dressed, but disheveled from some hours of sleep;

Meserve, belittled in the great skin coat he wore.

Meserve was first to speak. He pointed backward

Over his shoulder with his pipestem, saying,

"You can just see it glancing off the roof

Making a great scroll upward toward the sky,

Long enough for recording all our names on. —

I think I'll just call up my wife and tell her

I'm here — so far — and starting on again.

           I'll call her softly so that if she's wise

And gone to sleep, she needn't wake to answer."

Three times he barely stirred the bell, then listened.

"Why, Lett, still up? Lett, I'm at Cole's. I'm late.

I called you up to say Good-night from here

Before I went to say Good-morning there. —

I thought I would. — I know, but, Lett — I know —

I could, but what's the sense? The rest won't be

So bad. — Give me an hour for it. — Ho, ho,

Three hours to here! But that was all uphill;

The rest is down. — Why no, no. not a wallow:

They kept their heads and took their time to it

Like darlings, both of them. They're in the barn. —

親愛的，我早上會回來。我給你
打電話可不是要你邀請我回家——」
他等了等她不肯說出的那兩個字，
最後自己將其說出，「晚安，」另一頭
還是沒回應，於是他掛上了電話。
三個人圍著桌子站在燈光之中，
大家都垂著目光，直到他開口說：
「我去看看那些馬怎麼啦。」

             「去吧，」
科爾夫婦齊聲說。隨後科爾太太又
補充說：「看過之後才好作出判斷——
弗雷德，我要你在這兒陪我。讓他
留下吧，梅澤夫兄弟。你能找到
從這兒去牲口棚的路。」

                     「我想我能，
我想我知道能在那兒發現我的名字
刻在牲口棚裡，這樣即使我不知道
我在哪兒，也知道我是誰。過去我
習慣玩——」

             「你料理完馬就回來。
弗雷德，你打算讓他走？」

                   「難道你不？
你能容他留下？」

                   「我剛才叫他兄弟啦。
知道我為什麼那樣叫嗎？」

                   「這很自然。
因為你聽見周圍人們都那麼叫。
他好像已經失去了他的教名。」

My dear, I'm coming just the same. I didn't

Call you to ask you to invite me home. —"

He lingered for some word she wouldn't say,

Said it at last himself, "Good-night," and then,

Getting no answer, closed the telephone.

The three stood in the lamplight round the table

With lowered eyes a moment till he said,

"I'll just see how the horses are."

        "Yes, do,"

Both the Coles said together. Mrs. Cole

Added: "You can judge better after seeing. —

I want you here with me, Fred. — Leave him here,

Brother Meserve. You know to find your way

Out through the shed."

                "I guess I know my way.

I guess I know where I can find my name

Carved in the shed to tell me who I am

If it don't tell me where I am. I used

To play —"

"You tend your horses and come back. —

Fred Cole, you're going to let him!"

                "Well, aren't you?

How can you help yourself?"

                "I called him Brother.

Why did I call him that?"

                "It's right enough.

That's all you ever heard him called round here.

He seems to have lost off his Christian name."

「我倒覺得那樣叫頗有教會味兒。
他沒注意到,是嗎?好吧,至少
我那樣叫並不是出於對他的喜歡。
老天作證,一想到他有十個孩子就
令我厭惡,而且最大還不到十歲。
我也討厭他那個小得可憐的教派,
就我所聽到的,那個教派不怎麼樣。
但這也難說——瞧,弗雷德,現在
都十二點了。他來這兒才半個小時,
而他說他是九點離開鎮上雜貨店的。
三小時走四英里路——一小時一英里
或稍稍多一點兒。這是為什麼?
似乎一個男人不可能走得那麼慢。
想想在這段時間裡他走得多吃力。
而他還有三英里路要走!」

　　　　　　　　　「就別讓他走了。
留住他,海倫。讓他回答你的問題。
那種人向來口快,說起來就沒完,
只要他自己談起一件什麼事情,
其他任何人說什麼他都充耳不聞。
不過我該想到,你也能讓他聽你說。」
「這樣的夜裡他在外邊幹什麼呢?
他幹嘛不能待在家裡呢?」

　　　　　　　　　「他得佈道。」

「這不是出門的夜晚。」

"Christian enough I should call that myself.

He took no notice, did he? Well, at least

I didn't use it out of love of him,

The dear knows. I detest the thought of him —

With his ten children under ten years old.

I hate his wretched little Racker Sect,

All's ever I heard of it, which isn't much.

But that's not saying — look, Fred Cole, it's twelve,

Isn't it, now? He's been here half an hour.

He says he left the village store at nine:

Three hours to do four miles — a mile an hour

Or not much better. Why, it doesn't seem

As if a man could move that slow and move.

Try to think what he did with all that time.

And three miles more to go!"

                                      "Don't let him go.

Stick to him, Helen. Make him answer you.

That sort of man talks straight-on all his life

From the last thing he said himself, stone deaf

To anything anyone else may say.

I should have thought, though, you could make him hear you."

"What is he doing out a night like this?

Why can't he stay at home?"

                                  "He had to preach."

"It's no night to be out."

　　　　　「他或許卑微，
他或許虔誠，但他肯定很堅韌。」
「而且壯得像根煙草。」
　　　　　　「他能夠克服困難。」
「你只是説説而已。要知道從這兒
到他們家，路上再沒有別的房子或
過夜處，我得再給他妻子打個電話。」
「等等，也許他會自己打，
看他會不會再一次想到他的妻子，
不過我認爲他未必會想到。
因爲他不把這種天氣當回事的。」
「他不能走——你瞧！」

　　　　　　　「那是夜空，親愛的。」
「至少他沒把上帝拉扯進這件事。」
「他不會認爲上帝與這件事有關係。」
「你這樣想，是嗎？你不了解這種人。
他現在正準備創造一個奇蹟。
悄悄的——只有他知道，此刻他在想
要是他成功了，他就證明了一種關係，
但要是失敗就保持沉默。」
　　　　　　　「永遠保持沉默。
他會被凍死——被雪埋掉。」
　　　　　　　　「如此嚴重！
不過如果他這樣做只會使那些
道貌岸然的惡棍表現出幾分僞裝的
虔誠，那我仍然有一千條理由
不在乎他會出什麼事。」

"He may be small,

He may be good, but one thing's sure, he's tough."

"And strong of stale tobacco."

"He'll pull through."

"You only say so. Not another house

Or shelter to put into from this place

To theirs. I'm going to call his wife again."

"Wait and he may. Let's see what he will do.

Let's see if he will think of her again.

But then, I doubt he's thinking of himself.

He doesn't look on it as anything."

"He shan't go — there!"

"It is a night, my dear."

"One thing: he didn't drag God into it."

"He don't consider it a case for God."

"You think so, do you? You don't know the kind.

He's getting up a miracle this minute.

Privately — to himself, right now, he's thinking

He'll make a case of it if he succeeds,

But keep still if he fails."

"Keep still all over.

He'll be dead — dead and buried."

"Such a trouble!

Not but I've every reason not to care

What happens to him if it only takes

Some of the sanctimonious conceit

Out of one of those pious scalawags."

「胡說！你希望看到他平平安安。」
「你喜歡這小矮人。」
　　　　　「你不也有點喜歡？」
「這個嘛，我不喜歡他正在做的事，
而這是你喜歡的，並因此而喜歡他。」
　　　　　　　「哦，你一定喜歡。
你像任何人一樣喜歡有趣的事；
只是你們女人不得不裝模作樣，
好給男人留下印象。你們使我們
男人感到害臊，以致我們看見有趣
的爭鬥也覺得有義務去加以制止。
我說，就讓那個人凍掉他的耳朵吧——

　　　　　　　　他來了。我把他交給你。設法
　　　　　　　　救他一條命吧。——請進，梅澤夫。
　　　　　　　　請坐，請坐。你那些馬怎麼樣？」
　　　　　　　　「很好，很好。」
　　　　　　　　　　　「你還要再往前走？我妻子
　　　　　　　　說你不能走。我看你也必須放棄。」
　　　　　　　　「能給我個面子嗎，梅澤夫先生？
　　　　　　　　要是我說求你呢？我讓你妻子來決定。
　　　　　　　　你妻子剛才在電話裡都說些什麼？」
　　　　　　　　梅澤夫好像只是在注意桌上的燈，
　　　　　　　　或注意離燈不遠的一樣什麼東西。
　　　　　　　　他放在膝蓋上的那隻手活像一隻

"Nonsense to that! You want to see him safe."

"You like the runt."

    "Don't you a little?"

"Well,

I don't like what he's doing, which is what

You like, and like him for."

    "Oh, yes you do.

You like your fun as well as anyone;

Only you women have to put these airs on

To impress men. You've got us so ashamed

Of being men we can't look at a good fight

Between two boys and not feel bound to stop it.

Let the man freeze an ear or two, I say. —

    He's here. I leave him all to you. Go in

And save his life. — All right, come in, Meserve.

Sit down, sit down. How did you find the horses?"

"Fine, fine."

"And ready for some more? My wife here

Says it won't do. You've got to give it up."

"Won't you to please me? Please! If I say Please?

Mr. Meserve, I'll leave it to your wife.

What did your wife say on the telephone?"

Meserve seemed to heed nothing but the lamp

Or something not far from it on the table.

By straightening out and lifting a forefinger,

起皺的白蜘蛛，他抬起那隻手，
伸直胳膊翹起食指指著燈下說：
「看那頁書，在你攤開的那本書中！
我想它剛才在動。它一直豎立著，
就在這桌上，自從我進屋後
它一直在試圖自己朝前或朝後翻，
我也一直盯著它想看出個結果：
要是朝前，那它是懷著朋友的焦急
（你明白我知道）要你繼續看某些字句，
它想看你如何理解這些字句；如果向後，
那是因為它惋惜你翻過了某些字句
但未能體會其中妙處。但不用擔心，

在我們領會事物之前，它們肯定會
一次次地向我們展現──我說不清
具體有多少次，那得看情況而定。
有一種謊言企圖證明：凡事
都只能在我們的眼前顯現一次。
但真要是那樣，我們最終會在哪裡呢？
我們的生命依賴於萬事萬物的重現，
直到我們從內心作出回應。
第一千次重現也許會證明其魅力。
那書頁！沒風幫忙它自己不能翻動，
但它剛才動了，卻不是被風吹動。
它是自己動的，因為這裡壓根兒沒風。
風不可能使一樣東西動得那樣細膩，

He pointed with his hand from where it lay

Like a white crumpled spider on his knee:

"That leaf there in your open book! It moved

Just then, I thought. It's stood erect like that,

There on the table, ever since I came,

Trying to turn itself backward or forward,

I've had my eye on it to make out which:

If forward, then it's with a friend's impatience —

You see I know — to get you on to things

It wants to see how you will take; if backward,

It's from regret for something you have passed

And failed to see the good of . Never mind,

Things must expect to come in front of us

A many times — I don't say just how many —

That varies with the things — before we see them.

One of the lies would make it out that nothing

Ever presents itself before us twice.

Where would we be at last if that were so?

Our very life depends on everything's

Recurring till we answer from within.

The thousandth time may prove the charm. — That leaf!

It can't turn either way. It needs the wind's help.

But the wind didn't move it if it moved.

It moved itself. The wind's at naught in here.

It couldn't stir so sensitively poised

風不可能鑽進燈裡讓火苗噴出黑煙；
風不可能把這條柯利犬的長毛吹皺。
你們使這四四方方的一小團空氣
靜謐，明亮而溫暖，儘管四周是
無邊無際的黑暗、寒冷和風雪，
憑著營造這環境，你們讓身邊的
這燈這狗和這書頁享有了安寧。
雖說人人都能看出這種安寧也許
是你們沒有的東西，但你們卻能給予。
所以不擁有便不能給予是無稽之談，
認為話說一千遍即成真理，亦屬謬論。
我要翻這頁書了，若沒人願意的話。
它不願平放，那就讓它立著吧。
誰會在乎呢？」

「我並不想催促你，梅澤夫先生，
但要是你想走──請說你會留下。
不過讓我拉開這窗簾看看外面，
並讓你看你面前的雪如何在堆高。
你沒看見這冰天雪地一片白茫茫嗎？
問問海倫，從我們剛才量過之後，
窗框上的雪又增高許多。」

　　　　　「看上去像是
某個白乎乎傢伙壓扁了它的五官
並過於急切地閉上了它的眼睛，
不想看人們相互間發現什麼那樣
有趣，然後它由於愚蠢和不理解

A thing as that. It couldn't reach the lamp

To get a puff of black smoke from the flame,

Or blow a rumple in the collie's coat.

You make a little foursquare block of air,

Quiet and light and warm, in spite of all

The illimitable dark and cold and storm,

And by so doing give these three, lamp, dog,

And book-leaf, that keep near you, their repose;

Though for all anyone can tell, repose

May be the thing you haven't, yet you give it.

So false it is that what we haven't we can't give;

So false, that what we always say is true.

I'll have to turn the leaf if no one else will.

It won't lie down. Then let it stand. Who cares?"

"I shouldn't want to hurry you, Meserve,

But if you're going — say you'll stay, you know.

But let me raise this curtain on a scene,

And show you how it's piling up against you.

You see the snow-white through the white of frost?

Ask Helen how far up the sash it's climbed

Since last we read the gauge."

"It looks as if

Some pallid thing had squashed its features flat

And its eyes shut with overeagerness

To see what people found so interesting

In one another, and had gone to sleep

Of its own stupid lack of understanding,

而酣然入睡，或是折斷了它白蘑菇
般的短脖子，靠著窗玻璃死去。」
「梅澤夫兄弟，當心這可怕的夢魘
會嚇住你自己，遠遠超過嚇住我們。
與這有關係的是你，因為正是你
非要一個人走出這房子進入雪夜。」
「讓他說，海倫，也許他會留下。」
「在你放下窗簾前——我記起來了：
你還記得有年冬天跑到外面去
呼吸新鮮空氣的小伙子嗎——住在
南邊埃弗里家的那個小伙子？對啦，
那是個晴朗的上午，在暴風雪之後，
他路過我家發現我在屋外用雪護牆。

我為了保暖正把自己深深地埋起來，
把積雪一直堆到與窗台一般高。
堆上窗台的白雪吸引了他的目光。
『嘿，這真是個好主意』他說，
『這樣你既可以想到外邊積雪六英尺，
又可坐在暖和的室內研究均衡配給。
在冬天，你卻感覺不到太多寒意。』
這些就是他的話。他回到住處後幾乎
用雪把陽光擋在埃弗里家的窗戶外。
現在你們和我不會做出那樣的事。
不過，你不能否認，我們三個人
坐在這兒發揮我們的想像力，讓
外面的雪線高高地橫過窗格，這也
並不會使天氣更糟，哪怕糟一點點。

Or broken its white neck of mushroom stuff

Short off, and died against the windowpane."

"Brother Meserve, take care, you'll scare youself

More than you will us with such nightmare talk.

It's you it matters to, because it's you

Who have to go out into it alone."

"Let him talk, Helen, and perhaps he'll stay."

"Before you drop the curtain — I'm reminded:

You recollect the boy who came out here

To breathe the air one winter — had a room

Down at the Averys'? Well, one sunny morning

After a downy storm, he passed our place

And found me banking up the house with snow.

And I was burrowing in deep for warmth,

Piling it well above the windowsills.

The snow against the window caught his eye.

'Hey, that's a pretty thought' — those were his words —

'So you can think it's six feet deep outside,

While you sit warm and read up balanced rations.

You can't get too much winter in the winter.'

Those were his words. And he went home and all

But banked the daylight out of Avery's windows.

Now you and I would go to no such length.

At the same time you can't deny it makes

It not a mite worse, sitting here, we three,

Playing our fancy, to have the snow-line run

So high across the pane outside. There where

在茫茫冰天雪地中有一種隧道——
那更像隧道而不像洞——你可以
看見隧道遠方的盡頭有一種微動
或顫動，就像巷道磨損的邊在風中
飄動。我喜歡那景象——我喜歡。
好啦，現在我該走了，朋友。」

　　　　　　　　「喂，梅澤夫，
我們還以爲你打算決定不走了呢——
你剛才還用那種方式稱讚你此刻
待的地方舒適，你是想留在這兒的。」
「我得承認下這樣一場雪，很冷。
除了你們這個房間，這整幢
房子都快被凍裂。要是你們以爲
風聲遠去，那也不是因爲它消失；

屋頂上的雪越厚（那才是原因）你們
越感覺不到。聽那些鬆軟的雪炸彈，
它們正在煙囪口和屋簷上衝著我們
爆炸。我喜歡躲在屋裡，而不
喜歡暴露在外面。但那些馬已經
得到休息，而且已到告別的時間，
你們回床上繼續睡覺吧。晚安，
原諒我闖進來驚了你們的好夢。」
「你闖進來算你運氣。你眞走運，
選我們家作爲你中途的休息站。
如果你是那種願意尊重女人意見
的男人，你就應該聽我的忠告
並爲了你家人的緣故而留下不走。

There is a sort of tunnel in the frost —

More like a tunnel than a hole — way down

At the far end of it you see a stir

And quiver like the frayed edge of the drift

Blown in the wind . I like that — I like that.

Well, now I leave you, people."

        "Come, Meserve,

We thought you were deciding not to go —

The ways you found to say the praise of comfort

And being where you are. You want to stay."

"I'll own it's cold for such a fall of snow.

This house is frozen brittle, all except

This room you sit in. If you think the wind

Sounds further off, it's not because it's dying;

                You're further under in the snow — that's all —

                And feel it less. Hear the soft bombs of dust

                It bursts against us at the chimney mouth,

                And at the eaves. I like it from inside

                More than I shall out in it. But the horses

                Are rested and it's time to say Good-night,

                And let you get to bed again. Good-night,

                Sorry I had to break in on your sleep."

                "Lucky for you you did. Lucky for you

                You had us for a halfway station

                To stop at. If you were the kind of man

                Paid heed to women, you'd take my advice

                And for your famliy's sake stay where you are.

但我這樣苦口婆心又有什麼用呢？
你的所爲已超過了你有權認爲你
能夠做的──剛才。而你也清楚
繼續走所要冒的風險。」

　　　　　　　　「一般説來，
我們這兒的暴風雪不會置人於死地。
雖説我寧願當一頭藏在雪下面冬眠
的野獸，讓大雪把洞口封上並掩埋，
也不願當一個在上面與雪搏鬥的人，
但想想那些棲在樹枝上而不是待在
窩裡的小鳥吧。難道我還不如牠們？
在今晚的大雪中，牠們被弄濕的身軀
頃刻間就會被凍成冰塊。但到明天
牠們又會跳躍在林間發芽的樹枝上，
撲動牠們的翅膀，唱出歡樂的歌，
彷彿不知我們説的暴風雪有何意義。」

「你爲什麼要走？沒有人要你走啊！
你的妻子──她不想你走。我們也不想，
你自己也不想。此外還有誰呢？」
「讓我們免於被一個女人問倒吧！
哦，此外還有──」她後來告訴
弗雷德，在他停頓之時，她以爲他
會説出「上帝」這個令人敬畏的字眼。
但他説的是：「此外還有──暴風雪。
它説我得繼續走。它需要我就像
戰爭需要我一樣（若是戰爭降臨）。
去問問任何一個男人吧。」

But what good is my saying it over and over?

You've done more than you had a right to think

You could do — now. You know the risk you take

In going on."

    "Our snowstorms as a rule

Aren't looked on as man-killers, and although

I'd rather be the beast that sleeps the sleep

Under it all, his door sealed up and lost,

Than the man fighting it to keep above it,

Yet think of the small birds at roost and not

In nests, Shall I be counted less than they are?

Their bulk in water would be frozen rock

In no time out tonight. And yet tomorrow

They will come budding boughs from tree to tree,

Flirting their wings and saying Chickadee,

As if not knowing what you meant by the word storm."

      "But why, when no one wants you to, go on?

      Your wife — she doesn't want you to. We don't,

      And you yourself don't want to. Who else is there?"

      "Save us from being cornered by a woman.

      Well, there's — "She told Fred afterward that in

      The pause right there, she thought the dreaded word

      Was coming, "God." But no, he only said,

      "Well, there's — the storm. That says I must go on.

      That wants me as a war might if it came.

      Ask any man."

　　　　　　他扔下最後一句話
讓她發呆，直到他走出了房門。
他讓科爾陪他到牲口棚與他道別。
科爾回屋時發現妻子仍然站著，
在那張桌邊，挨近那本攤開的書，
但並不是在讀它。

　　　　　　「好啦，」她説，
「你覺得他是個什麼樣的人？」

　　　　　　　　「我應該説
他有語言天賦，或者説能言善辯？」
「這種人一向喜歡相似比擬嗎？」

「或是愛忽略人們提的世俗問題──
什麼？我們一小時內對他的了解
比我們看他從這路上經過一千次所
了解的還多。他要這樣佈道就好啦！
畢竟你剛才並不認爲你能留得住他。
哦，我不是責備你。他並沒有給你
多少説話的機會，再説我很高興
我們用不著陪他一夜。他留下來也
不會睡覺，最小的事也會使他興奮。
他一走這裡靜得像空盪盪的教堂。」
「事實上，這樣比他沒走好多少呢？
我們得坐在這兒等他平安到家。」
「是嗎？我猜你想等，但我不想。
他知道他的能耐，不然他不會走。
我説上床去吧，好歹休息一會兒。

He threw her that as something

To last her till he got outside the door.

He had Cole with him to the barn to see him off.

When Cole returned he found his wife still standing

Beside the table, near the open book,

Not reading it.

         "Well, what kind of a man

Do you call that?" she said.

         "He had the gift

Of words, or is it tongues I ought to say?"

"Was ever such a man for seeing likeness?"

         "Or disregarding people's civil questions —

         What? We've found out in one hour more about him

         Than we had seeing him pass by in the road

         A thousand times. If that's the way he preaches!

         You didn't think you'd keep him after all.

         Oh, I'm not blaming you. He didn't leave you

         Much say in the matter, and I'm just as glad

         We're not in for a night of him. No sleep

         If he had stayed. The least thing set him going.

         It's quiet as an empty church without him."

         "But how much better off are we as it is?

         We'll have to sit here till we know he's safe."

         "Yes, I suppose you'll want to, but I shouldn't.

         He knows what he can do, or he wouldn't try.

         Get into bed I say, and get some rest.

他不會回來的，而要是他來電話，
那也得一兩個小時之後。」
「好吧。我想我們坐在這兒等他
穿越暴風雪也無濟於事。」
科爾在沒開燈的外屋打電話。
科爾太太的聲音從裡屋傳來：
「是她打過來的，還是你打過去的？」

          「她打過來的，
你要不想再睡就把衣服穿好。
我們本該早就睡著了。都三點多了。」
「她已說了好一陣話嗎？我馬上穿睡袍，
我要和她通話。」

                「她只說了
他還沒到家，並問他真的走了嗎？」
「他走了都快兩個小時了。」
「他帶著雪鏟，他大概得鏟雪開路。」
「我剛才為什麼要允許他離開呢？」
「別這麼說。你已經竭盡全力
留過他了——不過你也許的確
沒掩飾你希望看到他不聽你勸告
的勇氣。他妻子會因此責怪你的。」
「弗雷德，畢竟我說了！你不能
撇開我的話本身而隨意去理解。
她剛才的話中沒流露出要怪我
的意思吧？」

He won't come back, and if he telephones,

It won't be for an hour or two."

"Well then —

Well can't be any help by sitting here

And living his fight through with him, I suppose."

Cole had been telephoning in the dark.

Mrs. Cole's voice came from an inner room:

"Did she call you or you call her?"

   "She me.

You'd better dress: you won't go back to bed.

We must have asleep: it's three and after."

"Had she been ringing long? I'll get my wrapper.

I want to speak to her."

     "All she said was,

  He hadn't come and had he really started."

  "She knew he had, poor thing, two hours ago."

  "He had the shovel. He'll have made a fight."

  "Why did I ever let him leave this house!"

  "Don't begin that. You did the best you could

  To keep him — though perhaps you didn't quite

  Conceal a wish to see him show the spunk

  To disobey you. Much his wife'll thank you."

  "Fred, after all I said! You shan't make out

  That it was any way but what it was.

  Did she let on by any word she said

  She didn't thank me?"

　　　　「當我告訴她『走啦』，
她說：『好呀，好呀』——像一種威脅。
然後她用變得很低的聲音說：『哦，
你們，你們幹嘛放他走呢？』」
　　　　「問我們幹嘛放他走？
你讓開。我倒要問問她幹嘛要放他
出來。他在這兒時她還不敢說哩。
他們的號碼——二一？電話不通。
有人摘下了話筒。這搖柄太緊。
這破玩意兒，會把人的手弄傷！
通了！她已丟下話筒走開了。」
「你說話試試看。說『喂！』」
　　　　　　　　「喂。喂。」
「聽到什麼嗎？」

　　　　　　　　　　「聽到一個空房間——
你知道——聽上去是空房間。對啦，
我聽見——我想是鐘響，還有窗響。
但沒腳步聲。她要是在屋裡也是坐著。」
「大聲點，她也許會聽見。」
　　　　　　　　　「大聲也沒用。」
「你繼續喊話。」
　　　　　　　　　「喂。喂。喂。
你不會認為——她不會出門去吧？」
「我有點擔心那正是她可能做的。」
「丟下那些孩子？」

"When I told her ˙Gone,˙
˙Well then,˙ she said, and 'Well then' — like a threat.
And then her voice came scraping slow: ˙Oh, you,
Why did you let him go?˙"

"Asked why we let him?
You let me there. I'll ask her why she let him.
She didn't dare to speak when he was here.
Their number's — twenty-one? — The thing won't work.
Someone's receiver's down. The handle stumbles.
The stubborn thing, the way it jars your arm! —
It's theirs. She's dropped it from her hand and gone."
"Try speaking. Say ˙Hello!˙"

"Hello. Hello."
"What do you hear?"

"I hear an empty room —
You know — it sounds that way. And yes, I hear —
I think I hear a clock — and windows rattling.
No step, though. If she's there she's sitting down."
"Shout, she may hear you."

"Shouting is no good."
"Keep speaking, then."

"Hello. Hello. Hello. —
You don't suppose? — she wouldn't go outdoors?"
"I'm half afraid that's just what she might do."
"And leave the children?"

「等會兒再叫吧。
你就聽不出是否她讓房門敞開著，
是否風已經把燈吹滅，是否壁爐
已熄火，是否那屋子裡又冷又黑？」
「我只能聽出她要麼上床睡了，
要麼出門去了。」
　　　　　「這兩種情況都沒辦法。
你知道她長什麼樣？你見過她嗎？
真奇怪，她不想和我們說話。」
「弗雷德，你來，看你能不能聽見
我聽見的那種聲音。」
「也許是鐘響。」
　　　　　「你就沒聽見別的？」
「沒人說話？」
　　　　　　　　　　　　　「沒有。」
　　　　「啊，我聽見了──是什麼？」
「你說是什麼？」
　　　　　「一個嬰兒的哭聲！
哭得真凶，儘管聽上去隱隱約約。
當母親的絕不會讓孩子這樣啼哭，
如果她在的話。」
　　　　　「你認為這說明什麼？」
「這只能說明一種情況，那就是，
可以假定──她已經出門去了。
不過她當然沒出去。」他倆一籌莫展地
坐了下來，「天亮以前我們毫無辦法。」

"Wait and call again.

You can't hear whether she has left the door

Wide open and the wind's blown out the lamp

And the fire's died and the room's dark and cold?"

"One of two things, either she's gone to bed

Or gone outdoors."

"In which case both are lost.

Do you know what she's like? Have you ever met her?

It's strange she doesn't want to speak to us."

"Fred, see if you can hear what I hear. Come."

"A clock maybe."

"Don't you hear something else?"

"Not talking."

"No."

"Why, yes, I hear — what is it?"

"What do you say it is?"

"A baby's crying!

Frantic it sounds, though muffled and far off.

Its mother wouldn't let it cry like that,

Not if she's there."

"What do you make of it?"

"There's only one thing possible to make,

That is, assuming — that she has gone out.

Of course she hasn't, though." They both sat down

Helpless. "There's nothing we can do till morning."

「弗雷德，我不允許你想到出去。」
「別出聲。」這時電話鈴聲開始響。
他倆驚跳起來。弗雷德抓過話筒。
「喂，梅澤夫。這麼說你到了！——
你的妻子呢？很好！我幹嘛問這個——
剛才她好像一直不接電話。—— 他
說她剛才到牲口欄接他去了。——
我們很高興。哦，別客氣，朋友。
歡迎你路過時順便再來看看我們。」
「好啦，這下她終於擁有他了。
不過我看不出她為什麼需要他。」
　　　　　「可能不是為她自己。
她需要他也許只是為了那些孩子。」

「看來剛才我們完全是大驚小怪。
我們折騰這一夜只會讓他感到好笑。
他來幹什麼呢？——只是來聊聊？
不過他倒是來過電話說今晚在下雪。
要是他認為他打算把我們家作為
往返鎮上時中途休息喝咖啡的地方——」
「我認為你會覺得剛才過分擔心了。」
「你認為剛才你自己就不擔心？」
「要是你想說他太不替人家著想，
半夜把我們從床上叫起來為他擔心，
然後對我們的忠告又置若罔聞，
那我同意你。但讓我們原諒他吧，
我們已分享了他生命中的一個夜晚。
他會再來的，你用什麼跟我打賭？」

"Fred, I shan't let you think of going out."

"Hold on." The double bell began to chirp.

They started up. Fred took the telephone.

"Hello Meserve. You're there, then! — and your wife?

Good! Why I asked — she didn't seem to answer. —

He says she went to let him in the barn. —

We're glad. Oh, say no more about it, man.

Drop in and see us when you're passing."

"Well,

She has him, then, though what she wants him for

I don't see.

    "Possibly not for herself.

Maybe she only wants him for the children."

        "The whole to-do seems to have been for nothing.

        What spoiled our night was to him just his fun.

        What did he come in for? — to talk and visit?

        Thought he'd just call to tell us it was snowing.

        If he thinks he is going to make our house

        A halfway coffee house 'twixt town and nowhere — "

        "I thought you'd feel you'd been too much concerned."

        "You think you haven't been concerned yourself."

        "If you mean he was inconsiderate

        To rout us out to think for him at midnight

        And then take our advice no more than nothing,

        Why, I agree with you. But let's forgive him.

        We've had a share in one night of his life.

        What'll you bet he ever calls again?"

樹聲

我對那些樹感到疑惑。
爲什麼比起另一種噪聲
我們更希望永遠忍受
它們的瑟瑟沙沙簌簌，
而且緊挨著家門口？
我們天天忍受樹聲，
直到喪失了步伐的節奏
和歡樂中的永恆，
並具有了傾聽的神情。
它們總談到要離去，
但卻從不挪動；
等它們更睿智更老成，
它們仍在談想長見識，
但這話現在意謂著不走。

有時當我從窗口或門洞
注視那些樹搖曳生姿，
我的腳會用力地踢地板，
我的頭會偏向一邊。
哪天它們嗓子好的時候，
哪天它們搖晃得甚至會
嚇走天上白雲的時候，
我將宣布要去某個地方，
我將作出不顧後果的選擇。
我將沒有太多的話要說，
但我將會離去。

The Sound of Trees

I wonder about the trees.

Why do we wish to bear

Forever the noise of these

More than another noise

So close to our dwelling place?

We suffer them by the day

Till we lose all measure of pace,

And fixity in our joys,

And acquire a listening air.

They are that that talks of going

But never gets away;

And that talks no less for knowing,

As it grows wiser and older,

That now it means to stay.

My feet tug at the floor

And my head sways to my shoulder

Sometimes when I watch trees sway,

Form the window or the door.

I shall set forth for somewhere,

I shall make the reckless choice

Some day when they are in voice

And tossing so as to scare

The white clouds over them on.

I shall have less to say,

But I shall be gone.

新罕布夏

NEW HAMPSHIRE

新罕布夏

我遇見位從南方來的女士，她說
（你不會相信她說的，但她說了）：
「我們家誰也沒做事兒，也沒有
任何東西可賣。」我並不認爲幹活兒
有多要緊。你可以替我全部做完。
我考慮過我必須自己做事情的時間。
至於有任何東西可賣，那正是
一個人、一個州或一個國家的恥辱。
我遇見位來自阿肯色州的旅遊者，
他誇耀說他的阿肯色州很美，
因爲那兒有鑽石和蘋果。「鑽石
和蘋果的數量有商業價值嗎？」
我警覺地問。「哦，是的。」他隨口
回答。當時是夜晚，在一列火車上。
我告訴他：「服務員已替你鋪好了床。」

我遇見過一位加利福尼亞人，
他老談加利福尼亞——說那個州
的天氣是如何得天獨厚，以致
死者均非自然死亡，於是不得不
成立些治安維持會爲墓地備貨，
同時也證明該州人性沒有扭曲。
我嘀咕道：「簡直就像斯蒂芬森
對北極喋喋不休一樣。這都是
因爲把氣候和市場連在了一起。」

New Hampshire

I met a lady from the South who said
(You won't believe she said it, but she said it):
"None of my family ever worked, or had
A thing to sell." I don't suppose the work
Much matters. You may work for all of me.
I've seen the time I've had to work myself.
The having anything to sell is what
Is the disgrace in man or state or nation
I met a traveler from Arkansas
Who boasted of his state as beautiful
For diamonds and apples. "Diamonds
And apples in commercial quantities?"
I asked him, on my guard. "Oh, yes," he answered,
Off his. The time was evening in the Pullman.
"I see the porter's made your bed," I told him.

    I met a Californian who would
    Talk California — a state so blessed,
    He said, in climate, none had ever died there
    A natural death, and Vigilance Committees
    Had had to organize to stock the graveyards
    And vindicate the state's humanity.
    "Just the way Stefansson runs on," I murmured,
    "About the British Arctic. That's what comes
    Of being in the market with a climate."

我遇見過一位另一個州的詩人，
一個滿腦子流動著靈感的狂熱者，
他憤怒地以流動著的靈感的名義，
但卻用劣等推銷術的最佳方式，
企圖讓我對沃爾斯特德法案
提出書面抗議（我想是用詩體）。
直到我要求來杯酒替他消消氣，
他才終於想到為我買杯酒喝。
這就是常說的有個主意可賣。
這種事絕不可能發生在新罕布夏。

在古老的新罕布夏，我碰上的
唯一一個被買賣玷污的人就是
一個在加利福尼亞做過買賣
剛剛羞愧滿面地回來的傢伙。
他修了幢君士坦丁壁式的房子，
房頂是折線式，塔樓尖是球形，
房子在樹林中，離火車站有十英里，
好像正如我們所說，他心中已
永遠放棄了再被人接納的希望。
一天日近黃昏的時候，我發現他
站在他那個開著門的牲口棚裡，
像個孤獨的演員在昏暗的舞台上；
當時光線暗得只能看清他的眼睛，
透過那昏暗的光線，我認出他是
我少年時代的朋友，實際上我倆
曾在去布萊頓的路上一起趕過牛。

I met a poet from another state,

A zealot full of fluid inspiration,

Who in the name of fluid inspiration,

But in the best style of bad salesmanship,

Angrily tried to make me write a protest

(In verse I think) against the Volstead Act.

He didn't even offer me a drink

Until I asked for one to steady him.

This is called having an idea to sell.

It never could have happened in New Hampshire.

The only person really soiled with trade

I ever stumbled on in old New Hampshire

Was someone who had just come back ashamed

From selling things in California.

He'd built a noble mansard roof with balls

On turrets, like Constantinople, deep

In woods some ten miles from a railroad station,

As if to put forever out of mind

The hope of being, as we say, received.

I found him standing at the close of day

Inside the threshold of his open barn,

Like a lone actor on a gloomy stage —

And recognized him, through the iron gray

In which his face was muffled to the eyes,

As an old boyhood friend, and once indeed

A drover with me on the road to Brighton.

他的農場不是農場，而是「庭園」，
與周圍簡陋的小木屋相比，他的
房子就像貿易站代理商的高樓。
他已是富翁，而我還是個窮光蛋，
因此我忍不住非常冒昧地問他：
這些年都在哪兒？在幹些什麼？
怎麼會有今天？（當然是說有錢）
他說他一直在舊金山銷售「破爛」。
啊，這真是要多可怕便有多可怕，
我倆恐怕進了墳墓也閉不上眼。
新罕布夏擁有的全都是標本，
就像陳列櫃裡的展品每樣就一件，
所以她當然不願意把它們賣掉。

她有一個總統（請管他叫錢包，
而且無論好歹都請對他充分利用。
他是你抨擊這個州的唯一機會）。
她有一個丹尼爾·韋伯斯特。他過去
或將來都永遠是丹尼爾·韋伯斯特。
她有造就他所必需的達特茅斯學院。
我說她古老，因為她有一個家庭
在開拓殖民地之前就在那裡定居，
甚至早在對北美的探險時代之前，
所以他們的主權要求無可爭議。
當約翰·史密斯沿蕭爾斯群島
岸邊航行時，他曾看見他們在
一個碼頭邊懸著腳捕魚，他高興
地看出他們不是印地安人，而是

His farm was "grounds," and not a farm at all;

His house among the local sheds and shanties

Rose like a factor's at a trading station.

And he was rich, and I was still a rascal.

I couldn't keep from asking impolitely,

Where had he been and what had he been doing?

How did he get so? (Rich was understood.)

In dealing in "old rags" in San Francisco.

Oh, it was terrible as well could be.

We both of us turned over in our graves.

Just specimens is all New Hampshire has,

One each of everything as in a showcase,

Which naturally she doesn't care to sell.

        She had one President. (Pronounce him Purse,

        And make the most of it for better or worse.

        He's your one chance to score against the state.)

        She had one Daniel Webster. He was all

        The Daniel Webster ever was or shall be.

        She had the Dartmouth needed to produce him.

        I call her old. She has one family

        Whose claim is good to being settled here

        Before the era of colonization,

        And before that of exploration even.

        John Smith remarked them as he coasted by,

        Dangling their legs and fishing off a wharf

        At the Isles of Shoals, and satisfied himself

        They weren't Red Indians but veritable

道道地地的白種人，白人的祖先，
就像那些爲亞當的子孫娶妻的祖先；
但雖說他們早在我們的歷史之前，
然而他們也許從來就不愚鈍。
當時他們在那兒已住了一百多年。
可惜他當時沒問既然碼頭已建成
他們還要做什麼，也沒問他們名字。
後來他們把他們的名字告訴了我——
一個今天在諾丁漢受人尊敬的名字。
至於他們除了捕魚還會忙些什麼——
且讓他們沒按清教徒的方式行事，
讓他們尚未開始爲成爲上流而戰，
人類也尚未開始去度公休假日。
對別人的事情不要探究得太深，
這才符合一個深刻的探究者的身份。

你肯定聽說過他，新罕布夏唯一
眞正的改革家，他要改變這世界，
以便這世界可以被兩類人接受，
一類是剛能自稱爲藝術家的藝術家，
也就是說在他們自己被接受之前；
另一類是剛逃出大學門的小伙子。
我禁不住認爲他們是應遵循的標準。

她還有一個我叫不出名字的人，
此人每年都要從費城來這兒，
帶著一大群品種都很珍稀的雞，
他想讓這些雞享受教育的好處，

Pre-primitives of the white race, dawn people,

Like those who furnished Adam's sons with wives;

However uninnocent they may have been

In being there so early in our history.

They'd been there then a hundred years or more.

Pity he didn't ask what they were up to

At that date with a wharf already built,

And take their name. They've since told me their name —

Today an honored one in Nottingham.

As for what they were up to more than fishing —

Suppose they weren't behaving Puritanly,

The hour had not yet struck for being good,

Mankind had not yet gone go on the Sabbatical.

It became an explorer of the deep

Not to explore too deep in others' business.

Did you but know of him, New Hampshire has

One real reformer who would change the world

So it would be accepted by two classes,

Artists the minute they set up as artists,

Before, that is, they are themselves accepted,

And boys the minute they get out of college.

I can't help thinking those are tests to go by.

And she has one I don't know what to call him,

Who comes from Philadelphia every year

With a great flock of chickens of rare breeds

He wants to give the educational

Advantages of growing almost wild

讓牠們在鷹和隼銳利的目光下
成長爲和野雞差不多的品種——
像喬叟筆下所描寫過的杜金雞，
或赫里克詩中出現過的蘇塞克斯雞。
她還有點黃金，新罕布夏黃金——
這你大概已聽說過。我有一座
前不久才到手的農場，在柏林；北邊，
農場上有座可開採黃金的礦山，
但黃金蘊藏量沒有商業開採價值，
因爲其數量只夠農場的擁有者
製作他們的訂婚戒指和結婚戒指。
人還能得到比這更清白的金子嗎？

最近從安多弗和迦南運回來
一些礦砂，我的一個孩子在篩選時
從中發現了一種綠柱石標本，
一種含有微量鐳的綠柱石標本。
我知道那點鐳的含量肯定是痕量，
絕對低於商業開採價值的標準；
但請相信，新罕布夏不會有
足夠的鐳或任何東西可以出售。
我說過，每樣東西都只是標本。
她有個女巫（老式的）住在科爾布魯克。
〔我遇見另一個女巫是最近在
波士頓吃一頓精緻的晚餐的時候。
當時有四個人，桌上有四支蠟燭。
那女巫很年輕，很漂亮（新式的），

Under the watchful eye of hawk and eagle —

Dorkings because they're spoken of by Chaucer,

Sussex because they're spoken of by Herrick.

She has a touch of gold. New Hampshire gold —

You may have heard of it. I had a farm

Offered me not long since up Berlin way

With a mine on it that was worked for gold;

But not gold in commercial quantities,

Just enough gold go make the engagement rings

And marriage rings of those who owned the farm.

What gold more innocent could one have asked for?

        One of my children ranging after rocks

        Lately brought home from Andover or Canaan

        A specimen of beryl with a trace

        Of radium. I know with radium

        The trace would have to be the merest trace

        To be below the threshold of commercial;

        But trust New Hampshire not to have enough

        Of radium or anything to sell.

        A specimen of everything, I said.

        She has one witch — old style. She lives in Colebrook.

        (The only other witch I ever met

        Was lately at a cut-glass dinner in Boston.

        There were four candles and four people present.

        The witch was young, and beautiful (new style),

思想也開放，她很坦率地懷疑
她閱讀鎖在信箱裡的信件的能力。
爲什麼金屬信箱時，那種能力更大，
而木製信箱時，那種能力就更小？
它使這個世界顯得如此神秘。
心靈研究學會也認識到了這點。
她的丈夫是個百萬富翁。我想
他擁有一些哈佛大學的股份。〕
過去在新罕布夏的塞勒姆鎮
有一家我們叫做「白血球」的公司，
他們的職責是在夜裡的每時每刻
只要聞到哪裡稍有點可疑的氣味，
便衝去讓某人坐「艾爾森船長的大車」。

每樣東西都是陳列櫃裡的樣品。
你也許會說她有足夠多的土地，
不止是樣品，但在這一點上會有
另一種東西來對她加以保護。
那就是其質量抵消了其數量。
她甚至沒有什麼農場可以出售。
我安家的那座在山裡的農場
與其說是買的，不如說是搶的。
那是在剛過完冬天的時候，我在
那農場主人的門口抓住他，並說：
「我要打發你走，我想要這農場。」
「你要打發我上哪兒去？上馬路？」
「我準備打發你去毗鄰那座農場。」

And open-minded. She was free to question

Her gift for reading letters locked in boxes.

Why was it so much greater when the boxes

Were metal than it was when they were wooden?

It made the world seem so mysterious.

The S'ciety for Psychical Research

Was cognizant. Her husband was worth millions.

I think he owned some shares in Harvard College.)

New Hampshire used to have at Salem

A company we called the White Corpuscles,

Whose duty was at any hour of night

To rush in sheets and fool's caps where they smelled

A thing the least bit doubtfully perscented

And give someone the Skipper Ireson's Ride.

One each of everything as in a showcase.

More than enough land for a specimen

You'll say she has, but there there enters in

Something else to protect her from herself.

There quality makes up for quantity.

Not even New Hampshire farms are much for sale.

The farm I made my home on in the mountains

I had to take by force rather than buy.

I caught the owner outdoors by himself

Raking up after winter, and I said,

"I'm going to put you off this farm: I want it."

"Where are you going to put me? In the road?"

"I'm going to put you on the farm next go it."

「那你自己幹嘛不要毗鄰的農場？」
「我喜歡這座。」這座的確更好。
蘋果？新罕布夏當然有蘋果，
但從不噴農藥，梗子和花萼裡
都沒有絲毫的硫酸鹽或砷酸鉛，
所以除了榨果汁沒什麼別的用處。
不修枝的葡萄像套馬繩一樣猛竄，
竄上白樺樹，叫人伸手也摘不著。
一個出產貴金屬和寶石的州
還出產──作品；而也許只有
這些數量多質量好的文學珍品
令這位出產者操心，操心這些
作品種類的配置。你可知道，
由於考慮到市場，那兒出產
的詩比其他體裁的作品都多？

怪不得有些時候詩人都不得不
顯得比生意人還更像生意人。
他們的產品也非常難以處理。
她是合眾國最好的兩個州之一。
另一個州是佛蒙特。很久以來
它們就像在許多三月裡掛上一棵
槭樹的兩只吊桶，它們又像兩根
楔形球棒互相用其粗端挨著細端，
而它們挨在一起的形狀好像是說
心靈之堅強與體魄之健壯應該相襯，
你粗的地方我細，你細的地方我粗。

"Why won't the farm next to it do for you?"

"I like this better." It was really better.

Apples? New Hampshire has them, but unsprayed,

With no suspicion in stem end or blossom end

Of vitriol or arsenate of lead,

And so not good for anything but cider.

Her unpruned grapes are flung like lariats

Far up the birches out of reach of man.

A state producing precious metals, stones,

And — writing; none of these except perhaps

The precious literature in quantity

Or quality to worry the producer

About disposing of it. Do you know,

Considering the market, there are more

Poems produced than any other thing?

No wonder poets sometimes have to seem

So much more businesslike than businessmen.

Their wares are so much harder to get rid of.

She's one of the two best states in the Union.

Vermont's the other. And the two have been

Yokefellows in the sap yoke from of old

In many Marches. And they lie like wedges,

Thick end to thin end and thin end to thick end,

And are a figure of the way the strong

Of mind and strong of arm should fit together,

One thick where one is thin and vice versa.

在靠近加拿大的一個鮭魚孵化場
新罕布夏養育了康乃迪克河，
但很快就把河的一半分給了佛蒙特。
這兩個州都有些小得可笑的城鎮——
洛斯特內申、邦格、馬迪布、
波普林、斯蒂爾科勒（這麼叫並非
因那個地方整天靜悄悄的，也不是
因爲它還有一種威士忌——而是
因爲它當初被規劃成一座城市，
可如今仍只是樹林中的荒僻之處）。
我還記得這些地名中的一個
曾出現在銀幕上的畫面之間，
那是弗朗科尼亞一個選舉日之夜，
當共和黨已得到它該得的全部選票，
而民主黨正迫切需要最後的支持，

這時伊斯頓鎮倒向民主黨，結果
威爾遜勝了休斯。於是人人
都哈哈大笑，大地方嘲笑小地方。
紐約（五百萬人）嘲笑曼徹斯特，
曼徹斯特（六萬或七萬人）嘲笑
利特爾頓，利特爾頓（四千人）笑
弗朗科尼亞，弗朗科尼亞（七百人）
笑——我擔心它那晚笑的就是——
伊斯頓。可伊斯頓該嘲笑哪兒呢？
像那個女演員驚呼的：「哦，天哪？」
那兒還有邦格，邦格有些鎮區，
所有鎮區都有鎮名但沒有人口。

New Hampshire raises the Connecticut

In a trout hatchery near Canada.

But soon divides the river with Vermont.

Both are delightful states for their absurdly

Small towns — Lost Nation, Bungey, Muddy Boo,

Poplin, Still Corners (so called not because

The place is silent all day long, nor yet

Because it boasts a whisky still — because

It set out once to be a city and still

Is only corners, crossroads in a wood).

And I remember one whose name appeared

Between the pictures on a movie screen

Election night once in Franconia,

When everything had gone Republican

And Democrats were sore in need of comfort:

> Easton goes Democratic, Wilson
>
> Hughes 2. And everybody to the saddest
>
> Laughed the loud laugh the big laugh at the little.
>
> New York (five million) laughs at Manchester,
>
> Manchester (sixty or seventy thousand) laughs
>
> At Littleton (four thousand), Littleton
>
> Laughs at Franconia (seven hundred), and
>
> Franconia laughs, I fear — did laugh that night —
>
> At Easton. What has Easton left to laugh at,
>
> And like the actress exclaim "Oh. My God" at?
>
> There's Bungey; and for Bungey there are towns,
>
> Whole townships named but without population.

關於新罕布夏我能說的一切
幾乎都同樣適合於佛蒙特州，
除了這兩個州的山勢各不相同。
佛蒙特的格林山脈筆直地伸延，
新罕布夏的懷特山脈則圍成一圈。
我曾多次談起新罕布夏的山。
但此時此刻我該說些什麼呢？
我的話題在這兒變得令人難堪。
愛默生說：「創造了新罕布夏的
上帝也譏笑那片高地上小小的人。」
另一位麻塞諸塞州的詩人則說：
「我再也不去新罕布夏過夏天。
我已放棄了在都柏林的消暑別墅。」

但當我問她新罕布夏有啥毛病時，
她回答說她沒法忍受那地方的人，
小小的人（這是麻塞諸塞人的說法）。
而當我問她那地方的人有啥毛病時，
她說：「到你自己的書中去找答案。」
作為幾本書的作者，我最好說明
那幾本書是從整體上批評這個世界。
如果認為它們批評的是某個州
或某個國家，那就曲解了我的本意。
我是人們所謂的特別敏感的人，
要不然就是環境保護主義者。
我不願讓自己去適應從熱到冷或
從冷到熱、從濕到乾或從乾到濕、
從窮到富或從富到窮的變化。

Anything I can say about New Hampshire

Will serve almost as well about Vermont,

Excepting that they differ in their mountains.

The Vermont mountains stretch extended straight;

New Hampshire mountains curl up in a coil.

I had been coming to New Hampshire mountains.

And here I am and what am I to say?

Here first my theme becomes embarrassing.

Emerson said, "The God who made New Hampshire

Taunted the lofty land with little men."

Another Massachusetts poet said,

"I go no more to summer in New Hampshire.

I've given up my summer place in Dublin."

But when I asked to know what ailed New Hampshire,

She said she couldn't stand the people in it,

The little men (it's Massachusetts speaking).

And when I asked to know what ailed the people,

She said, "Go read your own books and find out."

I may as well confess myself the author

Of several books against the world in general.

To take them as against a special state

Or even nation's to restrict my meaning.

I'm what is called a sensibilitist,

Or otherwise an environmentalist.

I refuse to adapt myself a mite

To any change from hot to cold, from wet

To dry, from poor to rich, or back again.

我甘願從發生在我周圍的每一件
事物中忍受我非忍受不可的痛苦。
換句話說，我知道我在什麼地方，
既然身為我已經是的詩人作家，
我就不會缺少使我保持清醒的痛苦。
基特‧馬洛教會我如何做祈禱：
「哪怕這是地獄，我也不會出去。」
我抱怨薩摩亞、俄羅斯和愛爾蘭，
也抱怨英格蘭、法蘭西和義大利。
我在新罕布夏寫出我的作品
並不證明它們只針對新罕布夏。
多年前我在夜裡離開麻塞諸塞，
當時我為何沒去康乃迪克或羅德島，
為何沒去紐約州或佛蒙特，而偏偏
到了新罕布夏？那原因只是

如果我住在新罕布夏，我就有
最近的邊界線供我逃避時跨越。
當時我旅行包裡並沒有幻想，並不
以為那裡的人會比我留在身後的
那些人更好。我以為他們不會也
不可能更好。然而他們確實更好。
我敢說在麻塞諸塞不會有這種朋友：
如溫德姆的霍爾、阿特金森的蓋伊、
雷蒙德的（現在科羅拉多）巴特利特、
德里的哈里斯和貝塞爾漢姆的林奇。

I make a virtue of my suffering

From nearly everything that goes on round me.

In other words, I know wherever I am,

Being the creature of literature I am,

I shall not lack for pain to keep me awake.

Kit Marlowe taught me how to say my prayers:

"Why, this is Hell, nor am I out of it."

Samoa, Russia, Ireland I complain of,

No less than England, France, and Italy.

Because I wrote my novels in New Hampshire

Is no proof that I aimed them at New Hampshire.

When I left Massachusetts years ago

Between two days, the reason why I sought

New Hampshire, not Connecticut,

Rhode Island, New York, or Vermont was this:

Where I was living then, New Hampshire offered

The nearest boundary to escape across.

I hadn't an illusion in my handbag

About the people being better there

Than those I left behind. I thought they weren't.

I thought they couldn't be. And yet they were.

I'd sure had no such friends in Massachusetts

As Hall of Windham, Gay of Atkinson,

Bartlett of Raymond (now of Colorado),

Harris of Derry, and Lynch of Bethlehem.

麻塞諸塞州榮耀的詩人們似乎
是想要改造新罕布夏的居民。
他們譏笑這高高山上有小小的人。
關於這裡的人我不知該說什麼。
為了藝術的緣故，我幾乎可以
希望他們過得更糟而不是更好。
要是美國人的生活總是安居樂業，
我們怎麼能寫出那種俄國小說呢？
迄今為止，我們的文學作品能發出
的唯一呻吟均來自小小的不舒服。
我們因沒有理由感到痛苦悲傷，
而獲得我們能獲得的一點悲苦。
一方面除了幸運舒適什麼也沒有，
一方面又想產生杜斯妥也夫斯基，
這使得美國小說家協會憂心忡忡。

不過這不是痛苦，只是憂鬱症，
如今新政權統治下的俄國自己
就這麼認為，於是憂鬱被禁止。
如果這對俄國沒事，那就坦然地
這麼說，或坦然地站到牆根被人
槍斃。現在不是波利安娜就是死亡。
所以這就是我們聽說的新自由，
而且合情合理。在無溫飽之虞
的康樂中，任何國家都營造不出
既合情合理又椎心泣血的文學。
要表現我們美國人的智力水平
還得靠我們沃倫鎮的一個農夫，

The glorious bards of Massachusetts seem

To want to make New Hampshire people over.

They taunt the lofty land with little men.

I don't know what to say about the people.

For art's sake one could almost wish them worse

Rather than better. How are we to write

The Russian novel in America

As long as life goes so unterribly?

There is the pinch from which our only outcry

In literature to date is heard to come.

We get what little misery we can

Out of not having cause for misery.

It makes the guild of novel writers sick

To be expected to be Dostoievskis

On nothing worse than too much luck and comfort.

This is not sorrow, though; it's just the vapors,

And recognized as such in Russia itself

Under the new regime, and so forbidden.

If well it is with Russia, then feel free

To say so or be stood against the wall

And shot. It's Pollyanna now or death.

This, then, is the new freedom we hear tell of;

And very sensible. No state can build

A literature that shall at once be sound

And sad on a foundation of well-being.

To show the level of intelligence

Among us: it was just a Warren farmer

有一天在路上，他的馬突然停在
我這個與他素不相識的陌生人跟前，
當時因為尷尬而沒有合適的話説，
於是他對我説出了下面這番話：
「你聽見穆西勞克山上的獵狗叫嗎？
牠們倒使我想起了我們聽見過的
反對觀念守舊者的抗議吶喊聲，
但直到拜倫退出政壇參加合唱隊[
我才算眞正明白了抗議的目的。
那些守舊派所面臨的問題好像是
一個名叫約翰‧L‧達爾文的人。」
「走吧。」我對他説，他對他的馬説。

我認識一個經營農場失敗的人，
他燒掉自家農舍騙取火災保險金，
然後他用那筆錢買了架天文望遠鏡]
以滿足他終身的好奇心——關於
我們在無垠宇宙中所處的位置。
多麼關心那無邊無際的冥冥世界！
如果我必須選擇該抬高什麼——
是抬高人還是抬高已算高的山脈，
我將抬高那已經算高的山脈。
我發現新罕布夏唯一不足的
就是她的山峰還不夠高大巍峨。
我並非歷來如此，是後來發現的。
唉，我怎麼會達到一個令我悲哀
的高度，竟能居高臨下睥睨群山？

Whose horse had pulled him short up in the road

By me, a stranger. This is what he said,

From nothing but embarrassment and want

Of anything more sociable to say:

"You hear those hound dogs sing on Moosilauke?

Well, they remind me of the hue and cry

We've heard against the Mid-Victorians

And never rightly understood till Bryan

Retired from politics and joined the chorus.

The matter with the Mid-Victorians

Seems to have been a man named John L. Darwin."

"Go'long," I said to him, he to his horse.

        I knew a man who failing as a farmer

        Burned down his farmhouse for the fire insurance,

        And spent the proceeds on a telescope

        To satisfy a lifelong curiosity

        About our place among the infinities.

        And how was that for otherworldliness?

        If I must choose which I would elevate —

        The people or the already lofty mountains,

        I'd elevate the already lofty mountains.

        The only fault I find with old New Hampshire

        Is that her mountains aren't quite high enough.

        I was not always so; I've come to be so.

        How, to my sorrow, how have I attained

        A height from which to look down critical

        On mountains? What has given me assurance

是什麼使我如此自信，竟敢說什麼
樣的高度才適合新罕布夏的山
或任何山？難道那是某種力量，
某種我覺得像地震震撼我全身、
能把群山舉得和星星一般高的力量？
難道那是登過阿爾卑斯山的經歷？
或難道是因見過林肯、拉斐特峰
和自由峰這些可憐的山峰後面
那些巍巍岩岩的雲嶺雲峰，並
一時間以為它們是實實在在的山峰？
或難道是因這樣一種感覺：覺得
泉噴多高才能與水池形成比例？
不，使我理性的不滿達到頂點的
不是這些，而是一次不幸的意外，

那就是我曾偶然見到過一幅地圖，
那幅早期的地圖把新罕布夏
山峰的實際高度多標了一倍——
用一萬英尺代替了五千英尺——
這說明一次意外會使人多麼傷心。
從此我不再覺得五千英尺夠高。
雖說對改造這個世界上的人們
我從不曾有過令人滿意的想法，
但對改造山我卻滿腦子奇思異想，
我禁不住日夜不停地設想規劃
我該把那些夏日雪峰升得多高
才能觸到天空，並從天上的星星
把寒冷的氣流引到夜幕籠罩的
山谷間使露珠兒凍成滿谷繁星。

To say what height becomes New Hampshire mountains,

Or any mountains? Can it be some strength

I feel, as of an earthquake in my back,

To heave them higher to the morning star?

Can it be foreign travel in the Alps?

Or having seen and credited a moment

The solid molding of vast peaks of cloud

Behind the pitiful reality

Of Lincoln, Lafayette, and Liberty?

Or some such sense as says how high shall jet

The fountain in proportion to the basin?

No, none of these has raised me to my throne

Of intellectual dissatisfaction,

But the sad accident of having seen

        Our actual mountains given in a map

        Of early times as twice the height they are —

        Ten thousand feet instead of only five —

        Which shows how sad an accident may be.

        Five thousand is no longer high enough.

        Whereas I never had a good idea

        About improving people in the world,

        Here I am overfertile in suggestion,

        And cannot rest from planning day or night

        How high I'd thrust the peaks in summer snow

        To tap the upper sky and draw a flow

        Of frosty night air on the vale below

        Down from the stars to freeze the dew as starry.

我越是敏感，我似乎就越希望
我的山不尋常；就像那個瘦小結實
的伐木隊長希望河上的木材堵塞。
在打開水閘讓木材開始漂動之後，
他拼命要躲開一根像一條手臂
伸向天穹要砸斷他脊梁的原木，
於是他東避西閃，左蹦右跳，
要從咆哮的河水亂竄的原木中逃命；
他在彎曲的河道上叫嚷的無疑
就是他漂近時我們所聽清的話：
「難道她不是一個理想的混血兒？
你完全可以說她就是個理想。」
儘管她的山峰是稍稍矮了一點，
但她的人民的藝術水平卻不低，
她仍是新罕布夏，一個寧靜的州。

最近與紐約一個叫亞歷克的人聊天，
談到了那個假陽具崇拜的新學派，
談話中我發現自己陷入了一種困境：
我不得不作出一個可謂滑稽的選擇。
「請你選擇是故作正經還是令人作嘔，
令人作嘔地在公眾懷裡啼哭嘔吐。」
「但為了那些山我無需作任何選擇。」
「要是你不得不選呢，你選什麼？」
我不會當個恐懼自然的正人君子。
我認識一個人，他曾帶著雙刃斧
獨自一人朝一片小樹林走去；

The more the sensibilitist I am

The more I seem to want my mountains wild;

The way the wiry gang-boss liked the logjam.

After he'd picked the lock and got it started,

He dodged a log that lifted like an arm

Against the sky to break his back for him,

Then came in dancing, skipping with his life

Across the roar and chaos, and the words

We saw him say along the zigzag journey

Were doubtless as the words we heard him say

On coming nearer: "Wasn't she an i-deal

Son-of-a-bitch? You bet she was an i-deal."

For all her mountains fall a little short,

Her people not quite short enough for Art,

She's still New Hampshire, a most restful state.

Lately in converse with a New York alec

About the new school of the pseudo-phallic,

I found myself in a close corner where

I had to make an almost funny choice.

"Choose you which you will be — a prude, or puke,

Mewling and puking in the public arms."

"Me for the hills where I don't have to choose."

"But if you had to choose, which would you be?"

I wouldn't be a prude afraid of nature.

I know a man who took a double ax

And went alone against a grove of trees;

但他失去了勇氣，他丟下斧子去找
藏身處，口中念著阿諾德的詩句：
「『自然是殘酷的，人厭惡鮮血』；
即使我不流血已有夠多的人流血。
記住勃蘭森林！那森林會移動！」
他對那種移動有一種特別的恐懼，
那種恐懼本身表現爲樹木恐懼症。
他說最合適的樹早已經進了
鋸木場，並被加工成爲薄木板。
由於某種可能的用途，他十分清楚
那條人止步而自然開始的分界線，
而且除了在夢中從不跨越那條線。
他站在分界線安全的一邊說話；

而這是十足的馬修·阿諾德崇拜，
崇拜那個承認自己是「歷經坎坷
挫折的流浪漢」的人，崇拜那個
「沮喪地在理智的王位就坐」的人。
他贊同這些臨時搭建的祭壇，
如今這種祭壇在樹林中比比皆是，
就像當初亞哈斯爲拜異教邪神
公開在林間綠樹下建起的祭壇。
我幾乎每走一英里就會碰上一座：
一塊黑石碑加一根雨淋過的灰木椿。
即使爲了安全而說這些樹林是上帝
最初的殿堂，那也幾乎與亞哈斯同罪。
神聖之物當然都是由雙手創造。
但卻沒有人問一問什麼是神聖，

But his heart failing him, he dropped the ax

And ran for shelter quoting Matthew Arnold:

"'Nature is cruel, man is sick of blood';

There's been enough shed without shedding mine.

Remember Birnam Wood! The wood's in flux!"

He had a special terror of the flux

That showed itself in dendrophobia.

The only decent tree had been to mill

And educated into boards, he said.

He knew too well for any earthly use

The line where man leaves off and nature starts,

And never overstepped it save in dreams.

He stood on the safe side of the line talking —

       Which is sheer Matthew Arnoldism,

       The cult of one who owned himself "a foiled

       Circuitous wanderer," and "took dejectedly

       His seat upon the intellectual throne" —

       Agreed in frowning on these improvised

       Altars the woods are full of nowadays,

       Again as in the days when Ahaz sinned

       By worship under green trees in the open.

       Scarcely a mile but that I come on one,

       A black-cheeked stone and stick of rain-washed charcoal.

       Even to say the groves were God's first temples

       Comes too near to Ahaz' sin for safety.

       Nothing not built with hands of course is sacred.

       But here is not a question of what's sacred;

或問問該面對什麼，或逃避什麼。
我不願做一個逃避自然的正人君子。
我也不會選擇當個令人作嘔的人，
因那種人從不在乎他在人群中幹什麼，
而當他什麼也做不了時，他會依靠其
口舌，聲嘶力竭地使他的語言
勝於行為，而且有時還果真奏效。
這似乎是時代所主張的狹隘選擇。
比如我說當一名好希臘人怎麼樣？
他們會告訴我今年不開希臘語課。
「得啦，可這不是在選擇——你

　　到底選故作正經還是令人作嘔？」
好吧，如果我不得不作出一種選擇，
我選擇當個平凡的新罕布夏農民，
來點現金收入，比方說一千美元
（比方說錢來自紐約的一個出版商）。
作出一個決定會使人感到寧靜。
想到新罕布夏會使人感到寧靜。
此時此刻我正住在佛蒙特州。

Rather of what to face or run away from.

I'd hate to be a runaway from nature.

And neither would I choose to be a puke

Who cares not what he does in company,

And when he can't do anything, falls back

On words, and tries his worst to make words speak

Louder than actions, and sometimes achieves it.

It seems a narrow choice the age insists on.

How about being a good Greek, for instance?

That course, they tell me, isn't offered this year.

"Come. but this isn't choosing — puke or prude?"

Well, if I have to choose one or the other.

I choose to be a plain New Hampshire farmer

With an income in cash of, say, a thousand

(From, say, a publisher in New York City).

It's restful to arrive at a decision,

And restful just to think about New Hampshire.

At present I am living in Vermont.

星星切割器

「你知道獵戶座總是從天邊升起。
先是一條腿抬過我們的山巒屏障,
接著舉手探腦,然後它會看見
我正在屋外邊點著燈邊忙,
做某件我本該在白天幹完的活兒。
若是在地面結冰之後,則是做
我本該在冰凍之前就做完的事情,
一陣風會把幾片枯葉颳向我燻黑
的燈罩,像是取笑我幹活的架勢,
不然就是取笑獵戶座令我著迷。

我倒想問問,難道一個人無權
考慮這些冥冥中注定的影響力?」
布拉德·麥克勞林總是這麼隨便地
把星星和他混亂的農事攪在一起,
直到他亂糟糟的農場難以維持,
他燒掉自家房屋騙取火災保險金,
並用那筆錢買了台天文望遠鏡
以滿足他的好奇心──關於
我們在無垠宇宙中所處的位置。
「你要那該死的玩意兒幹什麼呢?」
我事前曾對他說。「你千萬別要!」

The Star-Splitter

"Yow know Orion always comes up sideways.

Throwing a leg up over our fence of mountains,

And rising on his hands, he looks in on me

Busy outdoors by lantern-light with something

I should have done by daylight, and indeed,

After the ground is frozen, I should have done

Before it froze, and a gust flings a handful

Of waste leaves at my smoky lantern chimney

To make fun of my way of doing things,

Or else fun of Orion's having caught me.

Has a man, I should like to ask, no rights

These forces are obliged to pay respect to?"

So Brad McLaughlin mingled reckless talk

Of heavenly stars with hugger-mugger farming,

Till having failed at hugger-mugger farming

He burned his house down for the fire insurance

And spent the proceeds on a telescope

To satisfy a lifelong curiosity

About our place among the infmities.

"What do you want with one of those blame things?"

I asked him well beforehand. "Don't you get one!"

「別罵它該死。」他當時回答說：
「只要不是人類戰爭使用的武器，
任何東西都不該受到這樣的詛咒。
要是我能賣掉農場我一定買一台。」
在一個他要耕地就得清理亂石、
只能在搬不開的岩石間耕種的地方，
農場很難賣掉；所以他不是花了
許多年來賣農場而最終沒賣出去，
而是燒掉那房子騙了筆火災保險金，
然後用那筆錢買了天文望遠鏡。
有好幾個人都曾聽他說過：
「人世間最有趣的事就是觀看，
而能讓我們看得最遠的就是天文
望遠鏡。在我看來，每個鎮區
都該有人覺得一個鎮應該有一台。
而利特爾頓的這人最好就是我。」
有過這種信口開河，他後來燒掉
房子騙得保險金也就不足為奇。

那天全鎮到處都是輕蔑的冷笑聲，
好讓他知道我們絲毫沒被他矇住，
他就等著吧──我們明天再關照他。
可第二天一早醒來，我們首先想到
要是對每個人所犯下的小小過失
我們都毫不留情地逐一清算，
要不了多久我們都會形單影隻，

"Don't call it blamed; there isn't anything

More blameless in the sense of being less

A weapon in our human fight," he said.

"I'll have one if I sell my farm to buy it."

There where he moved the rocks to plow the ground

And plowed between the rocks he couldn't move,

Few farms changed hands; so rather than spend years

Trying to sell his farm and then not selling,

He burned his house down for the fire insurance

And bought the telescope with what it came to.

He had been heard to say by several:

"The best thing that we're put here for's to see;

The strongest thing that's given us to see with's

A telescope. Someone in every town

Seems to me owes it to the town to keep one.

In Littleton it may as well be me."

After such loose talk it was no surprise

When he did what he did and burned his house down.

Mean laughter went about the town that day

To let him know we weren't the least imposed on,

And he could wait — we'd see to him tomorrow.

But the first thing next morning we reflected

If one by one we counted people out

For the least sin, it wouldn't take us long

To get so we had no one left to live with.

因爲要互相交往就得互相寬恕。
比如那個經常偷我們東西的小偷，
我們也沒說不讓他參加教堂晚餐會；
而只是找他討回我們被盜之物，
他也總是爽快地將其物歸原主，
只要東西沒被吃掉、穿壞或丟棄。
所以爲台望遠鏡對布拉德過分嚴厲
實在沒道理。畢竟人家已上了年紀，
不可能收到這樣一份聖誕節禮物，
他只能用他所知道的最好辦法
替自己找尋一台。而我們也只能說
他認爲一件怪事被矇混過去。
有人徒然爲那幢房屋感到可惜，

那是一幢年代久遠的原木房子，
但房子沒有知覺，它不會感覺到
任何事情。而假設它眞有感覺，
爲什麼不把它看成一種祭品？
看成一種老式火壇上的祭品，
而不是新式的虧本拍賣的商品。
一根火柴劃掉了房子，也劃掉了
一座農場，於是布拉德不得不
改行到康科德鐵路公司謀生，
在一個車站當上一名售票員，
當他不賣票的時候他就開始瞎忙，
當然不像是在農場上時忙著農事，
而是忙著觀看天上的各種星星，
各種顏色，從紅色到綠色的天體。

For to be social is to be forgiving.

Our thief, the one who does our stealing from us,

We don't cut off from coming to church suppers,

But what we miss we go to him and ask for.

He promptly gives it back, that is if still

Uneaten, unworn out, or undisposed of.

It wouldn't do to be too hard on Brad

About his telescope. Beyond the age

Of being given one for Christmas gift,

He had to take the best way he knew how

To find himself in one. Well, all we said was

He took a strange thing to be roguish over.

Some sympathy was wasted on the house.

A good old-timer dating back along;

But a house isn't sentient; the house

Didn't feel anything. And if it did,

Why not regard it as a sacrifice,

And an old-fashioned sacrifice by fire,

Instead of a new-fashioned one at auction?

Out of a house and so out of a farm

At one stroke (of a match), Brad had to turn

To earn a living on the Concord railroad,

As under-ticket-agent at a station

Where his job, when he wasn't selling tickets,

Was setting out, up track and down, not plants

As on a farm, but planets, evening stars

That varied in their hue from red to green.

他花六百美元買了台挺棒的望遠鏡。
他的新工作使他有閒暇觀看星星。
他經常邀請我去他的住處，透過
內襯黑色天鵝絨的黃銅製的鏡筒
看某顆星星在鏡筒的另一端哆嗦。
我還記得一個滿天碎雲的夜晚，
腳下的積雪融化成水又凍結成冰，
冰在風中繼續融化成泥濘。
布拉德和我一起搬出那台望遠鏡，
讓它三腳叉開，我們則又開雙腿，
並把我們的心思對準它對準的方向，
天亮之前我倆一直悠閒地站著，
談了一些我倆從不曾談過的事情。
那台望遠鏡被命名為星星切割器，

因為它唯一的功能就是把一顆
星星一分為二或一分為三，就像
你用一根指頭從中一擊，把掌中
的一滴水銀分成兩滴或三滴。
若真有星星切割器，它便是之一，
而如果切割星星可以和劈木柴
相提並論，那它應該有點用處。
我們光是看，搞不清自己在哪兒？
我們比以前更清楚我們在哪兒嗎？
今夜它又是怎樣架在夜空和那位
有一個燻黑了的燈罩的人之間？
它的架設方式和以前有什麼不同？

He got a good glass for six hundred dollars.

His new job gave him leisure for stargazing.

Often he bid me come and have a look

Up the brass barrel, velvet black inside,

At a star quaking in the other end.

I recollect a night of broken clouds

And underfoot snow melted down to ice,

And melting further in the wind to mud.

Bradford and I had out the telescope.

We spread our two legs as we spread its three,

Pointed our thoughts the way we pointed it,

And standing at our leisure till the day broke,

Said some of the best things we ever said.

That telescope was christened the Star-Splitter,

Because it didn't do a thing but split

A star in two or three, the way you split

A globule of quicksilver in your hand

With one stroke of your finger in the middle.

It's a star-splitter if there ever was one,

And ought to do some good if splitting stars

'Sa thing to be compared with splitting wood.

We've looked and looked, but after all where are we?

Do we know any better where we are,

And how it stands between the night tonight

And a man with a smoky lantern chimney?

How different from the way it ever stood?

楓樹

她的老師肯定地說那無疑是梅布爾，
這使梅普爾第一次留心自己的名字。
她問父親，父親告訴她「是梅普爾——
梅普爾沒錯。」
　　　　　　「但老師對全校說
沒這個名字。」
　　　　「關於名字，老師不比
當父親的知道得多，你去告訴她。
告訴她你的名字就拼成 M-A-P-L-E。
你問她知不知道有一種楓樹。
好吧，你就是用楓樹取名的。
是你媽給你取的名。你可知道
你和她只在樓上房間裡見過一面，
當時你正呱呱墜地來到這世上，
而她則撒手人寰去另一個世界。
所以你對她不可能有什麼記憶。
她走之前曾久久地把你凝視。
她用指頭摁你的臉蛋，你的酒窩
想必就是她摁的，她說『楓樹』，
我重覆了一遍，她點點頭說：『對，
作她的名字。』所以這名肯定沒錯。
我不知她替你取這名有何含義，
但這名似乎是她的遺言，想要你
做個好姑娘——像棵美麗的楓樹。
如何像棵楓樹則需要我們去猜，

Maple

Her teacher's certainty it must be Mabel
Made Maple first take notice of her name.
She asked her father and he told her, "Maple —
Maple is right."
　　　　"But teacher told the school
There's no such name."
　　　　　"Teachers don't know as much
As fathers about children, you tell teacher.
You tell her that it's M-A-P-L-E.
You ask her if she knows a maple tree.
Well, you were named after a maple tree.
Your mother named you. You and she just saw
Each other in passing in the room upstairs,

　　　　One coming this way into life, and one
　　　　Going the other out of life — you know?
　　　　So you can't have much recollection of her.
　　　　She had been having a long look at you.
　　　　She put her finger in your cheek so hard
　　　　It must have made your dimple there, and said,
　　　　'Maple.' said it too: 'Yes, for her name.'
　　　　She nodded. So we're sure there's no mistake.
　　　　I don't know what she wanted it to mean,
　　　　But it seems like some word she left to bid you
　　　　Be a good girl — be like a maple tree.
　　　　How like a maple tree's for us to guess.

或有時候需要一個小姑娘去猜,
但不是現在,我現在不想傷腦筋。
以後我會慢慢告訴你我知道的一切,
關於不同的樹,還有關於你母親
的每件事,那也許會對你有用。」
把這種謎播入孩子心中極其危險,
幸好她當時探究自己的名字,
只是想第二天能反駁她的老師,
用父親的話把那位老師鎮住。
任何進一步的解釋對她都是白費,
或他曾試圖這麼認為以避免出錯。
她會忘掉這件事,她幾乎也忘了。

他播下的種子和她一起久久沉睡,
在她蒙昧的歲月裡幾乎已死去,
以致當它復甦並生根發芽開花,
花與她父親播下的種子迥然有異。
有一天它隱隱約約地突然閃過,
當時她正在鏡子前念自己的名字,
它慢慢地閃過她低垂的眼前,
使之與她探求的方向完全一致。
她的名字是怎麼回事?它怪就怪在
有太多的意義。其他名字,如
卡羅爾、萊斯利、伊爾瑪和瑪喬麗
沒什麼含義。羅斯可以有個意思,
但實際上沒有。(她認識一個羅斯。)
正是她名字與眾不同之處,使人人都
注意到它──而且對她加以注意。
(他們要麼注意它,要麼拼錯它。)

Or for a little girl to guess sometime.

Not now — at least I shouldn't try too hard now.

By and by I will tell you all I know

About the different trees, and something, too,

About your mother that perhaps may help."

Dangerous self-arousing words to sow.

Luckily all she wanted of her name then

Was to rebuke her teacher with it next day,

And give the teacher a scare as from her father.

Anything further had been wasted on her,

Or so he tried to think to avoid blame.

She would forget it. She all but forgot it.

What he sowed with her slept so long a sleep,

And came so near death in the dark of years,

That when it woke and came to life again

The flower was different from the parent seed.

It came back vaguely at the glass one day,

As she stood saying her name over aloud,

Striking it gently across her lowered eyes

To make it go well with the way she looked.

What was it about her name? Its strangeness lay

In having too much meaning. Other names,

As Lesley, Carol, Irma, Marjorie,

Signified nothing. Rose could have a meaning,

But hadn't as it went . (She knew a Rose.)

This difference from other names it was

Made people notice it — and notice her.

(They either noticed it, or got it wrong.)

她的問題是要發現擁有此名的姑娘
應該怎樣穿著，應該有何舉止。
要是她對母親有個概念該有多好！
她想像中的母親既可愛又優雅。
這裡就是她母親曾經度過童年的家：
這幢房子的正面是高高的一層樓，
朝向公路的這邊則有三層。（這種
結構造出了一個陽光充足的地下室。）
她母親的臥室現在是她父親的，
她在那兒能見到母親褪色的照片。
有一次她在大開本聖經中發現了
一片用做書籤的楓葉。她認為
楓葉肯定是為她留的。於是她

逐字逐句讀了楓葉隔開的那兩頁書，
彷彿每個字都是母親留給她的話。
但她合上書時忘了把楓葉放回，
結果再也找不到她讀過的兩頁。
不過她確信那兩頁書裡沒說什麼。
像每個人多少都要到外面去尋找
自我一樣，她也開始尋找自我。
雖說她的自我追尋斷斷續續，但
可能仍然使她讀了些書，想了些
問題，並受了一點城市教育。
她學會了速記，不管速記與她的
自我追尋有什麼相干──有時候
她也對此感到納悶，直到她發現
自己在一個因為叫梅普爾，

Her problem was to find out what it asked

In dress or manner of the girl who bore it.

If she could form some notion of her mother —

What she had thought was lovely, and what good.

This was her mother's childhood home;

The house one story high in front, three stories

On the end it presented to the road.

(The arrangement made a pleasant sunny cellar.)

Her mother's bedroom was her father's still,

Where she could watch her mother's picture fading.

Once she found for a bookmark in the Bible

A maple leaf she thought must have been laid

In wait for her there. She read every word

     Of the two pages it was pressed between,

     As if it was her mother speaking to her.

     But forgot to put the leaf back in closing

     And lost the place never to read again.

     She was sure, though, there had been nothing in it.

     So she looked for herself, as everyone

     Looks for himself, more or less outwardly.

     And her self-seeking, fitful though it was,

     May still have been what led her on to read,

     And think a little, and get some city schooling.

     She learned shorthand, whatever shorthand may

     Have had to do with it — she sometimes wondered.

     So, till she found herself in a strange place

     For the name Maple to have brought her to,

而吸引她前去的陌生地方，
正在記錄某人的口授，
停頓之間她抬起雙眼從十九層樓的
一扇窗戶朝外觀看一只不像艇的
飛艇正費力地前進，
越過這座人類建造的最高的城市，
一種隱約的轟鳴聲響在那條河上。
這時有人用那麼自然的聲調說話，
以致她差點把那句話寫在速記本上，
「你知道嗎，你讓我想起一棵樹——
一棵楓樹？」

　　　　　「就因爲我叫梅普爾？」
「你不叫梅普爾？我還以爲是梅布爾哩。」
「你肯定是聽辦公室的人叫我梅布爾。
我只能由他們想怎麼叫就怎麼叫。」

他倆都感到激動，他居然不憑
那名字就發現了她的個人隱私。
似乎名字中有某種她不曾
發現的秘密。於是他倆結了婚，
並把那個猜想帶回家和他們一起生活。
有一次他倆旅行去她父親家
（去那幢正面是高高的一層樓、
朝向公路的一邊是三層樓的房子），
去看那兒是不是有一棵她也許曾經
忽略的樹。結果他們什麼也沒發現，
甚至連一棵能遮陰的樹也沒看見，
更不用說什麼能生產楓糖的楓樹林。

Taking dictation on a paper pad

And, in the pauses when she raised her eyes,

Watching out of a nineteenth story window

An airship laboring with unshiplike motion

And a vague all-disturbing roar above the river

Beyond the highest city built with hands.

Someone was saying in such natural tones

She almost wrote the words down on her knee,

"Do you know you remind me of a tree —

A maple tree?"

                    "Because my name is Maple?"

"Isn't it Mabel? I thought it was Mabel."

"No doubt you've heard the office call me Mabel.

I have to let them call me what they like."

                  They were both stirred that he should have divined

                  Without the name her personal mystery.

                  It made it seem as if there must be something

                  She must have missed herself. So they were married,

                  And took the fancy home with them to live by.

                  They went on pilgrimage once to her father's

                  (The house one story high in front, three stories

                  On the side it presented to the road)

                  To see if there was not some special tree

                  She might have overlooked. They could find none,

                  Not so much as a single tree for shade,

                  Let alone grove of trees for sugar orchard.

她對他說了那片大開本《聖經》中
當書簽用的楓葉，但關於那兩頁書
的內容她只記得——「獻搖祭，
是說關於獻搖祭的一些事情。」
「難道你從來沒直接問過你父親？」
「問過，但我想是被他支吾過去了。」
（這是她對多年以前有次她父親
一時不想多動腦筋的依稀記憶。）
「這很難說，說不定那只是
你父親和母親之間的什麼事情，
對我們毫無意義。」

          「對我也沒意義？
給我取一個要伴隨我終生的名字，
但永遠不讓我知道這名字的秘密，
這公平嗎？」
        「它也許是一個
父親不能對他女兒說明的秘密，
當然母親也不能說。或許它
只是你父母當時的一種幻覺，
如今你父親年事已高，舊事重提
對他很不合適，會使他感到難過。
他會覺得我們在他周圍探尋什麼，
從而毫無必要地與我們保持距離，
看來他並不知道會有什麼東西
能引導我們去發現一個秘密。

She told him of the bookmark maple leaf
In the big Bible, and all she remembered
Of the place marked with it — "Wave offering,
Something about wave offering, it said."

"You've never asked your father outright, have you?"

"I have, and been put off sometime, I think."
(This was her faded memory of the way
Once long ago her father had put himself off.)

"Because no telling but it may have been
Something between your father and your mother
Not meant for us at all."

                              "Not meant for me?
            Where would the fairness be in giving me
            A name to carry for life and never know
            The secret of?"

                              "And then it may have been
            Something a father couldn't tell a daughter
            As well as could a mother. And again
            It may have been their one lapse into fancy
            ' T would be too bad to make him sorry for
            By bringing it up to him when he was too old.
            Your father feels us round him with our questing,
            And holds us off unnecessarily,
            As if he didn't know what little thing
            Might lead us on to a discovery.

從他過去理解此名的情況來看，
他是盡可能地把它視為你的隱私；
至於你母親，如果她還活著的話，
也許更說不出那有什麼確切含義。」

「讓我們記住你的話再來找一遍，
然後我們就放棄。」最後的尋找也徒然。
雖說他倆現在已永遠放棄了探尋，
可總也忘不了對方曾偶然發現的。
這說明她名字中的確有某種東西。
當一排排楓樹都掛起吊桶，當樹脂
的蒸氣和雪花在槭樹廠上空翻滾，
他倆都會避免去想她名字的含義。

而當他們把她與楓樹連在一起時，
他們想的是已被秋火燒透了每一片
樹葉，但樹皮沒被烤焦，甚至連
樹幹也沒被濃煙燻黑的楓樹。
他倆總是在秋天外出度假。
有一次他們在一片林間空地見到
一棵楓樹，傲然獨立，枝幹挺拔，
它曾有過的每一片深紅或淡紅的
樹葉，當時都已飄落在它的腳下。
樹齡打消了他們對它的猜疑，
二十五年前梅普爾被取名的時候
它最多只是一株只有兩片樹葉、
不夠旁邊牧場上的牛塞牙縫的幼苗。
可能是另一株像它這樣的楓樹嗎？

It was as personal as he could be

About the way he saw it was with you

To say your mother, had she lived, would be

As far again as from being born to bearing."

"Just one look more with what you say in mind,

And I give up" ; which last look came to nothing.

But though they now gave up the search forever,

They clung to what one had seen in the other

By inspiration. It proved there was something.

They kept their thoughts away from when the maples

Stood uniform in buckets, and the steam

Of sap and snow rolled off the sugarhouse.

When they made her related to the maples,

It was the tree the autumn fire ran through

And swept of leathern leaves, but left the bark

Unscorched, unblackened, even, by any smoke.

They always took their holidays in autumn.

Once they came on a maple in a glade,

Standing alone with smooth arms lifted up,

And every leaf of foliage she'd worn

Laid scarlet and pale pink about her feet.

But its age kept them from considering this one.

Twenty-five years ago at Maple's naming

It hardly could have been a two-leaved seedling

The next cow might have licked up out at pasture.

Could it have been another maple like it?

他倆在附近徘徊、搜尋了一陣，
充分發揮想像力想看出那個象徵，
但卻不敢相信任何象徵對不同
時代的不同人會具有同樣的意義。
也許多少是一種子女的羞怯阻止了
他們認為它會是一種很喜氣的東西。
再說意識到這點對梅普爾也太遲。
她用雙手矇住了自己的眼睛，說：
「即使我們現在能看到那秘密，我們
也不看了；我們將不再尋找那秘密。」
就這樣，一個有含義的名字促成了
一個姑娘的婚姻，支配了她的生活。
這種含義模糊不清也無關緊要。
有含義的名字可以培養一個孩子，
同時也把那孩子從父母手中奪去。
所以我得說人名沒有意思更好，
因為留給天性和機遇的東西會更多。
不如隨便給孩子取個名，看他們會怎樣。

They hovered for a moment near discovery,

Figurative enough to see the symbol,

But lacking faith in anything to mean

The same at different times to different people.

Perhaps a filial diffidence partly kept them

From thinking it could be a thing so bridal.

And anyway it came too late for Maple.

She used her hands to cover up her eyes.

"We would not see the secret if we could now:

We are not looking for it any more."

Thus had a name with meaning, given in death,

Made a girl's marriage, and ruled in her life.

No matter that the meaning was not clear.

A name with meaning could bring up a child,

Taking the child out of the parents' hands.

Better a meaningless name, I should say,

As leaving more to nature and happy chance.

Name children some names and see what you do.

保羅的妻子

要想把保羅趕出一座伐木區小鎮，
所需要的就只是問：「嗨，保羅，
你的妻子好嗎？」
——他馬上就會消失。
有人說這是因為他沒有妻子，
而又不喜歡為這事被人家嘲笑；
有人說這是因為他曾經差點結婚，
但在結婚前一兩天被未婚妻甩了；
有人說這是因為他曾有個漂亮妻子，
但她早已和別人私奔，離他而去；
還有人說他現在就有一個妻子，
只是需要人家提醒他才會想到——
想到後他的責任感便油然而生，
所以必須馬上跑去把她看望，
好像是說：「是呀，我妻子好嗎？

真希望她這會兒不是在搗蛋淘氣。」
其實沒有人急著要除掉保羅。
因為自從那次他顯示絕招之後，
他一直都是山區各小鎮的英雄，
那是在四月裡一個星期天，在
牧場上乾涸的小溪旁，他一口氣
剝光了一整棵落葉松的樹皮，
乾淨得就像核桃做柳枝剝的柳枝。
人們問他似乎只是想看他離去，
「你妻子好嗎，保羅？」於是他離去。
他從不曾停下來殺掉任何提這個

Paul's Wife

To drive Paul out of any lumber camp.

All that was needed was to say to him.

"How is the wife, Paul?" — and he'd disappear.

Some said it was because he had no wife,

And hated to be twitted on the subject;

Others because he'd come within a day

Or so of having one, and then been jilted;

Others because he'd had one once, a good one,

Who'd run away with someone else and left him;

And others still because he had one now

He only had to be reminded of —

He was all duty to her in a minute:

He had to run right off to look her up,

As if to say, "That's so, how is my wife?

I hope she isn't getting into mischief."

No one was anxious to get rid of Paul.

He'd been the hero of the mountain camps

Ever since, just to show them, he had slipped

The bark of a whole tamarack off whole,

As clean as boys do off a willow twig

To mark a willow whistle on a Sunday

In April by subsiding meadow brooks.

They seemed to ask him just to see him go,

"How is the wife, Paul?" and he always went.

He never stopped to murder anyone

問題的人。他只是突然消失──
一時間誰也不知道他去了哪裡，
但通常要不了多久，人們便會
聽說他在某個新興的採木區市鎮，
依然是那個幹伐木老本行的保羅。
人們到處問，保羅究竟為什麼
不喜歡人家問一個禮節性的問題──
只要不惡語傷人，你幾乎可以對
別人說任何話，你會得到答覆的。
還有一種對保羅不甚公平的說法：
說他已娶了個配不上他的妻子，
保羅替她感到害臊。要配一個英雄，
那她也得是個女英雄，可她非但
不是女英雄，反倒是個怪胎。
要是墨菲講的故事真實可靠，
那她壓根兒就不該讓人替她害臊。

你們都知曉保羅能夠創造奇蹟。
人人都聽說過他制服馱馬的故事，
當時負重的馬一步也不動，他只讓
大伙兒把生牛皮挽具拉長直到營地，
他對伐木隊長說貨物會安然無恙，
「太陽會把貨物送回」──果真如此──
就憑著使生牛皮收縮成自然長度。
有人覺得這故事有點誇張。但還
有一個故事，說他雙腳一跳就站在
天花板上，然後又安全地站到牆上，
最後跳回地面，我認為這故事若非

Who asked the question. He just disappeared —

Nobody knew in what direction,

Although it wasn't usually long

Before they heard of him in some new camp,

The same Paul at the same old feats of logging.

The question everywhere was why should Paul

Object to being asked a civil question —

A man you could say almost anything to

Short of a fighting word. You have the answers.

And there was one more not so fair to Paul:

That Paul had married a wife not his equal.

Paul was ashamed of her. To match a hero

She would have had to be a heroine;

Instead of which she was some half-breed squaw.

But if the story Murphy told was true,

She wasn't anything to be ashamed of.

You know Paul could do wonders. Everyone's

Heard how he thrashed the horses on a load

That wouldn't budge, until they simply stretched

Their rawhide harness from the load to camp.

Paul told the boss the load would be all right,

"The sun will bright your load in" — and it did —

By shrinking the rawhide to natural length.

That's what is called a stretcher. But I guess

The one about his jumping so's to land

With both his feet at once against the ceiling,

And then land safely right side up again,

千眞萬確，差不多也接近事實。
好吧，眼下這事是段奇聞：講保羅
從一塊五針松木裡鋸出了他的妻子。
墨菲當時在場，如你會說的那樣，
他看見了那女士出生。伐木場的活兒
保羅樣樣能做。當時他正努力搬運
木板。因爲——我差點兒忘了——
那個最愛炫耀的鋸工想知道他是否
能用搬不完的板材壓得保羅告饒。
他們鋸開了一根大椿木的表皮背板，
那個鋸工砰地一下將滑動支架放回，
並使勁讓支架末端重新緊貼鋸齒。
當他們順便留心評判木材質量時，

他們發現了那根木材出了什麼事，
想必他們當時都有種有罪的期待，
他們的魯莽草率造成某種後果。
在那根新鋸開的木材的整個表面
有一道又寬又長的黑漆漆的油漬，
也許只有兩端的各一英尺除外。
但當保羅伸出手指去摸那油漬，
卻發現那不是道油漬，而是條狹縫，
那木頭是空的。當時他們在伐松樹，
於是那鋸工嚷道：「我可是第一回
看見空心松樹，這都是因爲有保羅
在這裡，把它給我搬到地獄去吧！」
每個人都把那松木看上一眼，

Back on the floor, is fact or pretty near fact.

Well, this is such a yarn. Paul sawed his wife

Out of a white-pine log. Murphy was there

And, as you might say, saw the lady born.

Paul worked at anything in lumbering.

He'd been hard at it taking boards away

For — I forget — the last ambitious sawyer

To want to find out if he couldn't pile

The lumber on Paul till Paul begged for mercy.

They'd sliced the first slab off a big butt log,

And the sawyer had slammed the carriage back

To slam end-on again against the saw teeth.

To judge them by the way they caught themselves

When they saw what had happened to the log,

They must have had a guilty expectation

Something was going to go with their slambanging.

Something had left a broad black streak of grease

On the new wood the whole length of the log

Except, perhaps, a foot at either end.

But when Paul put his finger in the grease,

It wasn't grease at all, but a long slot.

The long was hollow. They were sawing pine.

"First time I ever saw a hollow pine   .

That comes of having Paul around the place.

Take it to hell for me," the sawyer said.

Everyone had to have a look at it.

然後告訴保羅他該拿它怎麼辦。
（他們認爲松木該還他）「你只要用
一把折刀削寬這道縫，就可以
得到一條釣魚用的獨木舟。」但保羅
發現那空洞毫無腐損並乾淨勻稱，
不可能是什麼禽獸或蜜蜂的窩巢，
原木上也沒有供牠們出入的洞口。
他覺得那似乎是一種全新的空洞，
他認爲他最好是削開它看個明白。
於是當晚幹完活兒後他回到那裡，
用刀削寬縫口好照進足夠的燈光，
看裡邊是否空空如也。他隱約看見
裡邊有一節木髓。可眞是木髓嗎？

說不定是一條蛇蛻下的蛇皮，
或原本豎立著留在那棵樹的樹心，
而那棵樹肯定已有上百年的樹齡。
保羅繼續削寬縫口，用雙手取出
那東西，看看它又看看附近的池塘，
他想知道那東西對水有什麼反應。
當時並未起風，但他慢慢行走時
引起的空氣流動一度使它飄離
他的雙手，而且差點兒使它破碎。
他把它放到池邊，讓它能吸到水。
它一吸水就窸窣作響並漸漸變軟。
吸完第二口水它開始漸漸隱去。
保羅心想它肯定融化了，便伸手
去抓它的影子。但它已不在那裡。

And tell Paul what he ought to do about it.

(They treated it as his.) "You take a jackknife,

And spread the opening, and you've got a dugout

All dug to go a-fishing in." To Paul

The hollow looked too sound and clean and empty

Ever to have housed birds or beasts or bees.

There was no entrance for them to get in by.

It looked to him like some new kind of hollow

He thought he'd better take his jackknife to.

So after work that evening he came back

And let enough light into it by cutting

To see if it was empty. He made out in there

A slender length of pith, or was it pith?

It might have been the skin a snake had cast

And left stood up on end inside the tree

The hundred yeas the tree must have been growing.

More cutting and he had this in both hands.

And looking from it to the pond nearby,

Paul wondered how it would respond to water.

Not a breeze stirred, but just the breath of air

He made in walking slowly to the beach

Blew it once off his hands and almost broke it.

He laid it at the edge, where it could drink.

At the first drink it rustled and grew limp.

At the next drink it grew invisible.

Paul dragged the shallows for it with his fingers,

And thought it must have melted. It was gone.

接著在池塘對面蠓蟲飛舞的暗處，
在水漂木材被柵欄網攔住的地方，
它慢慢變成了一個人——一個姑娘，
她濕漉漉的頭髮像頭盔戴在頭上，
她斜靠在一根木頭上回頭看保羅。
這使得保羅也掉過頭來朝後張望，
看是否有什麼人在他身後，而她
正在看的是那個人，而不是他。
當時墨菲一直都在那附近偷看，
但是從一座他倆都看不見的棚屋。
那姑娘誕生後有一陣子令人擔憂，
她好像溺水太久，沒法活過來，
但她終於透過氣來並發出了笑聲。
然後她慢慢站起身來試著走動，
跨過那一根根像鱷魚背的木材，

開始對她自己或是對保羅說話，
於是保羅繞過那池塘上前追她。
第二天晚上，墨菲和另一些傢伙
喝醉了酒，循著那對新人的足跡
上了野貓山，從那光禿禿的山頂
他們可望見一條幽谷對面的群山。
在天色黑盡之後，照墨菲的說法，
他們看見保羅和他的造物正在安家。
自從墨菲在磨坊水池邊透過夜色
看見他倆相親相愛以來，這是唯一
的一次再有人看見保羅和他妻子。

And then beyond the open water, dim with midges,

Where the log drive lay pressed against the boom,

It slowly rose a person, rose a girl,

Her wet hair heavy on her like a helmet,

Who, leaning on a log, looked back at Paul.

And the made Paul in turn look back

To see if it was anyone behind him

That she was looking at instead of him.

(Murphy had been there watching all the time,

But from a shed where neither of them could see him.)

There was a moment of suspense in birth

When the girl seemed too waterlogged to live.

Before she caught her first breath with a gasp

And laughed. Then she climbed slowly to her feet,

> And walked off, talking to herself or Paul.
>
> Across the logs like backs of alligators
>
> Paul taking after her around the pond.
>
> Next evening Murphy and some other fellows
>
> Got drunk, and tracked the pair up Catamount,
>
> From the bare top of which there is a view
>
> To other hills across a kettle valley.
>
> And there, well after dark, let Murphy tell it,
>
> They saw Paul and his creature keeping house.
>
> It was the only glimpse that anyone
>
> Has had of Paul and her since Murphy saw them
>
> Falling in love across the twilight millpond.

越過荒山野谷一英里多路之外，
在一道懸崖半山腰的一個小小的
凹洞中，他倆坐在一起，那姑娘
光彩照人，像舞台上表演的明星，
保羅則暗淡無光，像是她的影子。
光彩都發自那雖說並非明星的姑娘，
正如後來發生的事所證明的那樣。
那群大惡棍一齊扯開嗓門吶喊，
並且朝那道懸崖扔過去一個酒瓶，
作爲他們對美的一種粗暴的讚頌。
當然那酒瓶不可能扔出一英里遠，
但吶喊聲驚嚇到姑娘並減了她的光彩。
她像隻螢火蟲飛走，從此不見蹤影。

所以有目擊者證明保羅已經結婚，
而且他在任何人跟前都無須害臊。
人們對保羅的各種評判全都錯了。
墨菲告訴我說，保羅爲妻子的事
裝出各種姿態只是爲了金屋藏嬌。
保羅是人們常說的那種鐵公雞，
他的妻子就應該絕對歸他擁有。
她與其他任何人都毫不相干，
你既不能讚美她也不能提她的名字，
甚至你只是想想她他也不會允許。
墨菲是想說世上有保羅這樣的男人，
你不能用這世間已知的任何一種
交談方式對他說起他的妻子。

More than a mile across the wilderness

They sat together halfway up cliff

In a small niche let into it, the girl

Brightly, as if a star played on the place,

Paul darkly, like her shadow. All the light

Was from the girl herself, though, not from a star,

As was apparent from what happened next.

All those great ruffians put their throats together,

And let out a loud yell, and threw a bottle,

As a brute tribute of respect to beauty

Of course the bottle fell short by a mile,

But the shout reached the girl and put her light out.

She went out like a firefly, and that was all.

So there were witnesses that Paul was married,

And not to anyone to be ashamed of.

Everyone had been wrong in judging Paul.

Murphy told me Paul put on all those airs

About his wife to keep her to himself.

Paul was what's called a terrible possessor.

Owning a wife with him meant owning her.

She wasn't anybody else's business,

Either to praise her or so much as name her,

And he'd thank people not to think of her.

Murphy's idea was that a man like Paul

Wouldn't be spoken to about a wife

In any way the world knew how to speak.

野葡萄

從什麼樹上不可以摘到無花果？
難道從白樺樹上就摘不到葡萄？
你對葡萄或白樺樹的了解就這些。
作爲某年秋天曾把身體掛在葡萄
之間並從白樺樹上被摘下的姑娘，
我應該知道葡萄是什麼樹的果實。
我猜想我的出生也和其他人一樣，
然後慢慢長成一個男孩似的姑娘，
一個我哥哥沒法總摺在家裡的姑娘。
但這段身世已在那次驚恐中被抹去，
那天我和葡萄一起懸在空中晃盪，
後來像攸里底斯那樣終於被找到
並被安全地從半空中接回到地面；

所以我現在這條命完全是撿來的，
我喜歡誰就可以爲誰消耗這一生。
所以要是你看見我一年過兩次生日，
而且爲自己報出兩個不同的年齡，
記住其中一個比我看起來年輕五歲。
一天哥哥把我帶到一片林間空地，
他知道有棵白樺樹獨伶伶在那裡，
披著一張掌狀葉編織的薄薄頭巾，
薄而密的頭巾下面是它濃密的頭髮，
它脖子上掛著一串串葡萄作裝飾。
自打前一年見過之後我已認得葡萄。

Wild Grapes

What tree may not the fig be gathered from?

The grape may not be gathered from the birch?

It's all you know the grape, or know the birch.

As a girl gathered from the birch myself

Equally with my weight in grapes, one autumn,

I ought to know what tree the grape is fruit of.

I was born, I suppose, like anyone,

And grew to be a little boyish girl

My brother could not always leave at home.

But that beginning was wiped out in fear

The day I swung suspended with the grapes,

And was come after like Eurydice

And brought down safely from the upper regions;

And the life I live now's an extra life

I can waste as I please on whom I please.

So if you see me celebrate two birthdays,

And give myself out as two different ages,

One of them five years younger than I look —

One day my brother led me to a glade

Where a white birch he knew of stood alone,

Wearing a thin headdress of pointed leaves,

And heavy on her heavy hair behind,

Against her neck, an ornament of grapes.

Grapes, I knew grapes from having seen them last year.

先是一串，然後在我周圍開始有
無數串葡萄在白樺樹枝葉間生長，
就像它們曾在幸運的萊夫周圍生長；
可惜幾乎都長在我伸手不及的地方，
就像我更小的時候心目中的月亮，
你想痛快地擁有它就必須爬上去。
我哥哥爬上去了。起初他摘些葡萄
扔下來給我，但全都散落在地上，
我只好在香蕨木和繡線菊間尋找；
這使他有些時間自個兒在樹上吃，
但也許這對一個男孩還不夠痛快，
於是他爲了讓我能完全自食其力，
便往高處爬，把樹壓彎到地面，
讓我用手抓住樹枝自己摘葡萄。

「嘿，抓住樹梢，我去下面的樹枝。
我鬆手的時候你可得用力抓住。」
我說我抓住樹了，可這話不對。
應該倒過來說，是樹抓住了我。
就在我哥哥鬆開手的一瞬間，
樹猛然把我釣起，就好像它是根
釣魚竿，而我是條魚。於是哥哥
的聲聲呼喊變成了尖叫：「鬆手，
傻丫頭，難道你不知什麼是鬆手！」
但爲了活命我卻忍痛把樹抓得更緊，
顯出嬰兒抓住什麼就不放的本性，
這種本性就是從這種樹上傳下來的，
因爲遠古時代那些未開化的母親──
比今天最野蠻的母親還野蠻的母親

One bunch of them, and there began to be

Bunches all round me growing in white birches,

The way they grew round Leif the Lucky's German;

Mostly as much beyond my lifted hands, though,

As the moon used to seem when I was younger,

And only freely to be had for climbing.

My brother did the climbing; and at first

Threw me down grapes to miss and scatter

And have to hunt for in sweet fern and hardhack;

Which gave him some time to himself to eat,

But not so much, perhaps, as a boy needed.

So then, to make me wholly self-supporting,

He climbed still higher and bent the tree to earth

And put it in my hands to pick my own grapes.

"Here, take a treetop, I'll get down another.

Hold on with all your might when I let go."

I said I had the tree. It wasn't true.

The opposite was true. The tree had me.

The minute it was left with me alone,

It caught me up as if I were the fish

And it the fishpole. So I was translated,

To loud cries from my brother of "Let go!

Don't you know anything, you girl? Let go!"

But I, with something of the baby grip

Acquired ancestrally in just such trees

When wilder mothers than our wildest now

Hung babies out on branches by the hands

就曾讓她們的嬰兒雙手吊在樹上，
不知是為了洗淨晾乾還是曬太陽
（對此你得去請教一位進化論學者）。
我哥哥想把我逗笑以幫助我放鬆。
「你高高的在葡萄串中間幹嘛呢？
別怕，幾串葡萄傷不著你，我是說
你不去摘它們，它們也不會摘你。」
這時候我還去摘人家真是不要命了！
事到如今，我早已無可奈何地接受
了一種人生哲學：自己吊也讓人家吊。
我哥哥繼續說：「這下你可嘗到了
當一串人們所說的酸葡萄是啥滋味：
本以為長在不該生長的白樺樹上，
早已逃脫了被狐狸吃掉的命運，
因為狐狸壓根兒想不到來此覓食，
而且即使被牠發現也夠不著——
可這時候你我偏偏來這兒摘葡萄。
不過在有一點上你比那些葡萄強，
一串葡萄只有一梗，你卻有雙手，
採摘者要把你摘下來就更不容易。」
我的帽子和鞋子都先後掉下樹去，
可我依然吊在樹上。我仰著頭，
閉眼不看頭頂的陽光，充耳不聞
哥哥的胡言。「鬆手吧，」他說，
「我會用雙臂接住你。這不算高。」
（照他的身高來看那也許不算高。）

To dry or wash or tan, I don't know which

(You'll have ask an evolutionist) —

I held on uncomplainingly for life.

My brother tried to make me laugh to help me.

"What are you doing up there in those grapes?

Don't be afraid. A few of them won't hurt you.

I mean, they won't pick you if you don't them."

Much danger of my picking anything!

By that time I was pretty well reduced

To a philosophy of hang-and-let-hang.

"Now you know how it feels, " my brother said,

"To be a bunch of fox grapes, as they call them,

That when it thinks it has escaped the fox

By growing where it shouldn't — on a birch,

Where a fox wouldn't think to look for it —

And if he looked and found it, couldn't reach it —

Just then come you and I to gather it.

Only you have the advantage of the grapes

In one way: you have one more stem to cling by,

And promise more resistance to the picker."

One by one I lost off my hat and shoes,

And still I clung. I let my head fall back,

And shut my eyes against the sun, my ears

Against my bother's nonsense. "Drop, "he said,

"I'll catch you in my arms. It isn't far."

(Stated in lengths of him it might not be.)

「快鬆手，要不我就搖樹把你搖下來。」
可我一聲沒吭，儘管身子更往下墜，
兩隻手腕拉長得像五弦琴的琴弦。
「唉，她要不這麼死心眼該有多好！
那就抓緊吧，等我想想該怎麼辦。
我再把這樹壓彎到地上讓你下來。」
當時是怎麼下來的我也鬧不清楚，
只記得我只穿長襪的腳觸到大地時，
當這個地球又重新在我腳下旋轉時，
我只顧久久地打量我蜷曲的十指，
好半天才伸直它們並把樹皮渣拭去。
我哥哥說：「難道你就不會用腦子？
下次遇到這種情況你得動動腦筋，
免得又被白樺樹拉到半天上去。」

其實那並不是因為我不會用腦子，
甚至不是因為我對世事還一無所知，
儘管以前哥哥一直都比我更正確。
當時我還沒有邁出求知的第一步；
當時我還沒有學會如何鬆開雙手，
就像我迄今還沒有學會敞開心扉，
而且我沒這種願望，也沒有必要，
這我能意識到。而心事不是心扉。
所以我或許會像其他人一樣，為
睡得安隱而奢望拋開煩人的心事；
但從來沒有任何事情告訴過我
說我有必要學會向別人敞開心扉。

"Drop or I'll shake the tree and shake you down."

Grim silence on my part as I sank lower,

My small wrists stretching till they showed the banjo strings.

"Why, if she isn't serious about it!

Hold tight awhile till I think what to do.

I'll bend the tree down and let you down by it."

I don't know much about the letting down;

But once I felt ground with my stocking feet

And the world came revolving back to me,

I know I looked long at my curled-up fingers,

Before I straightened them and brushed the bark off.

My brother said: "Don't you weigh anything?

Try to weigh something next time, so you won't

Be run off with by birch trees into space."

        It wasn't my not weighing anything

        So much as my not knowing anything —

        My bother had been nearer right before.

        I had not taken the first step in knowledge;

        I had not learned to let go with the hands,

        As still I have not learned to with the heart,

        And have no wish to with the heart — nor need,

        That I can see. The mind — is not the heart.

        I may yet live, as I know others live,

        To wish in vain to let go with the mind —

        Of cares, at night, to sleep; but nothing tells me

        That I need learn to let go with the heat.

第三個妻子的墓地

對以前的那些婚姻都隻字不提！
她第三次結婚成了他第三個妻子。
他倆交了個平手，比分是三比三。
但臨死前她發現自己非常擔憂：
她想起了一排墳墓中的那些孩子，
一排墳墓中的三個孩子令人傷心。
一排墳墓中一個男人的三個女人
不知怎的使她受不了那個男人。
於是她對拉班說：「你已經做對了
許多事，請別把最後一件事做錯。
別把我和另外兩個女人埋在一起。」

拉班說不會，除非她自己願意，
他不會把她與任何人埋在一起，
如果她覺得願意，當然就不會。
於是她撒手而去。但拉班已經
瞥見了伊麗莎彌留之際的樣子，
並急於根據自己所記得的往事
盡可能地揣摩透她的全部心思，
他努力想怎樣能比諾言做得更好，
為亡妻竭盡全力，雖已沒有感謝。
她是怎麼想的呢，他不停地自問。
顧慮重重之中他首先想到的是
最近她自己經手新買的一塊墓地；
他不在乎為她豎一塊多大的墓碑，
為此他可以賣掉兩頭拉犁的公牛。

Place for a Third

Nothing to say to all those marriages!
She had made three herself to three of his.
The score was even for them, three to three.
But come to die she found she cared so much:
She thought of children in a burial row;
Three children in a burial row were sad.
One man's three women in a burial row
Somehow made her impatient with the man.
And so she said to Laban, "You have done
A good deal right: don't do the last thing wrong.
Don't make me lie with those two other women."

Laban said, No, he would not make her lie
With anyone but that she had a mind to,
If that was how she felt, of course, he said.
She went her way. But Laban having caught
This glimpse of lingering person in Eliza
And anxious to make all he could of it
With something he remembered in himself,
Tried to think how he could exceed him promise
And give good measure to the dead, though thankless.
If that was how she felt, he kept repeating.
His first thought under pressure was a grave
In a new-boughten grave plot by herself,
Under he didn't care how great a stone:
He'd sell a yoke of steers to pay for it.

難道墓畔不可以種些特別的花木？
悲痛可以開始滋生，也可以休假，
而此時花木即可代替悲痛寄托哀思，
這樣誰也不會被冷落或冷落了誰。
深謀遠慮的悲痛不會看不起幫助。
於是他想到了常青樹和永久花。
但接著他想到了一個更好的主意。
亡妻的第一個丈夫肯定就埋在什麼
地方，那小伙子當年娶她與其說是
娶妻子不如說是找玩伴，有時候
他還嘲笑他倆之間的關係。不過，
她會有多想與他永遠長眠在一起？
他的墓在哪兒？拉班知道他名字嗎？

他在一兩個鎮區外找到了那座墳，
墳前墓碑上刻著：亡夫約翰之墓，
墓邊有塊空地，其決定權在死者
的一個從來沒結過婚的妹妹手裡，
伊麗莎來這兒安息會受到歡迎嗎？
死者理當沉默，只有去問他妹妹。
於是拉班見到了那個妹妹，但他
隻字未提伊麗莎不願埋在何處之事，
也沒說想到她埋在這兒是誰的主意，
而只是坦率地懇求得到那塊空地。
責任心使那個妹妹臉上堆滿皺紋。

And weren't there special cemetery flowers,

That, once grief sets to growing, grief may rest:

The flowers will go on with grief awhile,

And no one seem neglecting or neglected?

A prudent grief will not despise such aids.

He thought of evergreen and everlasting.

And then he had a thought worth many of these.

Somewhere must be the grave of the young boy

Who married her for playmate more than helpmate,

And sometimes laughed at what it was between them.

How would she like to sleep her last with him?

Where was his grave? Did Laban know his name?

        He found the grave a town or two away,

        The headstone cut with John, Beloved Husband,

        Beside it room reserved; the say a sister's,

        A never-married sister's of that husband,

        Whether Eliza would be welcome there.

        The dead was bound to silence: ask the sister.

        So Laban saw the sister, and, saying nothing

        Of where Eliza wanted not lie,

        And who had thought to lay her with her first love,

        Begged simply for the grave. The sister's face

        Fell all in wrinkles of responsibility.

她想公平行事，她不得不考慮。
拉班又老又窮，但看上去很在乎；
她又窮又老，對這事也很在意。
他倆坐著，她用呆滯的目光看了他
一眼，然後叫他出去到村裡走走，
去處理她說他可能要處理的事情，
好讓她自個兒決定她有多麼在意——
拉班有多麼在乎——爲什麼在乎，
（她敏銳地意識到他何時娶伊麗莎。）

她第二次去看望伊麗莎的時候，
伊麗莎正站在她第二個丈夫的墳頭，
她還接伊麗莎回來住了一段時間，
才讓她回那個可憐的男人家守寡，
並爲一個不是丈夫的男人料理家務。
她和伊麗莎自始至終都是朋友。
在這《聖經》對婚姻都莫衷一是的
世上，她有什麼資格評判婚姻？
她以前從未碰見過這位拉班——
一個由生活熨斗熨出的正經男人；
她絕不可讓他久等。人死之後
和葬禮之間的時間總是很緊迫。

She wanted to do right. She'd have to think.

Laban was old and poor, yet seemed to care;

And she was old and poor — but she cared, too.

They sat. She cast one dull, old look at him,

Then turned him out to go on other errands

She said he might attend to in the village,

While she made up her mind how much she cared —

And how much Laban cared — and why he cared.

(She made shrewd eyes to see where he came in.)

She'd looked Eliza up her second time,

A widow at her second husband's grave,

And offered her a home to rest awhile

Before she went the poor man's widow's way,

Housekeeping for the next man out of wedlock.

She and Eliza had been friends through all.

Who was she to judge marriage in a world

Whose Bible's so confused in marriage counsel?

The sister had not come across this Laban;

A decent product of life's ironing-out;

She must not keep him waiting. Time would press

Between the death day and the funeral day.

所以當她看見他拐進街口的時候，
她已匆匆做出了決定，打算在
門口迎住他，告訴他她的答覆。
從她那張老嘴要開口說話的方式，
拉班已知道她最終會說些什麼，
等她開口說話，果然不出所料。

她讓緊閉的紗門隔在他倆之間，說
「不，不能在約翰身邊。這沒道理。
伊麗莎有過那麼多其他的男人。」

拉班被迫回頭實施他自己的計劃，
爲伊麗莎買了塊地讓她獨自安息；
這也爲他自己提供了選擇餘地，
當他大限來臨，需要長眠之時。

So when she saw him coming in the street

She hurried her decision to be ready

To meet him with his answer at the door.

Laban had known about what it would be

From the way she had set her poor old mouth,

To do, as she had put it, what was right.

She gave it through the screen door closed between them:

"No, not with John. There wouldn't be no sense.

Eliza's had too many other men."

Lanban was forced to fall back on his plan

To buy Eliza a plot to lie alone in:

Which give him for himself a choice of lots

When his time comes to die and settle down.

兩個女巫（二首）

一、科阿斯的女巫

我曾在山後邊的一座農場上過夜，
農場主人是一個母親和她的兒子，
兩個老迷信。他倆都特別健談。
母親：人們認為一個能呼喚精靈
但卻不召它們來共度冬夜的女巫
應該在火刑柱或別的柱子上被燒死。
但召喚精靈不是喊「鈕扣，鈕扣，
誰有鈕扣」，這我本該讓他們明白。
兒子：我媽能讓一張桌子豎立起來，
並讓它像騾子一樣用雙腿往後踢。

母親：我那樣做會有什麼好處呢？
與其豎桌子給你看，不如給你講講
蘇管員拉里有次怎麼告訴我。
他說死人有鬼魂，但當我問他怎麼
會呢──我認為死人就是鬼魂──
他驚走了我召來的鬼魂。這難道不
使你懷疑鬼魂總是躲著某種東西？
的確如此，鬼魂總是躲著某種東西。
兒子：媽，你難道不想告訴他
我們閣樓上有什麼嗎？
母親：屍骨──一具骷髏。

Two Witches

1. THE WITCH OF COÖS

I stayed the night for shelter at a farm

Behind the mountain, with a mother and son,

Two old-believers. They did all the talking.

MOTHER. Folks think a witch who has familiar spirits

She could call up to pass a winter evening,

But won't, should be burned at the stake or something.

Summoning spirits isn't "Button, button,

Who's got the button," I would have them know.

SON. Mother can make a common table rear

And kick with two legs like an army mule.

MOTHER. And when I've done it, what good have I done?

Rather than tip a table for you, let me

Tell you what Ralle the Sioux Control once told me.

He said the dead had souls, but when I asked him

How could that be — I thought the dead were souls —

He broke my trance. Don't that make you suspicious

That there's something the dead are keeping back?

Yes, there's something the dead are keeping back.

SON. You wouldn't want to tell him what we have

Up attic, mother?

MOTHER. Bones — a skeleton

兒子：但我媽那張床的床頭板
抵著閣樓門，而且那門已被釘死。
它不會有害的。夜裡我媽常聽見
它停在門和床頭板這道屏障後面
不知如何是好。它一心想的就是
重返地窖，它就是從地窖出來的。
母親：我們絕不會讓它回去，
你說是吧，兒子！絕不讓它回去！
兒子：它是四十年前鑽出地窖的，
當時它看上去像一只會飛的盤子，
先是從地窖裡一下子飛進廚房，
接著從廚房一下子飛進臥室，
然後又從臥室飛上了那個閣樓，
其間它曾從爸爸媽媽面前飛過，
但他倆誰也沒能把它攔住。
當時爸爸已上樓，媽媽在樓下，
我還是嬰兒；不知道當時我在哪裡。

母親：我丈夫覺得我唯一的缺點
就是我往往在上床之前就已入睡，
尤其是在冬天，當床鋪比冰還涼，
身上的衣服比雪還冷的時候。
骷髏從地窖樓梯上來的那天晚上，
托夫勒早已丟下我獨自上了床，
但他讓一扇門開著使廚房變冷，
可以說是故意要把我趕出廚房。
就在我慢慢醒來，清醒得足以
納悶冷風從何處吹進廚房的時候，
我聽見托夫勒在樓上的臥室裡，
但我以為聽見他在樓下的地窖。

SON. But the headboard of mother's bed is pushed

Against the attic door: the door is nailed.

It's harmless. Mother hears it in the night,

Halting perplexed behind the barrier

Of door and headboard. Where it wants to get

Is back into the cellar where it came from.

MOTHER. We'll never let them, will we, son? We'll never!

SON. It left the cellar forty years ago

And carried itself like a pile of dishes

Up one flight from the cellar to the kitchen,

Another from the kitchen to the bedroom,

Another from the bedroom to the attic,

Right past both father and mother, and neither stopped it.

Father had gone upstairs; mother was downstairs

I was a baby: I don't know where I was.

MOTHER. The only fault my husband found with me —

I went to sleep before I went to bed,

Especially in winter when the bed

Might just as well be ice and the clothes snow.

The night the bones came up the cellar stairs

Toffile had gone to bed alone and left me,

But left an open door to cool the room off

So as to sort of turn me out of it.

I was just coming to myself enough

To wonder where the cold was coming from,

When I heard Toffile upstairs in the bedroom

And thought I heard him downstairs in the cellar.

春天裡地窖下面總會有積水，
為了不濕鞋我們在那兒鋪有木板，
當時木板碰響了地窖堅硬的地面。
接著有人開始上來，一步發兩聲，
就像是一個獨腿人柱著T形拐杖，
或像一個孩子。那不是托夫勒，
其實地窖裡根本不可能有什麼人。
屋外的地窖出口門加有兩道鎖，
而且門扉受潮脹緊並被積雪掩埋。
地窖的窗戶都被堆積的鋸木遮住，
同時也受潮脹緊並被積雪掩埋。
是那具骷髏。我有充分的理由確信。

我的第一個念頭就是去抓住門柄
把門壓住。但那具骷髏並沒推門，
它只是茫然不知所措地停在門下，
等待著什麼有利於它的事情發生。
它全身不停地發出輕微的窸窣聲。
我真想看看屍骨怎麼會站起來行走，
而要不是這種願望是那麼的強烈，
我肯定不會做我後來所做的事情。
我想像出一堆白骨湊在一起的樣子：
不像是一個人，倒像盞枝形吊燈。
於是我突然打開了它頭頂上的板門。
它一時間激動得站在那裡直搖晃，
差點忘乎所以。（一條火焰般的
舌頭伸出來舔著它的上排牙齒。
兩個深陷的眼窩裡翻捲著煙霧。）

The board we had laid down to walk dry-shod on

When there was water in the cellar in spring

Struck the hard cellar bottom. And then someone

Began the stairs, two footsteps for each step,

The way a man with one leg and a crutch,

Or a little child, comes up. It wasn't Toffile:

It wasn't anyone who could be there.

The bulkhead double doors were double-locked

And swollen tight and buried under snow.

The cellar windows were banked up with sawdust

And swollen tight and buried under snow.

It was the bones. I knew them — and good reason.

My first impulse was to get to the knob

And hold the door. But the bones didn't try

The door; they halted helpless on the landing,

Waiting for things to happen in their favor.

The faintest restless rustling ran all through them.

I never could have done the things I did

If the wish hadn't been too strong in me

To see how they were mounted for this walk.

I had a vision of them put together

Not like a man, but like a chandelier.

So suddenly I flung the door wide on him.

A moment he stood balancing with emotion,

And all but lost himself. (A tongue of fire

Flashed out and licked along his upper teeth.

Smoke rolled inside the sockets of his eyes.)

然後它伸出一隻手直衝我撲來，
它活著時也這樣朝我撲來過一次；
但這次我把它那隻手擊碎在地板上，
我自己也往後一跌，倒在地板上。
當時那些手指碎片滑得到處都是。
（我最近還在什麼地方見過一塊？
把鈕扣盒遞給我，它肯定在盒裡。）
我從地板上坐起來大聲喊：「托夫勒，
它上樓衝你來了。」它當時可以選擇，
要麼是回到地窖，要麼是進門廳。
它為了看新鮮而進了通往門廳的門，
對那麼一個笨傢伙來說，它的行動

堪稱輕快，但由於我剛才的一擊，
它在門廳裡朝四面八方一陣亂竄，
看上去像是一道閃電或一陣旋風。
我聽見它從門廳去樓上那個唯一
裝修過的臥室，在它差不多要
爬上樓梯時我才從地板上站起來，
然後我邊追邊喊：「關上臥室門，
托夫勒，為了我！」「有客人？」他說，
「別讓我起來，在被窩裡真暖和。」
於是我無力地匍匐在樓梯扶手上
掙扎著上了樓，我不得不承認
在燈光下我什麼也沒能看見，（剛才
廚房裡沒燈）「托夫勒，我看不見
那具骷髏，可它就在這房間裡。」
「什麼骷髏？」「地窖墓中的那具骷髏。」

Then he came at me with one hand outstretched,

The way he did in life once; but this time

I struck the hand off brittle on floor,

And fell back from him on the floor myself.

The finger-pieces slid in all dircctions.

(Where did I see one of those pieces lately?

Hand me my button box — it must be there.)

I sat up on the floor and shouted, "Toffile,

It's coming up to you." It had its choice

Of the door to the cellar or the hall.

It took the hall door for the novelty.

And set off briskly for so slow a thing,

Still going every which way in the joints, though,

So that it looked like lightning or a scribble,

From the slap I had just now given its hand.

I listened till it almost climbed the stairs

From the hall to the only finished bedroom,

Before I got up to do anything;

Then ran and shouted, "Shut the bedroom door,

Toffile, for my sake!" "Company?" he said,

"Don't make me get up; I'm too warm in bed."

So lying forward weakly on the handrail

I pushed myself upstairs, and in the light

(The kitchen had been dark) I had to own

I could see nothing. "Toffile, I don't see it.

It's with us in the room, though. It's the bones."

"What bones?" "The cellar bones — out of the grave."

這下托夫勒把兩條光腿伸出被窩，
坐到我身邊並緊緊地把我抓住。
我想把臥室的燈吹滅，好看看
我能不能看見它，或是讓托夫勒
和我一道蹲下身子伸出雙臂猛揮，
把那堆白骨擊倒。「我會告訴你
怎麼辦——它正在找另外一道門。
這罕見的深深積雪使它想起了
它那支老歌，《殖民地的野孩子》，
它過去總愛在馬車道旁唱這支歌。
它想找一扇開著的門好逃到野外。
讓我們把閣樓門打開為它設個圈套。」

托夫勒同意這樣做，果然不出所料，
幾乎與閣樓門被他打開的同時，
上閣樓的樓梯上就響起了腳步聲。
我聽見了，但托夫勒好像沒聽見。
「快！」我砰地關上門並抓住把手。
「托夫勒，找釘子。」我讓他把門釘死
並把床推到門前用床頭板把門抵住。
然後我倆才互相問，閣樓上是否
有什麼我們可能還用得著的東西。
與地窖相比閣樓對我們不那麼重要。
如果那骷髏喜歡閣樓，就給它吧。
讓它就待在閣樓上。當它有時候
在夜裡走下樓梯，站在那扇門和
床頭板後面，不知如何是好地
用它的白骨手搔著它的白骨頭皮、

That made him throw his bare legs out of bed

And sit up by me and take hold of me.

I wanted to put out the light and see

If I could see it, or else mow the room,

With our arms at the level of our knees,

And bring the chalk-pile down. "I'll tell you what —

It's looking for another door to try.

The uncommonly deep snow has made him think

Of his old song, 'The Wild Colonial Boy,'

He always used to sing along the tote road.

He's after an open door to get outdoors.

Let's trap him with an open door up attic."

        Toffile agreed to that, and sure enough.

        Almost the moment he was given an opening,

        The steps began to climb the attic stairs.

        I heard them. Toffile didn't seem to hear them.

        "Quick!" I slammed to the door and held the knob.

        "Toffile, get nails." I made him nail the door shut

        And push the headboard of the bed against it.

        Then we asked was there anything

        Up attic that we'd ever want again.

        The attic was less to us than the cellar.

        If the bones liked the attic, let them have it.

        Let them stay it the attic. When they sometimes

        Come down the stairs at night and stand perplexed

        Behind the door and headboard of the bed,

        Brushing their chalky skull with chalky fingers,

發出百葉窗發出的那種嚓嚓聲時，
我就會從床上坐起來對托夫勒説：
既然它上了閣樓，就讓它待在閣樓。
自從托夫勒死後我就只能對黑暗説。
我答應過托夫勒對它要毫不留情，
所以要幫它就是對托夫勒無情。
兒子：我們認爲它在地窖有個墳墓。
母親：我們知道它在地窖有個墳墓。
兒子：我們不可能查出這骷髏是誰。
母親：不，兒子，我們能。就此説
破眞相吧。那是他父親爲了我而殺
的一個男人。我是説他殺了那男人，
而不是我。我能做的就是幫他掘墓。

有天晚上我們在地窖裡挖了那個墓。
我兒子知道這事，但假若該説的時
辰已到，也不該由他來説出眞情。
見我道出眞相我兒子顯得很驚訝，
這麼多年來我倆一直保守著這秘密，
以致隨時都準備著對外人撒謊。
但今晚我一點兒都不想説謊話——
我記不得我爲什麼一直掩蓋眞相。
我相信，要是托夫勒還活著的話，
他也沒法告訴你他爲什麼要撒謊⋯⋯
她把盒子裡的鈕扣一古腦倒在懷中，
但沒找到她想找的那塊手指碎片。
第二天上午我核實了托夫勒這個名字，
鄉村郵政信箱上寫著托夫勒・拉維。

With sounds like the dry rattling of a shutter,

That's what I sit up in the dark to say —

To no one anymore since Toffile died.

Let them stay in attic since they went there.

I promised Toffile to be cruel to them

For helping them be cruel once to him.

SON.   We think they had a grave down in the cellar.

MOTHER.   We know they had a grave down in the cellar.

SON.   We never could find out whose bones they were.

MOTHER.   Yes, we could too, son. Tell the truth for once.

They were a man's his father killed for me.

I mean a man he killed instead of me.

The least I could do was help dig their grave.

We were about it one night in the cellar.

Son knows the story: but t'was not for him

To tell the truth, suppose the time had come.

Son looks surprised to see me end a lie

We'd kept up all these years between ourselves

So as to have it ready for outsiders.

But tonight I don't care enough to lie —

I don't remember why I ever cared.

Toffile, if he were here, I don't believe

Could tell you why he ever cared himself....

She hadn't found the finger-bone she wanted

Among the buttons poured out in her lap.

I verified the name next morning: Toffile.

The rural letter box said Toffile Lajway.

二、克拉夫頓的乞丐女巫

既然他們已確認我是誰家的人，
那我就打算說些他們不愛聽的話：
他們認錯了，我可以證明這點。
使兩個鎮子爭著把我作爲禮物
互相贈送，這肯定是太恭維我了。
這兩個鎮子都休想使我有心爲
他們消災彌禍。因爲不管怎麼說，
雪上加霜永遠都是女巫的格言。
我要加重他們的災禍，你就瞧吧。
他們將發現他們已使一切都得重來，
我是說如果他們想忽略事實的話。

他們憑一份記錄，說阿瑟・埃米
曾在沃倫鎮三月會上投過里夫一票，
就安排一個人的命運（不是嗎？）。
我本可以在今年的任何時候告訴
他們，和我結婚的這個阿瑟・埃米
不可能是他們說的那個參加沃倫鎮
三月會的阿瑟・埃米，因爲在他們
說的那個年份他還不滿十五歲。
曾與我結爲夫妻的這個阿瑟・埃米
只參加過他曾參加過的幾次投票，
次數不太多，全都在文特沃思鎮。
而且其中一次還是受大夥兒委托，
去看鎮上是不是想接收那條通往
我們住的那片林間空地的馬車道。
我告訴你誰記得這事——哈曼・拉皮什。

2.THE PAUPER WITCH OF GRAFTON

Now that they've got it settled whose I be

I'm going to tell them something they won't like:

They've got it settled wrong, and I can prove it.

Flattered I must be to have two towns fighting

To make a present of me to each other.

They don't dispose me, either one of them,

To spare them any trouble. Double trouble's

Always the witch's motto anyway.

I'll double theirs for both of them — you watch me.

They'll find they've got the whole thing to do over,

That is, if facts is what they want to go by.

They set a lot (now don't they?) by a record

Of Arthur Amy's having once been up

For Hog Reeve in March Meeting here in Warren.

I could have told them any time this twelvemonth

The Arthur Amy I was married to

Couldn't have been the one they say was up

In Warren at March Meeting, for the reason

He wa'n't but fifteen at the time they say.

The Arthur Amy I was married to

Voted the only times he ever voted.

Which wasn't many, in the town of Wentworth.

One of the times was when'twas in the warrant

To see if the town wanted to take over

The tote road to our clearing where we lived.

I'll tell you who'd remember — Heman Lapish

他們的阿瑟・埃米是我的阿瑟的父親。
所以他們已爲這事上過一次法庭，
我想他們還是再上一次法庭爲好。
文特沃思和沃倫都是居住的好地方，
只是我碰巧更喜歡從今往後
就住在文特沃思鎮；歸根到底，
權利就是權利，當我能夠憑這樣做
而傷害某人的時候，公正對待
的誘惑對我來說實在是太過分。
我知道有些人喜歡有個著名女巫
住在他們鎮上，並會因此而得意；

但大多數人都不得不考慮花費多少，
甚至有我的費用。他們應該知道，
作爲一名女巫，我得經常擠蝙蝠奶，
而且一次要擠夠供好幾天用的。
這會使我的地位更加鞏固，想想吧，
我是否應該答應顯示出某種標記，
以此來進一步證明我是個女巫？
我認爲馬利斯當年就曾是標記，
它說明我在牠年老體衰的時候
還騎著牠到處走並讓它承載重負，
直到我使牠消瘦得皮包骨頭，
還說明既然我曾經不給牠蓋毯子
就把牠拴在一個鎮公所門前，那我
就曾把牠拴在全縣每個鎮公所門前。
有些人曾指責我不給牠蓋毯子，
那個可憐的老傢伙。這本來也沒

Their Arthur Amy was the father of mine.

So now they've dragged it through the law courts once,

I guess they'd better drag it through again.

Wentworth and Warren's both good towns to live in,

Only I happen to prefer to live

In Wentworth from now on; and when all's said,

Right's right, and the temptation to do right

When I can hurt someone by doing it

Has always been too much for me, it has.

I know of some folks that'd be set up

At having in their town a noted witch:

> But most would have to think of the expense
>
> That even I would be. They ought to know
>
> That as a witch I'd often milk a bat
>
> And that'd be enough to last for days.
>
> It'd make my position stronger, think,
>
> If I was to consent to give some sign
>
> To make it surer that I was a witch?
>
> It wa'n't no sign, I s'pose, when Mallice Huse
>
> Said that I took him out in his old age
>
> And rode all over everything on him
>
> Until I'd had him worn to skin and bones,
>
> And if I'd left him hitched unblanketed
>
> In front of one Town Hall, I'd left him hitched
>
> In front of every one in Grafton County.
>
> Some cried shame on me not to blanket him.
>
> The poor old man. It would have been all right

什麼要緊，要不是有一個聰明人
指出牠愛啃拴馬樁，在樁上留下牙印，
以便人們一眼就能認出那些標記。
人們能聽說的拴馬樁都被牠啃過。
他們讓牠啃呀啃呀，直到牠發牢騷。
於是那同一個聰明人又說，看呀——
他敢打賭馬利斯是匹有咬槽癖的馬，
牠已經咬碎了馬廄裡的飼料槽——
千真萬確，人們發現牠已把馬廄的
四根木樁咬成碎片。這說明什麼呢？
這並不說明牠沒咬過外面的拴馬樁。
因為對我來說，一匹馬在馬廄裡咬
東西並不證明牠不咬馬樁柵欄。

但人人都誤把這一點當作證明。
那時候我是個二十歲的健壯姑娘。
而那個把每樣事都弄糟的聰明人
就是阿瑟・埃米。你知道他是誰了。
他就是那樣開始向我獻殷勤的。
我們結婚後他對往事很少提起，
但我不相信他一點兒也不為他當年
干涉馬利斯啃拴馬樁的事感到得意。
我猜他是發現了若讓我當女巫，
他就更容易躲開我，要不然是
什麼東西碰巧使他變了。他開始
說一些與他從前所為相反的話，
譬如說：「不，她還沒飛回來哩。

If someone hadn't said to gnaw the posts

He stood beside and leave his trademark on them,

So they could recognize them. Not a post

That they could hear tell of was scarified.

They made him keep on gnawing till he whined.

Then that same smarty someone said to look —

He'd bet Huse was a cribber and had gnawed

The crib he slept in — and as sure's you're born

They found he'd gnawed the four posts of his bed,

All four of them to splinters. What did that prove?

Not that he hadn't gnawed the hitching posts

He said he had, besides. Because a horse

Gnaws in the stable ain't no proof to me

He don't gnaw trees and posts and fences too.

But everybody took it for a proof.

I was a strapping girl of twenty then.

The smarty someone who spoiled everything.

Was Arture Amy. You know who he was.

That was the way he started courting me.

He never said much after we were married,

But I mistrusted he was none too proud

Of having interfered in the Huse business.

I guess he found he got more out of me

By having me a witch. Or something happened

To turn him round. He got to saying things

To undo what he'd done and make it right,

Like, "No, she ain't come back from kiting yet.

昨晚是她外出的夜晚。她在飛。
她認爲既然風能痛快地玩上一夜，
她自己也能痛快一宵。」但他最愛
聲稱他被我折磨得要死。他說要是
有誰能像他在後半夜經常遇到的
那樣，看見我騎著掃帚，翻過屋脊，
從半空中回家，那他認爲人們
就可以了解他不得不忍受什麼生活。
好吧，我向阿瑟顯示過夠多的標記，
從我們曾經盡力維持的家中，
從即使用了七個年頭的全部雨雪
也沒法從耕地裡沖洗掉的穀倉味中，

我不是說穆西克勞山上羅杰斯騎兵
的頭骨，我是說女人對男人的示意，
只有迷住他我才能與他多過些日子。
在樹都挺直而矮苔蘚卻老高的地方，
我曾叫他去瀑布邊滑溜的岩石上
爲我採摘濕漉漉的白色漿果。
我是讓他在夜裡爲我做這件事的。
他曾喜歡做我叫他做的任何事情。
如果這時他在看得見我的地方，
我希望他離遠點，別看見我的模樣。
誰都可能從聲名顯赫變得一文不名。
關鍵是當我年輕、充滿活力的時候
我是否曾知道這就是我的結局。
看起來我好像不會有勇氣當著
大家的面這般無禮如此放肆。
我可能有勇氣，但看起來好像沒有。

Last night was one of her nights out. She's kiting.

She thinks when the wind makes a night of it

She might as well herself." But he liked best

To let on he was plagued to death with me

If anyone had seen me coming home

Over the ridgepole, stride of a broomstick,

As often as he had in the tail of the night,

He guessed they'd know what he had to put up with.

Well, I showed Arthur Amy signs enough

Off from the house as far as we could keep

And from barn smells you can't wash out of plowed ground

With all the rain and snow of seven years;

And I don't mean just skulls of Rogers' Rangers

On Moosilauke, but woman signs to man,

Only bewitched so I would last him longer.

Up where the trees grow short, the mosses tall,

I made him gather me wet snowberries

On slippery rock beside a waterfall.

I made him do it for me in the dark.

And he liked everything I made him do.

I hope if he is where he sees me now

He's so far off he can't see what I've come to.

You can come down from everything to nothing.

All is, if I'd a-known when I was young

And full of it, that this would be the end,

It doesn't seem as if I'd had the courage

To make so free and kick up in folks' faces.

I might have, but it doesn't seem as if.

我要歌頌你喔——「一」

那天夜裡，我
久久地睜眼躺著
希望那座鐘樓
會報出時辰
並告訴我能否
把當時算作白天
（儘管天還沒亮）
從而放棄睡眠。
伴著呼呼的風聲
雪下得很厚；
兩股風將相遇，
一股順著一條街，
一股順著另一條，
將在一陣紛亂
的飛雪中廝殺。
我嘴上不能說
但心裡卻擔心
嚴寒會捆住

鐘樓上那個鐘
的鍍金指針，
進而停止它們
前進的步伐。

這時傳來一聲鐘響！
雖說冷淡而低沉，
卻是人世風雲的
一個平穩的音符。
那鐘樓說：「一！」
隨之一座尖塔也說。
它們對自己說，
也對少數可能
被風從溫暖的被窩
驚醒（但不會被
逐出屋外）的人說。
它們沒注意那場
像一張飾有珠子的毛皮
猛烈撞擊我的玻璃窗
的暴風雪。

I Will Sing You One-O

It was long I lay
Awake that night
Wishing the tower
Would name the hour
And tell me whether
To call it day
(Though not yet light)
And give up sleep.
The snow fell deep
With the hiss of spray;
Two winds would meet,
One down one street,
One down another,
And fight in a smother
Of dust and feather.
I could not say,
But feared the cold

Had checked the pace
Of the tower clock
By tying together
Its hands of gold
Before its face.

Then came one knock!
A note unruffled
Of earthly weather,
Though strange and muffled.
The tower said, "One!"
And then a steeple.
They spoke to themselves
And such few people
As winds might rouse
From sleeping warm
(But not unhouse).
They left the storm
That struck en masse
My window glass
Like a beaded fur.

在那聲莊嚴的「一」中，
它們說到了太陽，
說到了月亮和星星──
土星和火星
還有木星。
更加無拘無束，
它們丟開有名字的星星
說到了以字母稱呼的星：
各個星座中那些
σ 星和 τ 星。
它們讓自己的聲音中
充滿了最遙遠的天體：
那些引人類
遐思的天體，
那些離上帝更近的天體。
那些望遠鏡鏡頭中的
宇宙塵埃。
它們莊嚴的聲音
不屬於它們自己：
它們代表另一個鐘說話，
因那個鐘巨大的齒輪
連著它們的齒輪。

在那個單獨發出的
莊嚴的字眼中
這個最大的星球
顫抖並移動，
不過迄今爲止
它讓它旋轉的瘋狂
顯得像是保持在
一種自我靜止狀態中。
自從人類開始
使人類墮落，
自從人群開始
使人群墮落，
它一直都沒變化；
在四面八方
上下左右的
那些行星上的
人類眼中，
除了它曾
變大爲一顆新星
的奇蹟之外
它一直都沒變化。

In that grave One

They spoke of the sun

And moon and stars.

Saturn and Mars

And Jupiter.

Still more unfettered,

They left the named

And spoke of the lettered,

The sigmas and taus

Of constellations.

They filled their throats

With the furthest bodies

To which man sends his

Speculation,

Beyond which God is;

The cosmic motes

Of yawning lenses.

Their solemn peals

Were not their own:

They spoke for the clock

With whose vast wheels

Theirs interlock.

In that grave word

Uttered alone

The utmost star

Trembled and stirred,

Though set so far

Its whirling frenzies

Appear like standing

In one self station.

It has not ranged,

And save for the wonder

Of once expanding

To be a nova,

It has not changed

To the eye of man

On planets over,

Around, and under

It in creation

Since man began

To drag down man

And nation nation.

火與冰

有人說這世界將毀於烈火，
有人說將毀於堅冰。
據我對欲望的親身感受，
我支持那些說火的人。
但如果世界得毀滅兩次，
我想我對仇恨也了解充分，
要說毀滅的能力
冰也十分強大，
足以擔負毀滅的重任。

Fire And Ice

Some say the world will end in fire,

Some say in ice.

From what I've tasted of desire

I hold with those who favor fire.

But if it had to perish twice,

I think I know enough of hate

To say that for destruction ice

Is also great

And would suffice.

在一座荒棄的墓園

生者愛踏著荒草而來，
來讀山坡上這些碑銘；
墓園仍吸引活著的遊客，
卻再也不能把死者吸引。

墓碑上的韻文千篇一律：
「今日來此的活著的人們，
讀完碑文又離去的人們
明天將來這裡長眠安息。」

對死亡如此有把握的碑文
卻禁不住一直暗暗留心
怎麼沒有死者來的跡象。
畏縮什麼呢，活著的人？

這樣回答也許不乏機敏——
告訴墓碑人們憎惡死亡，
從今以後永遠不再死去。
我想墓碑會相信這彌天大謊。

In a Disused Graveyard

The living come with grassy tread
To read the gravestones on the hill;
The graveyard draws the living still,
But never anymore the dead.

The verses in it say and say:
"The ones who living come today
To read the stones and go away
Tomorrow dead will come to stay."

So sure of death the marbles rhyme,
Yet can't help marking all the time
How no one dead will seem to come.
What is it men are shrinking from?

It would be easy to be clever
And tell the stones: Men hate to die
And have stopped dying now forever.
I think they would believe the lie.

雪塵

一隻烏鴉
從一枝鐵杉樹上
把雪塵抖落到
我身上的方式

已使我抑鬱的心情
為之一振
並從我懊悔的一天中
挽回了一部分。

Dust of Snow

The way a crow

Shook down on me

The dust of snow

From a hemlock tree

Has given my heart

A change of mood

And saved some part

Of a day I had rued.

金子般的光陰永不停留

大自然的新綠珍貴如金，
但金子般的色澤難以保存。
初綻的新芽宛若嬌花，
但花開花謝只在一剎那。
隨之嫩芽便長成綠葉，
樂園也陷入悲涼淒惻。
清晨轉眼就變成白晝，
金子般的光陰永不停留。

Nothing Gold Can Stay

Nature's first green is gold,

Her hardest hue to hold.

Her early leaf's a flower;

But only so an hour.

Then leaf subsides to leaf.

So Eden sank to grief,

So dawn goes down to day.

Nothing gold can stay.

逃遁

那年當第一場雪開始飄灑的時候，
我們在一片山地牧場見過一匹小馬，
那匹小摩根馬將一隻前蹄踏在牆上，
另一隻蜷在胸前。當時牠把頭一低，
向我們噴了個響鼻，然後轉身逃去。
我們聽見牠逃去的方向有隱隱雷聲，
我們看見或以爲看見那張飛雪構成
的巨大簾幕襯映著牠灰濛濛的身影。
「誰家的馬駒？我想牠是害怕下雪。
牠肯定還沒經歷過冬天。牠可不是
在和雪花玩耍嬉戲，牠是在逃遁。

我看牠媽媽也未必能跟牠講清，『唷，
這只是天氣變化。』牠會以爲她不懂！
牠媽媽在哪兒呢？牠不該獨自在外。」
現在伴著硻硻叩石聲，牠又回來了，
又躍上那道石牆，眼睛上覆著白雪，
尾巴除短毛豎立處也蓋著一層雪霜。
牠抖擻身上的雪花像是要抖掉蒼蠅。
「這麼晚了，其他牲口都早已回棚，
不管把牠留在外邊挨凍的到底是誰，
都應該被叫出來把牠牽回家去。」

The Runaway

Once when the snow of the year was beginning to fall,

We stopped by a mountain pasture to say, "Whose colt?"

A little Morgan had one forefoot on the wall,

The other curled at his breast. He dipped his head

And snorted at us. And then he had to bolt.

We heard the miniature thunder where he fled,

And we saw him, or thought we saw him, dim and gray,

Like a shadow against the curtain of falling flakes.

"I think the little fellow's afraid of the snow.

He isn't winter-broken. It isn't play

With the little fellow at all. He's running away.

I doubt if even his mother could tell him, 'Sakes,

It's only weather.' He'd think she didn't know!

Where is his mother? He can't be out alone."

And now he comes again with clatter of stone,

And mounts the wall again with whited eyes

And all his tail that isn't hair up straight.

He shudders his coat as if to throw off flies.

"Whoever it is that leaves him out so late,

When other creatures have gone to stall and bin,

Ought to be told to come and take him in."

雪夜在林邊停留

我想我知道這樹林是誰的。
不過主人的家宅遠在村裡,
他不會看見我在這兒停歇,
觀賞這片冰雪覆蓋的樹林。

想必我的小馬會暗自納悶:
怎麼未見農舍就停下腳步?
在這樹林與冰凍的湖水間,
在一年中最最黑暗的夜晚。

小馬輕輕抖搖頸上的韁鈴,
彷彿是想問主人是否弄錯。
林中萬籟俱寂,了無回聲,
只有柔風輕拂,雪花飄落。

這樹林真美,迷濛而幽深,
但我還有好多諾言要履行,
安歇前還須走漫長的路程,
安歇前還須走漫長的路程。

Stopping by Woods on A Snowy Evening

Whose woods these are I think I know.

His house is in the village, though;

He will not see me stopping here

To watch his woods fill up with snow.

My little horse must think it queer

To stop without a farmhouse near

Between the woods and frozen lake

The darkest evening of the year.

He gives his harness bells a shake

To ask if there is some mistake.

The only other sound's the sweep

Of easy wind and downy flake.

The woods are lovely, dark, and deep,

But I have promises to keep,

And miles to go before I sleep,

And miles to go before I sleep.

見過一回，那也算幸運

其他人老嘲笑我跪在井欄邊時
總是弄錯光的方向，所以從未
見過井的深處，只是看見陽光
照耀的水面映出我自己的影像，
那上帝般的影像在夏日的天空
從一圈蕨草和雲圈中朝外張望。
有一回，試著將下巴貼著井欄，
我如願以償地透過那影像
看見了一個不確定的白色物體，
某種比深還深的東西——但它
轉瞬即逝。水開始制止太清澈
的水。蕨草上滴下一滴水，瞧，
一陣漣漪模糊了井底的白東西
並將它抹去。它是什麼？真理？
水晶？見過一回，那也算幸運。

For Once, Then, Something

Others taunt me with having knelt at well-curbs

Always wrong to the light, so never seeing

Deeper down in the well than where the water

Gives me back in a shining surface picture

Me myself in the summer heaven, godlike,

Looking out of a wreath of fern and cloud puffs.

Once, when trying with chin against a well-curb,

I discerned, as I thought, beyond the picture,

Through the picture, a something white, uncertain,

Something more of the depths — and then I lost it.

Water came to rebuke the too clear water.

One drop fell from a fern, and lo, a ripple

Shook whatever it was lay there at bottom,

Blurred it, blotted it out. What was that whiteness?

Truth? A pebble of quartz? For once, then, something.

藍蝴蝶日

這便是此地春天裡的藍蝴蝶日
隨著一陣陣藍色薄片紛紛落下
這種飛翔中的毫無混雜的顏色
比地上將逐日開放的野花還多。

但這些就是雖會飛但不會唱的
野花。因已克制了高飛的欲望，
它們在四月的和風中合翅停飛，
依戀泥淖中剛留下車轍的地方。

Blue-Butterfly Day

It is blue-butterfly day here in spring,

And with these sky-flakes down in flurry on flurry

There is more unmixed color on the wing

Than flowers will show for days unless they hurry.

But these are flowers that fly and all but sing:

And now from having ridden out desire

They lie closed over in the wind and cling

Where wheels have freshly sliced the April mire.

襲擊

總是這樣，當聚足力量的暴風雪
終於在一個命定的夜晚向下傾瀉，
襯著黑魆魆的樹林顯得分外潔白，
並攜著一首它整冬不會再唱的歌，
嗖嗖歌聲掠過尚未被覆蓋的大地，
這時四下張望的我便會張口結舌，
就像一個突然被死神抓住的傢伙
放棄他的使命，任憑死亡降臨到
他的頭上，他一生從未幹過任何
壞事，卻也不曾立下豐功偉績，
簡直就像那生命從來就不曾開始。

可是喲，所有的先例都對我有利：
我知道欲置全人類於死地的冬天
每次都會失敗，在漫長的風暴中
皚皚白雪可堆積四英尺而風吹不動，
壓上紅楓、白樺和橡樹的樹身，
但卻止不住小鳥兒銀鈴般的歌聲；
而我終將看到所有積雪滑下山丘，
融匯進四月裡那條細細的溪流，
閃著尾巴穿過去年的草荒林莽，
宛若一條長蛇漸漸隱沒在遠方。
白色都將消失，除這兒一株白樺，
那兒一座教堂，再加上幾戶人家。

The Onset

Always the same, when on a fated night
At last the gathered snow lets down as white
As may be in dark woods, and with a song
It shall not make again all winter long
Of hissing on the yet uncovered ground,
I almost stumble looking up and round,
As one who overtaken by the end
Gives up his errand, and lets death descend
Upon him where he is, with nothing done
To evil, no important triumph won,
More than if life had never been begun

Yet all the precedent is on my side:
I know that winter death has never tried
The earth but it has failed: the snow may heap
In long storms an undrifted four feet deep
As measured against maple, birch, and oak,
It cannot check the peeper's silver croak;
And I shall see the snow all go downhill
In water of a slender April rill
That flashes tail through last year's withered brake
And dead weeds, like a disappearing snake.
Nothing will be left white but here a birch,
And there a clump of houses with a church.

朝向地面

嘴唇間的愛曾是我
能夠經受的甜蜜接觸；
它一度顯得過分甜蜜，
使我生活在香氣之中，

香氣從馨香之物向我襲來，
一陣流動的——難道是
暮色中沿山坡從神秘的
葡萄藤中飄來的麝香氣味？

忍冬藤的小花枝
使我感到眩暈和渴望，
當我攀折花枝時
它們把露珠滴在我手上。

我渴望濃郁的芬芳，但我
年輕時那些都顯得濃郁；
玫瑰花的花瓣
那真是沁人心脾。

如今歡樂無不伴有
那種攪和著痛苦、厭倦
和罪過的滋味；
於是我渴望淚痕，

渴望差點兒過頭的愛
留下的隱痛，
渴望苦樹皮的清香，
渴望燃燒丁香的蘚澤。

當使勁兒撐在
草叢和沙間的手
僵直、酸痛或被劃破，
我會將其縮回，

這種傷痛還不夠，
因為我渴望重量和力量，
好讓我的全身
感受到泥土的粗糙。

To Earthward

Love at the lips was touch
As sweet as I could bear;
And once that seemed too much;
I lived on air

That crossed me from sweet things,
The flow of — was it musk
From hidden grapevine springs
Downhill at dusk?

I had the swirl and ache
From sprays of honeysuckle
That when they're gathered shake
Dew on the knuckle.

I craved strong sweets, but those
Seemed strong when I was young;
The petal of the rose
It was that stung.

Now no joy but lacks salt,
That is not dashed with pain
And weariness and fault;
I crave the stain

Of tears, the aftermark
Of almost too much love,
The sweet of bitter bark
And burning clove.

When stiff and sore and scarred
I take away my hand
From leaning on it hard
In grass and sand,

The hurt is not enough:
I long for weight and strength
To feel the earth as rough
To all my length.

不能久留

他們要把他還給她。那封來信
這麼說……她可以再次擁有他。
她還來不及確定字裡行間是否
藏有壞消息，他已經回到家裡。
他們把活生生的他還給了她——
然後呢？他們送回的不是屍體——
而且沒有明顯的傷殘。他的手？
他的臉？她得看看，邊看邊問，
「怎麼回事，親愛的？」她給予了
一切還擁有一切，他們真幸運！
難道她不高興？看來事事如意，
餘下的日子對他們將會很舒適。
但她得問：「能待多久，親愛的？」

「夠久，但不夠久。一顆子彈穿透
了我的胸部。只有治療和休息
再加上你一個星期的精心護理
才能夠使我傷癒，並重返戰場。」
這種可怕的給予他們得來兩遍。
這下她只敢用她的目光問他
他第二次上戰場結果將會怎樣，
而他也用目光求她別再提問。
他們把他還給她，但不能久留。

Not To Keep

They sent him back to her. The letter came
Saying.... And she could have him. And before
She could be sure there was no hidden ill
Under the formal writing, he was there,
Living. They gave him back to her alive —
How else? They are not known to send the dead. —
And not disfigured visibly. His face?
His hands? She had to look, to look and ask,
"What is it, dear?" And she had given all
And still she had all — they had — they the lucky!
Wasn't she glad now? Everything seemed won,
And all the rest for them permissible ease.
She had to ask, "What was it, dear?"

"Enough,
Yet not enough. A bullet through and through,
High in the breast. Nothing but what good care
And medicine and rest, and you a week,
Can cure me of to go again." The same
Grim giving to do over for them both.
She dared no more than ask him with her eyes
How was it with him for a second trial.
And with his eyes he asked her not to ask.
They had given him back to her, but not to keep.

城中小溪

那幢農舍依然存在，雖說它厭惡
與新城街道整齊劃一，但不得不
掛上了門牌。可是那條小溪呢？
那條像手臂環抱著農舍的小溪呢？
我問，作為一個熟悉那小溪的人，
我知道它的力量和衝動，我曾經
把手伸進溪水讓浪花在指間跳舞，
我曾經把花拋進水中測它的流速。
六月禾可以被堅硬的水泥覆蓋，
在城市的人行道下再也長不出來；
蘋果樹可以被塞進壁爐當作柴燒。

水紅木對於小溪是否還同樣需要？
此外對不再需要的永恒力量
又該如何處置呢？難道溯流而上
用一車車煤渣築堤堵住它的源頭？
後來小溪被拋進了石板下的陰溝，
在臭烘烘的黑暗中依然奔流不息──
也許除了可以使它忘記恐懼之外，
它這樣日夜奔流永遠是徒勞無益。
除了舊時的地圖沒有一個人知曉
有這樣一條小溪。但我真想知道
是不是由於小溪永遠被埋在地下
其記憶就不可能冒上來重見天日，
使這座新城沒法幹活也沒法休息。

A Brook in The City

The farmhouse lingers, though averse to square

With the new city street it has to wear

A number in. But what about the brook

That held the house as in an elbow-crook?

I ask as one who knew the brook, its strength

And impulse, having dipped a finger length

And made it leap my knuckle, having tossed

A flower to try its currents where they crossed.

The meadow grass could be cemented down

From growing under pavements of a town;

The apple trees be sent to hearthstone flame.

Is water wood to serve a brook the same?

How else dispose of an immortal force

No longer needed? Staunch it at its source

With cinder loads dumped down? The brook was thrown

Deep in a sewer dungeon under stone

In fetid darkness still to live and run —

And all for nothing it had ever done,

Except forget to go in fear perhaps.

No one would know except for ancient maps

That such a brook ran water. But I wonder

If from its being kept forever under,

The thoughts may not have risen that so keep

This new-built city from both work and sleep.

覓鳥，在冬日黃昏

西天正脫下輝煌的金衣，
空氣早已在嚴寒中凝滯，
漫步回家，踏茫茫白雪，
似見有隻鳥在枝頭棲歇。

當我夏日裡經過這地方，
我總得停步，抬頭仰望；
一隻小鳥放開美妙歌喉，
如天使一般在樹上啁啾。

此刻樹上沒有鳥兒鳴囀，
唯有一片枯葉殘留枝端，
我久久徘徊，繞樹三匝，
只看見這幅清冷的圖畫。

憑高遠眺，在小山之頂，
我斷定這水晶般的寒冷
不過是白雪上再添嚴霜，
如金上敷金，難以增光。

自北向南橫過蒼茫碧空，
一顆小小流星劃破天穹，
星尾遺留下迤邐的一閃，
似縹緲流霞，隱約殘煙。

Looking For A Sunset Bird
in Winter

The west was getting out of gold,

The breath of air had died of cold,

When shoeing home across the white,

I thought I saw a bird alight.

In summer when I passed the place.

I had to stop and lift my face;

A bird with an angelic gift

Was singing in it sweet and swift.

No bird was singing in it now.

A single leaf was on a bough,

And that was all there was to see

In going twice around the tree.

From my advantage on a hill

I judged that such a crystal chill

Was only adding frost to snow

As gilt to gold that wouldn't show.

A brush had left a crooked stroke

Of what was either cloud or smoke

From north to south across the blue;

A piercing little star was through.

無限的瞬間

他迎著風停下腳步——那是什麼，
在楓樹林中，白乎乎但不是幽靈？
他站在那兒讓三月緊貼他的思緒，
但卻極不願意相信那最美的美景。

「啊，那是繁花盛開的樂園。」我說。
它的確也美得足以被人看成繁花，
只要三月裡的我們能在心中想像
那是五月裡如雪似銀的一樹春華。

我倆在一個奇異的世界站了片刻，
我自己也像他發呆那樣心醉神迷；
最後我說出了真相（我倆繼續走）。
那是棵還留著去年枯葉的山毛櫸。

A Boundless Moment

He halted in the wind, and — what was that
Far in the maples, pale, but not a ghost?
He stood there bringing March against his thought,
And yet too ready to believe the most.

"Oh, that's the Paradise-in-Bloom," I said;
And truly it was fair enough for flowers
Had we but in us to assume in March
Such white luxuriance of May for ours.

We stood a moment so, in a strange world,
Myself as one his own pretense deceives;
And then I said the truth (and we moved on).
A young beech clinging to its year's leaves.

糖楓園之夜

在三月裡風暴停息的時候，在我
喜歡的一個夜晚，我逗留在糖廠
門外，小心翼翼地招呼那燒火工，
叫他離開煉鍋去為拱爐添些木柴：
「嗨，聽我說，請把火弄得更旺些，
讓更多的火星順著煙囪冒上天空。」
我想有些火星也許會像往常一樣
糾纏在周圍楓樹林光禿禿的枝間，
在山上稀薄的空氣中久久不熄滅，
這樣便可以裝飾夜空中那輪月亮。

那夜月色雖朦朧但仍然足以映出
掛在每一棵糖楓樹上的取脂吊桶
和黑黝黝大地上那張雪白的地毯。
火星都無意升上高空去充當月亮。
它們滿足於在樹上扮星星的角色，
如獅子座、獵戶座和七姐妹星團。
所以枝叢間不一會兒就群星閃爍。

Evening In A Sugar Orchard

From where I lingered in a lull in March

Outside the sugarhouse one night for choice,

I called the fireman with a careful voice

And bade him leave the pan and stoke the arch:

"O fireman, give the fire another stoke,

And send more sparks up chimney with the smoke."

I thought a few might tangle, as they did,

Among bare maple boughs, and in the rare

Hill atmosphere not cease to glow,

And so be added to the moon up there.

The moon, though slight, was moon enough to show

On every tree a bucket with a lid,

And on black ground a bear-skin rug of snow.

The sparks made no attempt to be the moon.

They were content to figure in the trees

As Leo, Orion, and the Pleiades.

And that was what the boughs were full of soon.

收落葉

用鐵鍬去鏟落葉
簡直就像用鐵勺，
成包成袋的落葉
卻像氣球般輕飄。

我整天不停地鏟，
落葉總窸窣有聲，
像有野兔在逃竄；
像有野鹿在逃遁。

但我堆起的小山
眞令我難以對付，
它們遮住我的臉，
從我雙臂間溢出。

我可以反覆裝車，
我可以反覆卸貨，
直到把棚屋塞滿，
但我得到了什麼？

它們幾乎沒重量；
它們幾乎沒顏色；
因爲與地面接觸，
它們已失去光澤。

它們幾乎沒用處。
但收成總是收成，
而且又有誰敢說
這收穫何時能停？

Gathering Leaves

Spades take up leaves
No better than spoons,
And bags full of leaves
Are light as balloons.

I make a great noise
Of rustling all day
Like rabbit and deer
Running away.

But the mountains I raise
Elude my embrace,
Flowing over my arms
And into my face.

I may load and unload
Again and again
Till I fill the whole shed,
And what have I then?

Next to nothing for weight;
And since they grew duller
From contact with earth,
Next to nothing for color.

Next to nothing for use.
But a crop is a crop,
And who's to say where
The harvest shall stop?

谷間鳥鳴

唯一的響動是你關上外屋的房門。
你的腳步在草地上沒有一點聲音，
你剛出房門不久，還沒有走多遠，
可你已經讓第一聲鳥鳴響徹谷間；
而它又喚醒了晨星下的其他鳥兒。
但牠們充其量也只能多睡一會兒，
因為按部就班的黎明已開始讓晨光
穿過雲層熹熹微微地投射到地上，
欲強行揭開籠罩山川大地的面紗；
欲釋放被禁錮壓抑了一夜的喧譁。
但黎明不想那天始於「點點珍珠」

（有人形容拂曉前的雨點像珍珠，
天亮後在陽光照耀下則變成鑽石），
也沒打算讓那天的鳥鳴自己開始。
讓它開始的是你，若這需要證辭——
當時我就在那滴水的屋頂下安眠，
而且我的窗簾飄上窗台被雨淋濕；
但我有責任醒來把你的說法證實，
我有責任樂意宣稱並幫著你宣稱
那天是你讓山谷裡的鳥開始啼鳴。

The Valley's Singing Day

The sound of the closing outside door was all.

You made no sound in the grass with your footfall,

As far as you went from the door, which was not far;

But you had awakened under the morning star

The first songbird that awakened all the rest.

He could have slept but a moment more at best.

Already determined dawn began to lay

In place across a cloud the slender ray

For prying beneath and forcing the lids of sight,

And loosing the pent-up music of overnight.

But dawn was not to begin their "pearly-pearly"

(By which they mean the rain is pearls so early,

Before it changes to diamonds in the sun),

Neither was song that day to be self-begun.

You had begun it, and if there needed proof —

I was asleep still under the dripping roof,

My window curtain hung over the sill to wet;

But I should awake to confirm your story yet;

I should be willing to say and help you say

That once you had opened the valley's singing day.

擔憂

都在喊：「我們要跟你去，哦，風！」
葉片和葉柄都跟著風一道往前走；
可當它們行進時，一陣睡意壓來，
它們止步，並求風也與它們同留。

自從在春天裡隨風東搖西晃以來，
它們就一直期待著這次遠走高飛，
可現在它們寧願尋一道避風的牆，
覓一片叢林或一塊凹地昏昏入睡。

眼下它們正以越來越曖昧的移動
來敷衍搪塞疾風摧枯拉朽的召喚，
迫不得已時才勉勉強強扭動一下，
這扭動只能使它們在原地打個轉。

我只希望，當我像這些樹葉一樣
獲得自由，當我能夠去探索尋找
知識，當我已擺脫了生活的羈絆，
安歇對於我不會顯得比追求更好。

Misgiving

All crying, "We will go with you, O Wind!"
The foliage follow him, leaf and stem;
But a sleep oppresses them as they go,
And they end by bidding him stay with them.

Since ever they flung abroad in spring
The leaves had promised themselves this flight,
Who now would fain seek sheltering wall,
Or thicket, or hollow place for the night.

And now they answer his summoning blast
With an ever vaguer and vaguer stir,
Or at utmost a little reluctant whirl
That drops them no further than where they were.

I only hope that when I am free,
As they are free, to go in quest
Of the knowledge beyond the bounds of life
It may not seem better to me to rest.

山坡雪融

簡直難以想像，熟悉那個地方卻不
熟悉那道山坡——那道被春日太陽
從雪中釋放出千萬條銀蜥蝪的山坡！
雖說我以前也常見山坡雪融的場面，
卻不敢誇口能描繪銀蛇狂奔的景象。
那看上去像是太陽施展出某種魔法
揭開了那層繁殖出銀色蜥蝪的雪毯，
結果溫暖的陽光使它們朝山下逃竄。
但要是我打算去阻止這場蜥蝪潰逃，
那到頭來我肯定一條蜥蝪也攔不住；

我若伸手去抓蛇尾無疑是枉費心機，
要用腳去踩蛇頭也只會是白費力氣，
面對數十條蜥蝪扭著纏著猛撲而來，
看著數百條銀蛇閃著白光蜿蜒而去，
我只會在雪水中手忙腳亂連滾帶爬；
而且春歸的鳥兒也會來湊這場熱鬧，
嘰嘰喳喳嚶嚶噝噝巴不得亂上添亂。

A Hillside Thaw

To think to know the country and not know

The hillside on the day the sun lets go

Ten million silver lizards out of snow!

As often as I've seen it done before

I can't pretend to tell the way it's done.

It looks as if some magic of the sun.

Lifted the rug that bred them on the floor

And the light breaking on them made them run.

But if thought to stop the wet stampede,

And caught one silver lizard by the tail,

And put my foot on one without avail

And threw myself wet-elbowed and wet-kneed

In front of twenty others' wriggling speed —

In the confusion of them all aglitter,

And birds that joined in the excited fun

By doubling and redoubling song and twitter —

I have no doubt I'd end by holding none.

只有月亮能制止這混亂。我剛才説
太陽是名術士；但月亮則是個女巫。
她會從高高的西天灑下冷浸的清輝，
轉眼之間，既沒有掙扎也沒有抽搐，
一條條銀蜥蜴便會被她的符咒鎮住。
我相信，我六點鐘看那片山坡之時，
銀色的蛇群還在瘋狂飛奔急速逃竄。
當時月亮正在等她的寒光產生作用。
到九點鐘再看：蛇群已變成了頑石，
每條石蛇都保持著栩栩如生的姿勢；
有的甚至凝固在幾乎垂直的坡壁上，
它們磕頭碰尾橫七豎八滿山坡臥躺。

那種能使飛龍變成僵蛇的神奇魔力
就這樣自上而下無聲無息穿過樹枝，
如果枝頭有樹葉，樹葉也不會搖曳。
這是月亮的魔力，她讓每一縷寒光
都凍住一條銀蛇，直到白晝又來臨。
我想達到的目的就是這樣一種暫停。

It takes the moon for this. The sun's a wizard

By all I tell; but so's the moon a witch.

From the high west she makes a gentle cast

And suddenly, without a jerk or twitch,

She has her spell on every single lizard.

I fancied when I looked at six o'clock

The swarm still ran and scuttled just as fast.

The moon was waiting for her chill effect.

I looked at nine: the swarm was turned to rock

In every lifelike posture of the swarm,

Transfixed on mountain slopes almost erect.

Across each other and side by side they lay.

      The spell that so could hold them as they were

      Was wrought through trees without a breath of storm

      To make a leaf, if there had been one, stir.

      It was the moon's: she held them until day,

      One lizard at the end of every ray.

      The thought of my attempting such a stay!

耕犁人

他們所說的犁是指除雪。
他們不可能指耕耘種植——
除非他們故意尖酸刻薄
嘲笑說一直在耕耘岩石。

Plowmen

A plow, they say, to plow the snow.

They cannot mean to plant it, no —

Unless in bitterness to mock

At having cultivated rock.

關於一棵橫在路上的樹

（請聽我們說）

那棵被狂風暴雨卡嚓一聲折斷
並轟然橫著倒在我倆面前的樹，
不是要把我們的旅程永遠阻攔，
而只是要問我們認為自己是誰，

為何總是堅持走我們自己的路。
它只是希望我倆暫時停止前進，
讓我們下車在厚厚的雪中小佇，
為沒有斧子該怎麼辦進行討論。

它知道任何阻礙都會徒勞無功，
因為我們不可能偏離最終目標，
這目標早已深深藏在我們心中，
哪怕我們不得不追到天涯海角。

厭倦了漫無目的的在一處打轉，
我們義無反顧地駛向新的空間。

On A Tree Fallen Across The Road (To hear us talk)

The tree the tempest with a crash of wood

Throws down in front of us is not to bar

Our passage to our journey's end for good,

But just to ask us who we think we are

Insisting always on our own way so.

She likes to halt us in our runner tracks,

And make us get down in a foot of snow

Debating what to do without an ax.

And yet she knows obstruction is in vain:

We will not be put off the final goal

We have it hidden in us to attain,

Not though we have to seize earth by the pole

And, tired of aimless circling in one place,

Steer straight off after something into space.

我們歌唱的力量

下雪了，在春天乾燥溫暖的地上，
雪花找不到可以落腳成形的地方。
為把大地變濕變冷，雪花
前撲後繼，但它們難以占有永久陣地。
白色的雪片一近黑土就立即融化，
彷彿大地把它們全都送回了老家。
直到夜闌人靜，霧霧漠漠的雪塵
已差不多形成了斑駁的雪堆雪埂，
草地和菜園終於承認冬天未離，
紛紛縮回去過冬，除了那條大路。
翌日的景象是雪山銀海一派死寂。

綠草在巨大的腳下卑躬屈膝。
每一個初綻的嫩芽都托著一個雪球，
細長的枝椏提前讓白色果實掛滿枝頭，
樹枝被壓彎觸地彷彿要入地生根。
唯有那條路在泥濘中保持著原形，
也不知這奧秘是因為地心的烈火，
還是因為白天人來車往留下餘溫。

春日裡這片土地上總是歌手雲集：
歌鶇、烏鶯、藍鳥、朱雀和黃鸝，
但牠們並不是全都屬於這個地區；
有些鳥將繼續北上直到哈德遜，
有些則向北飛，等到秋天再回返，
真要在這兒築巢建窩的不到一半。
牠們顯然不喜歡這場遲來的大雪。

Our Singing Strength

It snowed in spring on earth so dry and warm

The flakes could find no landing place to form.

Hordes spent themselves to make it wet and cold,

And still they failed of any lasting hold.

They made no white impression on the black.

They disappeared as if earth sent them back.

Not till from separate flakes they changed at night

To almost strips and tapes of ragged white

Did grass and garden ground confess it snowed,

And all go back to winter but the road.

Next day the scene was piled and puffed and dead.

        The grass lay flattened under one great tread.

        Borne down until the end almost took root,

        The rangey bough anticipated fruit

        With snowballs cupped in every opening bud.

        The road alone maintained itself in mud,

        Whatever its secret was of greater heat

        From inward fires or brush of passing feet.

        In spring more mortal singers than belong

        To any one place cover us with song.

        Thrush, bluebird, blackbird, sparrow, and robin throng;

        Some to go further north to Hudson's Bay,

        Some that have come too far north back away,

        Really a very few to build and stay.

        Now was seen how these liked belated snow.

牠們在原野上已找不到地方停棲。
若老在天上飛翔很快會精疲力盡，
牠一踏上樹枝會引起一場雪崩，
那樣嘗試一次就已經叫牠們受夠。
除了那條路牠們找不到落腳之處。
於是牠們只好壓縮其生存的空間，
壞天氣使萬千同胞同類親密無間。
大路很快就變成了一條流動的河，
羽毛光滑的鳥群猶如石上的水波。
我試圖驅趕牠們成群成群地逃走，
可牠們無動於衷，仍把陣地堅守，
並且差點和我爭論逃走是否妥當，
嘰嘰喳喳地說牠們既然來就要歌唱。
有幾隻鳥肯定是被我驅趕得太急，
牠們飛快地閃開，但只騰空而起
到或粗或細的樹枝間轉一個圈，
然後又非常溫順地飛回到我的跟前，
樹林像一座被鏤空的大理石廣廈，
被翅膀尖輕輕一碰就會轟然倒塌，
可鳥兒寧願被我驅趕再去受驚嚇。
這樣一場雪永遠別想把牠們教會：
雪季之後再北上就不會這般受罪；
牠們甚至不飛到我身後圖個清靜。
好吧，大雪總算展示了某種力量，
這塊土地歌唱的力量就這般聚集，
雖說暫時還受制於這惡劣的氣候，
但牠們仍然準備著一旦獲得自由，
使用其歌聲讓野花開遍原野山丘。

The fields had nowhere left for them to go;

They'd soon exhausted all there was in flying;

The trees they'd had enough of with once trying

And setting off their heavy powder load.

They could find nothing open but the road.

So there they let their lives be narrowed in

By thousands the bad weather made akin.

The road became a channel running flocks

Of glossy birds like ripples over rocks.

I drove them underfoot in bits of flight

That kept the ground, almost disputing right

Of way with me from apathy of wing,

        A talking twitter all they had to sing.

        A few I must have driven to despair

        Made quick asides, but having done in air

        A whir among white branches great and small,

        As in some too much carven marble hall

        Where one false wing beat would have brought down all,

        Came tamely back in front of me, the Drover,

        To suffer the same driven nightmare over.

        One such storm in a lifetime couldn't teach them

        That back behind pursuit it couldn't reach them;

        None flew behind me to be left alone.

        Well, something for a snowstorm to have shown

        The country's singing strength thus brought together,

        That though repressed and moody with the weather

        Was nonetheless there ready to be freed

        And sing the wild flowers up from root and seed.

沒有鎖的門

已經過去許多年頭，
終於又傳來敲門聲，
這使我突然想到
我那扇沒有鎖的門。

我匆匆把燈吹熄，
把雙腳踮得老高，
在胸前合攏十指
對那扇門做禱告。

但敲門聲又傳來。
我只好把窗戶打開，
悄悄爬上窗台，
縱身跳到了屋外。

然後我對著窗戶
應了一聲「請進」，
也不管那敲門者
可能是哪路客人。

因為那聲敲門聲，
我丟下一個空屋，
藏身於這個世界
並隨著時代變化。

The Lockless Door

It went many years,
But at last came a knock,
And I thought of the door
With no lock to lock.

I blew out the light,
I tiptoed the floor,
And raised both hands,
In prayer to the door.

But the knock came again.
My window was wide;
I climbed on the sill
And descended outside.

Back over the sill
I bade a "Come in"
To whatever the knock
At the door may have been.

So at a knock
I emptied my cage
To hide in the world
And alter with age.

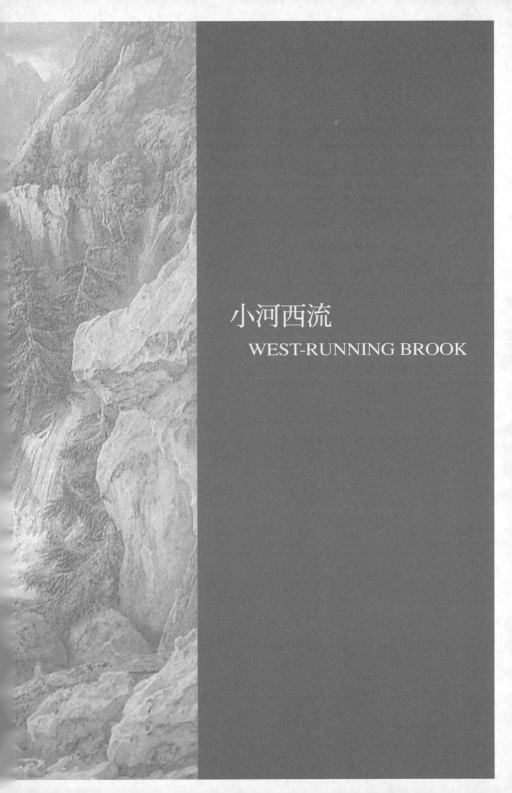

小河西流
WEST-RUNNING BROOK

春潭

春潭雖掩蔽在濃密的樹林，
卻依然能映出無瑕的藍天，
像潭邊野花一樣瑟瑟顫慄，
也會像野花一樣很快枯乾，
但潭水不是匯進溪流江河，
而將滲入根絡換蔥蘢一片。

把潭水汲入其新蕾的樹木
夏日將郁郁蔥蔥莽莽芊芊，
但是在潭渴枯槁之前，
不妨先讓它們多思考兩遍：
這如花的春水和似水的花
都因皚皚白雪消融在昨天。

Spring Pools

These pools that, though in forests, still reflect

The total sky almost without defect,

And like the flowers beside them, chill and shiver,

Will like the flowers beside them soon be gone,

And yet not out by any brook or river,

But up by roots to bring dark foliage on.

The trees that have it in their pent-up buds

To darken nature and be summer woods —

Let them think twice before they use their powers

To blot out and drink up and sweep away

These flowery waters and these watery flower.

From snow that melted only yesterday.

玫瑰家族

玫瑰就是玫瑰，
而且始終是玫瑰。
但如今有理論説
蘋果也是玫瑰，
梨也是玫瑰，所以
我想梅子也是玫瑰。
只有上天知道
還會證明什麼是玫瑰。
你當然是一朵玫瑰——
但卻是永遠的玫瑰。

The Rose Family

The rose is a rose,

And was always a rose.

But the theory now goes

That the apple's a rose,

And the pear is, and so's

The plum, I suppose.

The dear only knows

What will next prove a rose.

You, of course, are a rose —

But were always a rose.

忠誠

此心想不出還有何忠誠
堪比海岸對大海的忠貞——
守著那始終如一的曲線，
數著那永遠重覆的濤聲。

Devotion

The heart can think of no devotion
Greater than being shore to the ocean —
Holding the curve of one position,
Counting an endless repetition.

匆匆一瞥
致里奇利‧托倫斯寫在最近讀他的
《金蘋果園》之後

我常從火車的窗口看見野花繽紛，
但不待細看它們就早已無蹤無影。

我總想下車回到剛才看見花的地方，
看看究竟是些什麼花開在鐵路兩旁。

我用明知不對的花名稱呼那些花；
因爲火菊不喜歡樹林燒掉的山崖，

藍鈴花絕不會去裝飾隧道的洞口，
紫狼花也不會生長在乾旱的沙丘。

一個朦朧的念頭忽然閃過我腦際：
它們莫非是這人世間難覓的東西？

天國往往只在某些時候偶爾閃現，
即當觀者位置只能遠看不可近觀。

A Passing Glimpse

To Ridgely Torrence on last looking into his
"Hesperides"

I often see flowers from a passing car
That are gone before I can tell what they are.

I want to get out of the train and go back
To see what they were beside the track.

I name all the flowers I am sure they weren't:
Not fireweed loving where woods have burnt —

Not bluebells gracing a tunnel mouth —
Not lupine living on sand and drouth.

Was something brushed across my mind
That no one on earth will ever find?

Heaven gives its glimpses only to those
Not in position to look too close.

曾被擊倒

雨曾經對風說：
「你去風狂我來雨驟。」
於是它們襲擊花壇，
於是花兒紛紛低頭，
雖未死去，但被擊倒。
我了解花兒當時的感受。

Lodged

The rain to the wind said,
"You push and I'll pelt."
They so smote the garden bed
That the flowers actually knelt,
And lay lodged — though not dead.
I know how the flowers felt.

孤獨

我以前曾在何處聽見這風
像今天這樣變成一種低低的轟鳴？
它為什麼要使我站立到門邊，
在這兒推開一扇倔強的門，
凝望山下白浪擊岸的海濱？
夏日過去了，白晝過去了。
西天已聚集起大團大團的烏雲。
在屋外門廊下陷的地板上面
一團枯葉旋轉並發出嘶嘶之聲，
想撞我的膝蓋但未能得逞。
那嘶嘶聲中某種不祥的意味
說明我的秘密肯定已走漏風聲，
不知怎的四下裡肯定已有傳聞：
說我在這幢房子裡是形單影隻，
說我在我的生活中是孤家寡人，
說我除上帝之外已舉目無親。

Bereft

Where had I heard this wind before

Change like this to a deeper roar?

What would it take my standing there for,

Holding open a restive door,

Looking downhill to a frothy shore?

Summer was past and day was past.

Somber clouds in the west were massed.

Out in the porch's sagging floor

Leaves got up in a coil and hissed,

Blindly struck at my knee and missed.

Something sinister in the tone

Told me my secret must be known:

Word I was in the house alone

Somehow must have gotten abroad,

Word I was in my life alone,

Word I had no one left but God.

我窗前的樹

我窗前的樹喲，窗前的樹，
夜幕已降臨，讓我關上窗戶；
但請允許我不在你我之間
垂下那道障眼的窗簾。

夢一般迷濛的樹梢拔地而起，
高高樹冠伸展在半天雲裡，
你片片輕巧的舌頭喧嚷不停，
但並非句句話都很高深。

樹喲，我看見你一直搖曳不安，
而要是你曾看見過我在睡眠，
那麼你也看見過我遭受折磨，
看見我幾乎不知所措。

那天命運融合了我倆的思想，
命運女神也有她自己的想像，
原來你掛念著外邊的氣候冷暖，
我憂慮著內心的風雲變幻。

Tree at My Window

Tree at my window, window tree,

My sash is lowered when night comes on;

But let there never be curtain drawn

Between you and me.

Vague dream-head lifted out of the ground,

And thing next most diffuse to cloud,

Not all your light tongues talking aloud

Could be profound.

But, tree, I have seen you taken and tossed.

And if you have seen me when I slept,

You have seen me when I was taken and swept

And all but lost.

That day she put our heads together,

Fate had her imagination about her,

Your head so much concerned with outer,

Mine with inner, weather.

茅草屋頂

獨自出門走進冬日的雨中，
一心只想著互相給予的傷痛。
不過我並沒有走出多遠，
沒讓樓上的窗口離開視線。
那窗口的燈光是我的一切，
但我不會進去，除非燈光熄滅；
可我不進屋，那窗也不願熄燈。
好吧，就看到最後我倆誰贏，
我們會看到最後是誰先投降。
這世界是一片黑咚咚的牧場。
這雨實際上是冰涼的水雪；
這風則是又一層土的鋪放者。

最奇怪的是：那些於夏初
在厚厚的舊茅草屋頂中孵出、
然後漸漸羽毛豐滿的小鳥，
竟有一些還隱居在牠們的窩巢。
當我經過那道低矮的屋簷，
我不小心讓衣袖擦到了簷邊，
結果把藏在窩裡的鳥兒驚飛，
牠們飛進黑暗令我感到傷悲；
想到牠們的情況已沒法補救，
我舊的悲愁中又添新的悲愁——
鳥兒不可能再飛回來尋找
牠們築在這茅屋頂上的窩巢。

The Thatch

Out alone in the winter rain,

Intent on giving and taking pain.

But never was I far out of sight

Of a certain upper-window light.

The light was what it was all about:

I would not go in till the light went out;

It would not go out till I came in.

Well, we should see which one would win,

We should see which one would be first to yield.

The world was a black invisible field.

The rain by rights was snow for cold.

The wind was another layer of mold.

But the strangest thing: in the thick old thatch,

Where summer birds had been given hatch,

Had fed in chorus, and lived to fledge,

Some still were living in hermitage.

And as I passed along the eaves

So low I brushed the straw with my sleeves,

I flushed birds out of hole after hole,

Into the darkness. It grieved my soul,

It started a grief within a grief,

To think their case was beyond relief —

They could not go flying about in search

Of their nest again, nor find a perch.

牠們肯定在想該降在何處安身，
怎樣憑著牠們的羽毛和體溫
平平安安地熬到第二天黎明。
當我這樣想到牠們無家可歸，
出門前的傷痛反而大大消退。
下面就是我傷悲消散的緣故：
鳥兒使我想到我倆居住的茅屋，
它被風撕裂的屋頂已沒法修補，
它幾個世紀的生命已經結束，
因為此刻打在我身上的雨點
也同樣打在樓上房間的地板。

They must brood where they fell in mulch and mire,

Trusting feathers and inward fire

Till daylight made it safe for a flyer.

My greater grief was by so much reduced

As I thought of them without nest or roost.

That was how that grief started to melt.

They tell me the cottage where we dwelt,

Its wind-torn thatch goes now unmended;

Its life of hundreds of years has ended

By letting the rain I knew outdoors

In onto the upper chamber floors.

冬日伊甸

冬日菜園在檜樹叢生的窪地，
穴兔出洞在陽光下玩耍嬉戲，
此時的菜園最接近天國伊甸，
雪尚未融化，樹木還在休眠。

積雪把生存空間墊高了一層，
使菜園離頭頂上的天國更近，
鋪展在覆蓋大地的雪層之上，
去年的紅漿果在陽光下發亮。

消瘦但快活的野獸伸展身子，
這下很高的食物它也能夠著，
盡情享受野蘋果樹嬌嫩的樹皮，
那將是該年最高的環帶痕跡。

接近天國使動物停止了交媾：
無愛的鳥兒聚為冬天的朋友，
滿足於查看並猜測枝頭萌芽，
哪些會長成葉，哪些會開花。

一柄羽毛榔頭呼呼敲兩聲。
這伊甸園的白天於兩點告盡。
冬日白晝的時辰看上去太短，
似乎並不值得眾生醒來遊玩。

A Winter Eden

A winter garden in an alder swamp,
Where conies now come out to sun and romp,
As near a paradise as it can be
And not melt snow or start a dormant tree.
It lifts existence on a plane of snow
One level higher than the earth below,
One level nearer heaven overhead,
And last year's berries shining scarlet red.
It lifts a gaunt luxuriating beast
Where he can stretch and hold his highest feast
On some wild apple-tree's young tender bark,
What well may prove the year's high girdle mark.

So near to paradise all pairing ends:
Here loveless birds now flock as winter friends,
Content with bud-inspecting. They presume
To say which buds are leaf and which are bloom.
A feather-hammer gives a double knock.
This Eden day is done at two o'clock.
An hour of winter day might seem too short
To make it worth life's while to wake and sport.

熟悉黑夜

我已熟悉黑夜，熟悉黑夜。
我曾冒雨出去又冒雨回來。
我到過街燈照不到的郊野。

我見過城裡最淒涼的小巷。
我曾走過巡夜更夫的身旁，
不想解釋我為何垂下目光。

我曾停下止住腳步的聲音，
當時遠處傳來斷續的呼喊，
從另一條街道，越過房頂，

但不是叫我回去或說再見；
而在遠方一個神秘的高處
有只發亮的鐘襯映著天幕，

它宣稱時間沒錯，但也不正確。
我已經熟悉這黑夜，熟悉黑夜。

Acquainted With The Night

I have been one acquainted with the night.
I have walked out in rain — and back in rain.
I have outwalked the furthest city light.

I have looked down the saddest city lane.
I have passed by the watchman on his beat
And dropped my eyes, unwilling to explain.

I have stood still and stopped the sound of feet
When far away an interrupted cry
Came over houses from another street.

But not to call me back or say good-by;
And further still at an unearthly height
One luminary clock against the sky

Proclaimed the time was neither wrong nor right.
I have been one acquainted with the night.

小河西流

「弗雷德，哪兒是北方？」
「北方？這兒就是北方，親愛的。
這條小河流去的方向是西方。」
「那就把它叫做往西流的小河。」
（直到今天人們仍叫它西流河。）
「它以爲自己在幹嘛呢，往西去，
而其他所有的河川都東流入海？
它肯定是條非常自信的小河，
它敢背道而馳是因爲它能相信自己，
就像我能相信你──你能相信我──
因爲我們──我們是──我不知道
我們是什麼樣的人。
我們是什麼樣的人呢？」

「年輕人或新人？」
　　　「我們肯定是什麼人。
我們是說咱們倆，讓我們改說咱倆。
就像你和我我和你結婚一樣，咱倆
將一同與這條小河結婚。我們將
在這河上架座橋，而那橋將是我們
的助手，跨越這小河，睡在它身邊。
你看那兒，有團浪花在向我們招手，
它想讓我們知道它聽見了我們説話。」
　　　　　「嗨，我親愛的，
那團浪花是在避開這突出的河岸。」
（黑色的河水被一塊暗礁擋住，
於是回流湧起了一團白色的浪花，

West-Running Brook

"Fred, where is north?"

"North? North is there, my love.

The brook runs west."

"West-Running Brook then call it."

(West-Running Brook men call it to this day.)

"What does it think it's doing running west

When all the other country brooks flow east

To reach the ocean? It must be the brook

Can trust itself to go by contraries

The way I can with you — and you with me —

Because we're — we're — I don't know what we are.

What are we?"

                    "Young or new?"

                    "We must be something.

We've said we two. Let's change that to we three.

As you and I are married to each other,

We'll both be married to the brook. We'll build

Our bridge across it, and the bridge shall be

Our arm thrown over it asleep beside it.

Look, look, it's waving to us with a wave

To let us know it hears me."

                    "Why, my dear,

That wave's been standing off this jut of shore —"

(The black stream, catching on a sunken rock,

Flung backward on itself in one white wave,

白色浪花永遠在黑色水流上翻湧，
蓋不住黑水但也不會消失，就像
一隻白色的小鳥，一心要讓這黑河
和下游那個更黑的河灣有白色斑點，
結果它白色的羽毛終於被弄皺，
襯著對岸的檟木叢像一塊白色頭巾。)
我是想說，自從天底下有河流以來，
那團浪花就在避開這突出的河岸。
它並不是在向我們招手。」
「你說不是，但我說是。不是向你
也是向我——以一種宣告的方式。」

「噢，要是你把它搬到女性王國，
如果它屬於那個亞馬遜人的國度，
我們男人肯定會把你送過國境並把
你留在那兒，我們自己禁止入內——
這是你的小河！我已經無話可說。」
「不，你還有話說。繼續說吧。
你剛才想到了什麼事情。」
「說到背道而馳，你看在白浪處，
這條小河是怎樣和自己相向而流。
它來自我們來自的那個水中的地方，
早在我們被隨便什麼怪物創造之前。
今天我們邁著迫不及待的步伐，
正溯流而上要回到一切源頭的源頭，
回到永遠在流逝的萬事萬物的溪流。

And the white water rode the black forever,

Not gaining but not losing, like a bird

White feathers from the struggle of whose breast

Flecked the dark stream and flecked the darker pool

Below the point, and were at last driven wrinkled

In a white scarf against the far-shore alders.)

"That wave's been standing off this jut of shore

Ever since rivers, I was going to say,

Were made in heaven. It wasn't waved to us."

"It wasn't, yet it was. If not to you,

It was to me — in an annunciation."

"Oh, if you take it off to lady-land,

As't were the country of the Amazons

We men must see you to the confines of

And leave you there, ourselves forbid to enter —

It is your brook! I have no more to say."

"Yes, you have, too. Go on. You thought of something."

"Speaking of contraries, see how the brook

In that white wave runs counter to itself.

It is from that in water we were from

Long, long before we were from any creature.

Here we, in our impatience of the steps,

Get back to the beginning of beginnings,

The stream of everything that runs away.

有人說生存就像一個皮耶羅和一個
皮耶羅蒂，永遠在一個地方站立
並舞蹈，其實生存永遠在遠逝，
它嚴肅而悲傷地奔流而去，
用空虛去填充那深不可測的空虛。
它在我們身邊的這條小河裡流逝，
在一陣短促的恐慌中分開我們。
它在我們之上之間和我們一起流逝。
它是時間、力量、聲音、光明、
　　生命和愛——
甚至是流逝成非物質的物質；

這道宇宙間的死亡的大瀑布
消耗成虛無——而且不可抗拒，
除非是憑它自身的某種神奇抵抗，
不是憑偏向一邊，而是憑向後，
彷彿它心中感到惋惜，神聖的惋惜。
它自己具有這種逆流而行的力量，
所以這大瀑布跌落時通常都會
舉起一點什麼，托起一點什麼。
我們生命的跌落托起時鐘。
這條小河的跌落托起我們的生命。
太陽的跌落托起這條小河。
而且肯定有某種東西托起太陽。
正因為有這種逆流而上、回歸源頭
的向後運動，我們大多數人才在

Some say existence like a Pirouot

And Pirouette, forever in one place,

Stands still and dances, but it runs away;

It seriously, sadly, runs away

To fill the abyss's void with emptiness.

It flows beside us in this water brook,

But it flows over us. It flows between us

To separate us for a panic moment.

It flows between us, over us, and with us.

And it is time, strength, tone, light. life, and love —

And even substance lapsing unsubstantial;

> The universal cataract of death
>
> That spends to nothingness — and unresisted,
>
> Save by some strange resistance in itself,
>
> Not just a swerving, but a throwing back,
>
> As if regret were in it and were sacred.
>
> It has this throwing backward on itself
>
> So that the fall of most of it is always
>
> Raising a little, sending up a little.
>
> Our life runs down in sending up the clock.
>
> The brook runs down in sending up our life.
>
> The sun runs down in sending up the brook.
>
> And there is something sending up the sun.
>
> It is this backward motion toward the source,

自己身上看到了歸源長河中的貢品。
我們實際上就是從那個源頭來的。
我們幾乎全是。」
　　　　「今天該是你說這些
的日子。」
　　　「不，今天該是你說這條小河
被叫做西流河的日子。」
「今天該是咱倆說這些話的日子。」

Against the stream, that most we see ourselves in.

The tribute of the current to the source.

It is from this in nature we are from.

It is most us."

       "Today will be the day

You said so."

       "No, today will be the day

You said the brook was called West-Running Brook."

"Today will be the day of what we both said."

移民

所有這些使越來越多的人民
聚集到這個大陸的帆船輪船
無一不是由五月花號護航
在渴望的夢中駛向這片海岸。

Immigrants

No ship of all that under sail or steam

Have gathered people to us more and more

But, Pilgrim-manned, the Mayflower in a dream

Has been her anxious convoy in to shore.

最後一片牧草地

有一片被叫做偏遠牧場的草地，
我們再也不會去那兒收割牧草，
或者說這是農舍裡的一次談話：
說那片草場與割草人緣分已盡。
這下該是野花們難得的機會，
它們可以不再怕割草機和耕犁。
不過必須趁現在，得抓緊時機，
因爲不再種草樹木就會逼近，
得趁樹木還沒看到那塊地荒廢，
趁它們還沒有在那裡投下濃陰。
我現在所擔心的就是那些樹，
花兒在它們的濃陰下沒法開放；
現在我擔心的不再是割草人，
因草地已完成了被種植的使命。
那片草場暫時還屬於我們，
所以你們喲，躁動不安的花，
你們盡可以在那兒恣意開放，
千姿百態、五顏六色的花喲，
我沒有必要說出你們的名字。

The Last Mowing

There's a place called Faraway Meadow
We never shall mow in again,
Or such is the talk at the farmhouse:
The meadow is finished with men.
Then now is the chance for the flowers
That can't stand mowers and plowers.
It must be now, though, in season
Before the not mowing brings trees on,
Before trees, seeing the opening,
March into a shadowy claim.
The trees are all I'm afraid of,
That flowers can't bloom in the shade of;
It's no more men I'm afraid of;
The meadow is done with the tame.
The place for the moment is ours
For you, O tumultuous flowers,
To go to waste and go wild in,
All shapes and colors of flowers,
I needn't call you by name.

黑暗中的門

黑暗中從一個房間到一個房間，
我盲目地伸出雙手護著我的臉，
但多麼輕率，我忘了交叉十指
讓伸出的雙臂合攏成一個弧形。
結果一扇薄門突破了我的防衛，
給了我的腦袋狠狠一擊，以致
我讓我自然的比喻產生了衝突，
於是我筆下人與物的互相比喻
不再像從前那樣總是和諧匹配。

The Door in the Dark

In going from room to room in the dark

I reached out blindly to save my face,

But neglected, however lightly, to lace

My fingers and close my arms in an arc.

A slim door got in past my guard,

And hit me a blow in the head so hard

I had my native simile jarred.

So people and things don't pair anymore

With what they used to pair with before.

偶觀星宿有感

你得等上很久很久，才會看見變化
發生，在流霞浮雲所不及的天宇，
在像神經顫慄的北極光之外的太空。
太陽和月亮會相遇，但絕不會相觸，
不會碰出火花，也不會撞出聲音。
行星好像會互相干擾其曲線運動，
但卻相安無事，各自太太平平。
我們滿可以耐心地繼續過日子，
除日月星辰之外也看看別的地方，
尋找些震盪和變化使我們保持清醒。
千真萬確，百年乾旱終將止於甘霖，
中國的千年和平也將止於戰爭。
但觀星者徹底不眠仍得不到報償，
他無法看到天空的寧靜發生突變
在他的眼前，在他特定的時辰。
看來那種寧靜今宵肯定會持續。

On Looking up by Chance
(At The Constellantions)

You'll wait a long, long time for anything much
To happen in heaven beyond the floats of cloud
And the Northern Lights that run like tingling nerves.
The sun and moon get crossed, but they never touch,
Nor strike out fire from each other, nor crash out loud.
The planets seem to interfere in their curves,
But nothing ever happens, no harm is done.
We may as well go patiently on with our life,
And look elsewhere than to stars and moon and sun
For the shocks and changes we need to keep us sane.
It is true the longest drouth will end in rain,
The longest peace in China will end in strife.
Still it wouldn't reward the watcher to stay awake
In hopes of seeing the calm of heaven break
On his particular time and personal sight.
That calm seems certainly safe to last tonight.

見證樹

在我想像中的界線在樹林中
成直角轉彎的地方，一溜鐵絲網
和一道真實的石牆已被豎起。
而在離開這個角落的曠野裡，
在這些石塊被沖來並堆積的地方，
一株樹，因被深深地挫傷，
給人的印象也是一棵見證樹
並成了我並非不受約束的物證，
成了我記住這一事實的物證。
於是真理被確立並被證明，
儘管被曖昧和疑惑所包圍──
儘管被一個疑惑的世界包圍。

A Witness Tree

Where my imaginary line
Bends square in woods, an iron spine
And pile of real rocks have been founded.
And off this corner in the wild,
Where these are driven in and piled,
One tree, by being deeply wounded,
Has been impressed as Witness Tree
And made commit to memory
My proof of being not unbounded.
Thus truth's established and borne out,
Though circumstanced with dark and doubt —
Though by a world of doubt surrounded.

一棵幼小的白樺

那棵白樺開始褪去綠色的胎衣，
漸漸露出它胎衣下白色的樹皮，
若是你喜歡這幼小纖細的白樺，
那可能早就注意到了這種變化。
它不久就會一身素白高大巍然，
使白日成雙，把黑夜劈成兩半，
樹皮白皙如雪，唯有樹冠青翠，
這周圍的樹就數它最勇敢無畏；
憑著天生麗質它不怕依偎藍天，
恐怕輕信的美人也沒這麼大膽。
某個愛回憶往事的人將會回憶
有次在順著牆根砍除灌木之時
他大開殺戒卻偏對它刀下留情，
那時它的樹幹還細如一根蔓藤，
後來慢慢長得像釣魚竿那麼粗，
但最後終於長成那麼一棵大樹，
連你雇來的那位最能幹的幫工
也知道它在那兒就是讓人讚頌，
知道他若是趁你讀書或者外出時
將它砍倒，那他將會被解雇。
它是美的化身，是上天的賜予，
它將作為裝飾品度過它的時日。

Steeple Bush—A Young Birch

The birch begins to crack its outer sheath

Of baby green and show the white beneath,

As whosoever likes the young and slight

May well have noticed. Soon entirely white

To double day and cut in half the dark

It will stand forth, entirely white in bark,

And nothing but the top a leafy green —

The only native tree that dares to lean,

Relying on its beauty, to the air.

(Less brave perhaps than trusting are the fair.)

And someone reminiscent will recall

How once in cutting brush along the wall

He spared it from the number of the slain,

At first to be no bigger than a cane,

And then no bigger than a fishing pole,

But now at last so obvious a bole

The most efficient help you ever hired

Would know that it was there to be admired,

And zeal would not be thanked that cut it down

When you were reading books or out of town.

It was a thing of beauty and was went

To live its life out as an ornament.

總該有點希望

肯定會照目前的方式發生，
不久之後，牲口不愛吃的
白花繡線菊和絨毛繡線菊
就將擠掉牲口愛吃的牧草。

然後能做的事情就是等候，
等楓樹白樺雲杉破土而出
擠過頭頂的繡線菊屬灌木，
以類似的方式把它們擠走。

在這亂石中耕耘得不償失。
所以趁樹木在增長其年輪，
趁它們的長樹枝橫行霸道，
你最好去做些別的事情。

等樹木成材時再將其砍倒，
於是你的土地將恢復原貌，
將擺脫艷麗但無用的雜草，
再一次準備爲牧草所擁有。

我們可以設百年爲一周期。
這們深謀遠慮就不會干預
一種我們可能都有的美德，
除非有一個政府出面干涉。

要學會忍耐並學會向前看，
有些事我們只能聽其自然。
雖說希望不可能養殖牛羊，
但據說它可以把農人滋養。

Something for Hope

At the present rate it must come to pass,

And that right soon, that the meadowsweet

And steeple bush, not good to eat,

Will have crowded out the edible grass.

Then all there is to do is wait

For maple, birch, and spruce to push

Through meadowsweet and steeple bush

And crowd them out at a similar rate.

No plow among these rocks would pay.

So busy yourself with other things

While the trees put on their wooden rings

And with long-sleeved branches hold their sway.

Then cut down the trees when lumber grown,

And there's your pristine earth all freed

From lovely blooming but wasteful weed

And ready again for the grass to own.

A cycle we'll say of a hundred years.

Thus foresight does it and laissez-faire,

A virtue in which we all may share

Unless a government interferes.

Patience and looking away ahead,

And leaving some things to take their course.

Hope may not nourish a cow or horse,

But spes alit agricolam 'tis said.

PURE Robert Frost: selected poems
佛羅斯特詩選

文／羅伯特·佛羅斯特　譯／曹明倫
責任編輯／劉曉菁　美術編輯／蕭雅慧

出版發行／愛詩社出版事業部
地址／台北市新生南路二段20號6樓
電話／(02)2351-7251　傳真／(02)2351-7244

讀者服務中心／書虫俱樂部
讀者服務專線／(02)2500-7718～9　24小時傳真服務／(02)2500-1990～1
郵撥帳號／19863813　書虫股份有限公司　網址／www.readingclub.com.tw
讀者服務信箱E-mail／service@readingclub.com.tw

香港發行所／城邦（香港）出版集團
地址／香港灣仔軒尼詩道 235 號 3 樓　電話／852-25086231　傳真／852-25789337
E-Mail／hkcite@biznetvigator.com
馬新發行所／城邦（馬新）出版集團 Cite (M) Sdn. Bhd. (458372 U)
地址／11, Jalan 30D/146, Desa Tasik, Sungai Besi, 57000 Kuala Lumpur,Malaysia
電話／603-90563833　傳真／603-90562833　E-Mail／citecite@streamyx.com

ISBN10: 986-7388-47-X
ISBN13: 978-986-7388-47-6
2006年12月初版一刷
定價600元